I0825347

PHOENIX KNIGHT

THE LOST SON

JAMES UNGURAIT

Legacy Edition ISBN: 979-8-9993809-1-3
Ebook ISBN: 979-8-9993809-2-0

Library of Congress Control Number: 2021924003

Second Edition 2025

Published in the United States by IRONWAKE
an Imprint of Ungurait House LLC
Hattiesburg, Mississippi

For information contact:
sales@unguraithouse.com
www.unguraithouse.com

TO ADDISON, BETH, BLAIR, EMMA, AND LIZZY.
FOR EXPERIENCING THIS ADVENTURE FIRST.

Other Works By James Ungurait

I'm The Same

AUTHOR NOTE

There's something intimate—almost sacred—about returning to a story that once saved you. The Lost Son wasn't just the first novel I wrote. It was the first world I built, the first character who truly carried a piece of me, and the first time I dared to put something that vulnerable out into the world.

I began writing Phoenix's story in 2018. I was in college, still figuring out who I was, still carrying a lot I didn't have words for. The book, in many ways, became a place to sort through all of that. It held pieces of my questions about identity, belonging, purpose. And beneath all that, it held something even quieter—a grief I didn't know how to name yet.

Phoenix is the son of two academics, quiet on the outside but loud in thought. He lives in his head. He questions everything. And he carries a wound most people don't see. Sound familiar? He was never meant to be a hero in the traditional sense. He was built to wrestle with truth—his own and the world's.

When The Lost Son was first published in 2022, I was proud, but I was also still learning. I didn't yet know what I know now about writing, editing, design, or even what it means to build something that lasts. With the launch of Ungurait House, and now IRONWAKE—our imprint for myth, fantasy, and those beautifully weighty stories. I had the opportunity to return, sharpen, and honor this work the way it always deserved.

This second edition reflects that growth. We took a hard editorial look at the original manuscript. We preserved what mattered: the lore, the themes, the heart. But we also filled in the gaps. Added the weight. Brought the characters into clearer focus. The story hasn't changed at its core but it's deeper now. More lived-in. More honest.

We also made some big changes. The title now bears Phoenix's name front and center—because this is his story, and that name will matter more than you know soon enough. The cover is brand new, designed with intention and homage. And we're introducing a new format here at Ungurait House we're calling it the Legacy Edition—a line of books that mark turning points in our creative journey. This edition includes refined layout, interior flourishes, and just maybe, a few extra details hidden between the lines.

To everyone who read the first edition and told me they loved Phoenix—thank you. To those who saw themselves in him, or saw someone they loved—thank you. And to those of you discovering this story for the first time: welcome. Adventure is only part of what you'll find here.

More than anything, this second edition is a love letter. To Phoenix. To the version of me who needed him. And to every reader who's ever searched for something in the pages of a book and come away changed.

—James Ungurait

"The greatest journeys begin
not with courage
–but with the quiet decision to
keep going."

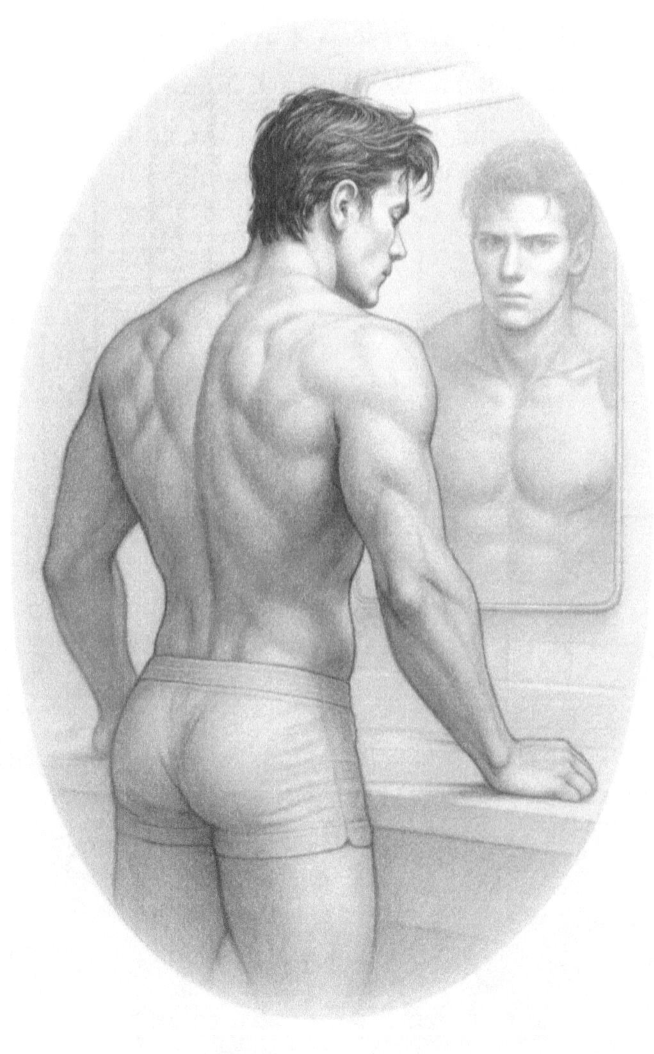

ONE

THE RUN

"WHERE FLAME FIRST FLICKERS"

I ran like something might catch me if I slowed—something ancient, patient, and waiting for me to name it.

The Mississippi trail curved ahead in loops of memory and mud, winding between oaks and pines swollen with summer heat. Cicadas shrieked like rusted gears in the trees above, their song vibrating through limbs that drooped with weight. The air was thick as old grief—heavy, damp, smelling of pine needles, cracked earth, and something vaguely metallic, like blood in the back of the throat.

I let it press into me. Let it choke the thoughts that never left me alone. Sweat soaked my shirt, clung to the arch of my spine, ran down my arms like ritual ink. Each step burned—heel to toe, breath to breath—a mantra of movement and muscle. My lungs ached. My thighs screamed. My mind was a war zone gone silent.

Above, sunlight fractured through the canopy in brilliant, holy shards— gold broken across green, slashed against bark, flickering as I moved. It was beautiful, almost cruelly so. But beauty didn't save you. It just watched.

This—this rhythm, this pain—was the only thing I still trusted.

Only a little further, Phoenix.

Her voice again. Not in my ears. In my bones. A whisper tangled in memory, like static from an old cathedral radio tuned just off the mark. My mother, the eternal scholar, the ghost who never left. Always urging me forward. To rise. To become.

But I hadn't. Not really. I'd failed—and she didn't even know.

The trail spilled suddenly into a clearing like lungs releasing their breath. Light exploded into the open, washing the world in gold and green and memory. Ahead, the recreation building sat wide and low, indifferent to time. Students strolled the quad—laughing, half-asleep, tangled in headphones and leash lines. A dog barked. Someone threw a frisbee. The world spun in slow, forgettable arcs.

I pushed through the final yards, everything burning. My body shuddered as I slowed. At the edge of the trail, I crouched low, hands on knees, breath clawing its way free.

Checked my watch. New best. Didn't matter.

A bitter smile. Progress. Whatever that meant.

The run got me through the morning. The ache in my muscles dulled the sharp edges in my mind. I moved on instinct, guided by routine. No destination—just the familiar loop back home.

The house on Broadview Lane greeted me with silence and stale coffee air. The A/C hummed like penance, wrapping its chill around my overheated skin. Brick exterior, gabled roof, ivy kissing the windows—our place looked like a professor's cottage dressed up as a student rental. It didn't belong to this stage of life. Then again, neither did I.

Upstairs, I peeled off sweat-soaked clothes and stepped under the blast of the cold shower. I didn't move. Just let the water erase me, inch by inch, until I felt less like smoke.

In the mirror: the aftermath.

Six feet of reconstructed ruin. Muscle clung where shame once curled. Olive skin stretched over a frame I had forged like armor—slowly, painfully, obsessively. The soft, breakable boy I had been was gone. Eaten alive by the version of me that refused to stay small.

Now, I had edges. Now, I had control.

Dark hair. Cropped close. No flair. No distraction. A hint of stubble across my jaw. Not style—just a way to feel time pass. And those eyes.

Brilliant. Silver. Unnatural. Impossible. Mine.

"Phoenix, you done yet?"

Lucas's voice cracked through the door like reality reasserting itself.

"Almost."

He barged in a moment later, towel-wrapped and groggy, already halfway to annoyed. Lucas was shorter, built like a tailback with the kind of natural athleticism that fit right in at Ole Miss—broad-chested, quick-footed, and louder than necessary. He had that Rebel swagger, the kind of charisma that made professors sigh and sorority girls swoon.

"It's about time," he muttered, shoving past.

"Good morning to you too."

The door slammed. I sighed.

We weren't friends, not really. Just orbiting bodies forced into proximity. But sometimes, when the frat-boy act slipped, I caught glimpses of the real him. Something delicate. Cracked. Too familiar.

I dressed in silence, grabbed my bag. The scent of detergent and burnt coffee clung to the kitchen as I passed through. The sun hit my face as I stepped outside.

Back in motion, I followed the path I always did—down streets etched with tradition, across sidewalks older than they looked. The hum of the town folded into the beat of my steps.

Oxford unfolded in layers— red brick buildings, oak-lined streets, porch swings, whispers of history thick in the air. The town wore nostalgia like a second skin. But the beauty was a mask. Like most Southern things, it came with a cost.

The University rose ahead, an intricate sprawl of manicured grounds and timeworn brick buildings, each one named after a figure whose legacy hovered somewhere between myth and burden. Pathways curled like veins through the campus heart, shaded by towering oaks and magnolias. The Grove stretched wide to my right, a cathedral of trees that transformed every fall Saturday into ritual and reverie. Beyond it, the iconic Circle framed the university's historic core—a quiet loop haunted by memory and tradition. My steps fell into familiar rhythm.

I passed the Lyceum. It loomed ahead like a sentinel of another era—its red brick façade crowned by six imposing white columns, framed by a pediment that seemed to listen more than speak. It was the oldest building on campus, once a Confederate hospital, now the administrative heart of the university. Students hurried past its steps, rarely looking up, as if acknowledging its history meant carrying it. Elegant. Watchful. Its red walls whispered secrets in the heat.

"Mr. Knight."

Dr. Dawson. Arms crossed. Brows lifted. Eyes that saw more than you ever wanted them to.

"Yes, ma'am?"

"Your paper on conservation theory—it was good. I'd like to see more of that this year."

A pause. "Thank you."

I didn't know how to take praise. Still didn't.

Latin followed like quicksand. Notes, sighs, minutes dragging their heels. My eyes fluttered. Survived.

Lucas found me near the steps afterward, flanked by two of his fraternity brothers. They wore the same uniform confidence—pressed polos, too-bright smiles, a scent of cologne and certainty that never quite belonged to me. One of them laughed too loud at something Lucas said. The other barely noticed me.

"Party tonight," Lucas said, like it was a commandment, not a question.

I hesitated.

He always did this—roped me into social rituals I had no real use for. He wasn't trying to torture me, not exactly. It was more like... he needed me there. As if my presence made his own feel more grounded. Or less fake.

"Maybe," I replied.

He tilted his head. That look he gave me sometimes, like he was reading a script he didn't quite believe in.

I'd show up. Smile. Nod. Leave early. It was a rhythm. A camouflage.

"Seven," he said. "Don't ghost."

I didn't answer, but he already knew I would. We both played our roles well enough.

As the others joked and moved ahead, Lucas lingered for a breath too long. I caught it—that flicker. A shift behind the eyes. Like something in him wanted to say more. Or less. But then the moment passed, and he turned to catch up, his laugh already back in place.

The circle stretched wide before me. Trees swayed. Light bled. And then—

Her.

Thirty feet away. Red hair. Familiar as a dream half-remembered.

My breath caught. No. No, it couldn't—

I blinked. She was gone.

But something stayed behind.

A hum beneath my skin. A ripple in the stillness.

I turned toward Bryant Hall, the stones steady beneath my feet. But the air? It was different now.

And so was I.

By the time I was home, it had rained and passed. The streets glistened faintly, puddles catching the last of the light like fallen mirrors. The air still held it—soft and metallic, like something recently broken. It smelled of wet pavement, upturned soil, and jasmine from a neighbor's overgrown hedge. Everything felt just a little more fragile.

I lay on the couch, half-lost in a dense chapter on the Roman imperial bureaucracy. Dry reading to most, but there was something calming in the structure of it all—order imposed on chaos. An illusion, maybe. But one I liked. The click of the clock, the rustle of turning pages, the world outside muffled and slow—this was peace in a different shape.

At six-thirty, I closed the book. I'd said I would show up. I should at least try.

I changed into something more appropriate, something neutral enough to fade into the noise: dark jeans, gray shirt, old jacket. Outside I took the usual route down university avenue and then turned towards the fraternities, the house across the street was pulsing—colored lights bleeding through the windows, bass rattling the siding. If there had ever been noise complaints on Fraternity Row, they were clearly lost in the mail.

At the door, a guy in a hoodie held a clipboard like it was a shield.

"Name," he mumbled, not looking up.

I said nothing. Just stood there.

"Name," he repeated, louder, glancing up this time.

Recognition hit his face like a delayed signal. "Oh. You're good. Go on in."

Inside was chaos—the kind that made your ears ring before the door even closed. People pressed into each other like atoms at boiling point. The scent of cheap beer, cologne, and sweat clung to every surface. Music throbbed at some unreadable BPM, bodies swayed, drinks sloshed, someone shouted something unrepeatable. It was, I assumed, a standard Oxford house party. Too many bodies for too little space, the walls breathing with sound.

"PHOENIX!" Lucas shouted from across the room, a red cup in hand. I made my way toward him, dodging elbows and beer breath. He handed me a drink—water, mercifully. A party trick. You hold a cup, no one asks questions.

"It's a little loud, don't you think?" I said, raising my voice above the noise.

He motioned to the door, and we slipped outside.

The air was thick but bearable. Above us, the sky had cleared, and the stars hung heavy—sharp, white, watchful. Even with the town's soft glow, you could make out the constellations. The sound dulled behind us, the quiet like a balm.

I tilted my head back.

I remembered nights like this. Lying in the grass beside my mother, naming stars while she whispered myth after myth—Orion, Cassiopeia, Andromeda. She'd travel for weeks at a time, sometimes months. But when she was home, she made the sky feel small enough to hold.

She was the reason I studied history. The reason I studied anything.

"See something interesting?" Lucas asked, his voice cutting into the quiet.

"Just the stars," I murmured, eyes still upward. "They don't judge."

He nodded like he understood.

"Seriously, thanks for coming," he said after a pause.

"Can I ask you something?"

His brow lifted. "Shoot."

"What are you hiding from?"

He flinched—just enough to notice.

"You're not yourself when you're around them," I added. "It's like you're playing a part."

He stared at the ground for a beat too long.

"Nothing," he said, and drank deep.

I didn't press. I could feel the wall go back up. I knew what it cost to scale your own.

"If you ever do want to talk," I said, "I'm here."

He didn't answer, but the silence wasn't rejection. Just armor.

Then—out of the corner of my eye—I saw her again.

Red hair. Illuminated faintly in the moonlight. Standing near the tree line in a black hoodie, still, watching something.

It can't be.

"What is it?" Lucas asked, following my gaze.

"There." I pointed. "See her?"

"Who the hell…?"

She was moving now—slowly, cautiously, like she was following someone. But her mistake was the same one most people make when they think no one's watching: she forgot to look behind her.

"I've got to check this out," I said, already moving.

"Oh no, you don't," Lucas said, setting his cup down. "You're not going without me."

I didn't argue.

Back inside, we pushed through the party crowd and slipped out the front. The street was quiet, the air thick with humidity and the faint smell of spilled beer and damp earth. The night had shifted—something about it taut, like string pulled too tight.

We caught sight of her again, walking toward the edge of campus—Paris Yates Chapel just visible in the near distance, its cross gleaming faintly against the dark. Trees loomed, casting long shadows across the path.

"Are we seriously following her?" Lucas asked.

I nodded.

"You know how that looks, right?"

"I don't care. Something's not right."

He groaned but didn't stop walking.

We crossed into the quad. The world fell into hush—the rush of water from the fountain, the static buzz of crickets, the old buildings sleeping under stars. The night was clean in a way the day never could be.

We saw her again, now across from the library, drifting toward the Circle like a shadow. Statues watched in silence, their bronze faces unreadable in the dark.

At first, I thought she was alone.

Then I saw what she saw.

Four figures, cloaked in black from head to toe, slipped silently up the steps of the Lyceum. Hoods covered their faces, their bodies moving as one—eerie in their synchronization. It was like watching a ritual unfold in secret.

"What the hell…" Lucas whispered, and we both instinctively ducked behind a hedge.

The girl stood maybe a hundred feet ahead of us. Unmoving. Watching.

And then she turned.

"Who's there?" she called out, her voice cutting the quiet like a blade. The accent hit first—English, unmistakable.

"I see you," she said again, stepping forward. "Who are you?"

Lucas and I exchanged a glance. I knew that voice.

I stood, heart pounding.

"Evelyn?"

She blinked, startled. Her face flickered through confusion, recognition, something like disbelief.

"How do you..." she began, then stopped.

"Phoenix?" she said.

And in that moment, it all returned.

The past. The weight. The beginning of whatever this was.

Two

Reunion

"Ghost of the Grove"

"You two know each other?" Lucas asked, his voice somewhere between confused and suspicious.

Standing in front of me was someone I never expected to see again. Evelyn Ramses—five-foot-five, flame-kissed hair cascading from a messy bun, fair skin with freckles only visible under soft light. London-born, sharp-tongued, and brilliant to a fault. Her presence pulled gravity into focus. She had always felt too big for the rooms she entered, like the air bent around her intellect. Fiercely independent, maddeningly stubborn, and impossible to forget.

"You could say that," Evelyn replied, stepping closer. Her eyes searched mine with a mixture of disbelief and calculation. "What are you doing here?"

"I go to school here—remember?" I said. It came out more defensive than intended. Evelyn never missed details. She catalogued everything. Yet under the flicker of the streetlamp, I could see she genuinely hadn't realized it. A rare crack in her precision.

"Oh. I forgot about that," she admitted. I rolled my eyes, knowing full well she'd file that reaction away. Or pretend not to. Either way, she'd win the memory.

"Okay," Lucas broke in, brows drawn. "How do you two know each other?"

I looked to Evelyn. She owed me that much.

"I'm his mother's graduate assistant," she said. It was the truth, but only part of it. She omitted the nights of late conversation over wine, the arguments about ethics and myth, the time we almost kissed and never spoke of it again. But Lucas didn't need all that. Not yet.

"What are you doing here?" I asked. Her presence felt out of place, like seeing a ghost in the wrong graveyard. Evelyn belonged in Memphis with my mother. Not here.

"When's the last time you heard from your mother?"

The question landed hard.

"A month ago, maybe? She said she was buried in research for her book. You know how she is."

It wasn't unusual for my mom to disappear into work. Field sites, locked archives, places where phones didn't work and time went soft. But a month... it was nearing her limit.

"A week ago, she told me she was coming down here to see you," Evelyn said. Her voice had cooled into something too still. Not accusing. Not afraid. Just certain.

My stomach dropped.

"What?"

"She never came?"

"No. I would know if my own mother came to see me," I said sharply. The lamplight caught the tension in Evelyn's shoulders. She wasn't playing.

"Then where is she?"

The question cut. Because I didn't have an answer.

"That can't be true," I muttered, trying to piece together reasons. Maybe she lied. But that wasn't her. Not with Evelyn. Not with me.

"Shh..."

Evelyn raised a finger and pointed back toward the Lyceum. More figures emerged from the darkness—hooded, faceless, silent. Moving with intent.

"We need to figure out what's going on," she said. "Your mother mentioned something before she left. Something about this."

"I agree."

Lucas looked between us like we were pulling him into a play without a script. He gave a theatrical sigh, then nodded.

"Just do a better job at it," Evelyn said to me, lips twitching in a half-smirk.

I scowled. She snickered. Of course she did.

We crept forward, finding cover behind a low brick half-wall beside a memorial stone etched with names of those long gone. From our position, we could still see into the Lyceum's portico.

Evelyn leaned further, cautious.

"You don't want them to see you," she whispered, pulling back. The group ahead—ten, maybe twelve people—formed a quiet ring, then moved in sequence.

And then, one by one, they stepped through a section of the wall.

"Where did they go?" Lucas asked.

"I don't know," Evelyn said, standing up. "But we're going to find out."

"Evelyn," I started, but she was already moving. Determined. Reckless.

Lucas gave me the look: *Are we really doing this?*

I gave him a nod. We followed.

The Lyceum towered above us now, its neoclassical columns glowing under campus lights. Inside, the entry hall was cool and echoing, all pale marble and echo. The ceiling arched high, built in a time before central air, when height alone had to invite the wind. Tall windows framed the night outside. Dust floated in the ambient glow.

Evelyn stood at the far end, hands brushing the stone where the figures had disappeared. A seam. A threshold.

Whatever this was, it wasn't ordinary. And we were already too deep to pretend otherwise.

"I don't get it. Where did they go?" Evelyn's voice was hushed but sharp, each word cutting the silence like a blade. She paced the hall, eyes scanning everything—the ornate wallpaper, the antique furnishings, the dust-veiled air. Her fingers brushed a side table, trailing along its filigree edge like she might reveal something hidden beneath the varnish. The creaking floorboards beneath her boots echoed like questions waiting for answers.

Lucas, still near the shelves, narrowed his eyes. "Look," he said, gesturing to the edge of a bookshelf. A tear—small, jagged—broke the pattern of wallpaper beside it.

I moved toward it carefully, feeling the cold in the air shift, the kind of draft that came from spaces not meant to exist. As I pressed my hand against the shelf, the chill deepened. The scent of mildew and stone crept through the seams.

With effort, I pushed. The bookshelf groaned, but then moved easily, as if it had been opened before. Behind it, a spiraling staircase descended into the ground, stone steps swallowed by darkness.

"Where do you think it leads?" Lucas asked, his voice low.

"Don't know," Evelyn answered, her tone too calm. "Let's find out."

She went first. Joy flickered in her voice, a scholar's delight bleeding through her resolve. It scared me. Lucas and I exchanged glances, then followed.

The air grew colder as we descended. Stone walls, slick with condensation, seemed to breathe around us. The faint scent of moss and rust filled our noses, mixing with something older—burned incense, perhaps, or time itself. Every few steps, torches flickered in built-out recesses, casting warped shadows that danced across our skin.

The stairwell twisted endlessly, stone beneath our feet worn by centuries. Then, just as I began to question how deep we'd gone, the walls widened into an archway—and beyond it, a corridor lined with marble columns.

"What is this place?" I whispered, though I knew no one had answers.

To the left, murals stretched across the walls, worn but magnificent. Scenes of ancient warfare—blazing skies, armies clashing, titans falling into ash. Fire bloomed from chariots, while clouds churned in oils of grey and blood-red. The painting style was old, older than anything I had seen in textbooks. Faded, but still alive.

To the right, the corridor opened into a vast chamber. A rotunda, circular and domed, with torches embedded high on the walls. Their flames glowed against soot-darkened stone, revealing intricate carvings etched into the room itself. It smelled of wax and earth and something sweetly metallic. The air was heavy—stagnant, old, sacred.

We crouched behind a wide stone ledge, half-shielded from view. From here, we could see the group that entered before us, gathered in a circle. In their center stood a pedestal of dark wood inlaid with gold symbols. Upon it, a square object wrapped in velvet and marked with symbols I didn't recognize.

"They're worshiping it," Evelyn whispered.

"Or protecting it," I said, though I wasn't sure why I did.

The group began to chant.

"We all serve," one voice declared.

"Till the end," the others answered in unison.

Their hoods shifted in flickering light, shadows hiding their faces. The words they spoke next were no longer English. The sound felt wrong—too fluid, too resonant. The syllables hung in the air like smoke.

"What language is that?" Lucas asked.

"I don't know." I turned to Evelyn.

"Neither do I," she admitted. "It doesn't match anything I've ever studied."

Still, we stayed. Drawn by something deeper. Wonder. Fear. Memory. I didn't know yet.

Then—crack.

The sound of stone breaking echoed like thunder. A piece of the ledge beneath Lucas's elbow broke loose, crashing onto the floor below. It hit with a sound too loud for secrecy.

The group recoiled. Hoods flew back. Gasps broke the silence.

"Who's there?" a voice rang out—familiar, commanding.

My stomach dropped.

Dr. Dawson.

I didn't need to see her face to know. The voice, the posture—it was her.

"We need to leave. Now," Evelyn hissed.

We ran.

The stairwell felt longer on the way back up, every step a scream of breath and burning calves. Behind us, footsteps rose like pursuit.

Back in the Lyceum's hall, we burst through the hidden door and slipped outside, diving into the bushes just beyond the portico. The campus lay still beneath the stars. The air, thick with humidity, clung to our skin like breath held too long.

I held Evelyn close. Lucas was beside me, panting.

The doors creaked open. Footsteps emerged.

"I swear, I saw someone up there," Dr. Dawson said. Her voice was close. Too close. She scanned the area with surgical precision.

"We better be sure. We don't need anyone meddling," another said.

We stayed still, barely breathing. The campus watched with us, old and silent. The wind moved just enough to cover the truth.

And then—silence.

They were gone.

But the questions? They were just beginning.

They stood a moment longer, watching the shadows retreat into silence. The Lyceum loomed behind them, its doors now closed as if nothing had happened. Slowly, they circled around to the back and entered through the rear. The moment the door clicked shut, all three exhaled—relief and disbelief mingling in their breath.

That's when I noticed Evelyn was still close—too close. Her back brushed against my chest, and my arms, instinctively protective, had wrapped around her. I pulled away fast, almost clumsily, as though the contact had burned.

It didn't work last time. I can't. Not again.

"We should get home," I said, breaking the silence. Lucas nodded.

"Do you have a place to stay?" Evelyn looked up at me, hesitant.

"I was planning to find a room somewhere." Her voice was even, but her eyes lingered just past mine, like she was already lost in another place.

"We have an extra room if you want to stay with us," Lucas offered, casual but kind. "Don't worry. It's far away from Phoenix's room."

She didn't laugh, not quite, but her lips curled with the effort of hiding it. I barely heard the words. My thoughts were still spinning—Dr. Dawson's voice, the hooded figures, the object, the language. I nearly missed the dig. When it landed, I glared at Lucas.

He smirked. Oblivious.

"Thanks, I appreciate it. If it's okay with you," Evelyn added, finally meeting my eyes.

"Of course," I said. "We can try to make sense of all this in the morning."

She nodded, a soft grin tugging at the corners of her mouth. Then we started walking.

The Grove stretched before us like a dream unraveling—warm lamp light scattering gold across grass and root, trees rising like sentinels. The moon filtered through the leaves in broken threads, casting living shadows that swayed with the breeze. The scent of loam, magnolia, and wet pavement lingered in the air.

Evelyn walked ahead, hands in her pockets, her silhouette quiet and composed. Lucas and I hung back, the crunch of gravel soft underfoot.

"So," Lucas said, nudging me. "What is with you two?"

"No, you don't," I replied, already bracing.

"Yes, I do."

"It's complicated."

"Complicated?"

I exhaled through my nose, the humid air clinging to my skin. I had hoped we'd make it home without this. But Lucas didn't let things go. Not when his curiosity was piqued.

"We may have gone on one date."

"Really?"

I nodded. "My mother set it up. Long story. Awkward one. Mistake number one—letting my mom play matchmaker. Mistake number two—letting her set me up with her grad assistant."

"And it was quite awkward, if I remember correctly," Evelyn called back over her shoulder.

Great. Just what I needed—commentary from the source.

We walked the rest of the way in silence. The houses grew darker, the streets emptier. Oxford had folded itself in for the night, leaving only the street lamps to burn gently against the sky.

As we neared the house, I let my mind drift again—to the chamber beneath the Lyceum, to the velvet-covered object, the whispered tongue. The idea of a secret society didn't seem so absurd now. But what were they? Guardians? Cultists? Scholars? Something darker?

And what did they want?

The questions trailed me like ghosts. They would wait until morning.

Until the weight of tonight settled in our bones and let us breathe again.

Once home, I gathered a few things to help Evelyn settle in. The guest room was at the end of the hall from mine—always clean, just in case. I'd always imagined my mother or maybe Lucas's parents crashing there. Never Evelyn. She didn't have much, just a single suitcase.

"Here are a few things," I said, handing them to her. "Lucas keeps the house pretty cold, so I added an extra blanket."

"Thank you."

"If you need anything, I'm right down the hall," I added, unsure why I said it. Maybe it was the night. Maybe it was her. Evelyn smiled faintly before slipping into the room, leaving me standing in the hall with too much quiet.

Lucas was already in bed, lights off, door shut. I tried to lie down, tried to rest, but the silence only made the noise louder. My mind spun—what we saw, what we heard, and most of all, what we didn't. I reached for my phone and called my mom. Straight to voicemail. Again. I tried my dad—same result. Typical. He was likely buried in fieldwork somewhere remote.

I dropped the phone on my nightstand and sat on the edge of the bed, breath tight in my chest. My knees bounced. My fists clenched and unclenched. Every inhale felt too short, every exhale too loud. My mother's voice should have been on the other end. She should've answered. She always did. Always.

My father—he'd just vanish into the field, no warning, no signal. I'd grown up used to that. But her? Her silence cut different.

My chest tightened, a pressure I couldn't push down. I stood. Then sat. Then stood again. My mouth was dry. My hands shook. Thoughts collided like speeding cars. Did she lie? Was she taken? Was she hurt? Was she—

No. I shut it down. I had to shut it down.

My throat burned. The familiar edges of panic wrapped around my ribs like vines pulling tight. I opened the window, sucked in humid air, but it only made the room feel smaller. I needed something physical. Something to jar the storm loose.

I changed into swim trunks and slipped out the back door.

Our yard wasn't big, but it was enclosed, quiet. Vines crept over the stone wall that framed the small pool. Deck chairs sat empty under a canopy of tree limbs, their shadows long in the moonlight. Pool lights glowed underwater, casting soft patterns that danced on the surface. A single cricket chirped.

I stepped to the edge and lowered myself in slowly, careful not to make a sound. The night was too still for splashes—this was not a moment for disruption.

The water was shockingly cold against the humid night. It peeled the thoughts back for a moment, gave my skin something else to feel. I let myself sink to the bottom, eyes open, the world above blurry and distant. When I surfaced, I took a slow breath. Then another. I floated on my back, watching the stars try to break through the southern haze.

This body—it was something I built. Every rep, every run, every drop of sweat had gone into remaking what I once hated. Now, in the glow of the pool, it looked sculpted, defined. But it didn't matter. Not really. Not now.

What if she was really gone?

I forced the thought away, tried to let the motion of the water carry it off. But grief didn't move like that. It lingered.

"Couldn't sleep?"

I turned sharply.

Evelyn stood at the edge of the deck in an oversized shirt, arms folded, eyes soft.

"Yeah," I said, pulling myself closer to the edge. She sat and dipped her feet into the water beside me.

I stayed a moment longer in the pool, then lifted myself out, sitting beside her. Water dripped from my arms, pooling at our feet. The air was thick, but it didn't touch the chill clinging to my skin.

"Bright blue trunks?" Evelyn smirked.

"Of course. They complement my eyes. Didn't you know?"

She laughed softly, then looked at me. Really looked.

"I always loved your eyes," she said.

That was one of the first things she'd ever told me. It was back in Memphis, in my mother's cluttered office, the one with too many books and not enough chairs. I was waiting for Mom to finish a meeting, leafing through a book on Mesopotamian symbols. Evelyn had walked in, noticed me, and without preamble said, "Your eyes. They're like mercury—like they know things no one else does." I remembered the way she'd said it—not like a compliment, more like an observation. It stuck with me. Maybe because it felt true.. Back when things felt less fragile.

"Trying to clear my head," I said, leaning back on my palms. "Sometimes this helps."

"I understand. I kind of unloaded on you tonight."

"It's okay," I said. "I needed to know. Now I just need to find her."

"We will." Her hand found mine—warm, steady. I didn't pull away at first.

But then I did.

She shifted slightly, the distance reasserting itself.

"Sorry," she whispered.

"Don't worry about it," I said, forcing a smile.

It wasn't her fault. It never had been. I just didn't know how to open doors I'd spent years learning to keep shut. That's why we didn't work. That's why so many things didn't.

We sat in silence, listening to the night—crickets, rustling leaves, the slow hum of Oxford asleep. It was intimate in a way that had nothing to do with touch. Just presence. Unspoken things.

"I'm going to try to get some sleep," I said, standing. The wet fabric clung to me as I reached for the towel.

"Goodnight. I'll be right behind you," she replied.

I stepped back inside, the door clicking softly behind me. My room waited in stillness, and for the first time all night, I hoped sleep might find me too.

OLE MISS

THREE

THE LYCEUM

"A DOOR BENEATH THE PILLARS"

I knew it was morning as the sunlight entered my room. Its rays peered through the cracks in the blinds, painting pale lines across the floor like a barcode of another day. I lay still, letting the cool draft from the ceiling vent brush against my skin, trying to savor the last few moments of peace before the day began.

My phone glared six o'clock from the nightstand. Saturday. Normally, I'd drift back into sleep. But after last night, rest was a foreign concept. My mother was missing. That thought alone struck like a metronome, steady and hard.

I pulled away from the sheets—still warm, still tethered to the illusion of safety and stood. In just boxers, I moved to the dresser and grabbed some gym shorts and a cutoff tee from a drawer. Old university shirt. Faded crest. It would do.

The house was wrapped in early morning silence, the kind that holds its breath. Only the faint chirping of birds and rustling of trees cut through. I sauntered into the living room. The light that filtered through the windows was soft, casting a bluish tint on the gray hardwood floors. This time of morning always felt somewhere between worlds.

In the kitchen, I poured a glass of orange juice and grabbed two small pastries from the pantry. My routine, a quiet ritual of familiarity. I took a seat and opened one of my books. I was halfway through a dense section on medieval power structures when I looked up. A light fog rolled lazily across the backyard, hugging the earth like a ghost that hadn't yet lifted.

It wasn't until around eight that Evelyn emerged from the hallway. She was dressed simply—tee, shorts, bare feet—but there was a calm in her face, a stillness that had nothing to do with rest.

"Good morning," she said, easing into the armchair across from me.

"Get some sleep?"

"What little I could." She looked around. "Lucas still asleep?"

"Give it another hour or two."

Evelyn gave a small, tired smile—the kind that tugged at the corners of her mouth without ever reaching her eyes. We sat in companionable silence for a while. I read. She sipped from a bottle of water. Every now and then, she glanced at the window like it might whisper something useful.

Around nine-thirty, she spoke again.

"I know there's not a lot you've told me," she said quietly. "And despite... everything, I just want you to know I'm here. If you ever need to talk."

I looked up from the page, unsure what to say. Could I trust her with that part of me? Could I trust anyone?

"Thanks," I said. "Maybe one day."

She nodded, no pressure, no disappointment. Just presence.

The back hallway creaked. Lucas finally emerged, groggy and blinking in the morning haze. He wore a long t-shirt and boxers and scratched at his hair like the night had given him more than he asked for.

"Good morning," I called.

"Hey," he mumbled, then spotted Evelyn and blinked fully awake. "Oh. Sorry, I should probably be more... dressed."

"It's fine, Lucas," Evelyn said, smirking. "Not the first time I've seen a guy half-dressed before breakfast."

Lucas shot me a look—half curious, half triumphant. I said nothing, raising an eyebrow instead. Let him wonder.

He flopped down into the chair beside her and grabbed a pastry off the table. "So… about last night?"

"I think it deserves more thought," I said.

Evelyn nodded. "We know there's a group meeting in secret. We know Dr. Dawson is one of them. That's not small."

"And they're meeting on campus," I added. "Right under our noses."

"I think we should go back," Evelyn said. "See if we missed anything. Today's Saturday—it'll be quieter. Safer."

It wasn't a bad plan. Risky, sure. But sitting around wouldn't help.

"Alright," I agreed. "We'll go once we're all ready."

While Lucas and Evelyn got dressed, I returned to the same book on medieval power structures. Not because I expected it to mention anything about the Lyceum or Ole Miss—the building was constructed in the 1800s, far removed from the era the book covered—but because I was hunting for echoes. Hidden influence. Unseen hierarchies. I wanted to understand how power like that could exist so openly and still remain invisible.

Nothing. Not a single reference to secret chambers or hidden doors. Of course there wasn't. That kind of truth doesn't get bound in spines or shelved in libraries. Whatever lives under that building—if anything—has been kept from the page on purpose. Hidden not just by time, but by intent. Sanitized before it could even make it into myth.

That was the answer in itself.

Secrets this deep don't live in documents. They live in people. In silence. In the kind of history that gets erased before it's ever written.

I closed the book, ran a hand through my hair, and stared out the window again. The fog was lifting, but it left behind something unsettled.

What the hell were we walking into?

It was around ten when everyone was ready. Evelyn was in shorts and a tee, Lucas the same. I stayed in what I was wearing—and as we stepped into the sweltering Mississippi heat, I was glad I did.

Our walk to campus was quiet. The air was thick, but the trees whispered overhead, casting shade along the sidewalks. Every few minutes a car passed, but otherwise, Oxford was asleep. Without a home game, the Grove stood empty, the canopy of oaks untouched except by squirrels and the occasional breeze.

"Is campus always this peaceful?" Evelyn asked, her gaze sweeping the empty lawns.

"When there's not a game, yes," Lucas answered.

"So what's it like on game day?"

"It's basically one big party," I said.

Evelyn raised an eyebrow. "And how would you know that, you bookworm?"

"That would be because I drag him to it," Lucas said proudly. "Otherwise he'd fossilize in the library."

She laughed, the sound light and familiar. "I'll have to see it one day."

"You should've seen his 21st," Lucas added with a wicked grin.

I shot him a look sharp enough to cut glass. "Nope."

Evelyn's grin widened, her laughter bubbling up again. I turned away before they could see the color rising in my face. Never let Lucas mix your drinks—that was a mistake I'd only make once.

We passed Ventress Hall, its red brick and Gothic silhouette piercing the leafy skyline. Unlike the columned buildings that dominated campus, Ventress stood smaller, prouder—more like a memory than a monument. Its conical roof caught the morning light, and for a moment, the campus felt like a place of stories.

Then the Lyceum came into view.

The building was open. We entered quietly and made our way to the bookshelf. It slid aside as easily as before, revealing the rough stone hallway.

"This is still creepy," Lucas muttered.

The air cooled as we descended into the open chamber. The stone steps groaned beneath our feet, worn by time, slick with moisture. Moss clung to the walls like stubborn secrets, and the smell—damp earth mixed with something faintly metallic—filled our noses. The torches that lined the walls flickered against the breeze, casting long shadows that danced across the stone. About halfway down, Evelyn paused beside a faded mural, barely visible behind layers of grime. It showed three figures—cloaked, arms outstretched—surrounding what looked like the same tree from the chamber. "Look at this," she whispered. Lucas brushed his hand along a carved groove in the wall, tracing a spiraling pattern like roots or veins. "Was this here yesterday?" he asked. I shook my head. Maybe we were too distracted last night. Maybe the darkness had hidden more than we realized. We continued down, slower now, more cautious. The silence deepened, pressing in. And then we reached the chamber again, but with new eyes. The murals loomed larger in the morning light that filtered through some unseen shaft. Evelyn stepped closer, her fingers brushing the stone.

"Amazing."

"It is," I agreed. "But what is it?"

The mural depicted a cataclysm—great armies clashing beneath a bruised sky, fire sweeping across hills, storm clouds clawing at the heavens. At the center of it all stood a colossal white tree, luminous even amid the chaos. Branches stretched across the mural like veins, and from its roots, faint lines spread outward, as if the tree itself held the world together. Flames licked at its bark, and three cloaked figures—one kneeling, one standing, one dissolving into ash—circled its trunk. The detail was breathtaking, layered and old, the kind of artistry that made you feel watched. Beneath it, lines of unfamiliar script glimmered faintly, etched in something metallic, not quite gold. Evelyn snapped pictures in silence, her gaze locked not on the battle, but on the figure crumbling into light.

"Guys—down here!" Lucas called.

We followed him to the lower chamber, each step down echoing off the ancient stone walls. The air grew colder, heavier, like it hadn't been stirred in centuries. I moved ahead slowly, brushing my fingertips along the stone as we descended, the dampness clinging to my skin. The scent was stronger here—wet moss, mineral, and something older, like burnt incense and rusted iron.

When we reached the bottom, the chamber opened before us, circular and immense, like stepping into the heart of something sacred. My footsteps softened on the stone floor, worn smooth in the center and rough near the edges. The space breathed, exhaled memory.

At the center rose a massive stone tree, its roots splitting the floor like fractures in the earth, reaching out in all directions. I walked around it slowly, one hand grazing its carved trunk. The patterns were too deliberate to be decorative—there was intention behind every groove. Symbols shimmered faintly where light from the torches caught them.

I stepped between two of the marble Ionic columns, each one slick with moss and carved in looping glyphs I didn't recognize. I circled the column slowly, brushing my fingers along its damp surface. When I pressed my palm against it, there was a faint hum—like a memory vibrating under my skin. I leaned in slightly, listening, half-expecting the stone to whisper back. The chill from the moss seeped into my skin, grounding me. This place wasn't just old—it was waiting.

The room smelled of damp earth and old iron, with a whisper of ash clinging to the edges. It settled into my skin, the way grief does—slow and unshakable.

Murals emerged next, half-swathed in shadow. I paused before one, watching the scene unfold beneath the torchlight: a sky torn open by flame, armies locked in battle, and a singular white tree standing untouched in the chaos. At its base, three figures—one raised in defiance, one on their knees, and one fading into fire—encircled its roots. I didn't know what it meant. But it felt like a memory not mine, returned to me all the same.

Another mural showed rows of people kneeling before a sealed door guarded by robed figures, silver shining where the paint hadn't faded. I stepped closer, the weight of the room pressing against my chest, not suffocating—just real. It wanted us to see. To remember. Even if we didn't understand.

Evelyn stepped lightly across the stone, her hand trailing along one column. Lucas crouched near a mural, inspecting its chipped surface.

"It feels sacred," she whispered.

And she was right. The space didn't just hold history—it held memory. And weight. Like stepping into a story that still remembered its ending, even if we didn't.

“What is this place?” Evelyn whispered.

Lucas pointed to a lectern. An old book lay open, its pages lined in faded Latin.

“Beneath a hollow grove is where we rest,” I translated.

“Could it mean people?” Evelyn asked.

“Or something worse,” Lucas muttered.

Evelyn photographed the pages. “It's safer to leave it. But at least we'll have something to study.”

Everywhere we looked, more questions. Symbols carved between the murals—stylized, alive. I didn't recognize any of them.

“Phoenix,” Evelyn called. I joined her at the center.

She pointed to the trunk of the tree etched into the floor.

“Isn't that the university seal?”

It was. The eye, hidden but unmistakable.

“What's it doing here?” Lucas asked, kneeling.

“Maybe it marks this as the center,” he said. “The tree's branches… they could lead to more chambers.”

“Very clever,” Evelyn said, impressed.

Lucas beamed. I rolled my eyes.

“I think we should research more before going further,” Evelyn said.

“You want to go deeper?” Lucas asked, stunned.

“Don't you?” she replied.

I looked around again. My mother's voice echoed in my mind. There was something down here—and we were only beginning to see it.

We climbed back to the upper chamber and moved the shelf into place. But the moment we stepped into the main room, we weren't alone.

Someone was waiting.

The air shifted before we even saw her. Dr. Miriam Dawson stood in the center of the Lyceum's main room, her posture straight as a blade. She wasn't just waiting—she was guarding.

"Mr. Knight," she said. Her voice held no warmth. Just my name, flat and edged. "May I ask what you are doing?"

I straightened instinctively, as if she were still my professor. Still my mentor.

"Investigating," I said. I tried to sound sure, confident. "What is all of this?"

"Something you should not be looking into." Her tone clipped each word like it offended her. She'd always been composed, even gentle, no matter how tense the topic. But now—there was a crack in that mask. Annoyance. No, disappointment. Something worse.

"The chamber below—it's just the beginning, isn't it?" I pushed. I needed her to give me something. Anything.

Her eyes flickered. Just for a second. "Phoenix, I am not at liberty to discuss this. You need to leave."

That's when it broke. All the restraint I had been holding, all the fear and confusion and anger that had been simmering since Evelyn showed up, since my mother disappeared—it snapped.

"Are you at liberty to tell me why my mother is missing?"

The words hit her like a slap. Her breath hitched, just a fraction, but I saw it. Saw the fear slip through.

"I'm sorry," she said softly. "Let's talk in my office on Tuesday. For now, please... leave this alone."

It was like watching a wall rebuild itself. The vulnerability, gone. The authority, back in place.

We left without another word.

Outside, the heat was no longer oppressive—it was grounding. Evelyn caught up beside me, her eyes searching mine.

"You're not dropping this, are you?"

I shook my head. "Why would I?"

Lucas jogged to join us. No one said anything for a few steps. Then I spoke.

"She knows something. And we're going to find out what it is. We're going to find my mother. I don't care what it takes."

Evelyn nodded. Lucas gave a half-smile, half-sigh. "Well then," he said. "Guess that means late nights."

"What do you think?"

"I guess I should go grocery shopping," Lucas groaned. "Only way I survive research is with snacks."

Evelyn let out a short laugh. "Do you always think with your stomach?"

Lucas winked. "Only when I'm awake."

But I didn't laugh. I kept walking. My fists clenched at my sides. Because beneath everything—Evelyn's calm, Lucas's humor, the heat of the Mississippi sun—was betrayal.

Dr. Dawson had known me for years. Had mentored me. Had held my hand through theory and grief.

And she lied.

Not by words—but by omission. By presence. By standing in that chamber like it wasn't made of ghosts.

That was what burned.

And the fire wasn't going out anytime soon.

OLE MISS

FOUR
QUESTIONS

"THE SILENCE BETWEEN US"

It was Tuesday morning, and I sat alone outside Dr. Dawson's office, fingers steepled, elbows resting on my knees. The corridor was empty, quiet except for the hum of ancient pipes groaning behind plaster and the faint rhythm of a janitor's mop against tile down the hall. A thin ray of light filtered through the small window, catching the dust in the air like frozen rain.

The weekend had passed in a blur of frustration and research. Evelyn had gone back to Memphis, combing through my mother's notes and office for anything—a scrap of paper, a name, a direction. I'd spent my nights calling the same number over and over, hoping this time her voice would answer. It never did.

Part of me wanted to file a missing person report. But what would that even do? The police would look in Memphis. They wouldn't know where to start. And the media frenzy would destroy what little space I had left to breathe.

I wasn't just here out of obligation. I needed answers. Not just about my mother, but about the chamber beneath the Lyceum—the murals, the tree, the impossible sense that the world I'd known was paper-thin, and I'd just seen through the cracks.

Dr. Dawson finally arrived, her tall frame shadowing the hallway as she strode toward me, papers cradled in one arm like a bundle of unfinished thoughts.

"Mr. Knight, early as usual," she said, offering a ghost of her usual warmth. Her smile didn't reach her eyes.

"Dr. Dawson," I greeted, rising.

She fumbled with her keys and opened the door. "Pardon the mess—you know I think better with a cluttered desk."

The smell hit me first: old paper, ink, a hint of lavender from her worn scarf. Her office was the organized chaos of someone who lived among history. Towers of books lined the walls, overflowed the shelves, and formed spires on the floor that threatened to collapse with a single breath. Her window barely caught the light through the overgrowth outside, casting long streaks of shadow across everything.

I took the familiar seat opposite her and tried to read her expression. There was tension in her jaw, a hesitation in her movement.

"I know you have questions," she said, fishing out a paper from her stack. "But first, your work."

She handed it to me. Barely marked. "It was thoughtful. Persuasive. An A, as expected."

"Thank you," I said, taking it. I didn't look at the grade. Not yet.

She set her bag aside and leaned back. Her demeanor shifted—subtle, but I noticed. This was no longer a conversation between student and professor.

"Phoenix," she said, voice softened, "what exactly did you see?"

I hesitated. How much could I share without tipping my hand?

"I found the chamber," I said. "Just stumbled on it."

Her eyes narrowed. She saw the lie in that. "You were there Friday night."

I held her gaze. "You recognized me?"

"I thought I did. I needed to be sure." She leaned forward slightly. "So I'll ask again. What did you see?"

I exhaled slowly. "A gathering. A mural. Something ancient. And I want to know what the hell it is."

She hesitated, folding her hands in her lap. "We are not what you think."

"What I think is that there's a group of faculty wearing hoods and chanting in a secret underground room."

She smiled—barely. "Yes. The hoods are ridiculous. That wasn't my idea."

"But you're part of it."

"I am. And there are things at play that I can't fully explain. Yet."

My jaw clenched. "Do you have anything to do with my mother disappearing?"

Her eyes widened, and for the first time, her composure cracked. "No. God, no. Phoenix... where was she last seen?"

"Here. In Oxford."

Something in her went cold. She leaned back, stunned.

"I had no idea." Her voice was soft. "She's my friend. And a brilliant historian."

I nodded, barely holding myself together. "She would've told me something. Anything."

"I know." She stood, moved around the desk, and without asking, pulled me into an embrace. Her arms were thin but firm, and the gesture felt honest. Real.

"We're on your side," she whispered. "And I promise you—we want the same answers."

She stepped back, gently but firmly. "Now go. I'll see you in class tomorrow."

It was the most I was going to get. For now.

I left the office, the door clicking shut behind me like a verdict. There was something else she wasn't saying—I felt it in my gut. She hadn't lied about not knowing where my mother was. But there was fear in her face. Fear and sorrow.

And that was almost worse.

Later that afternoon, I hunted shadows.

The third floor of the library was a vault of silence and dust. Shafts of light cut through tall arched windows, igniting motes in the air like a galaxy suspended in stillness. The smell—aged parchment, oak varnish, something mineral and earthy—clung to the back of my throat. I moved like a ghost through the stacks, fingers trailing the spines of books I could name by feel alone.

I wasn't just searching. I was chasing something hidden—beneath the surface, behind the obvious.

So I watched. Lurked in the shadows near the archive wing. I timed the librarian's coffee break and slipped behind the circulation desk, ducking beneath the swinging gate. The door to the back room was locked, but a faculty member had propped it ajar earlier.

A sliver was all I needed.

Inside, the room was close and humming with quiet machinery. Old maps. Filing cabinets. Metal drawers labeled with brittle masking tape. I crept to one marked "Architectural Records."

One drawer stuck slightly. I tugged harder. It gave, shrieking on rusted rails, revealing carefully filed tubes of parchment. I pulled a few at random, laying them out on the table beneath a green-shaded lamp.

Drawings of the Lyceum—some dating back to its earliest days. Floor plans, cross-sections, hand-inked with astonishing detail. I combed through each one, heart pounding, scanning for anything—a seam, a stairwell, an unaccounted space.

Nothing.

But something was off. The drawings were too clean. Too deliberate. No architectural plan is that tidy without revision—no notes, no margins, no alternate drafts. My eyes narrowed.

Someone had scrubbed the record. This wasn't a mistake. It was concealment.

Footsteps behind me—a sudden creak on the old floorboards—and my heart jolted. I turned sharply, tension coiled tight in my chest.

Lucas stood a few paces away, hands raised in mock surrender, coffee cup sloshing slightly. "Easy, man. Just me. Didn't mean to scare you."

I stared at him, confused. "How did you even get back here?"

He shrugged, flashing a mischievous grin. "Told the desk I was looking for a lost laptop. They let me through. Guess I've still got that innocent face." I just rolled my eyes at him as the smile increased in length.

Lucas crossed the room quietly, the echo of his steps muffled by thick carpet. Sliding into the seat across from me, he gave a wary glance around. "Didn't expect to find you up here. This place feels haunted."

"It is," I muttered, the adrenaline fading slowly as I turned back to the floor plan. "Just not in the way you think."

He leaned closer, eyes scanning the faded paper. "Any luck?"

I shook my head. "It's like someone sanitized the past. These aren't the real records. They're decoys."

Lucas raised a brow. "So what? Someone rewrote history to hide a basement crypt under the university's crown jewel?"

"Something like that."

He nodded slowly, then paused, looking thoughtful. "You know, back when I was a freshman, my roommate swore there were tunnels under campus. Secret ones. Like, old Confederate escape routes or Prohibition hideouts—total ghost story stuff. We'd laugh it off... but now I wonder."

I looked up, caught off guard. "You think there's truth in those stories?"

Lucas shrugged. "Sometimes the wildest stuff's got a kernel of truth. My dad used to say that stories are how people smuggle reality through time. Maybe what you're looking for isn't in the records—it's in the legends."

The words sat heavy between us, unexpected in their weight.

"That sounds like something my mother would've said," I murmured.

He smiled, lifting his coffee like a toast. "Then maybe you're on the right track."

Lucas gestured to the satchel at my feet. "You're going to keep digging till you fall in. Come on. Let's go eat before you forget what food tastes like."

I exhaled and began rolling the plans with careful precision.

"You're right. Just... let me bag these."

"To the Square," he said. "My treat."

We left the archives in silence. The echo of our steps lingered longer than they should have, like the library itself was holding its breath.

The Square was a pocket of normalcy in a world unraveling. Sunlight glazed the brickwork of the courthouse, turning it a molten amber. The first cool whisper of autumn threaded through the streets, brushing against our skin like a secret. Trees bordering the sidewalks rattled faintly, shedding early leaves like forgotten promises.

Lucas and I took a table on the patio of a local deli, the scent of toasted bread and herbs wafting from the open kitchen. A server set down two glasses of sweet tea, condensation already beading on the sides. The quiet rhythm of the square unfolded before us—cars meandering past, a street musician softly picking a blues riff near the corner, laughter drifting from the open doors of a boutique nearby.

Lucas bit into his sandwich like a man starved by the world's chaos.

"It floors me that you're not overweight," I said, watching him with mock judgment.

He smirked mid-chew, wiping his mouth. "You're just jealous I can eat like this and still rock skinny jeans."

I nudged my own sandwich. It was warm in my hands, the crust crisped just right—but it felt like too much. Like reality pressing down. My stomach twisted, not from hunger, but from everything else.

"You need to eat," Lucas said, quieter this time. His eyes didn't leave mine.

"Trying," I muttered, and forced a bite. The tomato was sweet, the cheese rich, but they turned to paste in my mouth.

A beat of silence.

"You ever think about just… vanishing for a bit? No secrets, no searching. Just bad TV and worse decisions?"

I gave him a half-smile. "That your subtle way of asking me to spend more time with you?"

"Maybe. You're a tough read, Phee." His voice faltered. "Used to think I had you all figured out. Not anymore."

Before I could respond, a voice cut through the hum of the square—sharp, sweet, unmistakably flirtatious.

"Hey, handsome."

Lucas kicked me under the table.

I looked up. She was all confidence and curves, framed by the sunlight—olive skin, hair cascading in waves, lips curled in amused challenge. The kind of presence that turns a street into a stage.

"Me?" I asked, stupidly.

She laughed, smoky and smooth. "Yes, you. Love the eyes."

"Uh… thanks."

She handed us a black card stock invite, embossed with gold foil. Thursday. Address, time, a teasing little 'don't be late.'

"Allison," she said, her gaze locking onto mine like a match to kindling. "Nice to meet you, Phoenix."

She turned, hips swaying, owning every inch of the sidewalk.

Lucas watched her go, then grinned. "Talk about a distraction."

I flicked a napkin at him. "Shut up."

But his eyes weren't following her. Not entirely. I caught the shift—barely—the way his gaze snagged for a breath too long on the barista cleaning a nearby table. It meant nothing to me then.

"Think Evelyn found anything?" he asked as we paid and gathered our things.

"I hope so," I said, my voice already distant.

We wandered through the golden haze of late afternoon. Conversation turned—light, then probing. Lucas brought up Evelyn again, a gentle prod into old wounds. I deflected, made it a joke, tossed it back.

He didn't push. Just gave me that same look—quiet, unreadable. A smile that didn't need to be anything else.

And I wondered, for the first time, if Lucas had a whole other story he was keeping close, waiting for someone to ask.

V,

I know what you'll say—that I'm acting from sentiment.
You're right.
But I also know the signs.
The seal is breaking. I can feel it.
He's not ready. He doesn't even know.
I've raised him. He is my son. And the Collective is closer than they realize. I fear it's only a matter of time before they discover what we did.
I'm going to Oxford. There's something we missed—something that's been there the whole time, right under our noses.
If I can draw them away, give him more time...
maybe that's enough.
If I don't return, keep him in the light.
Remind him who he is.
A life worth living.
Guard the Flame.

-Joanne

Five

Distractions

"Smoke and Surface"

It was Thursday. Still no word from Evelyn.

I tried to tell myself not to worry. She'd texted briefly Monday night to say she was back in Memphis chasing down something in my mother's notes. Nothing since. Rationally, I told myself she was fine. But logic doesn't always win against instinct.

Lucas watched me pacing with a book in hand, his arms crossed, a knowing smirk tugging at his lips.

"You're pacing."

"No, I'm not."

He pointed. "You've walked that exact circle at least eight times."

I stopped mid-step, glancing down at the worn path I'd made across the rug. Damn. I hadn't even noticed.

"Evelyn's fine," Lucas said. He was trying to be reassuring, but his voice carried an undertone of concern he didn't want me to catch. Maybe I wasn't the only one worried. Maybe neither of us wanted to admit how much she meant.

"I know," I muttered, settling on a stool at the kitchen counter. "Just… she should've called."

"Probably chasing a lead. Or she found something and lost track of time. You know how she gets."

I did. Laser-focused. Stubborn. Brilliant. Still, it gnawed at me.

Lucas nudged my elbow. "We've got a party to get ready for."

"Do we have to?" I let my forehead fall against the cold granite counter.

"Yes, Phee, you do. Be social. Come on. You'll survive."

I groaned. My idea of a good night was a book and a blanket. Not a party thrown by a gorgeous stranger who flirted like it was a martial art.

Outside, the sky hung low and heavy, a blanket of gray mist softening the edges of Oxford's red brick and wrought iron. The cool humidity kissed our skin as we stepped out, the distant rumble of traffic muffled under the shroud of drizzle. It was Mississippi pretending to be autumn, and I wanted it to last.

We walked through the misty streets, the air clinging damp and chill to our jackets, turning our breath into ghostly wisps. Each streetlamp we passed buzzed faintly in the fog, casting long golden halos on the slick pavement. Lucas brushed close beside me, his presence steady, humming a soft tune to calm his own nerves—or maybe mine. I noticed how his fingers tapped rhythmically against the seam of his jeans, a small, restless gesture.

The house loomed ahead, nestled just off the Square. A Victorian beauty with carved gables and stained glass that flickered like kaleidoscopes in the low light. Warm amber glow leaked from the windows like secrets. The gingerbread trim along the porch curled like frosting atop a haunted confection. Faint laughter rose from within, carried on the low throb of bass. The music wasn't just heard—it thrummed against our ribs, vibrating in the marrow.

I paused at the gate, heart racing. My stomach knotted.

Lucas nudged my shoulder. "Come on, Phee. It's just a party, not a battlefield."

But to me, they were sometimes the same thing.

"Why am I doing this again?"

"Because I said so," Lucas grinned.

The front door swung open, spilling light and bodies into the yard. Inside was chaos—a living kaleidoscope of sound and color. The air was thick with sweat, perfume, beer, and something smoky that stung the nose. People swayed and danced, clung and shouted over the music. Red solo cups in every hand. Laughter mingled with the pounding rhythm.

"This is not a party," I said. "This is a circus."

"An awesome circus," Lucas shouted, already disappearing into the crowd.

Typical. I sighed and moved through the crush of bodies, searching for solitude or at least a wall to lean against. Neon lights bounced off the ceiling fan, creating dizzying shadows. Every surface was sticky. Every conversation too loud.

"Glad you made it," a voice purred near my ear.

I turned to see Allison standing before me, the girl from the Square, radiating confidence and danger in equal measure. She looked like she'd stepped out of a perfume ad. Dress clinging, eyes glittering. Dangerous.

"Phoenix, right?"

"Yeah," I replied. "Allison?"

"Look at you," she said, handing me a cup with a wicked grin. "Drink."

I hesitated. It smelled sharp—too sharp.

"Come on, have a little fun."

I took a sip. Burned like fire and tasted like regret. She cheered like I'd won a challenge.

"That's better, handsome."

The word sent a chill down my spine. She guided me deeper into the party. Past dancing bodies and spilled drinks. Past someone throwing up in a sink. Into a sunken living room with mismatched couches and flickering fairy lights. The air was thick—hot breath, cheap cologne, the cloying tang of spilt liquor soaked into the carpet.

We sank onto one couch. She leaned in. Her perfume was heady, cloying, too much. A mix of jasmine and some darker note—patchouli or maybe musk. It wrapped around me like a noose.

Lucas stumbled by, waving dramatically. "This party is lit!"

"Your friend's enjoying himself," Allison said, slipping her legs over mine. Too close.

I tried to focus, but my head was spinning. My pulse surged. The drink was too strong. Something was wrong.

"I don't feel—"

"What's wrong, handsome?" Her tone had shifted. Too calm.

My vision blurred.

The music twisted. Lights swam.

Dark–

Pain—

Then silence.

And I fell.

Into the place I thought I'd left behind.

The place I feared most.

My vision began to return, sluggish and muddled. Everything was colorless, like being submerged underwater, shadows swimming at the edge of recognition. My head throbbed with the pulse of returning awareness. A dull ache radiated from my temples, matched only by the persistent, rhythmic plink of water dripping from some unseen pipe above. Each drop hit the concrete with a soft splatter, counting time like a metronome in a world otherwise drowned in stillness.

The air moved across my skin with the chill of abandonment—stale, metallic, edged with mildew and something faintly chemical, like old paint or decaying leather. I could taste it on the back of my tongue. As my vision sharpened, shapes resolved out of the murk: bare concrete walls veined with moisture, tagged by forgotten graffiti. The shadows clung like cobwebs between thick iron beams, vanishing upward into a ceiling shrouded in darkness.

I was upright. No, bound. Ropes bit into my waist and wrists, the fibers coarse and unyielding. My muscles screamed with pressure. I twisted instinctively—pain flared. My breath hitched. The steel beam at my back was unforgiving, its chill seeping into my spine. The sensation of damp rust kissed my clothes. I could feel every thread of the ropes grinding against raw skin.

How could I be so stupid? So careless?

Above, a single bulb hung from a cord, its light flickering with a sickly yellow stutter. Each swing of it cast jittery shadows that lunged and shrank around the cavernous warehouse. Massive girders arched around me, forming a skeletal frame that seemed almost organic, like the ribcage of some long-dead beast. Dust floated in the air like ash suspended in time.

This wasn't the house from the party. This wasn't anywhere familiar.

I'd been taken.

Footsteps echoed.

"Look who's finally awake," came a voice laced with sugar and steel.

Allison.

She stepped into the halo of the overhead light, dressed down now—just a white tee and dark cargo pants, her hair pulled back, no longer the temptress from the party. Her confidence hadn't lessened. If anything, it had solidified into something more dangerous.

"What is this?" I croaked.

"Oh, handsome, we kidnapped you. Can't you guess?"

I struggled, twisting against the ropes. She moved closer, circling me like a lioness.

"Why? What do you want?"

"You, Phoenix. For who you are. For what you are. You just don't know it yet." Her voice was almost wistful, like she regretted the necessity.

I kept her talking. Every second gave me another chance to test the knots, to map my cage.

"Need me for what?"

Allison smiled and stopped in front of me. "You think this is about college crushes and parties? You're part of something ancient, Phoenix. You carry something sacred inside you. Blood. Memory. Potential. And the Collective... we collect things. Especially rare ones."

Her hand ghosted along my cheek, icy and gentle. My skin crawled.

"You know about my mother," I growled.

She nodded. "She interfered. She's safe, for now. But she knows truths that no one should. And you, you've barely scratched the surface of what's inside you."

"You know nothing about me."

She tilted her head, eyes narrowing. "Don't I? Don't you wonder why your eyes flash silver when you're angry? Why your name was chosen? Why the Council hides you? We do. We watch."

I pulled sharply. One rope strand frayed. Almost there.

"You're exactly what we need, Phoenix. A key. A weapon. A bridge."

She leaned in, so close I could smell her perfume again—now tainted by blood and sweat.

"Don't you want to know why you survived?"

That was enough. I slammed my forehead into hers. Her head snapped back with a cry, blood spilling from her nose.

As she stumbled, the bindings slipped. I tore free. Pain flared, but freedom burned hotter.

Two goons burst from the shadows. Built like linebackers. Fast. But not trained.

The first threw a haymaker. I dipped under it and planted my palm into his chest—center mass. The blow reverberated through his ribcage, sending him crashing into a stack of crates.

The second came low, hoping to tackle. I pivoted on instinct, swept his legs clean out from under him, then drove my knee into his ribs as he gasped. He didn't rise.

Allison shrieked, fury painting her bloodied face. "Get him!"

I lunged and grabbed her collar, driving her into the same steel beam that had held me captive. The thud reverberated through both our bodies, metal groaning with the impact.

"Where is she?! Where's my mother?!" I shouted, voice raw, veins taut with fury. My knuckles whitened as I pressed her against the beam, lifting her slightly off the ground.

Her breath caught—more from surprise than fear. Her legs dangled just enough to remind her she wasn't in control. But then—she smiled. A sick, knowing grin that cut deeper than any blade.

"You'll never find her. The Collective sees all."

For a second, I didn't move. The weight of her words anchored me, twisted in my gut like barbed wire. My arm trembled with the force of restraint. Her eyes searched mine, daring me to finish what I started. But I couldn't cross that line.

Not yet.

I let her go. She crumpled to the floor, coughing and clutching her throat, her pride as bruised as her neck. Her eyes burned—not with fear, but promise.

She would remember this.

And so would I.

Footsteps thundered in the distance—more goons incoming.

I turned and sprinted, boots hammering the concrete.

A side door. Emergency exit. Rusted and barely ajar.

I slammed through it, into the cold grip of night—

Darkness—

The woods beyond were cloaked in a dense, moonless mist, thick as smoke and just as choking. Trees loomed like skeletal sentinels, their bark slick with rain, limbs reaching like twisted fingers. Each breath I took was cold and wet, drawing in the scent of moss, decay, and ozone.

Darkness—

Silence—

The drizzle wasn't just falling—it clung, sticky and persistent, soaking my clothes until they hung heavy against my skin. The chill gnawed through to my bones, and each step through the underbrush left icy water splashing up my calves. Behind me: distant voices, urgent and cruel, echoing like ghosts.

But I ran.

Branches clawed at my face and arms. Thorns scraped my legs. The earth sucked at my feet with every step. Fog swallowed everything a few feet out. My lungs burned. My heartbeat pounded in my ears, louder than the slapping of rain.

Eventually, I collapsed behind a gnarled tree trunk slick with lichen. The ground was soft and muddy, the damp stench of decomposing leaves thick in the air. I pressed my back to the bark, trying to vanish into it. My breath came in ragged gasps. Around me: nothing but the rhythmic drop-drop-drop of water falling from branches to the soaked earth.

A stillness settled. Not peace, but a hush—ominous, waiting. The kind of silence that makes the hairs on your arms rise, where the dark presses in and breath feels too loud.

Then—

A rustle. Subtle. Measured.

Something moved between the trees, just at the edge of vision. A flicker of shadow against deeper black.

A deer stepped into the clearing, its coat dappled with rain, steam rising faintly from its back. It stood perfectly still, ears twitching, eyes fixed on me. Ancient eyes. As if it saw something deeper than the surface. As if it knew me. As if it remembered something I hadn't yet learned.

I stared back, transfixed, heart slowing. The fog blurred its edges, but its gaze pierced through. It didn't flee. It watched. Studied. It bowed its head ever so slightly—an acknowledgment. Then—gone. A blur of muscle and grace disappearing into the mist.

I wasn't alone. Not entirely. And maybe, just maybe, the forest knew who I was.

Silence—

Cold—

Darkness—

Time passed. How long? Hours maybe. The fog seemed to bend time, stretching minutes into eternities. I walked, trembling, every step dragging like it weighed a hundred pounds. My breath came in shallow gulps, each inhale laced with the scent of rotting leaves and cold iron.

Thoughts spun like leaves in a storm. The Collective—they knew who I was. More than I did. My mother… held somewhere in shadow. My secret—something I had buried so deep even I struggled to name it. But Allison's words lingered like a toxin: the Council hid me. Protected me.

Why?

Each syllable of that question thudded in my skull. Why would they? Who were they really—these so-called keepers of truth? Scholars, mystics, spies? What was I to them? A mistake? A weapon?

What was I?

That question hit harder than any blow. My feet sank deeper into the mud with every step, the world narrowing to the rhythm of slosh and splatter. The cold was no longer just on my skin—it was inside me, wrapping around my ribs, squeezing.

I was unraveling. Not from the chase, not even from fear—but from the yawning hole opening inside me. I didn't know who I was anymore. And maybe, just maybe, I never had.

The trees leaned closer, their limbs skeletal in the mist. The dark pressed in like a breath held too long. I staggered over a root and caught myself on a branch slick with moss. My fingers had gone numb.

Was this still Mississippi? Was I even on Earth? Or had I stepped into some otherworldly borderland—between truth and madness, between man and myth?

"Phoenix!"

I froze.

Again: "Phoenix!"

British. Familiar.

"Bloody hell, Phoenix, where are you?!"

Evelyn.

I stepped from the shadows. Her voice, sharp and desperate, was a lifeline. I moved through the bramble, my breath ragged. When I reached her, she pulled me into a tight embrace, warmth radiating through her soaked coat.

"How did you find me?"

"Lucas called me when he realized you'd disappeared. I was already on edge after what happened in Memphis. It's only about ninety minutes—I drove like hell. Tracked your shoes as soon as I was close enough."

"Wait—you what?"

"I put a tracker in your shoes," she admitted, looking sheepish. "I didn't know what we were dealing with back then. And after seeing what we saw I just had a feeling. I'm sorry."

I blinked at her, mouth opening, then closing. Finally: "Remind me never to trust you with my laundry."

She half-laughed, half-sighed. "I'll take that over a screaming fit."

"Thanks," I said as we pulled apart. "Allison—she has my mother."

Her expression hardened instantly, lips pressing into a thin line. No words, only fury.

We stumbled over the ridge, dew-slicked and treacherous, to where Lucas paced with a flashlight, his face pale and strained. The beam jittered in his trembling hands, slicing through the mist in erratic arcs. When he saw us, his whole body sagged in relief. He sprinted forward with a muttered, "Holy hell—thank God," and wrapped me in a fierce hug before pulling back with a sharp breath.

"You okay? What the hell happened? I—I should've noticed sooner," he said, eyes scanning me as if to confirm I was real.

I nodded slowly, unsure where to begin. My throat tightened. "You called Evelyn?"

"Yeah. When you didn't come back and your phone just rang—I knew something was wrong. I panicked. I—I'm sorry, Phee."

There was guilt in his voice, genuine and heavy, pressing between us like fog. I clapped a hand on his shoulder, squeezing once. "You did good. I'm here. That's what matters."

Lucas swallowed hard, his jaw flexing. He looked like he wanted to say more, maybe yell, maybe cry, but he nodded instead. The flashlight quivered in his hand, the light catching the glint of unshed tears.

He looked down for a moment, then met my eyes. "You don't know how scared I was. I—" He stopped himself, exhaled, then added quieter, "You mean more than you realize, okay?"

I offered a soft smile, brushing it off with a weak chuckle, but something flickered beneath his gaze. A shadow of something unspoken.

The moment passed.

Then came the sound. Low, mechanical. An engine, cutting through the forest hush like a blade.

"They're coming," I hissed.

A toolshed stood nearby, half-collapsed and hidden by ivy and rot. I threw the door open and shoved Evelyn and Lucas inside.

"Stay down," I ordered, voice taut with urgency.

The musty air inside the shed reeked of old grass, oil, and mildew. My hand found a broom leaning in the corner—its wooden shaft long and dense, slick with damp. I snapped off the bristles with a sharp twist, the sound echoing like a crack of thunder in the confined space.

Outside, the forest pulsed with tension. Then they appeared—three men, shadows wrapped in black, emerging from the trees like predators. Their movements were sleek and menacing, water dripping from their hoods, the glint of something metallic at their hips.

"What, you gonna joust us with that stick?" one sneered, stepping forward with a cocky swagger.

"You'd be surprised," I said, voice low, every nerve alight. The staff wasn't just a stick to me—it was muscle memory, hard-earned discipline. Years ago, when I was a freshman. Dr. Dawson insisted I train. Said it would help ground the chaos inside. It's like she knew I was struggling and I didn't argue—I needed control. The dojo became my temple, the kata my ritual. Every strike, every breath, every pivot was inked into my bones. This wasn't bravado. This was survival sharpened into form.

They lunged.

I sprang into motion. The air split as I pivoted, the wooden shaft a natural extension of my arm. I ducked under the first punch, feeling the wind of it graze past, then drove my staff hard into the attacker's knee. A crunch—he howled and fell.

The second came fast, heavier. He clipped my shoulder with a glancing hit that sent pain singing down my side. I spun with the momentum, crouched low, and swept his legs. He crashed down. I followed through with a hard thrust to the chest, air whooshing from his lungs.

Two down. Mud splashed as they writhed.

The third froze, eyes wide, uncertain.

"Who the hell are you?" he rasped.

I stepped forward, heart hammering, rain dripping from my chin in rivulets. My grip tightened on the staff.

"Tell Allison... I'm coming for her."

He didn't wait for more. He turned and vanished into the woods.

The shed door creaked open behind me. Lucas stepped out, mouth agape, eyes reflecting the chaos. Evelyn was cautious as she slowly emerged. There was a hint of realization it seemed, but there was something else. Investigative, fear, and something darker.

"Damn," he breathed, voice half in awe. "Remind me never to tick you off."

Evelyn knelt beside one of the unconscious attackers, inspecting the small circular emblem stitched into the shoulder of his coat—deep blue, almost invisible in the dark.

"It's them. The Collective."

"Who are they?" I asked.

"I'll tell you everything once we get back, first lets get you home."

"Ok, but I don't..."

I dropped the staff, my hands trembling now that the adrenaline had faded and the world came crashing in from all sides. All I saw was Evelyn's face darken as she started to rush forward, but it was already to late.

Silence—

Dark—

Pain—

And I fell.

Six

Ashes of Truth

"Echo and Embers"

I woke to a hush, like the world had exhaled and was waiting for something. My body lay in the familiar contours of my bed, but nothing else felt familiar. My limbs were heavy, sore as if I'd been through a car crash—every muscle throbbed with quiet fury. As I tried to shift, pain flared across my ribs and spine, anchoring me in place. Light streamed through the slats of the blinds, casting golden lines across the floor. Morning, but late. The sun only hit this part of my room once a day.

Evelyn sat in the corner chair, legs folded beneath her, watching me with eyes like storm clouds barely holding back a downpour. She wore a soft sweatshirt and joggers, her hair pulled back into a loose ponytail that made her look younger, more raw. The moment she saw my eyes flutter open, she shifted forward.

"Hey, you," she said, voice low, touched with relief. "How are you feeling?"

"Like I got hit by a truck, then backed over," I muttered, trying to push myself up. Pain lanced through my chest. I winced.

"Slowly," she said, rising to gently place a hand on my shoulder. "Just because you managed to knock them all down doesn't mean they didn't land a few of their own."

I looked down. Still in the clothes from the night before—flannel shirt crusted with dirt, pants damp and flecked with mud. No blanket. I'd been dumped on the bed, not tucked in. I didn't even remember getting home.

"Did you carry me here?"

She smiled softly. "Lucas did most of the lifting. I just made sure you didn't bleed out on your sheets."

"Charming," I muttered.

"You're welcome," she added, then hesitated. Her hand brushed against mine, fingers tracing the bruised knuckles. "I was scared, Phoenix. You went dark so fast. And what we found in those woods..."

Her words trailed off. Something unspoken lingered there. I wanted to ask. But I also didn't.

"Thanks," I said finally. "Even if you were tracking me."

She smirked, but her eyes didn't match. "Had to keep tabs on you somehow. You attract trouble like it's a part-time job."

I huffed a laugh, but it came out as a wheeze. She squeezed my hand gently.

The bedroom door creaked open and Lucas stepped inside with two steaming mugs. He looked more exhausted than I felt—hair askew, hoodie wrinkled, eyes rimmed red.

"Look who's finally up," Lucas said, stepping in with two steaming mugs. He handed one to me, his expression somewhere between relief and lingering guilt. "Here. Figured you could use it."

I took the mug, the warmth seeping into my fingers, grounding me for a second.

"Your roommate has a point," Evelyn added, nodding toward Lucas, her tone shifting to something gentler—more united. Like this had bonded them in some silent, unspoken way.

"Great. Now you're both on the same side," I muttered.

Lucas shrugged. "We're not wrong. You look like you were thrown down a cliff and then kicked by a moose."

"Charming visual, thanks."

I tried to sit up more fully. Evelyn pushed back gently.

"God, you're a stubborn ass," she said.

"Let me at least get vertical," I grumbled. "I hate feeling useless."

With effort, I swung my legs off the bed and stood, wobbling slightly before finding balance. The dizziness faded slowly.

We migrated into the living room. Sunlight filtered through the windows, casting a lazy warmth that felt entirely at odds with the night I'd just lived through. I dropped onto the couch with a grunt.

"Okay," I said, looking between them. "What is the Collective?"

The room froze.

Evelyn set down her mug carefully, the ceramic clinking against the wood.

"That's... complicated," she said.

"Try me."

She glanced at Lucas. He nodded slowly.

Evelyn exhaled, shoulders sinking.

"They're old," she began. "Older than the Council, even. The Collective believes knowledge is power—but not in a protective sense. They hoard it. Twist it. Turn relics and myths into weapons. They see the world as a chessboard, and every bloodline like yours as a potential piece."

I swallowed. "They knew my mother. They knew about me."

"They always know," she said darkly. "The Council... they're not innocent, but at least they try to shield what matters. The Collective corrupts. And they've been watching you for a long time, Phoenix."

Lucas shifted, eyes low.

"You should've seen her after she got that call," he said. "She was out the door before I could even finish a sentence. I should've been faster. I should've—"

"Stop," I said firmly.

He looked up.

"You saved me. You called her. That was everything."

Lucas gave a tight nod, jaw clenched. Then, quietly: "I didn't sleep. Not once. Just kept checking the time, waiting for a call that didn't come. I was scared. For you."

There was something in his voice I couldn't place. Something deeper. But the moment passed too quickly.

I looked back to Evelyn. "What's the Council? You said they're not innocent. Are they who you were working with?"

She hesitated. Her gaze flicked to the floor, then to the window, watching the wind stir leaves across the sill.

"Yes," she said quietly. "I used to believe in them. That they were doing good. That they were protecting something sacred. But after what happened in Memphis... and after what Allison did—I don't know anymore."

"So you left them?"

"I defected," she said, voice hardening. "The moment I realized they were hiding the truth from even you, I knew I couldn't be a part of it."

"What truth?" I asked.

Before she could answer, a knock sounded at the door.

All of us turned.

Outside, the morning felt suddenly colder.

"Are we expecting someone?" Lucas asked, brows raised.

I shook my head, rising slowly and padding to the door. I opened it cautiously.

There, standing like she owned the world, was a woman in a sleek black coat. Her blond hair shimmered in the morning sun, styled with precision. Behind her, a matte black SUV idled, its driver waiting stoically.

"Good morning, Mr. Knight," she said smoothly. "I'm Veronica. May I come in?"

I stared. "Who are you?"

"A friend of Evelyn and your mother," she said, brushing past me into the living room with the poise of a queen returning to court.

Evelyn stiffened visibly. "Veronica?"

"Time to fill Mr. Knight in," she said briskly, settling into the dining room like it was her own.

Her presence shifted the air, sharp and commanding. Veronica Ashwood was elegance wrapped in authority, every word crisp with purpose. She was the storm after the silence.

"Your mother works for the Council of Keepers," she began, her tone clipped yet reverent. "She's a professor, yes—but that's only one of her faces. The Council safeguards relics, ancestral knowledge, and certain bloodlines from falling into the wrong hands. Your mother wasn't recruited—she co-founded the modern Council with me."

I blinked. "Wait, founder?"

Veronica's expression tightened, eyes narrowing with the weight of memory. "Yes. Dr. Knight is one of the original architects of the Council's mission in this age. Without her, there is no Council. She is the compass. The heart."

She paused, then added more quietly, "The Council began in a library. Late nights thick with dust and candle smoke, too much coffee staining old maps and dog-eared mythologies. Three people bound not by power, but by urgency—driven by a truth too dangerous to ignore. We weren't trying to change the world; we were trying to keep it from tearing itself apart. Joanne always believed in the myth. She was the first to trace its echoes in forgotten scrolls and half-burned codices. Her conviction lit the spark that would become the Council's mission."

Lucas sat down heavily, clearly trying to keep up. "So this is real. Like—secret organizations, relics, bloodlines?"

"It's all real, Mr. Jones. And Evelyn, well—she's walked both sides."

Evelyn winced. She wouldn't meet my eyes.

"She lied to me."

"To protect you," Veronica said without hesitation. "You've been under quiet observation your entire life, not out of suspicion—but out of necessity. You were hidden for a reason. The Collective is hunting for something, and they think it begins with you."

"Does this tie into my kidnapping?"

Veronica nodded. "Yes. The Collective took your mother. They believe she's protecting something—something ancient, buried, and bound to a lineage they've hunted for centuries. You may not just be a key, Phoenix. You may be the door itself."

"Why me?"

Veronica looked at me with a gaze that carried weight—unspoken history, unanswered prayers.

"Because they believe in blood. And yours... is marked."

The room was heavy with tension. Lucas leaned forward. "So what now?"

Veronica glanced at him, then back at me. "You know the university better than we do. There's something hidden on campus—something old. Evelyn and your mother were close to finding it. We believe your professor may know more."

"Then I'll talk to her," I said. "She owes me that much."

"But be discreet," Veronica warned. "We don't know who we can trust."

Lucas folded his arms. "Can we trust you?"

Evelyn snapped, "Lucas—"

"He's right to ask," Veronica said calmly. "Yes. You can. I've known Phoenix since he was in diapers."

My face flushed. "Seriously?"

"Oh, I have pictures," she said with a wink.

Evelyn chuckled. "I need to see those."

Lucas cracked a smile, but the undercurrent remained. Evelyn was distant now, wrapped in her own guilt. I could feel it building—a reckoning waiting just beneath the surface.

Veronica stood. "Keep me updated. I have to get to my son's soccer match."

"Tell Thoran I said hi," Evelyn murmured.

"Be safe," Veronica said, stepping back toward the SUV. "And Phoenix—be ready. This is just the beginning."

I stood at the door as she left, the sunlight too bright, the room too quiet.

Then the weight hit me.

I turned to Evelyn, voice low and tight. "She talks like she's in control of everything. Like she knows what's coming."

Evelyn nodded slowly.

I clenched my fists, my voice sharp now: "Then why hasn't she found my mother yet?"

Silence. Heavy. Sharp.

I looked to the door, then back. "If my mother is so important—if she's the heart of this Council—why isn't Veronica doing more? What the hell is she waiting for?"

Evelyn's eyes glistened. "Phoenix—"

But then I heard the door creak. Veronica had paused on the threshold, one hand still resting against the frame. Her voice, when it came, was no longer polished—it cracked.

"Because I can't lose her too."

The air shifted.

"I'm doing everything I can," Veronica whispered. "More than you know. I've called in every favor, opened every vault. She's not just my colleague. She's like a sister to me."

Her composure was gone. And for the first time, I saw the woman behind the power.

"Just... give me time. Please."

And with that, she stepped out, the door clicking softly shut behind her.

The room was silent. And somehow, heavier than before.

Evelyn turned to me slowly. "Phoenix—please—"

I backed away, eyes locked on hers. "You lied to me."

She flinched. Then, almost rehearsed, she gestured to the couch. "I couldn't tell you."

I stayed standing. "Couldn't, or wouldn't?"

Her lips parted, but her eyes didn't meet mine. "The Council has rules. Protocols. I was bound by them."

"And where did that leave me?" I said, my voice rising. "Chained up in a warehouse while everyone played keep-away with my life?"

"You think I wanted that?" she snapped, rising from the couch. "You think I didn't argue? That I didn't fight to bring you in sooner?"

"You lied. Just like my mother."

Silence.

I could see it—the sharp pain behind her eyes, the hit she took but refused to block. She looked smaller now, arms folded tight, knuckles white.

"Everything you said… all the times you were 'busy' or vague or just vanished—was that all just part of the act?"

"It wasn't an act," she whispered. "I was trying to keep you safe. That was real."

I shook my head. "You mean you were trying to keep your conscience clear while I lived in the dark. Evelyn, I trusted you. I—"

I stopped. Couldn't finish the sentence. Too much weight in the unspoken.

Lucas stood like a ghost between us, watching, not daring to speak. He didn't know what to say. He didn't have to.

"You don't understand," Evelyn said. "You have no idea the pressure we were under. Your mother made choices to protect you—"

"And what about my choices?"

"Phoenix—"

"I needed one person—just one—to be honest with me. And even you couldn't do that."

She closed her eyes. Her shoulders trembled. A tear slid down, unchecked.

"I'm sorry," she said, voice cracking. "I thought I was doing the right thing. I thought… if I could keep you out of it—"

"You already put me in it."

Her eyes finally met mine, red-rimmed and glistening. "You're right. You're absolutely right. But you're in it now. And I'm not walking away."

That stopped me.

I didn't want to forgive her. Not yet. Maybe not ever. But something about her—standing there, broken but unyielding—kept me from turning away.

Lucas finally stepped forward, voice soft. "You two should take a break before you burn the house down."

I gave a bitter laugh. Evelyn didn't.

"I'm going to email my professor," I muttered. "See what she knows. And tomorrow, I'm going to Memphis. To my mom's office."

"You sure that's smart?" Lucas asked.

"No," I said. "But it's what I have."

As I turned away, Evelyn didn't stop me.

"Yes." I lay on the couch so I could rest once I was finished, the worn fabric hugging the contours of my aching frame. Time trickled by. The room was still, save for the faint ticking of the clock in the kitchen and the slow, steady inhale of my own breath. Pain bloomed across my body like a slow sunrise—heat and ache rising in waves. My limbs felt like dead weight, my chest tight with every breath.

Eventually, curiosity—or maybe morbid fascination—compelled me. I lifted my shirt. The bruise across my side was massive, the skin a horrifying canvas of marbled purple, blue, and sickly yellow. It pulsed faintly with each heartbeat. Evelyn's handiwork was there too—a neatly wrapped bandage secured against a thin gash, clean and precise.

I sat there for a moment longer, allowing the silence to hold me. Then I reached for my phone, pulling it from the end table. I stared at the blank screen before composing a short email to Dr. Dawson. I kept it vague—asking if she had time to meet about the recent research we discussed. A harmless pretext. But my fingers hovered before hitting send. Something about it felt... irreversible.

Still, I tapped 'send.' Watched the screen confirm delivery. Then I leaned back, head against the couch cushion, and closed my eyes for a beat longer, letting the throb in my ribs sync with the clock's rhythm. Letting the waiting begin.

Then came the growl in my stomach. I made my way to the kitchen, finding Lucas already moving around, sleeves rolled up, an apron slung over his shoulder like he'd worn it so many times before.

"You better cook enough for me," I demanded, easing myself onto the barstool with a grunt.

"Already planning on it," he replied without missing a beat, stirring the pot with focused ease.

The scent hit me before I could see the dish—garlic, tomatoes, basil—like the memory of a late-night diner on some forgotten road trip, tucked into a corner booth laughing about nothing. The water boiled behind him, fogging the small kitchen windows.

"Where's Evelyn?"

"She went and took a nap," he said softly, not turning from the stove. "She stayed up all night making sure you were okay. Wouldn't even sit until you were breathing evenly."

That landed heavier than expected. My chest tightened—not just from bruises. I leaned on the counter, eyes fixed on the steam swirling upward.

Lucas finally glanced over, that same steady look he gave me in the woods, full of quiet knowing.

"Give her a break," he said. "She cares about you."

I nodded slowly. "I know."

“Look at you being the mediator.”

He chuckled, then tossed a pinch of salt into the pot. "Someone has to keep your dramatic ass grounded."

The house filled with the comfort of slow cooking—the kind that seeps into the walls and lingers long after the plates are empty.

"So why didn't it work?" he asked, slicing a bell pepper with careful precision.

"What?"

"You and Evelyn."

I exhaled, slow. “Mostly my fault.”

He glanced at me, waiting.

"I was young," I said. "And afraid. Mostly afraid. I didn't think I could be enough for her."

Lucas nodded without judgment, continuing his prep.

"What about your love life?" I asked, trying to shift the weight away from me.

He paused, just for a second, then said, "Eh—no one interesting."

But there was something behind his words. A hesitation. A flicker.

I studied him, noting how he avoided my gaze.

"High standards much?"

He smirked, eyes on the cutting board. "Like you don't."

"I'm offended," I said with mock indignation.

He just smiled, faint but sincere. The silence that followed wasn't awkward—it was thick with things left unsaid. When the food was finally plated, it was exactly what I needed. The warmth, the flavor, the ritual—it grounded me in the moment, a fragile peace amid the storm.

Even if everything else was unraveling.

SEVEN

FAMILY HISTORY

"THE THINGS WE INHERIT"

The pain had dulled to a manageable throb by the time we hit the highway to Memphis. It was a good hour and a half ahead of us, and Evelyn was behind the wheel. That fact alone unsettled me. My life, rattling down I-55, was quite literally in her hands. Not that she was a bad driver—just... assertive. The kind of person who treated merging as a test of dominance.

"Nice Audi," Lucas said from the backseat, stretching out with his hoodie bunched under his head. "Definitely beats Phoenix's Jeep."

"Hey," I said, not even bothering to look back, "don't make fun of my Jeep. It's got character."

Evelyn snorted. "That thing barely has brakes."

"Still has more soul than this metal pod."

She only grinned and hit the gas a little harder. The Audi purred like a beast trying to be polite.

The road stretched on in an endless ribbon of grey. On either side, fields blurred into each other—flat and sprawling, with trees clustered like quiet conspirators along the edges. A mist still hung low over the land, clinging to the ditches and fence lines. Every so often, we'd pass through the remnants of some forgotten town.

Signs that proudly read Five Star City or Gateway to the Delta, though none ever seemed to back up those claims.

"You feeling better?" Evelyn asked, breaking the silence as she kept her eyes on the road.

"Yeah," I said, rolling my shoulder. "Still sore in places."

"That means you're healing," she said, her voice softening.

I nodded, returning my gaze to the scenery outside. The power lines dipped and rose with the motion of the car, hypnotic in their rhythm. I followed them with my eyes like a thread pulling me forward, away from everything behind.

Lucas had fallen asleep at some point. His breathing was slow and even, his mouth slightly open in the kind of deep nap that only came from emotional exhaustion. I almost envied it.

"You two seem to be good friends," Evelyn said, her voice quieter now so as not to wake him.

"We weren't always," I replied, still watching the trees. "At first, we just sort of... coexisted. Roommates out of necessity. But then—something clicked. I don't know. He's been there. Really been there."

"Huh," she said, eyebrows lifting. "I always thought you'd been tight from the start."

"Nope. It was slow. Earned, I guess."

She smiled, her hands steady on the wheel. "Well, I'm glad you have someone like that."

Traffic thickened as we approached the city limits. The skyline rose slowly from the haze—low and broad, with the occasional flash of mirrored glass or brick chimney catching the light. Billboards dotted the edges of the highway: concerts, lawyers, a giant neon chicken advertising hot wings. Classic Memphis.

We veered north, following the signs to midtown before weaving through the familiar routes to the university district.

"Lucas," I said, turning to glance over my shoulder. "We're here."

He stirred, groaning. "Already?"

"Get up," Evelyn barked, and he sat upright, blinking like a startled owl.

The University of Memphis unfolded before us—red brick buildings framed by oaks and elms, walkways lined with fading banners, and students weaving between classes with backpacks slung over one shoulder. It looked exactly as I remembered and yet somehow impossibly distant, like a photograph faded at the edges.

I felt it then—the weight of memory pressing against my chest. This was home once. A different kind of home. I had run these halls as a kid, slipped into lecture rooms just to listen, been handed off to grad students who doubled as babysitters. The math department used to help with my homework because numbers and I had always been enemies.

Evelyn pulled into a faculty lot near the humanities building. We sat for a moment before any of us moved.

"You good?" she asked.

I hesitated. "Ask me when this is over."

Then I stepped out into the Memphis sun, the university looming around me like the echo of a forgotten life.

The school sprawled between Central Avenue and Southern, a condensed patchwork of brutalist buildings and aging infrastructure. It was a blend of the sixties' optimism and seventies' pragmatism—form over flourish. The history department stood just opposite the newer University Center, a squat rectangle of red brick and narrow windows.

We walked past the misting fountain near the admin building. The air smelled like wet concrete and pollen, thick with the scent of magnolia leaves baking in the sun.

"You haven't been here since you moved to Oxford, have you?" Evelyn asked.

"No, I haven't." I glanced around, familiar buildings pulling on old threads in my memory. The paths we took as we headed toward Mitchell Hall cut through both good memories and ones I had buried. I had let this place fade into the background of my life, too painful or too distant to return to.

"What's that?" I asked, pointing to a strange new tower on the south end of the quad.

"Land bridge," she replied. "They built it over the railroad tracks."

"Damn. That train made my parents all the time."

Mitchell Hall loomed up ahead, four floors arranged in a stacked puzzle. The main entrance was on the second floor, but the building sloped weirdly, the basement half-submerged.

"Phoenix?" A familiar voice boomed from the hallway. "My, have you grown."

It was Dr. Baker—one of the professors who used to help with my homework while my mom was in meetings.

"Dr. Baker, good to see you," I said, offering a handshake.

"How's Ole Miss treating you?"

"Good," I lied. "All quiet."

He smiled. "Need anything?"

"Just grabbing something from my mom's office."

"Well, you know the way. Tell her I can't wait to read her new book."

"Will do."

We headed down the stairs. Her office was in a corner near the break room. The door looked exactly the same: a brass plate reading Dr. Knight and a collage of absurd historical memes that Lucas chuckled at.

"I can't with these," he muttered.

"She takes her memes seriously," I said, pulling out my keys.

"Wait—you have a key?"

"Since I was thirteen."

Inside, the office was a time capsule. Bookshelves groaned under the weight of academic tomes. Photos lined her desk—one in particular caught my eye: the two of us atop a temple in Tikal, Guatemala. I remembered that trip vividly. It was just two years ago, a rare getaway amid one of her research visits. She had a colleague working a dig nearby, and we took a day to explore the ancient Mayan city. The ruins rose from the jungle like forgotten sentinels, wrapped in vines and echoing with time. I had always wanted to go—pestered her about it for months—but once we were there, I saw it in her eyes. The awe. The joy. She was more excited than I was, and that was saying something. We wandered through mossy plazas and climbed the stone steps to view the forest canopy stretching out forever. It had felt sacred. Like we were touching something eternal, together. beside some ancient monument, candid shots of dusty libraries and sun-drenched digs.

Lucas drifted toward the bookshelves. Evelyn scanned the desk.

"What are we looking for?" Lucas asked.

"Notes. A journal. Anything."

"Here." Evelyn pointed behind a line of books. A safe—tucked neatly into the shadows like it had always been part of the wall. I stepped forward, heart thudding. From my keyring, I pulled the small silver key Mom had given me back in high school. For emergencies, she'd said. I used to think that meant storms, or getting locked out. Not this.

The lock clicked open with a stubborn groan. Inside: a sealed envelope marked from a law firm, a worn leather journal whose edges were frayed from use, and a strange wooden box—carved with intricate symbols, almost Celtic in design. The wood felt aged, like it had soaked up the secrets it protected.

Lucas reached in and lifted the box, his fingers running across the seams. "What's this? Some kind of puzzle?"

Before I could respond, Evelyn cracked open the journal without asking. The sound of the spine creaking made something in me bristle. That was my mother's. A part of me wanted to snatch it away, but I held my tongue.

"She writes about a group of professors," Evelyn murmured as she skimmed. "Guardians of secrets. Protectors of something ancient—something hidden beneath layers of rewritten history."

"Maybe the ones under the Lyceum," I said, flipping through pages beside her. The ink was smudged in places, handwritten notes weaving into printed texts. My stomach twisted.

Lucas turned the puzzle box over in his hands. It had no obvious latch, just interlocking pieces that seemed designed to confuse. Evelyn stayed focused on the journal, her brow furrowed with every page.

The silence settled between us—not peaceful, but pregnant. Like the room was holding its breath.

I stared down at the envelope. Heavy in my hands. Waiting. Just like everything else she left behind.

A knock rattled the doorframe.

"Has Dr. Dawson gotten back with you?" Evelyn asked.

"No, not yet, which is pretty normal." She could take a couple of days unless it was about a graded assignment or draft paper. Other than what we had found, there was nothing here. I had hoped for at least something more. Why was my mother keeping these secrets?

Dr. Baker's head poked in the doorway, his expression taut. "Phoenix, I hate to interrupt, but there's a bunch of scary men coming into the building."

Evelyn's tone turned grim. "They're here. Can you stall them?"

"I'll try, Miss Ramses. Go. Out the back. Now."

We bolted, heartbeats pounding in unison. Evelyn grabbed my shoulder, steady and firm, pulling me toward the narrow back staircase.

As we surfaced into the misty courtyard, the air was damp and cold against my skin, thick with the scent of wet stone and grass. Shadows slid between buildings, not just silhouettes but shapes with purpose. I crouched instinctively, my fingers brushing the dew-slick concrete.

Wilder Tower loomed above us, its beacon light flickering erratically—less a guide, more a warning flare. The surrounding silence was unnatural, as if the whole campus had paused to breathe with us.

Evelyn pressed a hand to my chest, stopping me. Her eyes scanned the area like a hawk tracking prey. "They're patrolling," she whispered. Her breath curled into the mist. "This wasn't random—they knew we'd come. Look at their movements. Steady intervals. Wide arcs. Someone trained them."

The weight of her words pressed into my spine. She wasn't just guessing. She knew. And that certainty told me just how serious this had become.

"How?" Lucas asked, voice barely audible.

"Because someone's watching Phoenix. Tracking him. Maybe even someone inside the university," she answered. "We need to move."

Evelyn slipped away from us as we crouched behind a low wall bordering the courtyard. Her breath was shallow but steady, her body poised like a coiled spring. Her fingers brushed the ground, testing for vibrations. The sharp tang of ozone lingered in the air—like a storm was coming, or had just passed. Beneath the towering limbs of leafless trees, the chill seemed to settle in their bones, and even Lucas's normally casual demeanor was wound tight.

"They're communicating in cycles," Evelyn murmured, eyes darting between the distant patrols. "Two-minute loops. I'll draw them." Her voice was laced with a precision that demanded trust.

She whispered, "Cover me," and then slipped out from behind the wall with feline grace.

Lucas and I tensed as she stepped into the open, deliberately placing herself in a patch of light cast from a nearby lamppost.

"Hey! You there!" one of the dark-coated men barked, their attention snapping to her.

"Sorry! I'm just... lost. Looking for the library," she said, voice feathered with mock embarrassment, posture shrunk as if timid.

They advanced quickly—too quickly.

In one blink, her stance shifted. A whirlwind of motion. One assailant crumpled with a sickening crack as her boot connected with his knee; the second met her elbow, the temple impact collapsing him into unconsciousness. Their radios sputtered out garbled warnings.

She turned, fierce and controlled. "Move! Now!"

Lucas and I burst from cover, barely containing our shock.

"Did you see that?" Lucas hissed, half in awe, half in panic.

"I didn't know she could fight like that," I muttered, adrenaline scorching through me.

We followed her—our protector, our shadow—through frozen paths and echoing footfalls, hearts pounding to the rhythm of pursuit. Evelyn wasn't just a friend or an ally.

She was trained.

She was lethal.

And right now, she was the only reason we had a chance to make it out.

Suddenly—"There! By the library!"

A chorus of shouts erupted behind us—raw, commanding, full of threat. The slap of boots on pavement closed in fast, echoing between the concrete walls like war drums.

We burst into motion. I felt the air rip past my face as we sprinted, legs burning, lungs on fire. Evelyn's voice sliced through the chaos: "Get across!"

Her eyes locked onto the stream of traffic, scanning with razor focus. A blur of headlights and honking horns surrounded us as she gauged the timing like a battlefield tactician. Lucas hurdled a low railing, barely avoiding a student who spun around in surprise. Tires screeched somewhere to our right.

The smell of exhaust and scorched rubber filled the air as we darted into the street. My heart thudded like a drumline. Everything narrowed to the sound of our footsteps, the glare of headlights, and the hope we wouldn't get flattened by a car before a bullet found us.

We reached Evelyn's Audi. Breathless. Two figures approached from behind.

"Buckle up," Evelyn growled, slamming the car in reverse. The tires shrieked against the pavement, lurching us backward with such force that Lucas nearly collided with the seat in front of him. We clipped the edge of a trash can, launching it across the sidewalk like a missile, and nearly flattened one of the black-clad pursuers who dove aside at the last second.

"Holy—" Lucas cursed, gripping the oh-shit handle with white knuckles.

A sharp crack split the air—gunfire. One bullet shattered the taillight, sending a spray of red plastic into the air.

"They're shooting at us!" I shouted, ducking instinctively.

Evelyn yanked the wheel hard, veering onto Central Avenue like a possessed demon behind the wheel. Cars honked. Pedestrians screamed. More shots rang out, thudding into metal and ricocheting off street signs.

"Just another day in Memphis!" Lucas yelled, his voice bouncing off the windows.

"Now is not the time for commentary!" I snapped, clutching the side of the seat like it was a lifeline.

"You're both mad!" Evelyn barked, her accent sharpening with stress as she rocketed us onto Walnut Grove. The tires squealed in protest, narrowly missing a pickup that slammed on its brakes.

Another burst of gunfire. Missed—barely. A metal thud somewhere behind us told me the Audi had taken a hit, but it wasn't slowing.

My stomach flipped inside out, the g-forces relentless.

Lucas peeked through the rear windshield, wide-eyed. "They're still gaining!"

"How are they this fast?!" I asked, bracing as we flew past traffic.

Evelyn didn't answer. Her eyes were locked on the road, wild and laser-focused. She swerved between lanes like she was threading a needle at ninety miles an hour. A bead of sweat ran down her temple.

"Stop looking so ill," Evelyn said, noticing me sinking in the chair.

"You're driving like a crazy Brit," I said, trying to center myself in the madness. "This is why I drive always!"

"At least we drive on the correct side of the bloody road!" Evelyn shouted, just as another volley of gunshots rang out.

"This is you behind the wheel!" Lucas added.

"I'm saving your lives, thank you very much!" she snapped, veering onto a side street with enough force to throw us sideways in our seats.

"Dear God, you're going to kill us," Lucas groaned.

"Shut up!" Evelyn and I said in perfect unison.

I looked back—they were still trailing us. Swerving through traffic, horns blaring. Someone was going to get killed if this kept up.

"So, when did they teach you how to fight?!" I asked.

"Now is not the time!" Evelyn growled, cutting the wheel again. Two more turns. Lucas looked nauseous.

"Are all Keepers like you?" Lucas coughed. "Because, damn, that was—was that Krav Maga?"

"Let's say I took some classes," Evelyn muttered, then sighed. "We're not just historians. The Council trains us. Field ops. Tactical protocol. We're taught to protect knowledge and people."

"You're a spy!" Lucas said, half-awed, half-terrified.

"I prefer the term 'well-rounded scholar.'"

"Is that what they call it now?" I smirked.

"Oh, please—you've got some moves yourself, sir." Evelyn shot back, her grin flashing like a dare.

We swerved down a back road flanked with shadowy trees. No tail lights behind us anymore. No gunshots. Just the quiet hum of tires on asphalt and the thunder of our heartbeats.

"Where are we going?!" Lucas finally asked.

I saw it in Evelyn's eyes.

"No," I said flatly.

"It's safe. And you have the key."

"What's safe? Where?!" Lucas asked.

"My parents' house," I muttered.

The car fell silent.

We weren't just running. We were heading straight into memory—and maybe something worse.

The Collective hadn't just stumbled upon us—they were hunting with purpose.

And Evelyn Ramses was full of more secrets than I'd ever imagined.

As Evelyn took another sharp turn, the adrenaline began to ebb just enough for reality to set in. The silence in the car was louder than any of the bullets. The air hung thick with tension, punctuated only by the rasp of our breathing and the soft click of the turn signal—pointless, considering Evelyn hadn't actually used it.

Lucas leaned forward between the front seats, rubbing the back of his neck. "So… just to recap. We went to a college campus, got hunted by mercenaries, watched Evelyn take down two grown men like some MI6 assassin, and now we're heading to your childhood home. Did I miss anything?"

"Don't forget the box full of secrets and the journal that basically implies there's a secret society under our universities," I said, glancing at the wooden puzzle still clutched in his hands.

"Right. That too."

Evelyn's knuckles were white on the steering wheel. I watched her in the mirror—her jaw tight, her eyes darting between the road and the rearview like a soldier expecting an ambush.

"You okay?" I asked.

She didn't answer right away. Then: "This isn't how it was supposed to go. We weren't supposed to be seen. Not yet."

"You think someone leaked it?" Lucas asked.

"I think," she said slowly, "someone has been watching Phoenix for longer than we realized."

That cold feeling returned—like ice in my chest. "Why? I'm not… important."

Evelyn shot me a look. "Don't say that. Not again."

Her voice was fierce, protective. It startled me. I glanced away, letting my eyes drift to the blurred shapes of traffic lights, brick storefronts, and rows of trimmed hedges. Something twisted inside me—some half-formed memory from childhood. The way Mom would always glance over her shoulder on trips. The way she checked hotel windows twice. The way she never let me walk home alone, even in high school.

Maybe the truth had always been there. I just hadn't been willing to see it.

"Phoenix," Lucas said gently. "What if this goes deeper than your mom? What if you're part of whatever she was trying to protect?"

The question hit harder than I expected. Evelyn was silent. Her hands still white-knuckled on the wheel.

"I don't know what I'm part of," I said quietly. "But I'm going to find out."

We passed into the quiet calm of Germantown. Sidewalks stretched wide. Lawns manicured. The world pretending to be normal.

Evelyn eased off the gas, letting the quiet settle in.

And then, softly: "We're almost there."

There was weight in her words. Something final. As if the next step wasn't just a destination, but a door we couldn't close once opened.

And I couldn't shake the feeling that once we crossed that threshold… nothing would ever be the same again.

Ashwood Tower - High Keeper Transmission
CLASSIFIED: FLAME TIER - LOCK MODE DELTA
TO: Commanders, TRS Operatives, BSE Surveillance Leads
FROM: Veronica - High Keeper, Chair
SUBJECT: Activation of Protocol Thrice Lit Flame

At 04:17 CST, confirmed intelligence from LRI tracepoint convergence verifies the abduction of High Keeper Dr. Joanne Knight by an active Collective cell.
In accordance with Council Emergency Statute 7.1, Protocol THRICE LIT FLAME is now in effect.

EFFECTIVE IMMEDIATELY:
- All Knight-affiliated archives and field assets are sealed under Level II Lockdown.
- TRS is authorized to deploy Recovery Operation: MERIDIAN.
- BSE will initiate full-spectrum trace and initiate containment sweeps across Range V.

Under Protocol AEGIS FLAME, Subject Codename: SOLUS is now elevated to Tier II following verified Collective contact and trauma exposure.
- Keeper Ramses is reaffirmed as Active Guardian under Clause 7-B, with expanded clearance.
- Emotional bleed risk is logged. Observation is prioritized over recall.
- Subject remains unaware. This ignorance is to be preserved.

Surveillance must remain layered. Intervention requires High Keeper review.
The Root Remembers. The Flame Endures.

— Veronica
High Keeper, Council of Keepers

EIGHT

SANCTUARY

"SHELTER THAT REMEMBERS"

It was nearly nightfall as we turned down the drive I knew so well—every crack in the pavement, every bend in the road etched into my memory. The towering trees stretched toward the dusk-drenched sky like ancient guardians, their leaves rustling in a slow whisper, echoing memories I wasn't sure I was ready to revisit.

The houses lining the street were stately, pristine even in the fading light. I could see warm porch lights flickering on like constellations, some windows glowing gold with early dinner prep or flickers of TV light. I remembered walking these sidewalks with my parents, waving to neighbors during fall festivals or helping string up lights in the winter. I could almost hear the crunch of snow under boots from one of those rare snow days, and the laughter as kids built lopsided snowmen with mismatched scarves. But the shadows held other memories, too—dark ones. Nights when the power went out and silence settled over the neighborhood like a shroud, broken only by candlelight and whispered worry.

We lived in the eastern stretch of Germantown—a pocket of affluence where lawyers, doctors, and executives built their mini-empires behind trimmed hedges and wrought iron gates. I remembered a house two blocks down that looked like it had been pulled straight from a fairytale, all turrets and stone. My mother used to say a prince lived there. It took years for me to realize it was just some hedge fund manager with a flair for the dramatic. Even now, I wasn't sure how my family fit into this picture. Professors didn't usually afford this kind of life. Not on paper.

Our house, by comparison, was humbler—a craftsman-style home with warm wooden eaves and a wide front porch that looked like it belonged in a southern novel. But it had soul. My mother had just finished remodeling the kitchen and adding a patio out back. She was ridiculously proud of it. I could still hear her voice describing the stonework or gushing over the butcher block island. She'd also expanded the library, adding built-in shelves until books climbed the walls like ivy. A scholar's sanctuary. A fortress of pages and silence.

"We are here," Evelyn said, easing the car to a stop. The sky above was painted in molten hues—amber bleeding into crimson, the clouds streaked like brushstrokes over the rooftops. The air smelled of pine, fresh-cut grass, and something else—something metallic, maybe just in my head.

"You grew up here?" Lucas asked, stepping out and looking around with wide eyes. A bird rustled in the hedges. Somewhere down the street, a dog barked once before falling quiet again.

I nodded, unlocking the door. As it swung open, the scent of cedar and old paper drifted out to greet us. Home, haunted by silence.

The light cast long shadows across the floor, stretching over the familiar hardwoods and the worn runner rug that had been in the family for as long as I could remember. I stood still for a moment, taking it all in—the scent of cedarwood from the hall table, the subtle hum of the air conditioning, the quiet that only a house too empty can have.

Lucas stepped in behind me, eyes wide, taking everything in like it was a museum. "Feels...weird. Like it's been waiting."

"Yeah," I replied softly. "It does."

Evelyn moved past us and began securing the house—locks clicked, blinds were drawn. She moved like she'd done this before. Lucas and I exchanged glances.

"You sure this is safe?" he asked.

"For now," she answered. "But we won't be staying long."

"Make yourself at home. The guests' rooms are upstairs," I said, closing the door behind us. The house looked the same, as if it had never changed since the last time I walked through its door. The hardwood floors still gleamed beneath the warm overhead light, polished and unmarred. Evelyn and Lucas made their way upstairs to the bedrooms, their footsteps soft against the wood.

I drifted into my old bedroom, the grayish-blue walls still intact from when I had painted them at sixteen. It was neat and untouched, as if frozen in time. The scent of linen and faint cologne still lingered. The sheets were freshly laundered. My mother always kept the house ready, just in case. I was going to fulfill my mother's wish of staying here; mostly I came to visit and then headed back down to Oxford for the night. But I had stopped truly staying here long ago. Too many memories. Too much pain.

Silence—

Pain—

Shame—

The weight of it pressed down, so I left the room and wandered downstairs into the living room. The space welcomed me like an old friend, with soft lamplight and worn furniture. And there, nestled at the far end, was the baby grand piano.

I sat without thinking. The bench creaked faintly under my weight. My fingers hovered above the ivory keys—cool and familiar. Slowly, they descended.

A note. Then another. A melody began to unfurl, halting at first, then fluid, drawn from memory and muscle.

Each note was a confession. A plea. A breath.

The room filled with it—the piano's voice echoing off the walls, climbing the staircase, pressing against the quiet. My hands moved of their own accord, chasing something unspoken. The house, the shadows, the silence—they all bent around the sound.

The music became a moment suspended in time, dripping emotion into every measure. My chest ached, my breath shallow. For once, everything else faded.

Just me. And the song.

I played until I could no longer tell where I ended and the music began.

"I forgot you played." Evelyn's voice startled me as I stopped, turning around and seeing her behind me.

"I don't really anymore."

"Doesn't sound like it; that was wonderful," she answered, taking a seat next to me. Thinking back, I had never really played in front of her before. I hadn't in over three years. Must have been something my mother told her about. She had always enjoyed it when I played. She would always stand and listen from the kitchen or sitting in one of the chairs, reading. She said it relaxed her and that she was proud of me. Would she be proud of me now?

"Thanks," I said, breaking the little silence that was between us.

"I know that we are complicated," she started, her voice softer now, layered with something unspoken. "But can we at least, like, acknowledge that we care?"

I stared at the piano keys, letting the silence build. I did care about her—of course I did. But I had also spent years perfecting the art of shutting people out, and she had withheld so much. She had known the truth about the Council, about my mother, and she said nothing. That wasn't something I could just wave away.

"You kept things from me," I said. My voice was low but steady. "Things that could've changed everything."

Evelyn didn't flinch. She looked at me with those unreadable eyes, not defensive, just... tired. "I know. And I hate it. But I couldn't tell you, Phoenix. It wasn't just about loyalty or protocol. It was about protecting you. And yeah, maybe that wasn't my choice to make, but I didn't know another way."

I wanted to be angry, to push her away again—but there was a vulnerability in her voice that cut deeper than any deflection. We were complicated, yes, but maybe that didn't mean unsalvageable.

"You still should've told me."

"I know."

There was a beat of quiet. Her hand brushed the edge of the piano bench, uncertain.

"But can we... just start with admitting we still care? Not everything has to be fixed tonight."

I let the silence stretch before answering. The music still lingered in the air, a residue of something truer than words.

"Okay," I said at last.

She smiled—not triumphant, but soft, almost sad. She sat beside me, not touching, just close. We didn't need to say more. Not yet.

There was so much still unspoken between us. Wounds that hadn't closed, trust that hadn't been rebuilt. But maybe—just maybe—this was a start.

I looked at her from the corner of my eye. She looked forward, not pushing, just being there. And even though I could feel the ache beneath my ribs, the wall I'd spent years fortifying cracking ever so slightly, I didn't stop it.

A loud knock sounded at the front door. I got up and headed that way. Outside stood Veronica Ashwood. She didn't look entirely thrilled, but then again, could she ever smile? She seemed like she'd had a long day at the office, with the slight wrinkle of her pantsuit. It was still pristine elsewhere, but you could tell it had been used today.

"Glad to see you are all safe," she said, walking in. Lucas made his way down from upstairs to join us in the living room.

"They knew we were going to be there," Evelyn mentioned to Veronica, hoping to get an explanation.

"I realize that, which means there must be someone at the university who works for them," she exclaimed.

"We'll have to be more careful now," I said, trying to assert caution. I didn't want anyone to get hurt or worse. There was too much already at stake, and yet this organization would do anything to get what they wanted.

"Did you find anything?" Veronica asked.

"This," Lucas said, holding up the puzzle box we'd found. "I am trying to open it, but it has proven difficult."

"We also found a journal. They were all in a safe in her office," Evelyn interjected.

"That's a good start. Did you find anything else, Phoenix?"

It took me by surprise, like she knew there was something else in there. She was not overly impressed about what was left. Yet now she was asking if I'd found anything. She must be talking about the envelope, but I'd never opened or looked at it. I presumed it was a will or something in case my mother died. Which I chose not to even consider.

"Just an envelope, but I haven't opened it," I said, telling the truth. Not hiding it like I wanted to.

"I see. Let me know what you find and keep me updated," she said. Her voice held a curious gentleness now. "Phoenix, you don't have to open that envelope unless you wish, but I suggest you wait and ask your mother first. Sometimes truths come wrapped in legalese."

I shook my head in the way of understanding; it had to be what I thought at that point. It was best not to look at it unless I had to. I would rather not think about it, hoping to see my mother again. Veronica turned to leave, but before she stepped outside, she glanced back at me.

"Keep playing, Phoenix. Whatever's in that envelope will wait. Your mother would want you to live first."

And with that, she was gone.

"I'm going to try to do some reading and see what I find out from her journal," Evelyn said as she headed upstairs. Lucas was still trying to figure out his puzzle, which only left a small number of things to do. The only thing other than sleep was to relax.

Which ended up being my decision as I headed out to the backyard.

The pool was pristine as usual; my parents never let it get dirty even in the winter months. The soft glow of the patio lights shimmered on the surface, casting lazy golden waves that danced along the edges. The air was still warm and pleasant, carrying the faint perfume of gardenias from the flowerbed and the deeper, earthy undertone of damp stone and chlorine. A windchime clinked faintly from the back corner of the porch, the sound delicate and eerie in the hush.

Wearing some of my old trunks that still fit, I dived in, the cold water shocking and invigorating all at once. It wrapped around me like a veil, muting the world above into nothing but pressure and heartbeat. Down here, beneath the surface, everything was still. No threats, no questions—just the steady rhythm of lungs and thought. I broke through the waterline with a gasp, eyes drawn skyward. The moon watched overhead, pale and deliberate. The stars—fewer than in Oxford but still present—offered small sparks of comfort in the city haze.

Reflection crept in. I tried not to invite it, but solitude tends to unlock the corners I seal shut. Old memories surged forward—mocked laughter in a grade school hallway, lonely lunches, cold shoulders. That aching feeling of not fitting anywhere, not knowing why.

But then, there were the better memories too. Like the first time Evelyn came to the house. How awkward and formal we both were, like two actors fumbling through a script. And later, that first date—the small pub nestled into Cooper Young, tucked away like a secret only we knew. The evening stretched long into the night, the conversation as easy as the warm drinks in our hands. We laughed about my mother's quirks, teased each other about our favorite books. It had felt effortless.

As we walked under the amber streetlamps, our hands found each other. Near the car, her red hair glowed in the light, her blue eyes locking on mine. That moment—the way time seemed to stall, as if the universe itself were waiting. She leaned in, breath brushing against mine. I didn't move. Couldn't. Fear chained me. Fear that I'd ruin her, that my broken edges would tear her apart. So I stood there. Silent. Still.

Her eyes had opened slowly, confusion tinged with hurt. We never talked about it. Not until tonight, when the piano gave us both an opening.

I lay on my back now, floating beneath the stars. What if I'd kissed her? What if I'd let myself want something?

"Phoenix," Lucas called from the patio, pulling me from the haze.

"What's up?" I swam over to the edge.

"I got it open." He held the puzzle box like a trophy.

"What's in it?" I asked, hauling myself out and sitting beside him.

"This," he said, handing me a piece of parchment. The lost son is the key, it read.

I stared. "That makes no sense." I handed it back, careful not to drip on it. What did that even mean? A lost son? A key to what?

"I don't know. But I'm sure we'll figure it out." He looked at me, and then—wham—I was underwater again, laughter muffled and limbs flailing. Lucas grinned down at me.

That bastard.

I retaliated with a splash. "You know you want to join."

"You're right—I do." He peeled off his shirt and cannon balled in, drenching me again.

"You have to make a mess, don't you?" I grumbled.

"Only to annoy you."

We laughed, real and free. This wasn't something we'd done before—not really. And it hit me: this was the first time I felt like we were more than roommates. We were friends. Brothers in arms, or mischief at least.

"What is all the noise out here for?" Evelyn called, stepping onto the patio.

Lucas and I exchanged a glance.

"Just having fun?" Lucas offered.

Her brow furrowed, her lips twitching. "Oh no. No, no, no."

Too late.

We charged. She shrieked and tried to back away, but we caught her. She struggled, laughing despite herself.

"Put me down!" she demanded.

"Relax," I said.

Then, with a synchronized heave, we tossed her into the water. She surfaced, sputtering.

"I hate you both!"

"See? Isn't this better?" I asked, brushing wet hair from her face.

Lucas cackled.

"You know," she said with mock menace, "you're right." Then she lunged and dunked Lucas.

Her laughter rang out, clear and unguarded. And in that moment, under the stars, drenched and breathless, we forgot the world outside. For a little while, we were just three friends in a pool, surrounded by moonlight and memory.

But even as we splashed and laughed, I could feel it—a flicker of something deeper. A ripple in the calm. The message in the box clung to the back of my mind like wet fabric. The lost son is the key. What did it mean? Who was lost? And why did I feel like the answer was closer than I wanted it to be?

NINE

WATCHING

"EYES ARE ALWAYS WATCHING"

Birds chirped outside as the first moments of light stretched across the horizon. I had barely slept. Tossing and turning, my mind racing, it felt like my skin itched from the inside. The one moment I did drift off brought a dream—but it wasn't a dream, more of a memory. I woke breathing hard, sweat dampening my forehead, heart thrumming like I'd just run a mile. It took a second to reorient myself. I was in my childhood bedroom. No wonder I had the dream.

I slipped out of the sheets and stretched, joints creaking faintly. The air greeted my skin like ice, sharp and sudden, before mellowing into the familiar warmth of the old house. I opened the door to the hallway. It was dark and quiet, yet I knew the route by muscle memory. Eighteen years of moving through it, even during nights like this.

I walked carefully, not wanting to wake Evelyn and Lucas—both still asleep from the sound of it. For a moment I thought of my mother. Then I reminded myself: she wasn't here. She was still missing. The house felt wrong without her. Not empty. Altered. Like something essential had been misplaced.

In the kitchen, I turned on the soft under-cabinet light, casting a warm glow across the counter. My mother's tea kettle sat on the stove, exactly where she'd always left it. I filled it with water and set it to boil. In the pantry, the collection of loose-leaf teas waited, lined up in perfect rows—just like mine in Oxford. I selected the jasmine blend, measuring it out into a mug with practiced hands. As the kettle began to whistle, I removed it swiftly, pouring the hot water over the leaves. The steam rose, fragrant and calming.

I heard soft footsteps and turned toward the doorway just as Lucas appeared, yawning. He was in the same dried shorts from the night before, hair sticking up on one side.

"What are you doing up this early?" he asked.

"Could say the same for you," I said, watching the tea steep.

Lucas walked over and paused, then sat down. I poured a second mug and slid it to him.

"You didn't sleep, did you?"

"That easy to tell?"

"Yeah. I can see it in your eyes. Plus, you usually at least wear shorts when you're wandering around."

I glanced down. Just underwear. He had a point. I took a sip of tea, the warmth sliding down my throat, grounding me.

Lucas cradled his mug, blowing gently at the steam. "You always drink that jasmine stuff when you can't sleep."

I raised an eyebrow. "How would you know that?"

He smirked. "You made it the night after your Latin midterm. And that night you got the call about Dr. Dawson's grant getting pulled."

I blinked, caught off guard. "You remember that?"

"You think I don't pay attention? I just play dumb well," he said, sipping.

I stirred the tea slowly, watching the leaves spiral. "You ever feel like this house is too still? Like it's waiting to be loud again?"

Lucas didn't answer right away. Then he nodded. "Yeah. But maybe it's not waiting. Maybe it's mourning."

The words landed heavy. I stared into the mug. The scent of jasmine filled the air—soft, floral, aching.

"She's not coming home," I said finally. "Not like before."

Lucas set his mug down with a soft clink. "Then we find out why."

The silence that followed wasn't awkward. It was something else. A kind of pact. The kettle still radiated warmth behind us. The scent of tea lingered like memory.

Outside, the sun climbed higher. Inside, something between us held firm—quiet, real, unspoken.

By the time Evelyn emerged, sunlight was pouring through the kitchen windows in golden streaks. She moved with the precision of someone who'd already been awake for an hour, her eyes scanning the room before resting briefly on me and Lucas.

"We should head out soon," she said simply.

Lucas stood and stretched, finishing his tea in one last gulp. "Car's packed," he offered. "Just waiting on us."

I nodded, setting my mug down and moving through the quiet routine of preparing for departure. Backpack zipped. Jacket retrieved. Last check of the guest room.

We gathered by the front door. Evelyn adjusted the strap of her satchel with clinical ease. "Oxford by early afternoon if traffic's light."

Lucas popped the trunk and started loading. I glanced back at the house one last time. It looked smaller from the porch than I remembered.

As we pulled out onto the road, none of us spoke. Just the sound of tires on pavement and the low hum of the engine. The scent of jasmine still lingered faintly on my shirt.

And behind us, just for a moment, I thought I saw a dark sedan parked two houses down.

Watching.

The morning passed slowly as we made our way south on the expressway. Trees blurred past in streaks of pine and gold, the sun climbing steadily behind us. We hadn't said much. The radio played something soft and forgettable, the kind of sound meant to fill space but not memory.

I sat in the passenger seat, Lucas at the wheel—his turn to drive after Evelyn's intense handling the day before. We'd all silently agreed a change of pace might be good. Evelyn was in the back, eyes half-closed but never quite relaxed. Every so often, she'd glance out the window, fingers tapping a subtle rhythm on her thigh.

The longer we drove, the more I felt it—something off. A quiet, invisible weight pressing on the back of my neck. Like being watched, but from just outside the edge of vision.

Lucas changed lanes suddenly, breaking the quiet. "You see that?" he asked, eyes flicking to the mirror.

I turned, catching a glimpse of a black sedan a few car lengths behind us. Tinted windows. Steady speed.

"Same one from the neighborhood?" I asked.

"Could be. Might've been a coincidence."

"Twice doesn't feel like coincidence."

From the back seat, Evelyn's voice came low, sharp. "Keep driving. Don't change speed. Let's see how long they hold."

Lucas nodded, hands tightening on the wheel.

For the next ten miles, the car stayed behind us. Never too close. Never too far. Matching us turn for turn.

Then it changed lanes. Pulled alongside.

I held my breath.

But the windows stayed up. No glimpse of the driver. Just that blank, black glass like a mirror that refused to reflect.

Then it dropped back again. And followed.

Evelyn's hand moved subtly inside her coat. Not panicked. Ready.

Something was coming.

We just didn't know what.

Lucas took the next exit without signaling, turning down a quiet rural road flanked by trees and old fenceposts. The sedan mirrored the move, a few seconds behind.

"Alright," Lucas muttered, more to himself than anyone else. "Let's see if you're really after us."

He accelerated slightly, weaving through the curves. Evelyn sat up straighter, jaw clenched. "Lucas, don't lose the Audi."

"Relax. I'm not taking her off-road yet," he said, his tone clipped. "But I'm not letting them tail us into Oxford either."

The trees thickened as the road narrowed. The sedan followed, matching every turn, every rise and dip.

Lucas took another turn, sharper this time, onto a narrow paved backroad that looped through a small industrial area—abandoned warehouses, faded signage, rusted fencing. "Let's give them some static."

He swerved into an alley between two buildings, then doubled back onto the main road, eyes checking the mirrors constantly.

The sedan reappeared. Still with them.

"Persistent," I said.

Lucas grit his teeth, scanning ahead. "Hold on."

He veered off again, this time onto a gravel path that cut through a grove of pines. The Audi jolted, tires skimming loose stone. The sedan tried to follow—but this time, the dust, loose rocks, and tight turns slowed it.

Lucas took the next left, then another, zigzagging through backroads and country lanes until the sedan was no longer in sight.

We didn't stop. Not yet.

Only after we reached a long stretch of empty road bordered by farmland did Lucas finally ease off the gas and pull onto a dirt turnout partially hidden by brush.

"We'll wait here for a few," he said, voice low.

The engine idled quietly. Evelyn leaned forward between the seats, eyes scanning the rearview.

"Think we lost them," she said.

"I don't like that we had to," Lucas said.

I nodded slowly, heart still thudding. "Yeah. Because it means they're not done. The Collective doesn't just let go."

She exhaled through her nose. "And they know we're moving."

Lucas turned the car off. The silence pressed in again—hot, still, watchful.

I leaned my head back, the scent of gravel dust and pine settling into my senses. We hadn't outrun the danger. Just delayed it.

And something—or someone—was still looking.

Lucas stepped out to stretch his legs and walked back to the trunk. When he returned, he was crouched by the rear bumper, rummaging in Evelyn's emergency kit. A few moments later, he stood up with a screwdriver and a strip of metal—an old novelty plate she'd picked up years ago and never removed. Working quickly and quietly, he adjusted the plate mount, securing the novelty plate over the real one with a flipped bolt. From a distance, it would read as a different tag.

"Temporary measure," he said, brushing off his hands. "Might buy us time if they're checking cameras or road plates."

Evelyn raised an eyebrow but didn't argue.

I stayed in the front seat, still processing. The countryside was quiet, broken only by wind and the occasional bird call.

"Phoenix," Evelyn said softly. I turned, surprised by her tone. "There's something you should probably know."

She wasn't looking at me. Just out the side window, like the words were hard to push forward.

"When we met—back before your freshman year—it wasn't exactly chance. Your mom introduced us for a reason."

I narrowed my eyes. "What do you mean?"

Evelyn finally turned to face me. "I was her grad assistant at Memphis. She... asked me to keep an eye on you. Not as a spy. Just... someone she trusted to be nearby."

I let that sit for a beat. The silence between us was thick.

"So the bookstore thing?"

"Not random," she admitted. "She thought you needed someone who wouldn't treat you like glass. Someone younger, who understood what it meant to straddle both worlds. A Keeper, but not yet burdened by rank. That was me."

I didn't know how to feel. Part of me was angry. Another part was weirdly relieved.

"And after we broke up?"

"I kept my distance. Tried to. But I never stopped looking out for you."

Outside, Lucas was watching the road, but I could feel the weight of his listening.

"You could've just told me," I said.

Evelyn's voice softened. "I think part of me wanted it to become real on its own. And then it did. And then it didn't."

We sat in silence again, but it wasn't empty.

She broke it. "Your mother believed in you long before the Council did. She knew what might be coming—and what it might cost you."

I turned toward her, brows furrowing.

"She didn't tell me anything. Not about the Keepers. Not about what she was preparing for."

"She couldn't," Evelyn said. "Council rules. But she told me enough. Enough to know you'd be tested. That your bloodline wasn't just legacy—it was a tether."

I frowned. "Council rules? She founded the damn thing. Why not just change them?"

Evelyn gave a small, tight shrug. "Because she believed some things had to be earned. Even by her son. Especially by him."

I looked away, letting that land.

"So you've known all along," I said.

She shook her head. "Only pieces. I was a junior Keeper, brought in on strict need-to-know. But Joanne—Dr. Knight—she trusted me. Trained me. And when she introduced us, she asked one thing: 'Make sure my son isn't alone when the world begins to change.'"

We sat there in the silence that followed, no longer filled with everything unsaid, but everything known too late.

I studied her. The way her eyes didn't quite meet mine, how her hands rested perfectly still on her knees. Too still.

"So that's what I was to you," I said, quieter than I meant. "An assignment."

"It wasn't like that," she said quickly, too quickly.

"But it started like that. You were told to watch me. You agreed. And then what?"

She opened her mouth. Closed it again. "Then I got to know you. Then it became more. But yes—at first, I did what she asked. Because I believed in her."

"But you didn't believe in me. Not enough to tell me the truth."

Evelyn's jaw tightened. "You don't get it. I didn't know what I was protecting you from. I only knew your mother was scared. And if Joanne Knight was scared—really scared—then I followed orders."

I looked back out the window. The brush swayed gently, as if the world hadn't shifted.

"I'm still a Keeper," she said after a long pause. "But sometimes I wonder if what we're keeping is actually keeping us."

That caught me. I turned toward her, not angry anymore—just tired.

"So what now?" I asked. "You still looking after me? Still watching the assignment?"

She didn't smile. Didn't blink. "No. Now I'm with you. Because I chose to be."

For the first time since the conversation began, I believed her. But belief didn't unmake the past.

It just made the present more fragile.

Lucas started the engine again. The Audi eased back onto the road like nothing had happened. But everything had.

We drove in silence, letting the dust settle behind us and the miles stretch out in front.

By the time the town of Oxford came into view, the sun was leaning west, casting long shadows through the trees. Familiar roads greeted us, but they didn't feel like home. Not anymore.

Lucas pulled the car into the driveway of the house on Broadview Lane. It was quiet and unassuming, like it had no idea what we were bringing back with us—just another home in a neighborhood that didn't know how deep the shadows ran.

Evelyn stepped out first, scanning the street, her shoulders still tight.

I lingered a moment before getting out, hand on the door. This was the last pause before the next unraveling.

Inside, we'd regroup. Try to make sense of what we knew, what we feared—and what we still hadn't uncovered.

Because the Collective wasn't done.

And neither were we

Ten

Crossing Points

"Between Silence and Signal"

Oxford was precisely the same—quiet, still, like nothing had changed. We'd left my parents' house in Germantown late that morning, after a long night and an even longer conversation that still lingered in the air between us. The drive south had been tense, shadowed by the car that had followed us, the dust we kicked up, and the truths Evelyn had finally shared. The quiet of Oxford, for all its sameness, felt thinner now—like the calm before another storm. I was tired and ready to be back in my own bed. I never slept well there, not after I moved out. Not after it happened. Coming home to Oxford wasn't exactly comforting. It felt like returning to a former life, one I barely recognized anymore.

Evelyn had spent most of Sunday flipping through my mother's journal, searching for a reference, a clue, anything. I'd grown used to it—not feeling weird about her reading it anymore. Honestly, I didn't know what I felt when she first picked it up. Maybe resentment, maybe a strange kind of comfort. Mostly, I felt like I was just waiting. And I hated waiting when I knew I should be doing something. Everyone else had their tasks. Me? I was stuck in limbo—waiting for a phone call, an email, any word from my mother. So I tried to stay busy: reading for class, drafting papers, pretending I had control over something.

"I know," Lucas said into his phone, pacing between the living room and his room. His voice was tight, his steps sharper than usual. I looked over a few times, but he didn't seem to notice. The longer he talked, the more his face flushed. I'd seen a few of these calls before—just never this heated. His entire posture was rigid, like he was fighting to keep his tone civil.

"What's going on with him?" Evelyn asked as she sat beside me, her voice hushed.

"Don't know," I said. "You find anything?"

"Nothing. A lot of research notes, but no answers." She sounded defeated. Her gaze dropped slightly, a subtle tell. I could tell she was trying to hide her frustration, but it clung to her like static.

Lucas's voice escalated. "DAD, I will look at it. I do still have schoolwork!" A few more clipped words, then silence. I assumed he'd hung up.

Evelyn glanced at me. I shook my head—staying out of it. Lucas family drama wasn't my battlefield. It had its own landmines, ones I didn't want to trigger.

"I hate my family," he muttered, dropping into the chair across from us. His eyes locked on the floor like he was daring it to fight back. Evelyn stood, excusing herself with a knowing look.

"Guy talk," she said. "I've got more reading to do." She vanished down the hall, leaving me with the emotional fallout.

Lucas didn't hold back. He vented about expectations, family obligations, the invisible leash they kept tugging. I tried to listen. I really did. But some of it washed over me. Maybe that was wrong. Maybe I was too distracted by my own mess to give him what he needed.

"Why don't you just tell them to stop?" I asked.

"My dad would love that." His voice dripped with sarcasm, but there was something bitter underneath—something cracked.

"Lucas, it's your life. Not his."

"I know."

"Then stop worrying about it."

He gave me a look. "Like you don't worry about anything?"

"Hey—this isn't about me."

"Why not?"

"Because you're the one fuming right now. Focus."

He huffed, sank deeper into the couch, but didn't speak again for a moment.

When he did, it was quieter. "He keeps trying to arrange these introductions. 'Opportunities,' he calls them. Networking. Future-proofing the family legacy."

Lucas wasn't made to fit molds. That's what I respected most. He carved his own shape, even if it left him bruised. And the bruises were showing.

We sat in silence, the ceiling fan spinning its lazy circles, the hum in the air like a lullaby for discontent.

"I'm tired of the whole 'this is what a man does' thing," he said finally.

"What do you mean?"

He exhaled, shaking his head. "The performative crap. You've got to chase girls, own a truck, crush beer cans on your forehead. Be a 'guy's guy.' Like some checklist of insecurities we're supposed to perform."

I nodded slowly. "And if you don't, you're less of a man."

"Exactly. My frat brothers talk about sex like it's conquest. Like women are trophies. And if you don't play that game? They look at you sideways. Ask if something's 'wrong' with you."

"What did your dad say?"

Lucas looked away. "He set me up with a girl. Said she was good for optics. Polished. Well-connected. Said she'd 'look good' beside me."

I felt the heat rise in my chest. "Like a prop."

"Like a campaign poster," he muttered.

"That's messed up."

Lucas didn't answer right away. Then: "I don't want to perform to be respected. I want to exist. Just exist. And still be enough."

"You are," I said, without hesitation. "You've always been enough. Just not to people who don't know how to see you."

He blinked, surprised. Then gave a soft laugh—half relief, half disbelief.

"Thanks," he said. But it landed deeper than thanks. Like he might actually believe it, someday.

I leaned back, let the silence fill the space again. "You're allowed to rewrite the rules, you know."

"Maybe. Still feels like I'm playing chess in a game that was supposed to be baseball."

"Then flip the board."

Lucas chuckled again. "You sound like your mother."

"I'll take that as a compliment."

A pause. Then I smirked. "At least... was she pretty?"

He chuckled despite himself. "Yeah. Probably lovely. Still not my choice."

"Then say that. 'I'll find someone—on my terms.'"

Lucas stared at the ceiling. "I'll try."

"Let's go for a run," I said, standing.

"Are you serious?"

"Very. Not asking."

He shot me a glare—the same one he gave before dragging me to that party. The one where I got kidnapped. He paused for a beat, then added, "You think the Collective's still watching us?"

I shrugged, trying to sound more confident than I felt. "If they are, they've got a weird way of showing it."

Lucas gave a dry laugh. "Great. Just wanted to make sure I'm not jogging into an ambush."

"Nah. Worst thing waiting out there is probably a squirrel. Maybe two."

"Fantastic," he muttered. "Can't wait to get mauled by a woodland creature."

I gave him a look. "You'll survive. Probably."

"Fine," he said with a theatrical sigh. "Let me change."

He walked off toward his room, and I stayed seated for a beat longer. The light from the living room window spilled across the floor like an invitation. Or maybe a warning. We weren't safe. Not really. And no run would fix that. But maybe—for a little while—it could help us breathe.

The air was warm with no breeze in sight. Heat clung to our skin the moment we stepped out of the Jeep, a wet Mississippi kind of heat that didn't ask permission—it just wrapped around you and stayed. The dirt trail crunched beneath our sneakers as we broke into a jog, the sound of our footfalls syncing into an easy rhythm. Trees pressed in close from both sides, tall and swaying, the late-summer leaves casting dappled shadows that danced across our bare shoulders.

By the time we stepped out of the Jeep and onto the gravel at the trailhead, the heat was already rising like steam off the pavement. I tugged at the hem of my shirt and peeled it off, slinging it into the backseat. The sun hit my skin immediately—hot, unrelenting, and already drawing out a sheen of sweat that slicked across my shoulders and chest. The Mississippi humidity didn't wait for an invitation. It wrapped around every inch of bare flesh, heavy and wet, the kind of air that made you feel like you were breathing through cotton.

I wore black running shorts, lightweight and loose, and my old sneakers that had seen more miles than most cars in Oxford. They were molded to me now—comfort in the midst of heat and pressure.

Lucas shut his door and looked at me with a shake of his head. "Already shirtless?"

"Better now than soaked two minutes in," I said, stretching out my arms with a groan.

He gave a small chuckle but kept his faded tee on, even as we started down the trail. The dirt crunched beneath us, trees hemming in the path on both sides, casting shadows that shifted with every step. The heat pressed in, relentless. I could hear his breathing pick up by the half-mile mark, and sweat had started to bead at his temples.

After the first lap, Lucas's shirt clung to him like shrink-wrap, soaked clean through and turning a darker shade of gray. He pulled at the hem with one hand, yanked it over his head mid-stride, and grunted as he tucked it into his waistband. His breath came in hard puffs, chest rising and falling as he adjusted to the relief of exposed skin.

"You're not going to pass out on me, are you?" I teased, watching him settle back into rhythm.

"Not a chance," he muttered, then added with a smirk, "but I better be getting a damn smoothie after this."

I laughed, and for a second, the heaviness of the week lifted. As we ran side by side, I caught a better look—his torso catching the sunlight in brief flashes between the trees. He wasn't bulky like a lifter, but defined. Cut. The kind of build born from constant movement and discipline. Sweat rolled down from his collarbone, tracing over the soft ridges of muscle along his sternum, glinting like silver under the sun.

He flicked a glance my way, quick and unreadable, before looking straight ahead again. There was something there—fleeting, unsure. But he said nothing, and neither did I.

The air hung heavy between us—not just from the heat, but from whatever thread of tension had slipped silently into the space we shared.

I caught him casting a glance at me from the corner of his eye, but he said nothing. The air between us was thick—not just from the humidity but from something unspoken. A subtle shift, there and gone.

Neither of us mentioned the change. There was something freeing in it—the silence, the effort, the stripped-down version of ourselves we could only find on trails like this. We didn't have to say why we needed the run. We both knew.

We passed an elderly couple walking slowly in the opposite direction. They gave us small nods, amused maybe at our foolishness or impressed we hadn't collapsed yet.

The trail curved around a slope, and through a break in the trees, Sardis Lake glinted in the distance, its surface calm and sunlit. I'd picked this trail for a reason—it was far enough from Oxford to feel like we'd left our worries behind, and the lack of cell reception meant Lucas couldn't be interrupted by calls from his family.

"How do you do this?" Lucas jogged next to me, breath staggered as he forced the words out.

"Do what?"

"All of this running."

"Try doing this for ninety minutes straight on the pitch." I grinned, remembering all those games I had played in the dead of winter. Hearing my mother cheer from the stands, even if I completely missed or fell. She would still say she was proud and sing praises.

"Yeah, that's why I didn't play." He shook his head as I laughed between breaths. We hit a small downhill stretch, our feet moving faster, muscles burning. The trail crossed a shallow stream, the rush of water barely audible over our breath and the rhythmic beat of our pace.

We made our way around for another lap, pushing through the fatigue. As we neared the trailhead for the third time, Lucas slowed and finally stopped.

"You tired already?" I slowed down next to him.

"Yes, yes I am." He paused. "I'm not as in-shape as you are."

Lucas bent forward slightly, hands on his hips, chest rising and falling with each heavy breath. His curls stuck to his forehead, and sweat dripped from his chin.

"Need to pace yourself," I said, trying to offer some advice.

"Yes, but hard to do keeping up with you." We passed through a small wooden bridge with a stream passing underneath. I just looked over at him as he tried to stay next to me.

"Well, guess we should do more of this so you can."

"You're going to kill me." He laughed a bit, still catching his breath.

"Is it helping?" I hoped it was helping him to clear his head. To get all the family issues out of mind and him just focusing on a single task.

"Yeah, it is. Is this what you do? To forget?"

"Not to forget. It helps to focus."

"I see."

"Okay, come on, enough rest." I nudged him back into motion. The trees hung over us, so at least we weren't in the direct line of the sun. Otherwise, we would bake more than we already were.

"Ugh, you're killing me," Lucas grunted as we set off again down the trail for the rest of the laps. He trailed a little but was still able to keep up the pace. It seemed to be working for him, never mentioning his father or the situation. I know it was working for me, keeping my mind off the search for my mother, the document I still had un-opened that sat by my bed. All of it still bugged me, but right now it was just the run that was important.

We finished the remaining portion of our run and came back to the trailhead. The Jeep was not too far off in the parking lot as we walked towards it, sweat clinging to us like another skin.

"Thank you," Lucas said, almost reaching the Jeep.

"You're welcome. Drink?"

"Yes, you owe me that smoothie."

"We'll grab one on the way back." I opened the door to my Jeep. My phone was sitting on my seat with at least five missed calls from Evelyn.

"That can't be good." I showed Lucas the phone.

"You better call her."

I walked away, calling Evelyn back. I tried a few times to get ahold of her with no luck. Everything went straight to voicemail. I would have a better chance getting closer to town.

"No luck?"

"Yeah, let's get going," I said, and we drove off towards Oxford. It took us about fifteen to twenty minutes to be able to get back into town. The drive itself was nothing impressive; I had done this trip too many times to count. We did stop for refreshments before heading to the house, since by the time we made it back into Oxford, both of us were quite parched.

Evelyn was a little cross with us once we got back into the house.

"You could have called me back," she said.

"I did!"

"No?"

"Yes, I did, see." I showed her my phone. Evelyn still looked upset, but she calmed a little. It wasn't like I didn't try; it was just that cell service sucked at the lake.

"Your professor came by," she finally said, getting to the point.

"Dr. Dawson?"

"Yes, she wanted to speak to you, but you weren't here."

"Damn, did she mention anything?" I hoped that something could give me a clue. I was surprised that she had come to the house. How did she know where I lived? It was not something I advertised, and nowhere in the school records that I knew of.

"Just that she got your email."

I can't believe I'd missed her; it could have been important. She had to have some information about what the hell was going on. She needed to, for my sanity. Otherwise, I would spiral into the endless abyss of research. Searching endlessly for an answer, something that could help me make sense of all of this.

"So that's it?"

"Yeah, I'm sorry," she said and headed to the kitchen. Maybe the run wasn't the best idea. I would have been here for when she came by. I could have the information that I had been looking for. Then again, Lucas needed it, and I couldn't wish to have that taken away.

It was nearing the evening when Lucas had dinner prepared; he must have been in a better mood. As the food spread, he made my mouth water before I could even take a seat at the table.

"Your cooking is incredible," Evelyn said between bites.

"Thanks." Lucas put a little more salad on his plate. The smell of the food was intoxicating as it swirled in the air around us. It was the best part about cooking. The smell that carried throughout the house.

"Where did you learn to cook?" Evelyn asked.

"My mother. It was the one thing she made sure I knew how to do."

I was surprised to hear him talk of his mother. I had never heard him mention her at all. It was almost like she didn't even exist or was dead. Even though I knew that his mother was just down in Jackson.

"So, I take it the run helped," I said, joining the conversation after finishing my bite.

"It did, thank you," Lucas said. "I'm starting to realize why you do it so much." He had no idea.

"That's why you two came back all sweaty," Evelyn interjected.

"You know a run is good for you too," I interrupted.

"No need with my figure, plus less time for reading," she replied, and I just shook my head and smiled.

"Confident with our body, aren't we," Lucas said, trying to poke at her a bit. She seemed confident of her body. Granted, she had every right to be.

"Why, yes, it takes work."

"Is there a Vogue cover I missed?" I joked, and I almost thought Lucas choked as he let out a laugh.

"Very funny, Phoenix." She threw a napkin at me. It barely made it towards me, landing on the table.

"You deserved it." We all laughed a little, enjoying the rest of dinner. We sat there just talking and eating. Having a great time, something I hadn't done often. These last few weeks, despite all the problems, I found myself not alone. I felt like somebody again.

"Come on, Phoenix, you know you want to play at least one game," Lucas pleaded as the conversation switched to playing games after dinner.

"It will help take our mind off things," Evelyn said, absolutely on board with the idea. I was trying to retire early, since I was tired from the run, not to mention the week itself. However, his face was not really giving me a choice in the matter.

"Ugh, fine," I gave in. "What are we wanting to play?"

"Monopoly or Risk?" Lucas asked.

"Both of those take forever."

"Risk it is," Evelyn said, and Lucas went to grab the game from the closet. He returned, and we began to set up the game. Then my phone rang, and I looked down at the message on the screen.

"Who is it?" Evelyn asked.

"It's my professor."

ELEVEN

A PROMISE

"OATHS IN QUIET"

Everything was silent as the crisp autumn air cut through my jacket and sent shivers down my spine. Leaves, bronze and brittle, skittered along the brick pathways like tiny dancers spun by the wind. Squirrels darted from tree to tree, cheeks full, their tiny paws clutching acorns as if they could outpace winter. The air was colder than it should have been, sharp and alive, as if the earth itself held its breath. I walked alone through the tall grove of trees lining the old campus walkway. It should've been peaceful. Instead, every shadow whispered unease.

An email had dragged me out into the night:

Need to meet. Office @ 9.

That was it. No name, no subject, no punctuation. It was after hours for most professors, especially on a weeknight. My gut twisted. Did she find something? Some clue in my mother's records? Or was it another half-answer wrapped in apologies? I'd missed her visit earlier—guilt still sat heavy on my chest like damp wool. Maybe this was her way of making up for it. Maybe this was my second chance.

I passed the student union. It sat dark, the windows blank, save for the amber pool of a vending machine light inside. The whole campus felt drained of color, like someone had dialed the contrast down on reality. Just lamp posts and memory.

Bryant Hall loomed ahead. The oldest building on campus. Gothic and brooding with its stained-glass windows and ivy-clad face. Tonight, it looked like a mausoleum.

I descended the side steps and passed dimly lit offices—professors bent over stacks of papers, some tapping on keyboards, others reading slowly under harsh fluorescent lights. The hallway smelled of coffee and old books. Routine. Familiar. But her office—

Her office pulsed.

The light behind the frosted window flickered with movement. Pages rustled, shadows shifted. A storm was inside.

I knocked. "Dr. Dawson?"

The door burst open. She stood there, eyes wild, hair undone, blouse wrinkled, breath shallow.

"Phoenix. Come in."

I stepped into chaos.

Books spilled off shelves. Papers littered the floor like fallen snow. Files flared open across the desk. She was packing—frantic, deliberate. Not preparing for class. Fleeing.

"Dr. Dawson, what's going on?"

"There's more, Phoenix. More than I realized. It's all connected—the school, the Council, your mother."

My pulse jumped. "Wait—what?"

"They've been watching. Listening. They knew I was digging."

"Who? The Collective?"

Her eyes darted to the door. "Yes. Maybe. I don't know who exactly. But someone."

She shoved more papers into her leather satchel, then looked up and grabbed my shoulders with cold fingers.

"You have to trust those who guard. Promise me."

"I promise," I whispered.

Her body slackened. A brief moment of stillness washed over her. Like the tide pulling back.

"Phoenix… you hold the key. Your mother—she knew. You are—"

Then she froze.

Not like hesitation.

Like time stopped.

Her mouth opened, but no words came out. Her pupils dilated, her hands fell away.

She collapsed.

"Dr. Dawson!" I caught her. Her body folded in my arms, heavy and limp.

Her skin—ice.

Her breath—gone.

No pulse.

Nothing.

"Dr. Dawson! Please!"

Something wasn't right—something was horribly wrong.

I shook her. Called her name. Checked again for breath, heartbeat, anything.

Dead

Death—

Cold—

Limp—

Silence—

"SOMEBODY HELP!"

The scream tore out of me, primal and raw. It echoed down the hallway.

"SOMEBODY HELP!"

Doors opened. Footsteps rushed. Faces appeared, wide-eyed and horrified. A professor. Then a janitor. Then campus police.

Blue lights. Flashing. Blinding.

I backed away as they lifted her. As they declared her.

Gone.

I stood there, alone in the eye of the storm, staring at the place she had fallen. The tiles beneath my feet felt colder than they should have, like the room itself had turned against warmth, rejecting the echo of her last breath. My shadow stretched long in the flickering light, tethering me to that one still point in time—where everything changed.

It was like the world had blinked and missed something vital. A spark—snuffed. The air, once vibrantly humming with her breath, her voice, her presence, now hung thick and stale, a vacuum where life had been. Her office, her sanctuary of knowledge and ritual, had transformed into a mausoleum. Her scent lingered still—coffee with a hint of lavender, normally comforting—but now it curled in my nostrils like the remnants of a cruel memory refusing to fade.

My hands trembled uncontrollably. They still remembered her touch, her fingers wrapped tight around mine only moments ago. I looked down at them as if they might carry the truth she never finished, some secret etched in the fine lines of my skin. But there was nothing. Just warmth turning cold.

The weight of her final words spun around inside my skull like a riddle I couldn't untangle. She had been on the edge of revelation—on the brink of giving me the answer, of stitching together the seams of my fractured world. I could still see her eyes, how they flickered from panic to peace. That moment where she saw it, accepted it, and let go.

They did this.

They were watching.

She had been running—not just from fear, but from inevitability.

And I had been too late.

My knees buckled slightly, but I didn't fall. I couldn't. Not yet. The room pressed in around me, the shelves leaning inward like mourners, paper scattered like ash from some unseen fire. I was a statue in grief, paralyzed in the aftermath.

Somewhere, footsteps approached. Distant voices mumbled directives. But it all sounded underwater, muted and warped. My vision blurred—not from tears, but from the sheer force of loss.

The absence of her voice, her motion, her mind—it was too loud in its silence.

She had something to say. And now it was gone.

I clutched at the fragments, tried to piece together her last sentence, to give it shape, meaning. "Phoenix, you hold the key... Your mother... you are—" What? What was I supposed to be? What truth had she seen too late?

Everything in me screamed for it back. Just one more breath. One more word. One more second.

But there was only stillness. And the quiet, mocking weight of what might have been.

More people arrived—professors with wide, hollow eyes, students whispering behind cupped hands, and campus police scanning the scene with muted urgency. Some cried softly, the kind of tears that slipped down faces like rain on old windows. Others stood frozen, unsure of how to react to the sight of one of their own, lifeless, carried away in a zipped black bag.

All I could do was stare.

The world had become muffled. Someone spoke to me—I saw their lips move—but no sound reached my ears. Even the cold breeze brushing my cheeks felt distant, like I wasn't entirely inside my body. I nodded in response to questions from UPD, though I wasn't sure what I agreed to. My throat was dry, my jaw clenched. They wrote things down, scribbled in notepads, but none of it mattered.

She was trying to run.

She knew her life was in danger.

She had a story to tell.

She had been trying to give me something. A warning, a truth—maybe both. But now that thread was cut. Snapped like a twig underfoot. And whatever it was, whoever did this—

They did this.

They will pay.

It won't be for nothing.

I didn't see Evelyn at first. Just felt her—her arms wrapping around me, her scent of mint and vanilla grounding me. Her lips moved, her voice soft and strained.

"I got you," Evelyn said. "I got you."

I stood there, frozen in her arms, letting the warmth of her presence soak through my shock. My body trembled, but I held everything in. I had to.

"They killed her, Evelyn. They killed her," I whispered, voice cracking like brittle glass.

They did this.

They will pay.

It won't be for nothing.

"I know," she murmured, pulling me tighter. "I got you."

We stayed like that, statues in grief, while the scene around us churned. Sirens faded. Questions circled back. I answered mechanically, detached, watching as others offered condolences with glassy eyes and uncertain hands. A few professors touched my shoulder or pulled me into a brief hug. Each contact felt both too much and not enough.

Mourn, Death

Cold—

Limp—

Those were the sensations that etched themselves into my memory. Her hands going slack in mine. The color draining from her skin. The echo of her final moment, suspended in stillness. I couldn't stop replaying it. Couldn't silence it.

I should've been at home. I could've stopped it. I could've saved her. Guilt gnawed at my insides like something alive.

When Evelyn and I walked home, the world felt like a shadow of itself. We passed familiar buildings that now looked foreign. Trees rustled, but no birds sang. My body moved through the world, but my spirit lagged behind, tethered to that office.

"Don't try to think about it right now," Evelyn said gently as we approached the porch.

"But there has to be a reason."

"There is. But not tonight. You're mourning."

I nodded. It was all I could do.

"I should've been at home," I said again, voice barely a whisper.

"Don't say that. Don't go down that road, Phoenix."

"But what if—"

"Don't." Her voice was firm this time. "Even if you were there, they would've found a way. This isn't your fault."

Inside the house, the warm light should've brought comfort, but it didn't. It felt like I was stepping into a memory I no longer deserved to live.

"Phoenix, I heard," Lucas said, appearing from the kitchen. His eyes were red. "I'm so sorry."

"Thanks."

He handed me a glass of red wine. I took it, my fingers brushing his. It was warm, a small anchor in a sea of numbness.

"Thank you. I need this."

"Glad I could help. Let me know if you need anything."

"Will do."

We sat in silence—me, Evelyn, and Lucas. Not speaking. Not needing to. The weight of what had happened sat with us like another presence in the room.

Death—

Cold—

Limp—

Silence—

I sipped the wine, but it tasted like ashes. My thoughts drifted to my mother. Would she be next? Would I find her lifeless, too, with only a mystery and a trail of grief left behind?

Endless images swirled behind my eyes. Of Dawson collapsing. Of her words cut short. Of the way the air had turned still. The feeling was unnatural, like something sacred had been violated.

Murder, I thought. That's what it was. And tomorrow, it would be buried under headlines. Sanitized for the public.

We stayed like that for what felt like an eternity, each of us lost in our thoughts. The room dimmed. The silence thickened. Then, I couldn't bear it anymore.

"I'm going to bed," I said, voice barely audible.

"Good night," Evelyn replied, standing to hug me. Her arms were strong but soft. I didn't move.

"Get some rest," Lucas said, his voice low as he cleared the glasses.

In my room, I stripped out of my clothes as if they were armor I no longer needed. I could still smell her on them—the faint lavender, the sharp note of stress. I wanted to burn them. I wanted to scream.

I curled into bed, sheets crisp and clean, the pillow cool against my cheek. I listened for the quiet to fall over the house. Only then, in that perfect silence, did I let the sobs come.

Death—

Cold—

Limp—

Silence—

Outside, the wind picked up again. It rattled the windows and sighed through the trees like a ghost mourning a name it could no longer speak. Somewhere down the hall, a door creaked open then shut softly. A reminder that life, however fragmented, continued around me.

I stared at the ceiling, watching as shadows played against the plaster. My body ached in strange places—grief lodged itself in my bones like frost. I wanted to scream again, to tear something apart, but the exhaustion won out. The grief, so sharp earlier, dulled to a steady throb.

I didn't know what tomorrow would bring. Headlines, maybe. Whispers on campus. Another knock at the door. But for now, there was just this moment. This silence. This memory.

And the sobs—ragged and real—dragged me down like undertow, until nothing remained but silence, and the fire I could no longer ignore.

✉LEGACY FILE 11.5 – SEALED COMMUNIQUE

Classification: Internal Collective Directive – Redacted Tier

File Type: Encrypted Message Intercept

Recovered From: Burned cache near Oxford node

Date Stamp: [REDACTED] – Estimated hours after Incident Dawson

---

TO: UNKNOWN

FROM: Stratford, Allison [Designation: Field Commander, South Division]

SUBJECT: Dawson Interference

This wasn't me

. don't eliminate assets without permission, and certainl. .ıot ones who still had leverage. Dawson was noisy, but useful. Predictable. Her removal? It reeks of panic –or ego.

If someone inside ordered this, I want the chain. If it came from higher, why wasn't I looped in?

Either way, the cleanup is now mine. Again.

And I don't like being surprised.

Whoever made this call better hope it was worth it.

– A.S.

⚠ No.. Though ..signed .op le. ..oded metadata confirms this transmission originated from Field Commander Stratford. No return channel identified. Kane's name does not appear anywhere in the trace.

Twelve

Mourning

"Ashes on the Wind"

It had been three days since she died.

Classes didn't meet. The campus felt like a wound wrapped in caution tape—sealed off, sterile, pulsing beneath the surface. Most buildings stood quiet, their interiors dim and cold, as if holding vigil. Dr. Dawson's death was officially ruled an accident, though no one really believed that. The university clung to the word like a lifeline, keeping "murder" out of the headlines, afraid of what truth might do to donor checks and enrollment numbers. But an investigation was ongoing. At least, that's what they said.

Over those three days, I had become a ghost in my own life. Visitors came and went—university officials, law enforcement, grief counselors. They asked questions, polite and practiced. I gave answers, clipped and controlled. I told them she'd asked to meet about a grade. That she collapsed. That I called for help.

I never lied.

But I didn't tell the truth, either. Some things weren't meant for them. Some truths needed to be protected, like embers hidden beneath ash.

The days blurred together in shades of gray. I spent most of them in bed, wrapped in my blankets like armor. When I did move, it was mechanical—laundry, dishes, catching up on readings I couldn't concentrate on. I still prepared for Dr. Dawson's class, part of me pretending she would be there, waiting with that half-smile and a dry wit. But I knew better. I'd watched her die. I felt the life leave her body in my arms.

Lucas and Evelyn checked in daily. They didn't hover, just appeared—silent presences with coffee or dinner or a quiet look that said we're here. We'd eat lunch or dinner together. Sometimes, Lucas ran with me, our shoes beating rhythm into the silence. We never talked on those runs. We didn't need to.

Even Oxford itself had gone quiet. No parties. No music drifting from frat houses. No shouting students walking home after bars. Just wind, rustling leaves, and the ache of a town unsure of how to mourn.

It was nearing evening when I finally dragged myself to the closet. Tonight was the campus memorial service. A public goodbye held on the steps of the Lyceum. Faculty, students, alumni—all invited to stand beneath those white columns and pretend words could fill the space she left behind.

I stared at my clothes.

What do you even wear to something like this? A funeral, but not really. A performance of grief, maybe. I touched a hoodie. It would be easier. Comfortable. Familiar. But my father's voice rang in my head—Always be presentable.

Fine.

I picked out a dark button-up shirt and black jeans. No tie. I didn't have it in me to be polished. I just wanted to survive the evening.

As I buttoned my shirt, the door creaked open.

"You ready?" Evelyn asked softly. Her voice was careful, not fragile, but gentler than usual.

"Yeah," I said, tugging the last button through its loop. "I'll be out in a minute."

She nodded and closed the door.

The silence returned. I slipped on my coat, fingers fumbling with the sleeves like I was forgetting how to be in my body. The mirror reflected someone I barely recognized—tired eyes, tight jaw, shoulders hunched like the weight hadn't shifted in days.

A few minutes later, I stepped into the living room. Lucas and Evelyn were waiting. Both dressed simply. No fuss. Just like her—unpretentious, thoughtful. Lucas held something in his hand—small, black. A single lily, probably from the campus greenhouse. He didn't say anything. He didn't need to.

"Shall we go?" he asked.

"Yeah," I said, clearing my throat. "Might as well."

I grabbed my coat from the hook by the door. The night waited beyond it—cool and solemn. The kind of night that felt like a page turning in a book you didn't want to read anymore.

Together, we stepped out into the hush of Oxford, three shadows moving through a grieving town, toward a memorial that couldn't bring her back—but might, just for a moment, remind us of the fire she left behind.

The air was crisp. Autumn was settling in with purpose, and clouds hung low in the sky, painted in muted blues and grays. As we walked along University Avenue, the streetlights blinked to life one by one, their orange glow spilling soft halos across the pavement. The rhythm of our footsteps felt in sync with the breath of the town—measured, slow, reverent.

Crossing the bridge into the Grove, we weren't alone anymore. People had begun to gather, silent and bundled against the creeping chill. They moved like pilgrims, reverent and solemn, all drawn to the Lyceum's white columns that loomed at the center like a monument to something sacred.

By the time we reached the circle, the crowd had swelled. Thousands, it seemed, stretching from tree line to tree line. The space was dense, but still. Each person held a single candle, the flames trembling like stars caught in human hands. Their soft glow flickered across solemn faces, illuminating tear-streaked cheeks, knitted brows, lips held tight with grief.

A woman passed by us and gently handed over three candles. She lit them with practiced care, and we added our flames to the sea of light. No words were exchanged—none were needed.

The Lyceum itself remained dark. Not a single electric bulb burned within its windows. It stood in quiet tribute, as if refusing to outshine the glow of collective memory. The only light came from those candles—thousands of them—shining defiantly against the encroaching night.

Then, without announcement, a single voice broke the stillness.

A young man, perhaps a student, stepped forward near the front. He was dressed in black, his posture straight, his eyes fixed on something only he could see. His voice—deep, rich, and full—rose into the air like incense, carrying the opening notes of Franz Biebl's Ave Maria.

And then, one by one, others joined him. Hidden in the crowd, voices emerged—tenors, basses, each entering in harmony, weaving a tapestry of grief and reverence. The sound billowed outward, echoing off buildings, wrapping the campus in something holy.

"Breathtaking," Evelyn whispered beside me.

I nodded, too moved to speak.

The choral harmonies swelled, filling every corner of the night. As the voices climbed and layered, it felt less like a performance and more like a ritual—a collective release, a final farewell lifted toward the heavens.

Even strangers reached for each other's hands. Even those who didn't know her wept.

I closed my eyes and let the music wash over me. The ache in my chest expanded and softened, made room for grief to be something beautiful. For a few moments, we weren't mourning alone. We were bound by something sacred.

The final chord held in the air, long and luminous, before fading into silence. Not absence, but reverence.

Then came the speeches. One by one, her colleagues stepped forward. They shared stories—small, glowing vignettes of her kindness, her brilliance, her fierce loyalty to truth. The department chair spoke with trembling hands, voice thick with emotion. Finally, the chancellor stepped up.

He looked out at us—all of us—candles held high, eyes brimming.

"Dr. Mariam Dawson's light will not go out," he said. "From this day forward, the Department of History shall bear her name."

A hush fell heavier.

And then the candles burned a little brighter.

The Mariam Dawson Department of History. A name etched in stone and memory.

And in us.

In me.

And for a moment, just beneath the solemnity and sorrow, I felt it—an echo in the bones of the campus itself. Like something older than any classroom or title had been acknowledged. A stillness that wasn't silence, but witness. The Grove held its breath, as if it too had lost more than a professor. As if the earth beneath our feet knew a flame had gone out that was never meant to flicker.

I found it fitting; she would've hated the attention, complaining every day about how ridiculous it was to name things after people still breathing. She always said legacy was written in what we built, not in bronze plaques. But now, she'd have to deal with it. And she deserved it.

Then, out of the corner of my eye, a shadow twisted in the periphery—subtle, like a memory flinching to life. I turned, and there she was.

Her brown hair hung loose, catching the flicker of candlelight like the strands of some serpent. Her face—unmistakable. Pale, calculating. And around her neck, a bruise like a ghost, the same one my hands had left. My breath hitched. My fingers curled into fists. She stood among the mourners like a phantom in silk, not hiding, not apologizing. She met my gaze and winked—slow, cruel, like she was signing her name at the bottom of the evening's pain.

My body tensed. My feet itched to close the distance between us.

"It's not worth it," Evelyn said under her breath. Her arm slid in front of me like a gate. She had followed my stare and knew instantly.

"She did this," I growled, heat rising under my skin. My voice cracked with restraint. I tried to break free of Evelyn's grip, but her hand stayed firm.

"I know. But it's not what she would have wanted. Not here. Not now."

And Evelyn was right. Even if every atom in me wanted retribution, even if the woman across the crowd was the embodiment of everything wrong and vile—this night was sacred. This wasn't for vengeance.

So I stayed. Let her get away. Let her vanish back into the crowd like a smirk slipping behind a mask. She would answer for it, eventually. Just not tonight.

As the ceremony drew to a close, people began to disperse. Some lingered, murmuring to one another, touching shoulders, whispering memories. Others wandered toward the memorial table lined with flowers and photographs, heads bowed in quiet respect.

Tomorrow would bring the funeral. After that, papers, deadlines, exams—normalcy would be wheeled out like a prop on a cracked stage. But nothing would be the same. Not for me.

Not when my mind still burned with her last words. Not when I still hadn't found my mother. This all felt like a dream stitched from grief and secrets, and I was staggering through it without a map.

Then I noticed him—a professor. He moved through the thinning crowd like a shadow with purpose. Dressed in black, face unreadable. I recognized him from the halls of the history department, though I'd never taken one of his classes.

"Mr. Knight," he said, extending a hand. His tone was even, rehearsed. "I'm so sorry for your loss."

"Thank you," I replied, automatically. His handshake was firm—too firm. Not just condolence. A message.

"I look forward to hearing from you," he added. Then turned and walked away.

I frowned. It was a strange thing to say. What could he possibly want to hear from me?

That's when I felt it. The soft brush of paper against my palm.

I looked down. A small, torn note. My heart stuttered.

Meet us in the Chamber this Friday @ 9 pm
Alone

"What is it?" Evelyn asked, catching my change in expression.

I handed her the note. Her brow furrowed as she read. She looked back up at me.

"Who is 'us'?"

"I think… the society. The one she was part of." My voice felt distant, like it was coming from someone else. My thoughts raced. Maybe she told them about me. Maybe this was what she meant—Trust those who guard.

Still, the paper burned in my hand like a fuse. A summons or a trap. Or both. It could be the Collective, playing a deeper game. Or it could be them—her people—finally stepping out of shadow.

The walk home was steeped in silence, but tension threaded every step like a wire pulled taut. The gravel crunched beneath our feet, the air sharp with the smell of fallen leaves and distant woodsmoke. Streetlights cast long shadows, painting our figures across the sidewalk like ghosts following us home.

Evelyn walked beside me, her steps quicker than usual, purposeful. I could feel her glance at me repeatedly, as if measuring the best way to break the quiet.

"You saw what they will do, Phoenix," she finally said, her voice low but pointed. "They don't care who they hurt. This isn't a game."

We reached the front steps, and I paused, fumbling for the key. My hands were cold, clumsy.

"I did see," I said as I pushed the door open. The house greeted us with familiar stillness. "I saw it right in front of me. But this could help us. It might not be a trick."

Inside, Evelyn tossed her coat over a chair instead of hanging it up like she usually did. "But it could be. And I won't let you walk into something you can't walk out of."

Frustration rose in me like heat. "Just let me do it—even if I'm going anyway."

Her eyes flared. "If it were Lucas or anyone else, you'd say go ahead."

"That's not true."

"It is," I snapped, louder than I meant to. "It's because it's me. Because you care. Because you're not going to let the person you care about go!"

The words shattered the room like glass. I watched her stiffen. For a heartbeat, the silence roared.

"You're right," she said softly. "I'm not going to lose you. And you bloody better deal with it."

With that, she turned and walked to her room, the door closing with a final, echoing click. The hallway dimmed, the house holding its breath. I stood there, jaw clenched, staring at the door like it might open again. But it didn't.

Lucas sat on the couch, watching without judgment. "You might have gone too far," he said at last, his voice a low tenor that settled into the quiet.

"I know." I collapsed into the armchair across from him.

He leaned forward, elbows on knees. "She's scared, Phee. Scared for you. It could've been you on that floor instead of Dr. Dawson."

Then, more quietly, he added, "Just… be safe, alright?"

"But Dr. Dawson told me to trust them."

"Then trust them," he said. "But don't punish Evelyn for being scared to lose you. She doesn't get scared easily. If she's shaken, it means something."

I nodded, dragging a hand through my hair. The weight of the evening bore down hard. "When did you become wise?"

Lucas cracked a faint smile. "When you started to become stupid."

I snorted, some tension easing from my shoulders.

We stayed like that, the two of us, surrounded by soft lamp light and the distant creaks of the house settling around us. It was the first time I could breathe without the weight of grief pressing against my ribs. We talked—small things, strange things. Childhood vacations. The best candy bars. The absurdity of organized religion.

And through it all, I realized that Lucas wasn't trying to fix anything. He was just there, steady and solid, anchoring me while the world tilted.

Eventually, the conversation faded. I stood, stretching the stiffness from my limbs.

"I'm calling it," I said. "Long day."

He nodded. "Don't let guilt make your choices. You'll only regret them more."

I offered a weak smile, then turned down the hall.

In my room, I tried calling my mother again. Straight to voicemail. As always. I stared at the ceiling, wondering if this meeting would bring me closer to her—or drag me deeper into something I wasn't ready to face.

But one thing was certain.

I had to go.

And I had to be ready.

THE LYCEUM

THIRTEEN

GUARDIANS

"TRUST THOSE WHO GUARD"

Friday came faster than I could've imagined. Time, once sluggish in grief, had surged forward since the funeral. Maybe it was the structure of classes resuming—the comfort of routine—or maybe I was simply trying to outrun the weight pressing on my chest. I spent the day lost in coursework, finishing assignments, even getting a bit ahead. My focus had sharpened into a kind of survival.

Dinner was quiet. Lucas outdid himself again with a seafood pasta dish so good I half-joked he should open a restaurant—only half-joked if it meant I got free meals. Evelyn gave a tired smile. Afterward, we each drifted into our corners of the house, the silence between us more understanding than awkward.

Once the lights dimmed and footsteps faded, I slipped out. I didn't leave a note. If they knew, they might try to stop me.

The night air was unexpectedly warm—summer's last breath before winter's grip took hold. University Avenue glowed in a haze of amber and shadow. Leaves clung to branches, trembling in the still air, and the silence was deep, layered. No wind. No crickets. Just the soft hush of my footsteps.

I should've been scared. Part of me was. The rational part. This could be a trap. But then I heard her voice again, faint but firm in memory:

Trust them, promise me.

I had. I wasn't breaking that.

The questions were too loud now. Why was the Collective after me? What did they want with my mother? Why did Dr. Dawson think I held the key to anything? I couldn't just sit and rot in fear anymore. Answers were out there, and this—tonight—was the first thread I could pull.

Still, dread lingered. If Evelyn found out, would she walk away again? That thought gnawed at me harder than the fear of the unknown. I didn't want to lose her. Not now. Not again.

Campus was already buzzing. A game tomorrow meant the Grove was transforming. Tailgating tents stretched like patchwork canopies across the grass, each one an altar to football. I passed chandeliers being strung from tree branches, silverware being laid out like fine dining under open sky. Generators hummed. People laughed. The scent of charcoal and sweet bourbon drifted through the air.

It was surreal—days ago, this had been a place of mourning. Now it pulsed with life. I walked among students clad in red and navy, some in opposing purple and gold, voices rising in excitement. Fraternity and sorority houses were already in celebration mode, the Walk of Champions lined with coolers and speakers, bracing for two days of relentless noise.

It was all so loud.

But I felt like I was underwater.

Just ahead, past the thickening crowd and through the veil of lights, rose the Lyceum. Tall. Unmoving. The white columns glowed faintly in the moonlight, their shadows long and sharp. A breeze whispered through the trees now, as if the building had exhaled.

It stood like a sentinel, ancient and watchful. I slowed. This was where everything started. Where she died. Where I had begun to change.

I stared up at it, heart pounding. What truths waited inside? What lies had it buried? I had once thought it beautiful. Now, it looked like a gatekeeper.

A place where secrets lived.

And I was about to knock.

The building stood silent, shrouded in a stillness that felt heavier than usual, as though it knew secrets were about to unfold within its depths. The halls were abandoned, shadows stretching long across the tiles as I moved, my steps measured and cautious. I navigated the familiar turns, feeling the slight rise in adrenaline with each footfall. The bookshelf greeted me like an old sentinel, unmoved and waiting. I reached forward and slid it aside with practiced ease, revealing the hidden passage beyond.

The corridor stretched ahead, lit by the warm glow of sconces embedded in the stone walls. The air was cool and carried a mix of ancient dampness, the sharp tang of old parchment, and a faint whiff of sandalwood. I took a deep breath, steadying myself. They were expecting me now. I only hoped this wasn't a trap. If it was, Evelyn would never let me live it down. Or I might not live to hear her say it.

The passage widened into the grand chamber, its vaulted ceiling arching high overhead. Torches flared along the walls, their flames flickering in unseen drafts and casting golden light on the murals—those timeless paintings of warriors, nature, symbols, and celestial figures. The pigments shimmered like precious metals, telling stories older than any I had read.

I descended the staircase slowly, each step thudding in sync with my heartbeat. As I reached the lower floor, they came into view.

They stood in a semi-circle, draped in cloaks of deep green and black. Hoods concealed their faces, though I could feel their eyes on me. Their collective presence was imposing—like walking into a cathedral of judgment. Silence reigned, sacred and watchful.

"Phoenix, welcome," came a resonant voice from the center. It echoed like a hymn down the stone corridor. The speaker stepped forward and drew back his hood.

"Chancellor Wilkinson," I breathed, stunned.

One by one, the others followed. Professors. Lecturers. Researchers I'd passed in hallways, seen across lecture halls. All here.

"Yes. And we've been watching you for some time," Wilkinson said. "I imagine you have many questions."

"That's putting it mildly," I replied, eyes darting between the faces. My chest tightened—each revelation cracked open another chamber of uncertainty.

"We are the Order of Nemus," he continued. "Guardians of this sanctuary and what lies beyond it. For millennia, we have kept watch."

I absorbed the words, but they didn't settle. Not yet. Something in his voice hinted at more.

"And what exactly lies beyond?" I asked.

Wilkinson glanced toward the rear of the chamber. "Something born of an ancient bloodline—something powerful. Only one of that lineage can command it."

My skin prickled. The air felt charged, heavy.

"Did Dr. Dawson know? Did she figure it out?"

Wilkinson shook his head, solemn. "She died before she could tell us everything. We feared what she had uncovered, and now it's lost."

My fists clenched. Of course. Another thread snipped just before I could grasp it.

"And what do you know, Phoenix? About her death?"

I hesitated, then spoke. "Not names. But the group responsible is called the Collective. They've been after me since summer. They tried to kidnap me once."

Gasps and murmurs broke the silence. A palpable tension flooded the room.

"Since summer?" one member asked sharply. "Then they've already marked you."

"I think so," I said, voice flat. "They knew things. Personal things. And they're not giving up."

"Do they know of this chamber? Of us?" Wilkinson's voice was low, urgent.

"I don't believe so. Not yet. But they killed Dr. Dawson for getting too close. They're searching. I don't know how much they know."

Whispers rippled through the Order. Faces turned toward each other. Wilkinson raised a hand to still them.

"This changes everything," said a female voice near the back. "If they are moving openly, then the sanctity of this place is at risk."

"And if Phoenix is already entangled," another added, "we must decide what role he plays in all of this."

Wilkinson took a step closer, the gravity in his gaze making my spine straighten. "Phoenix. We must ask something of you. Something not lightly given."

I looked around, pulse roaring in my ears. "What is it?"

"Swear to protect this place and what lies beyond it. The power here belongs only to the rightful heir. We do not yet know who that is—but we suspect its call has already begun."

I swallowed hard. A strange energy coursed through me, half dread, half recognition.

"I swear," I said.

Wilkinson nodded, but his face darkened. "There are trials. If you ever enter you must prove yourself—strength, wisdom, will, and truth. Each trial has broken others. They are built to know, to test, to cull those who are not worthy."

My voice came stronger than I expected. "Then let them try. I swear on my life."

At that, the chamber shifted. The torches flared brighter. Somewhere deeper within, a door or mechanism groaned open—like the temple itself was acknowledging my vow.

But I wasn't sure if I had just stepped toward destiny, or into the jaws of something ancient that now had its eyes fixed solely on me.

"Good. You are now one of us," the chancellor said, his voice warm and ceremonial. "And might I say—the youngest and first-ever student of this order."

The room murmured with subdued approval, the candlelight flickering across ancient stone and curious eyes. My chest tightened at the weight of it. My name now tied to something far older and deeper than I could fully comprehend.

"Wait," I said, a nervous edge breaking through the awe. "Does that mean I have to attend meetings and wear that cloak?"

I gestured vaguely at the flowing robes worn by the older members. One, they looked like something out of a medieval drama; two, I could already picture Lucas never letting me live it down.

The chancellor chuckled, and the room joined him in soft laughter.

"No, you don't," he replied, smile lines deepening as the warmth returned to his gaze.

Relief passed through me like a breeze. Still, I wasn't entirely sure what being a part of this meant. I shifted on my feet, the stone floor suddenly colder beneath me.

"Can I ask one thing?" I said, my voice softer this time.

He nodded, eyes sharp now, listening closely.

"Why me? Why trust me with all of this?"

A beat of silence.

The chancellor folded his hands before him, the silver ring on his finger catching a flicker of candlelight.

"Phoenix," he said gently, "we trust you because someone believed in you. She saw that you didn't seek knowledge for prestige or power. You sought it to protect. You carried love like a shield, even when the world gave you every reason not to. She believed in that spirit."

My throat tightened.

"Wait—Dr. Dawson?"

"She named you," he said, with a reverent nod. "In her final hours, that was her last wish. To bring you into this fold. To ensure you wouldn't have to face what's coming alone."

I stood there, not knowing what to say. Emotion caught in my ribs like a hook. She had believed in me—even after everything. After the way I'd doubted, questioned, failed. She still thought I was worthy of something this sacred.

I managed a small smile, the kind you wear to keep from breaking. "Part of me thought she hated me. That I'd let her down."

"She saw you clearly, even when you couldn't see yourself," the chancellor said. "And now—we do too."

"Thank you for telling me," I murmured. "Really."

He nodded once more. "And if ever you need anything, all you need to do is ask. The Order of Nemus protects its own."

I turned to leave but paused as he added, with a mischievous glint, "And do keep Mr. Jones from doing anything reckless."

A laugh escaped me—quick and real. "I'll try. No promises."

They chuckled as I turned toward the staircase, the echo of my steps rising with me. Each footfall heavier with meaning than the last.

As I ascended, a strange peace wrapped around me. For the first time in a long while, I didn't feel like a shadow wandering through someone else's story. I felt tethered—to something ancient, something enduring. I belonged.

When I emerged from the hidden chamber, night had fully settled in. The sky was inked in navy and violet, the moon etched in silver above the trees. The crispness of the autumn air kissed my face, grounding me.

Campus buzzed in the distance. Strings of lights wound through the grove like veins of gold. Students hurried past with drinks in hand, laughter echoing off dorm walls. Music pulsed faintly from somewhere deeper in the quad.

None of them knew what lay beneath their feet. The world they passed through like sleepwalkers.

As I crossed University Avenue, leaving the bright chaos of campus behind, I felt different. Not just older—but changed. I wasn't sure what tomorrow held or what exactly this Order would ask of me. But one thing was certain: I wouldn't be facing it alone anymore.

I walked toward the house, under the open sky, beneath the silent stars, carrying the weight of a new beginning.

The lights were on, and I knew they were awake—probably furious with me since I left my phone in my room. The porch glowed with amber warmth as I trudged up the steps, the cold biting into my jacket, the air tasting of wet stone and wilted leaves. They'd told me not to go, but I needed to. And it was a good thing I did; otherwise, I wouldn't have learned what I did down there. Now, I knew what lay beneath the surface, and with that knowledge came a new purpose. A single, burning goal.

I paused at the threshold, took a deep breath, and opened the door.

Evelyn stood there, arms crossed like a fortress, eyes flaring with fury. "What the hell were you thinking?" she snapped the moment the door clicked shut behind me.

"It wasn't a trap," I replied, voice tight but calm.

"I can see that," she said, stepping toward me, "and it doesn't make it any better."

"Evelyn, at least—"

"No, Phoenix! You could have been killed." Her voice cracked, trembling under the weight of fear masked as anger. Her cheeks were flushed, her jaw tense. I saw it then—she wasn't just angry. She was scared. For me.

"I'm sorry," I said, my voice rising with an ache I hadn't processed until now. "I had to know. I had to know what was down there. I had to know what she died for!"

It erupted out of me like steam breaking a pressure valve. The house echoed with my words, and I stood there, breath shallow, heart pounding. Evelyn froze. Her lips parted slightly, as if stunned by the rawness. Lucas emerged from his room, bleary-eyed and tense.

"Then what did she die for?" Evelyn asked, her tone softened now.

I told them everything. What the Order said. What I saw. Evelyn listened, eyes wide with disbelief but also something else—understanding. Lucas leaned against the wall, arms folded tightly, visibly shaken by the part about the Chancellor's comment.

"So, you're in this Order now?" Lucas asked, his voice skeptical but not mocking. "You and a bunch of professors make up a secret organization guarding an ancient chamber under the school?"

"Yes," I said, then faltered. "I think? I swore to protect it, and honestly, it was the only way they'd let me know more."

"To think," Evelyn muttered, "I thought they were part of the Collective. So this place… it's protected by trials?"

I nodded slowly. The weight of it settled in again. That place—those halls and symbols—it wasn't just a vault. It was alive. Calling to me. Some part of me didn't want to leave it behind. Another part feared what else might be waiting beneath the surface.

"So what's the plan?" Lucas asked, a flicker of unease tightening his brow.

"We protect it. Make sure the Collective never touches it. And… we find my mother."

Evelyn stepped forward, her resolve steely but kind. "Then we protect it."

She paused, looking at me with something deeper in her gaze. "You know… you sound like a Keeper. Like your mother."

The words hung in the air. I didn't know what to say to that, only that something inside me stirred at her saying it.

"Veronica can't know. Not yet," I added. "Not until we're sure what side she's on."

Evelyn nodded. "You can trust her, but we'll keep it quiet. Just promise me one thing—don't do anything like that again. Please."

I met her eyes and smiled. "I promise."

Lucas lingered a moment longer before saying quietly, "Just… be safe, Phoenix. Seriously."

That struck me. Not just the words, but the weight behind them. For once, I saw not just concern—but fear. He was scared too.

Later, as Lucas headed back to his room and Evelyn curled into her chair with a book, we sat in silence, our lamps the only glow in the room. The world outside was cold, but inside, we found warmth in each other's presence. I read too—class notes, old texts, pages I barely absorbed but needed to touch. Anything to ground myself.

Evelyn kept looking at me when she thought I wouldn't notice. I finally broke the silence.

"I'm sorry. I should've told you."

She closed her book. "I shouldn't have yelled. I was just scared. I didn't want anything to happen to you."

"I know. But I'm okay."

She smiled faintly. "True. I should get to bed. See you in the morning."

"Good night," I said, watching her disappear into the hallway.

I stayed up, finishing my reading. The quiet crept in like a familiar blanket. I wasn't alone in this anymore. Not really. When I finished, I took a long shower. The hot water soaked into my muscles, scalding away grief and tension. Steam curled into the air like whispered prayers.

Staring into the mirror afterward, I saw a face that felt different. Older. Hardened. Not broken, but reshaped. This wasn't the boy who hid from the world three years ago. This was someone new.

To Phoenix three years ago: *Look how far you've come. Look what you've endured. Even in the darkest night, you found a spark. You held on. And now, you rise.*

CLASSIFIED FILE | LEVEL 4 ACCESS
Command Structure & Ranks

INITIATE TIER

Initiate
Civilian or academic aide flagged for recruitment.
Role: Surveillance, intel logging. No relic or vault access.

Novice
Operative-in-training under Keeper guidance.
Role: Support duties, research, supervised site entry.

KEEPER TIER

Acolyte Keeper
First field-ready rank.
Role: Local missions, intel relay, low-risk relic escort.

Keeper
Full operative status with autonomous command ability.
Role: Mission leadership, artifact retrieval, intel ops.

SENIOR TIER

Commander
Oversees strike teams and operations.
Role: Mission planning, field training, tactical overrides.

High Keeper
Executive rank. Oversees doctrine, intel strategy, and global operations.
(Veronica & Dr. Joanne Knight)

Ashwood Archive | Doc# ZN-1128-B

FOURTEEN

THE SIGNAL

"A KEEPER IN THE MAKING"

It was three days later, and Oxford had begun to trade its late-summer heat for the slow hush of fall. The air carried a new sharpness, a whispered promise of colder days ahead. School was back in full throttle, and the return to routine had been a strange kind of balm—a camouflage for the ache that lived just beneath my skin. I buried myself in coursework, attacked assignments like they were enemies in a trench, and focused on anything that wasn't the gnawing question that haunted my every breath.

Was she still alive?

Evelyn had returned to Memphis to catch up on her own research and teaching, leaving Lucas and me to hold down the fort. Our mornings settled into a quiet rhythm. Coffee brewed, textbooks opened, meals were shared—but the silence between conversations still held a charge. Like a storm building at sea. Lucas watched me like I might shatter, and I tried to pretend I didn't notice.

Then came the day that changed everything.

After class, I turned the corner onto our street and stopped cold.

SUVs. Four of them. Matte black, tinted windows, their engines purring low like wolves waiting to strike. It looked like a raid, or a high-stakes political extraction. My stomach dropped. My feet moved before I could think, jogging up the path, heart hammering.

Inside, the house buzzed with an intensity I'd never felt before. Agents in black tactical gear moved swiftly around our dining room, which had transformed into a mobile command center. Monitors glowed with traffic camera feeds and thermal imagery. Communications gear covered every surface.

"Phoenix, glad you're home," Evelyn's voice cut through the chaos. She looked tired. Pale. Determined.

"What the hell is happening?"

She didn't answer. Veronica did.

"We found her."

The words hit me like a bell toll.

"We found my mother?"

Veronica stepped forward, her expression grave but calm. "Yes. We believe she's here. In Oxford. In a safe house used by the Collective."

The world slowed. Something hot and dangerous swelled in my chest, a familiar fire—the same one that burned the night I escaped that warehouse, the night I learned just how far the Collective would go. "I'm going," I said, my voice low but resolute.

Evelyn stepped in sharply, her presence like a wall. "Absolutely not. Phoenix, you can't just throw yourself into a raid. This isn't some heroic fantasy—it's a tactical operation. One misstep, and they'll kill you."

"She's my mother," I snapped, louder than I meant to. "And I need to be there. I can't sit this out again. I won't. Not after what happened last time."

"You think I don't understand that?" Evelyn's voice cracked, emotion slipping through the cracks of her usually calm demeanor. "I know what you went through. I remember what it did to you. But this is different—this is war. And I've already lost too much. I'm not losing you, too."

Her words hit like a body blow, and for a moment, neither of us moved. The memory of that night—the drugs, the confusion, waking up in a concrete hell—flashed behind my eyes. But I pushed it down.

"Then help me make sure no one else ends up like that. Help me bring her home."

Veronica raised a hand. "He's going. We've prepared for this. He won't be alone."

Evelyn looked between us, her mouth a hard line, then finally sighed, defeated. "Just promise me you'll be careful."

"I promise."

Veronica nodded. "Come with me."

We loaded into one of the black SUVs, its engine growling as it peeled away from the curb and merged into the winding streets of Oxford. The city was awash in twilight, buildings and trees streaking past like faded watercolor paintings under the dusky light. Orange streetlamps flickered to life one by one, casting long shadows across brick façades and ivy-draped university buildings. It all blurred together as we turned toward the edge of downtown, where the familiar gave way to something colder.

Our destination emerged from the shadows—a nondescript structure nestled between a bank and a law office. Its facade, composed of reflective glass, steel, and deep red brick, bore the polished, impersonal look of corporate indifference. There were no signs, no markers—just the faint hum of security cameras following our arrival. It might have passed for any number of buildings in the city. But I knew better. This place wasn't for clients or press releases. It was a mask, hiding the beating heart of something far older and far more dangerous.

Inside, we descended via a secure elevator that required not one, but two biometric scans. The doors opened into a subterranean world that looked more like a classified military bunker than anything Ashwood Enterprises would admit to on paper. Fluorescent lights buzzed softly overhead, casting a pale glow over the command center. Rows of terminals displayed live satellite imagery and data streams. Tactical maps blinked with colored overlays. A massive digital screen dominated the far wall, showing camera feeds from across Oxford. The air smelled of ozone, machine oil, and determination.

"Welcome to our Oxford outpost," Veronica said, her voice steady. "Every major region has a facility like this. We activated this one the moment we confirmed your mother's location."

The space was alive with movement. Agents spoke in clipped tones, analyzing data, preparing for deployment. Evelyn seemed to slide into it easily—her bearing changed, sharper, commanding. A young operative passed and gave her a respectful nod. "Field Acolyte Ramses."

Lucas arrived moments later, ushered in by a pair of operatives. He looked half-dazed, pulled from campus mid-sentence, his expression a mix of disbelief and alarm.

"Phoenix, what is going on?" he asked, looking between me, Veronica, and the tactical screen.

"You'll find out soon enough," Veronica said. "Come with me. All of you."

We followed her through a secure corridor and into a briefing room—glass-walled, minimalist, and loaded with tech. A large central table displayed a holographic map of Oxford. The strike team was already assembled—six individuals in tactical gear, seated or leaning against the walls. The moment we entered, several of them looked up. A few smirked at the sight of me.

"Alright, listen up," Veronica began, stepping to the head of the room. "This is not a drill. We have a confirmed location on Dr. Joanne Knight. She is being held here." She gestured, and the holographic map zoomed in on a residence. "It's a known Collective safe house, lightly fortified. We strike tonight at 2100 hours."

She turned to the team. "Before we continue—this is Phoenix He'll be accompanying us."

A couple of the operatives raised eyebrows. One snorted softly. "Seriously?"

"Yes. Seriously," Veronica replied, without looking at him. "He is a black belt, has already survived a kidnapping attempt by the Collective, and escaped."

That quieted the room a bit.

Then she added, "And in case you still have doubts, he's Dr. Knight's son."

Silence. Heavy. Respectful.

"Yes, that Knight," she clarified.

The smirks vanished.

Veronica continued. "This is Phoenix Team. You are to provide cover, extraction, and protection. Mission is rescue and secure. Zero civilian casualties. We enter from the west alleyway. Phoenix has recognized the property as the one he was previously held in."

I stepped forward. "It's familiar. I didn't remember much at first, but I'm sure now. The kitchen, the hallway layout. I've been there."

The strike team nodded. One of them leaned over the table, fingers tapping lightly against the steel. "That intel will help. We'll build from it."

The leader of the team—a tall, broad-shouldered man with a silver streak in his buzz-cut hair—stepped forward. His presence commanded the room without theatrics. "Here's how this is going down. Call signs Phoenix One through Four will breach through the west alley entrance. Phoenix One leads the stack. Two will cover rear, three takes overwatch at the stairwell, four secures the lower hall."

He tapped a section of the holographic map. "We suspect Dr. Knight is being held on the second floor, northeast bedroom. Curtains drawn, no exterior movement. Intel suggests two to three guards inside, minimum. All armed. We hit hard, fast, and quiet."

He pointed to the adjacent building. "Extraction will occur here. Team Delta will be waiting with transport. We exfil through the southeast window—fast rope if needed."

Veronica stepped in, her tone crisp, commanding. "All standard protocols are in effect. Encrypted comms only. We operate on synchronized internal timers calibrated down to the second. If the op is compromised, you follow lighthouse code. Blue signal: relocate to secondary rally point. Red: abandon the site immediately and sever all digital connections. Gray: initiate the cover sequence—burn evidence, scrub comms, fallback to tertiary identities."

She let that hang in the air. "Each team member is responsible for their own cipher module. If your signal breaks pattern, we assume capture and initiate shadow lockdown procedures. No deviation. No improvisation unless authorized. And above all—no chatter outside of mission parameters."

The air shifted palpably. The chatter died. The strike team nodded, their expressions hardening into focus. This wasn't just another mission. This was the kind of op that lived in the dark corners of memory. The kind you came back from changed—or didn't come back from at all.

Then Veronica's voice rang out again.

"For the duration of this operation," she said, locking eyes with the team, "Phoenix Knight is to be treated as Keeper-Class Rank. Full authority within mission boundaries. His protection and authority are not up for debate."

There was a beat of stunned silence. I turned to her, my mouth half open, words dying on my tongue. I had no idea what this meant, but the gravity in Veronica's voice made my gut tighten. The room suddenly felt smaller, like the walls themselves understood the seriousness of what had just been declared.

Evelyn turned sharply toward her. "Veronica, are you serious? Keeper Rank?"

Veronica nodded. "Yes. It's what his mother would have done. And it's what the Council has authorized."

Lucas blinked. "Wait—what does that even mean?"

Evelyn turned to him, her voice hushed. "It means… he's not just part of the mission. He outranks everyone here—except Veronica."

"Wait, he outranks you?" Lucas asked, his brows raised halfway to his hairline.

Evelyn crossed her arms and let out a breath through her nose. "Technically, for this mission—yes."

Lucas blinked, clearly trying to absorb the implications. "That's... kinda wild."

"Wild doesn't even begin to cover it," Evelyn muttered, more to herself than anyone else. She shook her head slightly, clearly still coming to terms with it. Her voice lowered as she added, "He's never even seen the Council chamber, and now he's walking into combat with Keeper authority."

Veronica just smirked, eyes twinkling with some private amusement. "He's a Knight. You'd be surprised how fast the fire burns with that pedigree."

One of the operatives straightened. "He's Keeper Knight now?"

Veronica met his gaze. "That's correct. It's provisional, mission-bound—but yes. Keeper Knight."

The room stilled. Even the hum of tech seemed quieter.

And in that stillness, I felt the weight of every choice, every step, every name I carried.

There was no turning back now.

We descended deeper into the Oxford outpost after the briefing, and the full weight of what I was entering began to settle on my shoulders. This was real. This wasn't a campus secret society. This was war. Every fluorescent-lit corridor whispered with urgency, and the faint scent of ozone and industrial cleaner clung to the cool, recirculated air. The deeper we went, the further we were pulled from the world above—college life, football games, autumn breezes. That world felt like a different lifetime.

A staffer led me down a side hallway—its walls a dull titanium gray, humming softly with energy behind its panels—and stopped at a thick, reinforced door. A red scanner blinked. The staffer pressed a thumb to the panel, and the door hissed open.

Inside was the locker room. It looked nothing like any I had ever been in. Sleek and orderly, it resembled the prep space for a high-level special operations unit. Rows of tactical gear lined the walls—modular armor rigs, encrypted comms units, modular weapons holsters. Every item bore the same emblem: a stylized sunburst ringed by geometric glyphs. Everything had its place.

Veronica was waiting, standing tall with a clipboard in hand, her attire a sharp contrast to the field operatives—tailored black slacks, a dark blazer, and a crisp high-collared blouse beneath. Her hair was pulled back into a tight bun, not for utility, but command. She didn't need armor to hold authority; her presence alone did that. Her presence was a command in itself.

She handed me a black duffel. "This is your gear. Tactical vest reinforced with hybrid Kevlar, mask with built-in voice modulation, night optics, encrypted earpiece, biometric lock on your primary rig."

I opened the duffel and slowly pulled out each item. The material was matte, angular, and perfectly balanced. It wasn't just armor—it was a transformation. My fingers lingered on the vest. I could feel the tension in my chest, not just from nerves, but from the sheer weight of meaning behind this gear.

Then Veronica reached into her coat and withdrew a small velvet pouch. From it, she drew a patch—the Council's symbol of Keeper rank. A golden sunburst wreathed by ancient shamanic symbols.

"What's this?" I asked.

"Your insignia," she said. "Official Keeper rank—for this mission. It's not just a formality. It's your voice, your authority. The symbol lets everyone know you're acting with the Council's full weight behind you."

She stepped forward and carefully affixed it to the left shoulder of my gear. Her hands were steady, but her eyes lingered.

"Why me?" I asked, my voice quieter now. "Why give me this?"

"Because you're ready. Because your mother would have wanted it. And because the Council needs more than bloodlines—it needs heart. And courage. You've already faced the Collective and lived. Most can't say that."

She paused, then turned to a secure compartment embedded in the locker wall, revealing a matte-black sidearm nestled in precision-cut foam. Without needing to explain, she picked it up, checked the chamber with clinical ease, and offered it to me grip-first.

"A Sig M17. Modified safety. Your father trained you on something similar, didn't he?"

I froze for a moment, fingers brushing the barrel as I looked at her. "You remember that?"

She nodded, eyes gentler now. "I remember everything. He insisted on teaching you early—said it was a rite of passage. Your mother didn't love it, but… she understood. He believed you'd need it someday."

"And now it's someday," I muttered, taking the weapon and feeling the weight of it settle in my palm like an echo from another life.

I turned to the bench and began suiting up. Every buckle snapped like a countdown, every strap drawn tight a shift from who I was into who I had to become. The armor settled across my frame, heavier than I expected, but secure. The air smelled of oiled leather, steel, and adrenaline.

Footsteps echoed behind me.

"Hey," Lucas said, stepping in with wide eyes. His gaze swept the room, then landed on me. "You look like you're about to star in a Mission Impossible movie."

"How'd they get you down here?"

"Two agents stormed my poli-sci class like I was being drafted into a war. Which, apparently, I was. They said you'd need me. I didn't argue."

Evelyn followed close behind, arms crossed, eyes scanning. She didn't even blink at the operation around us. Of course she didn't. This was familiar to her.

"You good?" she asked.

"As I'll ever be."

She stepped closer and pulled a compact device from her pocket. "I'll be in your ear the entire time. We'll have a secure link. You call me if anything goes sideways."

"Copy that, Acolyte Ramses."

She rolled her eyes but smiled faintly. "Don't get used to it."

As they turned to leave, the door opened again. A tall, broad-shouldered man entered, silver-haired, his movements precise. His tactical gear bore the insignia of a Council field commander.

"I'm Commander Dallan," he said, extending a gloved hand. His voice was gravel, but not unkind. "I served with your mother. Berlin. 2007. She saved my life. Consider tonight my turn."

I shook his hand, the grip firm and steady.

"Thanks."

He gave a single nod, his gaze assessing. "We've got you, Keeper Knight. We'll make sure you both come back."

As the door shut behind them, I was left with the quiet hum of readiness. My breath fogged the mirror in front of me. I saw myself—not just a student or a son. Something more. Something forged.

A Keeper.

But that reflection wasn't just about titles or armor. It was about weight. Responsibility. The knowledge that I was stepping into something irreversible. That, by dawn, I could be someone else entirely—or not come back at all.

I closed my eyes and steadied my breathing, centering myself like I had in martial arts drills years ago. The world was chaos, but I could be still in it. That's what my father taught me—calm was a weapon, and clarity was survival.

My mind flicked to my mother. To her voice reading me bedtime stories about the old myths. To the soft cadence of her lectures from the other room. To the shadow she left in every memory. Tonight, I had a chance to pull her back into the light.

And to the Collective—I wasn't afraid of them. I had seen their face and survived. But this wasn't just about surviving anymore. It was about fighting. It was about showing them that I wouldn't run again.

Outside, the strike team would be prepping for departure. The corridor lights had shifted to amber. The mission was close.

I took one last look at myself in the mirror, adjusted the Keeper patch on my shoulder, and whispered under my breath:

"Time to rise."

And with that, I turned and walked into the fire.

FIFTEEN

RESCUE

"INTO THE MAW"

As night began to fall, we loaded up in the matte-black SUV parked in the narrow alley behind Ashwood's Oxford outpost. The alley was cloaked in shadows, the kind that seemed to breathe and close in as the sun slipped beneath the tree line. The vehicle itself looked like a beast lying in wait—armored, silent, exhaling the scent of oil, steel, and new leather. I slid into the rear seat, the door shutting with a finality that clamped around my chest like a vice. The air inside was cold and sterile, humming faintly with the thrum of high-end electronics tucked into the console. Every surface was matte, efficient. No comfort, only function.

I was sandwiched between the reinforced walls and the presence of men who radiated danger. The kind of danger honed by war and scarred by classified history. The kind of danger that wore no expression because it didn't need to. My armor felt tight, too tight—not just the bulletproof weave pressed against my chest but the emotional exoskeleton I was struggling to maintain. Every breath I drew seemed to catch halfway, each inhale a reminder of what we were about to do. Not a simulation. Not a council drill. Real combat. Real stakes.

The team—four of them—sat with grim focus. No chatter. No pre-game hype. Their eyes, cold and deliberate, scanned the world outside like birds of prey waiting for the first flicker of weakness. They were each former special forces operatives, now co-opted by the Council for missions that never made headlines. I could feel their evaluation. Not disdain, but assessment. Who was this kid with the silver eyes and the Council patch stitched over his chest? Who let him in the truck? What weight did he carry?

"When we enter," said the team leader, a mountain of a man with a build that made the armor seem ornamental, "you stay behind us. Do not deviate. We clear the space. You move with us."

His voice was gravel and thunder. It didn't threaten; it pronounced. There would be no second chances. No hero plays.

I nodded, my throat dry and tight. "Will do," I said, though it came out smaller than I wanted.

He gave a sharp gesture. The engine responded like a summoned beast, and the SUV glided forward into the Oxford streets—deserted, cold, and cloaked in night's indifference.

"Phoenix team en route," he said into the radio, his tone clipped, precise.

I gave him a sidelong glance, eyebrows raised. "Phoenix team?"

He smirked for the first time, something sharp and amused. "Had to name the op something cool. You made it easy."

He tapped his earpiece again. "Phoenix 1 ready."

"Phoenix 2 ready."

"Phoenix 3 ready."

"Phoenix 4 ready."

Each voice answered like a note in a deadly chord. The cadence of people who had done this before. Who had seen doors open to gunfire and walked out of buildings on fire.

The numbers fell into place like war pieces on a board. My stomach twisted in anticipation, nerves knotting like coiled rope.

Phoenix 1 looked over at me, eyes sharp but not unkind. "And now for the last piece."

I hesitated, feeling the pressure of being the anomaly once again.

"Phoenix is ready," he said for me, filling in the gap with a grin that didn't feel condescending—just steady. Assuring. "We got you. Let's go save her."

The drive was only a few blocks, but it felt like a slow spiral into another world. The windows showed a blur of shadows and yellowed streetlights. I tried to steady my breath, tried to remember my training, tried not to think of the last time I was in that house—drugged, helpless, violated. That memory haunted the edges of my vision.

The SUV came to a halt. Every man in the vehicle pulled down his mask.

I did the same.

"On my mark," Phoenix 1 ordered.

My earpiece buzzed. "Phoenix team, you are clear," Veronica's voice crackled. Calm, composed. A tether to everything outside this.

We moved.

Dark streets cloaked our approach. The block's power had been discreetly cut—Council interference. Every window was black, the silence thick as we crept up to the side entrance.

A Collective sentry stood beneath the porch light.

Phoenix 2 moved like a shadow, wrapping an arm around the man's neck and lowering him gently to the ground. Unconscious. No noise.

Phoenix 3 dragged him behind a bush. We stacked at the door. A quick signal. The latch clicked.

We slipped inside.

The air was stale, tinged with mold and something metallic—blood? The kitchen was empty, dimly lit by dying moonlight. I recognized the counter, the back wall. Fragmented memories danced on the edges of my vision.

"Two in the living room," Phoenix 1 whispered.

Phoenix 3 moved, silent and swift. Two suppressed shots—soft squeaks. Then: "Room clear."

We fanned out.

Phoenix 2 dragged the Collective bodies out of view. I recognized one. The same man who'd cornered me in the woods. I stared at him, conflicted.

This was real.

The living room hit harder. I remembered the couch. Allison. The blurred haze. My limbs leaden, her breath hot and cruel against my skin. Rage curled in my gut.

"You okay?" Phoenix 1 asked.

I nodded. "Just... remembering."

"Eyes forward. Upstairs."

The staircase groaned beneath our weight despite our effort to move silently. Each wooden step creaked like a scream threatening to rise from the shadows. I tread carefully, my boots placing as little weight as possible, but the echo still followed us like a guilty conscience. Adrenaline buzzed through my bloodstream, tightening my chest, making every breath feel like glass.

At the top, a lone guard patrolled the hallway, unaware. Phoenix 1 moved with terrifying grace—two strides forward, a twist of the arm, a muffled grunt—and the guard crumpled like paper. No sound. No struggle. Just quiet efficiency. We moved past him, and I kept my hand close to my sidearm, though my fingers trembled.

Each room we passed loomed with danger. Doors yawned open into darkness, the smell of mildew and sweat thick in the air. Phoenix 2 cleared one, Phoenix 3 another. I pressed my back to the cold plaster wall, heart pounding like war drums in my ears.

Then—

A breath behind me. Close. Hot.

"Why don't you just stay still?"

Time snapped.

An arm coiled around my chest like a vice. He was shorter, maybe banking on surprise. He didn't expect resistance. Big mistake. I dropped my weight, pivoted under his grip, catching the wrist and driving it forward in a practiced arc. He flipped over my shoulder, hitting the floor with a dull thud that vibrated through my boots. I straddled him before he could recover, palm pressing against his windpipe. He struggled once, then went still.

Phoenix 1 rounded the corner, eyes locking onto mine, then the downed man. He gave a sharp nod. "Nice job."

"Where'd you learn that?" Phoenix 2 asked, his voice tight with a mix of surprise and approval.

"Martial arts class," I muttered, the sarcasm masking the adrenaline spike still rolling through me.

We gathered near the final door. The master bedroom. I could feel the tension spike in the room like static.

"Expect three," Phoenix 1 whispered, raising his hand. "On my mark."

He signaled.

The door burst open.

Three hostiles surged forward like wolves scenting blood.

Everything fractured. Gunfire snapped in tight pops, thudding into drywall. Shadows leapt—then were wrestled to the ground. Phoenix 1 slammed his target into a desk, the wood cracking beneath the weight. Phoenix 2 and 3 moved with silent aggression, clearing their marks with brutal precision. I ducked low, sidearm in hand. A Collective thug lunged at me—too close. I sidestepped, slamming my shoulder into him and delivering a swift elbow to his temple. He dropped like a stone. My breath came in ragged bursts. My hand shook. But I was still standing.

Then I saw her.

Tied to a chair, framed in the flickering light of the hallway.

My mother.

Her head lifted slowly. Eyes glassy, cheek marred with a bruise. Her brown hair was streaked with gray at the temples, damp with sweat. Even now, even beaten and bound, she looked like someone who'd survived a storm and dared the sky for more.

"Phoenix?"

"Mom."

“I'd recognize those eyes anywhere.”

I tore off my mask. Her eyes widened—then softened. Recognition washed over her face like sunlight through fog.

I crossed the room in a rush and dropped to my knees. My hands were clumsy at the ropes, fingers slick with sweat, but I got them loose. The second they fell, she folded into me. I caught her, her frame lighter than I remembered, but her presence solid as ever.

"This has Veronica written all over it," she rasped, brushing her hand against the golden sun patch on my arm.

"Yeah. I'll explain everything later."

Phoenix 1's voice broke in through the coms. "Dr. Knight secure. Ready for extraction."

Then—

"Hey, handsome."

My blood iced.

Allison. Leaning in the doorway, flanked by two more Collective goons. Her smile was all venom and victory. The sight of her was like bile in my throat.

"Glad you could make it. How's Mommy?"

My hand moved toward my sidearm again.

"Allison. Maybe I should've finished what I started."

She tilted her head with mock disappointment. "Temper, temper. Let's not upset the lady."

"He can say whatever he wants about you," my mom cut in sharply, her voice slicing through the air like a blade.

Allison arched an eyebrow. "Cute. Still feisty. I like that. But I'm not here for her. I'm here for you, Phoenix."

"Not happening."

"Walk out with me, and your friends walk away. No more chases, no more accidents. Clean break."

My mother's fingers curled around mine. Her grip was weak—but insistent. A silent plea: Don't.

My anger flared.

"Oh, like Dawson? You killed her."

Something flickered behind Allison's eyes. "I didn't."

"Liar."

My mom flinched. Her breath caught in her throat. I felt it—something inside her folding in on itself. She knew. Dr. Dawson was gone. And now she understood.

I looked past Allison. The window. A way out.

"Extraction ready," the voice crackled through my earpiece.

Phoenix 1 didn't hesitate. He threw a flashbang to the side and signaled the breach.

The room erupted into movement. Gunfire. Shouts. A blur of fists and boots. Allison shouted something, but I wasn't listening anymore. I grabbed my mother and half-carried, half-dragged her toward the window.

"Mom, trust me."

"Phoenix—just go."

I pushed her out. The air rushed in as she disappeared below. A second later, the catch team signaled she was safe.

I dove through the frame. My boots hit the soft pad with a solid thud. Pain spiked through my ankles, but I kept moving. She was there, arms open, pulling me close.

"You did good," she whispered, trembling against me.

And for the first time in days, I believed it.

"Let's go home."

We made our way back to the house, the weight of the night still heavy in my chest. The sky above Oxford was deep velvet, stars barely visible through the canopy of autumn branches. Each step toward the porch felt heavier than the last, not from exhaustion, but from a sudden, overwhelming shift: my mother was alive. Here. With me.

The soft amber porch light cast a warm glow across Evelyn and Veronica, who stood waiting, silhouettes of steadiness against the dark. Evelyn stepped forward first, eyes wide with emotion, her usual calm replaced by visible relief.

"Dr. Knight," she said, and the title carried weight. She pulled my mother into a tight hug. "It's good to see you again. Did you get those readings done?"

"Yes, I did," Evelyn replied with a sheepish smile, knowing the consequences of a different answer.

My mom chuckled—quiet and a little raspy, but real. "Then not all is lost."

Even after being held captive, she hadn't lost her sharpness. Her eyes moved quickly, already scanning the house and us, measuring, absorbing. She was assessing Evelyn, Veronica, the situation—like the scholar and leader she'd always been.

"So, this is the cavalry?" she said, glancing at Veronica with a raised brow. "The full strike team? I take it someone thought I was important enough."

"You are," Veronica replied simply. "And yes. We weren't taking any chances."

Her eyes then settled on me with a seriousness that cut through the reunion haze. "And what I want to know is how my son got swept into it. I spent years keeping him out of this world."

I didn't have an answer that would satisfy her. But I stepped forward anyway.

"It wasn't a choice, Mom. They came after me. Kidnapped me. Hurt people I care about. I couldn't stay on the sidelines."

She searched my face. A hundred questions behind her eyes. But she said only one word. "Veronica?"

"He's Keeper Knight now," Veronica said. "Provisionally. For the operation."

My mother's face hardened—not with anger, but with realization. The weight of that title, provisional or not, was immense. She had fought for decades to protect people like me from needing to carry it.

Inside, the house smelled like home—garlic, rosemary, roasted vegetables. Comfort. Lucas was at the stove, apron tied awkwardly, spatula in one hand. He looked up, saw me still in gear, and smirked.

"You know, you don't look bad in black ops chic," he said.

"Hilarious, Lucas."

My mom crossed the room, extended her hand like she'd known him all her life. "So, you're Lucas. I've heard things. Good things."

Lucas took her hand and smiled. "It's an honor. Your son's been a wreck, by the way."

She laughed—this time louder, more herself. "That doesn't surprise me. He's always been the worrier."

"Love you too, Mom," I said with a grin, slipping away to change.

I peeled off the gear in the quiet of my room. My hands trembled slightly, the rush still fading. I stared at the Council patch on my shoulder before pulling it off gently, setting it on the dresser like something sacred.

When I came back downstairs in regular clothes, dinner had been served. The table was full—plates passed, voices low and warm. Veronica had stayed, now relaxed slightly, her usual steel softened around the edges.

My mother sat beside me, sipping water slowly, her fingers still trembling faintly. And then she spoke.

"So, you're Keeper Knight now. And this is the world I once kept from you."

"Not just in name," Veronica said. "In role. In deed. He stepped into fire tonight, and he didn't falter."

"He's one of us now," Evelyn added, her voice laced with admiration.

Dr. Knight looked between us. There was pride in her eyes, yes. But also grief—for the innocence lost, the childhood interrupted. She placed her hand over mine, fingers pressing firm.

"Then the fire really did pass on. You've walked into it, Phoenix. And you didn't burn."

I couldn't speak. I didn't need to.

Veronica let the moment linger before adding, "He's earned more than rank. He's earned our trust."

The weight of it all landed. The table felt smaller, more intimate. Like the world had shifted and we were the only ones holding it together.

Lucas cleared his throat. "So... does this mean he outranks Evelyn now?"

Evelyn glared. "Not funny."

My mother laughed again, and this time there was something stronger in it—resilience, pride, even hope.

"Well, technically I still outrank him," my mother said with a smirk, lifting her glass of water. "So yes, he may be a Keeper now, but he still has to take orders from his mom." Her voice was light, teasing, but there was a glint of pride in her eyes that she didn't bother to hide.

Dinner flowed into conversation. Into laughter. Into stories from when I was little, of the times before I'd even known the Council existed. My mother's voice never wavered when she spoke of the work. Her eyes flicked to Veronica often, the bond between them forged in shared secrets and peril.

Later, as we prepared sleeping arrangements and guards took their posts outside, I stood in the hallway watching my mother settle into the guest room. She caught my gaze.

"You look tired."

"I feel... everything," I admitted.

She came over and cupped my cheek in her palm. "You did good. Better than I could've imagined. You saved me, Phoenix. And you held your ground."

Her voice softened. "We'll talk more. There's a lot to say."

"I know. I'm just glad you're safe."

She pulled me into a hug—tight, warm, familiar. The kind I hadn't felt in what felt like a lifetime.

And for the first time in all of this madness, I let myself exhale.

Safe. Finally, truly safe.

I stayed in the hallway a little longer after she went in. The house had settled into a rare quiet—no Council chatter, no alerts, just the ticking of the old clock in the living room and the wind outside brushing against the windows. I leaned against the wall, letting the calmness seep in, if only for a moment. The storm had passed, but I knew the horizon still held more.

Now there was just one problem, that I just thought of.

Sixteen

Home

"Where Names No Longer Fit"

"She's settled in," Evelyn said quietly, closing the bedroom door behind her with a soft click. The hallway fell still around us, wrapped in the kind of silence that only came after a storm. The kind of silence that wasn't peace, but pause—an interlude between battles. The lights were dim, casting elongated shadows against the walls. Lucas had already turned in, and the only sounds were the ticking of the hallway clock and the faint hum of wind pressing against the windows.

I exhaled, slow and shaky. "Good," I said. "What about you?"

Evelyn tilted her head, a small shrug lifting her shoulders. "I can just get a room somewhere. It's late, but I'll figure something out."

I hated that. She shouldn't have to. Not after everything tonight. Not after she helped bring my mother home.

"Stay—stay with me," I said, the words tumbling out before I could weigh them.

She blinked. "Phoenix—"

"Stay. I can sleep on the floor, or the chair. Whatever. Just... stay. It's safer here."

Her eyes searched mine, something unreadable flickering behind them. "It's fine. I don't—"

"Evelyn, please," I said, quieter now. I reached for her hand. It was warm and steady, grounding me more than I expected.

She hesitated, then nodded. "Fine. But you're not sleeping on the floor."

She disappeared down the hall toward the bathroom, her silhouette briefly framed in the hallway light before the door clicked shut behind her.

I walked into my room like I was walking into a sanctuary. The space looked the same—neat, clean, familiar—but I didn't feel the same inside it. I changed into a t-shirt and shorts, the soft cotton brushing against skin that still felt wired, still felt too alive. The room was dim, lit only by the bedside lamp that cast a pool of warm light against the far wall, while the rest remained cloaked in hushed shadow.

I sat on the edge of the bed, elbows resting on my knees. The tension in my shoulders hadn't released. My fingers twitched, the adrenaline refusing to fade. I waited—though I didn't know for what. Maybe for her. Maybe for silence to feel comforting instead of crushing.

The door opened gently.

"What are you doing?" Evelyn asked, stepping inside with bare feet. Her reddish hair was tied in a bun, and she wore a simple nightgown, elegant in its plainness. Her presence softened the room instantly.

I looked up, managing a tired smile. "I have no idea."

She crossed the floor with slow, quiet steps and sat down beside me. Her knee brushed mine. Her presence was gentle but solid. No words, just a steady warmth in a cold world.

There was a tug in my chest—something deeper than nerves or fear. It wanted to pull me toward her, to let me fall, to let me rest. But I resisted. Because I had to. Because everything still felt fragile.

She didn't press. She just sat there beside me, hands folded in her lap.

The silence stretched—but it wasn't empty. It held everything: exhaustion, unspoken questions, the aftermath of violence, the slow return of safety.

Just one night, Phoenix.

Maybe that would be enough.

"What are you wearing?" Evelyn asked, a teasing lilt in her voice. Her eyes skimmed over the loose t-shirt I had thrown on hastily, her tone soft but inquisitive. "I'm positive you have never slept in a shirt."

"I don't want to make you uncomfortable," I replied, my gaze locked on the grain of the wooden floor. Her concern was written in the soft furrow of her brow, the way her hands fidgeted at her sides. It was more than curiosity—it was worry.

"You okay?" she asked, her voice tender.

"Yeah. She's safe." The words came out too quickly. I wanted them to feel like a balm, like a statement of triumph. But they didn't. They felt hollow. A lie I told myself so I wouldn't unravel. I wasn't okay. Not really. I was fractured, flooded with emotions that clawed at my chest, desperate to be acknowledged, and yet I shoved them deeper. I had to stay strong. I had to protect everyone.

Don't be vulnerable—no emotion can show.

"Then why do you look tense?" she pressed, leaning closer.

"I'm not."

"Yes, you are."

"No—I'm fine," I pushed back, rubbing my wrist with my opposite hand, grounding myself in the motion.

"Stop—stop pushing me out," she said, reaching forward and placing her hand over mine. The contact was immediate, electric, halting my motion with a gentleness that hurt.

"Let me in."

How could I? Everything inside me felt like wreckage—shattered glass and broken gears. I looked up at her, at those blue eyes that had seen through every defense I ever tried to erect. She had been patient. Always. Even when I had abandoned her, even when I couldn't face what I felt.

"I know there is more to all of this," I muttered. "More to why she was manipulating me all this time." I needed to redirect. Talking about Allison was easier than peeling back the layers of me.

"Hey," Evelyn said, resting her head against my shoulder. Her presence was anchoring. "Right now, don't worry about it. We can figure it out tomorrow."

"I know." The quiet settled around us, a comfortable pause in the storm. Sitting beside her, feeling her warmth, I wanted to freeze time. I wanted to stay in this moment, with her.

"Can I ask why?" she whispered. "Why... we never worked?"

I swallowed. That question was heavier than it seemed. There was no easy answer. No way to erase the pain of what I had done by hiding myself from her. But she deserved the truth.

"It's my fault," I admitted. The words felt foreign on my tongue.

"How?"

"I pushed you away. I was afraid. Afraid of what you'd think if I told you how I felt."

"Phoenix—"

"I'm broken," I said, quietly but firmly. "There are things in my past that I didn't want to burden you with."

"You are not broken," she said, firm, resolute.

"Yes, I am. And I didn't want you to carry that weight. I thought... if I let you in, it would be too much."

She cupped my face, her thumb brushing against the line of my jaw. Her eyes burned with intensity.

"Then let me be the one to help carry it. You don't have to do this alone."

I felt the tear fall before I knew it had escaped. Her hand wiped it away before I could react.

"I'm sorry," I whispered. "I thought no one could love someone as damaged as me."

"Don't be. If you're broken, let me help you rebuild."

The silence that followed was rich with understanding. Her hand on my face, her eyes searching mine—there was no judgment, only care. My chest ached with the swell of everything I'd buried. I had never let anyone see me like this.

She leaned in, close enough that her breath warmed my skin. "Phoenix, you don't have to talk. Just... feel."

That pull inside me surged, undeniable. I closed the distance, capturing her lips with mine. The kiss was soft at first, tentative, a gentle query wrapped in warmth—but it quickly grew more urgent, more desperate. Like both of us had been waiting too long, afraid too long. Her fingers tangled in my hair, threading through it like she'd done it a thousand times in her dreams. My arms wrapped around her, pulling her close, trying to erase every inch of space that had ever existed between us.

I leaned forward, gently guiding her down against the cool sheets. She yielded with a sigh, her body arching to meet mine, soft and strong all at once. The shadows in the room seemed to soften, the lamp casting golden halos over her skin. The room fell away until it was just the warmth of her breath, the hush of our exhales, the electric current dancing between heartbeats.

We paused, forehead to forehead, suspended in a moment that felt infinite.

"Phoenix—" she began, her voice a whisper of uncertainty.

I silenced her with another kiss—deeper this time, unspoken truths passed from lips to lips. The weight of my sorrow, the flood of my desire, the ache of years we never had—all of it poured into that single connection.

Hands explored, slow and reverent. Hers moved across my back, then over my chest, tracing the map of tension I wore like armor. My shirt came off in a fluid motion, discarded without ceremony. She didn't flinch. Instead, her fingers traced lightly over my skin, her touch like a whisper, a grounding force. Her eyes stayed locked on mine—not afraid, not pitying, but wholly present.

She guided me down, easing me into the bed as her blouse slipped from her shoulders and fell silently to the floor. I stilled, just long enough to take her in. The grace in her vulnerability, the power in her quiet, steady breath. Every inch of her a declaration of trust.

Her hand found mine and guided it to her cheek, anchoring me.

"I want you," she said, voice thick with longing and certainty. "All of you. Not just the parts you think are safe."

My breath hitched. My heart raced. And yet, for the first time, I didn't feel like I was falling. I felt like I was being caught.

And for the first time in a long time, I didn't run from the wanting.

I surrendered to it, pulling her close again, into the gravity of this shared moment—raw, whole, and ours.

The night held us gently, and the world outside faded away.

Later, the room was wrapped in soft silence. The only sound was the hush of our breathing, slowing to a steady rhythm as the storm inside me began to settle. Evelyn lay against my chest, her fingers tracing slow, sleepy circles along my arm. Her touch was featherlight, almost reverent, like she was drawing runes of safety and belonging into my skin.

"You're warm," she murmured, her voice muffled against my skin, drowsy and content.

I smiled faintly, brushing my fingers through her tousled hair. It was still slightly damp with the heat of our shared moment. "You make me feel that way."

She shifted slightly, pressing a little closer, her arm sliding over my ribs. A gentle quiet settled between us like a shared blanket. The light from the bedside lamp had dimmed to an amber glow, casting soft halos across the tangled sheets.

Then she stirred again, her breath warming my collarbone. "Can I ask you something?"

"Anything."

"Do you think we would've had this... if things had been different? If we'd been braver sooner, or maybe just less scared of hurting each other?"

I thought about it. About the versions of us that had lived in silences and stolen glances. The near-misses. The moments we should've spoken but didn't. "I don't know," I said honestly. "But I know I wouldn't trade this now for anything. Not even the perfect past."

She lifted her head, her eyes soft and heavy-lidded, and pressed her lips gently to my collarbone, a silent affirmation that curled into my chest and bloomed there.

"Good answer," she whispered.

She settled again, and I held her tighter, feeling the way her body molded to mine like puzzle pieces that had always belonged. For a long moment, we just breathed together. A slow duet of healing.

Then she whispered, quieter still, "You don't have to go through this alone anymore. I mean it. You have me."

I didn't respond in words. I didn't have to. I reached down and laced my fingers with hers, holding her hand against my chest where she could feel the truth pounding in my heartbeat.

She rested her cheek against me again, her breath steadying. We drifted there, in that fragile, golden quiet, not yet sleep but not fully awake either. Just two souls rediscovering peace.

I watched her as she finally drifted off. The steady rhythm of her breathing, the delicate rise and fall of her shoulders. I memorized everything—the weight of her in my arms, the way the night light caught in the fine strands of her hair. I wanted to press it all into memory like photographs.

Outside, the world remained dark, full of unknowns and lurking threats. But here, in the silence, in the warmth of her embrace, I felt something I hadn't allowed myself to feel in a long time.

Safe.

And maybe, for the first time in years, whole.

We drifted into a soft, in-between place—not quite sleep, not fully awake. Just two souls finally allowed to rest.

I watched her for a long time as she slept. Listened to the rise and fall of her breath. Let the weight of the day dissolve, moment by moment. My hand curled around hers, grounding me to this moment.

SEVENTEEN

FAMILY SECRETS

"TRUTH BURIED IN BLOOD"

Evelyn lay curled in my arms as morning light trickled through the slats in the blinds, painting golden stripes across the bed. My eyes opened slowly, adjusting to the gentle glow. The warmth of her body against mine was real, grounding. I had woken up a hundred times over the past few weeks wondering if the nightmare would end. Today, it had. Today, this was my reality—Evelyn's breath rising and falling in a slow rhythm beside me, her presence like gravity holding me in place.

Her auburn hair spilled across the pillow, wild and soft, and her features were calm in sleep—softer than I'd ever seen. There was no trace of the analyst, the scholar, the warrior. Just Evelyn. My Evelyn.

Part of me had feared this—feared we would cross a line we couldn't return from. But now, in the quiet aftermath, all I wanted was to stay here. To exist in this moment.

She stirred, and her eyes fluttered open, meeting mine with a sleepy, blue brilliance that stole my breath.

"Good morning," I whispered, smiling.

"Good morning," she echoed, her voice husky with sleep. Then she leaned in and kissed me, slow and soft. Her lips still held the memory of the night before. The heat between us hadn't faded—it simmered, deep and steady, like embers glowing beneath ash.

I cupped her cheek, brushing a strand of hair behind her ear. "How did you sleep?"

"Like a baby," she murmured, nuzzling closer. "Had a pretty good snuggle-mate."

Before I could respond, there was a knock on the door. We both froze. Then—

"Hey, breakfast..." Lucas's voice trailed off as he opened the door. He blinked. Stared. And instantly flushed bright red.

"Oh, sorry—um, I'm just going to go," he said quickly, backing out and shutting the door behind him with a clumsy thud.

A beat of silence.

"Guess the secret's out now," I muttered.

"Well, it was only a secret for a few hours," Evelyn said with a shrug, grinning. She leaned over and kissed me once more before slipping out of bed to find her clothes.

We dressed in quiet companionship. There was no awkwardness—just a shared energy that buzzed softly between us. When we emerged from the bedroom, the smell of coffee and eggs hit us immediately. But more potent was the gaze of my mother and Lucas, seated at the kitchen table.

They both looked up.

"Good morning," my mom said cheerfully, a knowing smile curling her lips. "Hope you two slept well."

We sat down, pretending not to notice the scrutiny.

"It's about time you got off your ass and told her," she added, sipping her coffee like it was just another Tuesday.

Lucas nearly choked on his orange juice, laughter sputtering out between coughs. Evelyn turned red, eyes fixed firmly on her plate.

"Glad to have you home, Mom," I muttered, reaching for some eggs.

"So, how long have you two been…?" she asked, raising her eyebrows.

"Just last night," I admitted, rubbing the back of my neck.

"Yeah, you should've seen the sexual tension between those two," Lucas chimed in, grinning like the traitor he was.

I glared at him. Evelyn tried to disappear into her toast.

"Dr. Knight..." Evelyn started, clearly searching for an escape route.

"If you're about to ask if it's okay to date my son, you already know the answer is yes, my dear," my mother said, waving a hand dismissively.

"Thank you, but I was going to ask if you'd like to see the chamber we found," Evelyn finished, still blushing.

My mom's face lit up with interest. "Oh, well, that would be wonderful. If we can."

The moment shifted. From intimate to professional. From family to mission. And I realized then—we could have both. We could hold onto love and still chase purpose.

We could be whole.

"I'm pretty sure I can arrange it. I need to update the Order anyway," I said, grateful for the change in topic.

After breakfast, I stepped into the study to send a secure message to the Order. My fingers hovered over the keys as I composed the note, keeping it short: informing them that Dr. Knight had been rescued and requesting a tour of the chamber. I added that she was one of the Council's original founders—a detail that likely needed no reminder but carried diplomatic weight.

An hour passed. During that time, we cleaned up breakfast, swapped stories, and tried—at least for a while—to pretend life was normal. Then the reply came. A single-line confirmation: We're honored to welcome Dr. Knight. The chamber will be open upon arrival.

My mother emerged from her room dressed casually but still dignified—blouse, jacket, jeans, and well-worn boots that had clearly seen fieldwork.

"So where is this chamber?" she asked, lifting her coffee mug.

"On campus," I replied, smirking.

She arched a brow. "Interesting."

"You'll never guess where."

She gave me a look. "I suppose I'll find out."

I ducked back into my room to change—dark jeans, a black V-neck tee, my olive field jacket, and a pair of boots that felt like armor. It was a good blend of casual and ready.

When I returned to the living room, sunlight poured in from the windows, bathing the hardwood floors in warm light. Evelyn stood by the bookshelf, skimming a title. Lucas leaned against the kitchen counter, arms crossed, sipping coffee. My mother sat near the window, eyes scanning the treetops outside as if seeing more than just leaves and sky.

"Are we ready?" I asked.

"As ever," Evelyn said, flashing me a smile.

Something in her voice—steady, familiar—told me we were stepping into something important. And this time, I wasn't walking alone.

The walk to campus was perfect. Autumn leaves crunched beneath our boots as the breeze teased the branches overhead. It was that rare balance of sunlight and wind that made everything feel fresh and alive. My mother and Lucas walked ahead, deep in quiet conversation. Evelyn and I trailed behind, our hands linked like a promise.

For the first time in what felt like forever, I was simply happy.

Not the fake, performative kind I'd worn like a mask—but something deeper. Genuine. I didn't feel haunted. I didn't feel hunted. I felt here.

"So, I was thinking maybe later tonight we could go have dinner," I said.

Evelyn glanced over, a teasing glint in her eye. "Another date, then? You're not going to run off again, are you?"

"No. I think we're past that."

"Then I'd love that," she said. "There's a place on the square I like. Cozy. Quiet. Good food."

"Oh, really? I guess that's where we should go then."

Her smile warmed me more than the sun overhead.

As we passed the museum and approached campus, the world bustled around us—students jogging, bicycles weaving between pedestrians, groups laughing over coffee. We moved through them like ghosts wrapped in ordinary skin.

The brick sign welcoming us to the university was framed in flowers and the timeless presence of ivy. The Ford Center loomed nearby, and its lot was packed. People darted between buildings, late for class or deep in conversation. It was easy to forget, in moments like these, the weight of the world we carried.

"This campus has always been beautiful," my mom said as we entered the Grove. Trees stretched overhead like ancient sentinels, leaves whispering stories only they remembered. Students lounged beneath them, laptops open, books sprawled. We were just four more souls on a lazy midday path.

At the student union, the food court was chaos incarnate. Lines snaked everywhere, particularly Chick-fil-A, as expected. We voted for McAlister's and took our food to-go. My mom suggested we eat beneath the trees, and none of us disagreed.

We found a quiet table in the Grove, far enough from the bustle to feel private. My mom had grilled cheese and tomato soup, Lucas a towering Reuben, Evelyn her usual loaded spud, and I stuck to my go-to club sandwich with mac and cheese.

"I have to ask," Lucas said, setting down his sandwich, eyebrows raised. "Why did you name him Phoenix?"

Here we go.

My mother set her spoon down and took a deep breath, her fingers lacing together as if bracing for something ancient to rise. When she spoke, her voice slipped into the cadence of the professor I remembered from lectures she never gave to students, only to time.

"Phoenix wasn't breathing when I first held him," she said, eyes locked on the distant middle distance of memory. "No cry.

No gasp. Just silence. The doctors couldn't explain it—his heart beat, his vitals were faint but steady, yet it was like... his soul was caught somewhere between. They said he wouldn't last the night."

Lucas's jaw tightened slightly. Evelyn's hand brushed against mine, grounding me.

"But I refused that answer," she continued, her voice quiet but edged with defiance. "Not because I had evidence. Not because I was a Keeper or a scholar. Because I was a mother, and I knew something no machine could read. I left that hospital in the dark, carrying him in a wool blanket and driving east. Toward a place I'd only ever found in footnotes and folk legends."

She paused, her eyes flicking to mine, then away. "In the Smoky Mountains, there's a cave. You won't find it on maps or in digital records. It exists in the interstices of belief—hidden by memory and the veils of shamanic bloodlines. It's called the Cave of the Phoenix Tear."

I swallowed, sensing how much she believed in what she was saying—or needed to.

"The cave's mouth was narrow, shielded by fallen rock and thick moss. Inside, the air shimmered with heat, as if the world had swallowed fire and never exhaled. I passed through a chamber of glowing stone—ribbons of molten orange and gold veined the walls, giving off a soft, pulsing light. The heat blistered my arms, but I held you close, shielding you with my body. I kept walking."

Her hands trembled as she described it. Not theatrically. Just memory creeping back through bone.

"Eventually, I reached the inner chamber. It was obsidian. Walls like mirrors, black and endless. At the center, a volcanic pedestal. And on it, a vial—glass so thin it looked spun from moonlight. Inside it, liquid shimmered silver, like liquid starlight. I took it. Three drops. That's all it took."

She looked at me. "You gasped. You cried. And when you opened your eyes, they were silver. Like now. You weren't just breathing, Phoenix. You had been... rewritten."

Evelyn let out a soft breath. Lucas blinked like he'd forgotten how. I sat there, not cold or afraid—just suspended in something I couldn't name.

"So that's why you named him Phoenix," Evelyn said, reverent.

"From fire and ash," my mother nodded. "From death, life again."

But something in her gaze made my stomach twist. Not a lie—but not the full truth. I remembered once, long ago, finding an old baby blanket that smelled faintly of smoke. I remembered waking from dreams where flames licked the walls and a woman's voice screamed. And I remembered the gray hair hidden at the back of my head—my only strand. I had found it not long after the darkest night of my life, after I stood on the edge and nearly gave everything away to silence and despair. It had appeared overnight, like a scar without blood, a quiet brand that no one else could see. I'd kept it hidden ever since, not just because it looked strange on someone my age, but because it marked something I couldn't explain—a moment the world nearly lost me, and somehow, I came back. Not reborn in fire, not like the cave—this time it was sorrow that birthed me again.

"Did the Council know?" Evelyn asked.

"Only Veronica," my mother said, voice suddenly iron. "And it must stay that way."

I looked at her, and for the first time, saw something not quite whole in her eyes. A grief older than my name.

"What else haven't you told me?"

She looked up at the trees, voice just above a whisper.

"Some truths you must live to understand. Some answers wait where even I cannot follow."

The wind picked up, rustling the leaves above us. Their whisper sounded like fire.

"You should write them down. It's the only way Phoenix would get them," Lucas joked, leaning back and chuckling.

"Ha ha," I replied dryly, but the truth stung more than I liked to admit. He wasn't wrong. Life had been so intense lately, I hadn't had time to breathe, let alone dive into the hidden libraries of Council lore my mother probably kept locked in her head.

"You know, you should've seen him when he was reading your dissertation freshman year," Lucas added, nudging my mother. "He read it like it was the final book in a fantasy trilogy. I think he quoted it at one point."

"Did he really?" my mom asked, a smile curling at the corner of her lips. "Which chapter?"

"The one about household amulets and their links to funerary rites," I muttered. "It was... surprisingly engaging."

Evelyn snorted. "That's the most Phoenix thing I've ever heard."

"He always was a scholar at heart," my mother said with pride, reaching over and brushing her hand over mine. There was something tender in her eyes—something almost relieved. That I was here. That we all were.

The wind shifted through the Grove, scattering golden leaves around our table like a blessing. Students walked by, oblivious to the sacred moment unraveling quietly in our small corner of the world. For a fleeting second, the sunlight caught Evelyn's hair and made it glow like copper fire. My mother looked content. Lucas was smiling.

Then everything changed.

I noticed it first in Lucas's expression—the subtle freeze in his features, like a tape reel had suddenly hit pause. My mother's shoulders tensed just slightly, her smile wilting at the edges.

Before I could react, something cold and hard pressed into my back.

"Hey, handsome, we should chat," came Allison's sultry, venom-laced voice as she jammed her gun deeper between my ribs.

My body locked. I turned slowly, heart pounding. There she stood, immaculate in her cruelty, flanked by four goons in black coats and mirrored shades. Her lipstick was too red. Her smirk too pleased.

"Why on earth would I want to do that with you?" I said, my voice calm but coiled.

"Because I have no trouble killing off the rest of your friends and your mom, of course. You do still call her that, don't you?" She leaned in, her breath cool against my cheek.

The others surrounded us, moving in smooth, practiced precision. There would be no running. Not now.

I glanced at Evelyn. She gave the smallest shake of her head, eyes sharp with silent panic. Lucas's fists clenched in his lap. My mother's gaze was steel.

"I guess we are chatting then," I muttered, disappointment thick in my throat. And fear—cold and blooming like a storm about to break.

EIGHTEEN

THE DECENT

"BENEATH THE LIVING GROVE"

Allison surrounded us as I stood to face her. Her posture was poised and confident, her smirk a dagger sheathed in lipstick. She knew she had the upper hand. Her eyes danced with satisfaction, the kind only predators wore. This would've been the perfect moment for UPD to drive by, for someone—anyone—to intervene. But the Grove was silent. No footsteps. No witnesses. Just us.

"So, what would you like to chat about?" I asked, my voice flat, my pulse steady but coiled. I needed to move this along. Every second counted if I hoped to make good on my promise to Evelyn.

"Oh, can't I just see how you and Mommy are doing?" Allison replied, her tone dripping with venomous charm.

"I don't take you for making wellness checks." My voice didn't shake, but I was tired—tired of the dry humor, tired of the games. This had to stop. One way or another.

"True," she admitted with a careless shrug. "I guess I can shoot straight with you." She lowered her weapon slightly, still dangling it in her fingers like a toy. "You're going to take me to this little chamber of yours. Then we're going to have ourselves an adventure."

"And if I don't?"

She gave a theatrical sigh, as if I were being deliberately difficult. Then her eyes hardened.

"They all die, of course." Her voice was so matter-of-fact it made my skin crawl. In unison, her men raised their weapons, each pointed squarely at the people I loved.

I was not amused. "How cliché of you."

She rolled her eyes. "Please. If it ain't broke, don't fix it. Now, shall we?"

The fury that brewed inside me threatened to boil over, but I tamped it down. There was only one option, and I hated it. I had to play along. For now.

"You—" Evelyn began, fire in her voice, but one of Allison's men shoved her back into her seat.

"Oh Evelyn," Allison purred, glancing her way, "you know why I'm here."

"I do. Doesn't mean I can't stop you," Evelyn spat. She stood slowly, eyes blazing. Power crackled at the edges of her aura. She was close to losing control.

"Get going," Allison snapped. Her men prodded us to our feet with the business ends of their rifles. I scanned the campus again. Empty. Too empty. Must be the middle of class change. No eyes on us. Perfect for an ambush. Perfect for a quiet kill.

They moved us quickly but without obvious force. Anyone who might see would think we were just a group of students walking together. A very tense group. Allison followed behind me like a shadow with teeth, relishing every step of her control.

We made our way to the Lyceum. Its white columns towered over us, proud and stoic against the midday sun. The bricks were chipped in places, the wood beneath the facade starting to peek through with age. The university would cover it with paint soon, masking history again.

But I didn't care about the bricks.

I cared about the small camera tucked discreetly under the eaves of the front column.

I'd seen it before. A security feed Veronica insisted on—one of many Council overlays embedded throughout campus. If anyone was watching, they'd see us now. I just had to trust someone was paying attention.

"It's here?" Allison asked, eyeing the building.

"Yes," I said softly. I gestured toward the camera, not too obviously. "I suggest you hide those if you don't want to be spotted."

She raised a brow, amused. "Trying to help me now?"

"Just offering advice. Might help me earn your trust."

"Nice try," she said, but lowered her gun anyway. Her men followed suit. One small victory. One seed of doubt.

We walked toward the doors. Just beyond them, the hidden chamber waited. And once we passed through, we would be alone. Trapped in legend. No help. No guarantees.

Just us and the myth that lived in stone and shadow.

And whatever waited in the dark beyond.

I had to believe we weren't entirely alone.

Not yet.

Seeing no one was around, I slid the shelf open. My fingers trembled only slightly as I left a napkin tucked by one of the books—a silent signal. Maybe someone would find it. Maybe not.

"After you," I said, gesturing.

"How about your friends go first?" Allison smirked. She motioned her thugs to escort them in. Evelyn and Lucas both hesitated. I gave a slight nod. Trust me.

They vanished into the darkness with two of Allison's goons behind them. Others followed with large duffel bags—equipment, supplies, I guessed. Whatever Allison planned, she was ready.

"After you," I said, gesturing.

"How about your friends go first?" Allison smirked. She motioned her thugs to escort them in. Evelyn and Lucas both hesitated. I gave a slight nod. Trust me.

They vanished into the darkness with two of Allison's goons behind them. Others followed with large duffel bags—

equipment, supplies, I guessed. Whatever Allison planned, she was ready.

Allison and I descended next, the stone staircase curving deep into the earth. The walls grew colder, damper, slick with condensation that glistened like dew on ancient stone. My mother followed close behind, her breathing slow and deliberate, every step a measured act of composure. But beneath it, I could feel her pulse—the rhythm of memory returning to a sacred place.

The chamber opened like a breath exhaled after centuries. Warm light from modern sconces mingled with an internal golden luminescence, a kind of living energy pulsing through the walls. The air was thick with age and secrets, the scent of damp stone mixed with something floral and long-extinct.

Dr. Knight stepped forward slowly, her hands trembling—not from fear, but reverence. "It's still here," she whispered, voice catching in her throat. Her eyes widened, reflecting the golden hues of the murals. She moved forward, reverently tracing the outlines of the carved glyphs with her fingertips. Her whole posture shifted—no longer the composed scholar, but the awestruck explorer. "These glyphs… some are older than anything in the Arctic archives. This site predates the earliest Keepers, possibly even the Shamanic root cultures."

She turned, brushing her hand across a faded relief etched into obsidian. Her eyes brimmed with tears. "This was once a sanctum. A place of transformation. I studied its existence for decades. But to stand in it… to feel it beneath your skin... it's like the walls are alive."

Even Allison seemed affected. Her smirk was momentarily absent as she stepped forward, eyes scanning the inscriptions. She motioned to one. "What's that say?"

My mother followed her gaze, then translated, voice flat. "A gate sealed by blood. Only the marked may pass. The unworthy will burn in shadow."

Allison blinked. "So it's trapped?"

"It's protected," Dr. Knight corrected. "There's a difference. This is not a place you simply walk into."

"And yet here we are," Allison said, her composure returning as quickly as it had slipped. She swept an arm toward us. Behind her, more of her men filtered in, duffel bags slung across their backs, eyes hungry with greed and awe.

"Showtime," she said.

I joined Evelyn and Lucas, who stood just behind my mother. She was still mesmerized, whispering to herself as she sketched mental notes and memorized the wall carvings. Her face was alight with scholarly wonder—but the tension in her jaw betrayed how deeply she understood the stakes.

"What are we doing?" Evelyn kept her voice low.

"Trying to stall as best as I can."

Evelyn gave me that look—sharp, analytical. She was trying to figure out exactly what I was planning. The problem was, so was I. Fighting would be suicide. Bluffing, for now, was our only card.

"Well, take all the time you need. You know, not much going on. Except us being held against our will." Her sarcasm was bitter and laced with worry.

Lucas leaned in close, his voice low and sardonic. "If you die on me, I swear I'll find a way to bring you back just to kick your ass."

Despite everything, I smiled. "Deal."

We moved toward the lower chamber. My footsteps felt heavier, as if the weight of history—and danger—pressed down with each step.

"Okay, this is all nice and all, but I am dying to see the rest," Allison said.

"Well, this is it." I hoped the lie would suffice. Allison's face was unimpressed—flat, calculating. Frustration simmered behind her eyes.

"Handsome, we both know you're lying," she said softly. "So, which one dies first?"

Three of her goons lunged forward, grabbing Lucas, Evelyn, and my mother. The others closed in on me.

"Phoenix, don't," Evelyn said quickly.

"No!" I yelled as Allison pressed her gun to Evelyn's head. My chest surged with panic.

"Tick-tock," she taunted.

"Fine, there is more," I said. Evelyn's eyes flicked to mine—fear and fury mingled. "But I don't know how to get there."

She studied me. I hoped the truth in my voice saved us.

Allison's lips curled into a scowl, but she lowered her gun.

"Then you better start figuring it out," she said. Her men shoved Lucas and my mother forward again. Evelyn rushed to my side.

"You okay?" she whispered.

"No. But I'll fake it."

I moved to my mother. Her eyes were wide but resolute.

"We need to figure out a way in," I said.

"Are you sure?"

"No. But we don't have a choice."

We began inspecting the walls. Carvings, cracks, textures—searching for anything. Lucas crouched, examining the floor, running his fingers along ancient grooves.

Nothing. Not yet. But the walls were watching. And somewhere, I felt it—the pull of something waiting for me to wake it.

"Phoenix," Evelyn said again, sharper this time. She was crouched now beside one of the stone pillars, fingers pressed flat against its surface. Her eyes darted, not with panic but calculation.

I moved to her side. "What is it?"

She didn't look up. "These etchings near the base—they're not decorative. They're... directional. This one faces due north, I think."

I knelt beside her. To the untrained eye, it looked like simple erosion. But now that she mentioned it, I saw it—the groove. Clean, precise. Intentional. I turned to the others.

"Check the rest of them. See if they're all like this."

Lucas and my mother spread out. I rose and moved to the next pillar. Its marking faced west. Another—southwest. Each one different.

"They're all facing different directions," I muttered.

Lucas pushed against his, and with a low groan, it rotated. "They move. Like dials."

"It's a puzzle," Evelyn said, standing beside me. "They're meant to be positioned. This isn't just a room—it's some kind of mechanism, maybe even a lock."

My heart started to race—not with fear, but with recognition. Something ancient stirred beneath our feet, waiting.

I turned to Allison. "You're the one who wants in. You can help—or stay out of the way."

She made a show of sighing. "Oh, I do love being volunteered. How gallant."

She sauntered to a pillar and began turning it lazily, as if it were a game. The rest of us got to work, trying combinations—compass patterns, opposing forces, mirrored alignments. Each movement echoed, but nothing triggered.

"What if they point inward?" Lucas suggested. "Like... to the center of the room?"

We all paused. I looked down. Embedded in the floor was a carved tree—its roots curling outward like veins.

"Try it," I said.

One by one, we adjusted the pillars. With each alignment toward the center, the room felt heavier. Like the air thickened.

The final pillar clicked into place. Silence.

Then a tremor.

The ground shuddered beneath us. Fine dust drifted from the ceiling. Cracks spider-webbed outward from the center of the floor.

"Maybe it's just—" my mother began, but her voice was lost in the groan of stone giving way.

The center began to sink, petals of rock groaning and splitting apart with the sound of grinding centuries. Dust billowed as stone plates folded in precise, spiraling succession, like the gears of some buried clock finally awakening. Beneath, a staircase revealed itself—not just cut from stone, but seemingly melted into place, its surface charred and jagged, glistening with dark mineral veins.

The air shifted instantly. A blast of cold surged up through the aperture, sharp as needles against our skin. It carried the smell of deep, unturned earth—damp, metallic, tinged with rot—and beneath that, something stranger: a sweetness that didn't belong, like the wilted perfume of a flower long extinct.

The light didn't reach far. The steps vanished into shadow after only a few coils, and the stone around the stairwell seemed to absorb the glow rather than reflect it.

We stood at the edge, the weight of silence pressing in. No one spoke.

Something ancient had stirred. And it wanted us to come closer.

Evelyn exhaled slowly. "That's... not ominous at all."

"Bravo," came Allison's voice, slow and smug. "You broke the seal. I'm impressed."

I turned to her. "Happy now?"

"Not yet," she said. Her tone shifted—silk turned to steel. "What I want lies below. And I don't need your entourage anymore."

Her agents stepped forward, hands drifting toward weapons.

I stepped between them and my friends. "Stop."

The word echoed, not loud but final.

"I'll take you," I said. "But you leave them alone."

Allison tilted her head. "You know the way?"

"I know enough."

"Phoenix, no," my mother said sharply. Her eyes were wide—fear and fury barely contained.

"Mom... I have to." I lowered my voice. "This isn't their fight."

Her hands trembled, just slightly. "It's yours, then? Alone?"

"It was always going to be."

Allison smiled like a predator. "So noble. But I'm not a fool. They come. Or you don't."

"Fine," I said. "But if anything happens to them, I'll burn this whole place to ash."

"Oh, Handsome," she purred. "That's what I'm counting on."

We descended.

The steps were wide enough for two. Evelyn walked beside me, her grip tightening around my hand. I didn't let go. Not this time.

"I don't know what we'll find," I whispered.

"We face it together," she replied, eyes forward. "No more secrets."

The deeper we went, the colder it became. The torches lining the walls were lit—already lit. Someone had prepared this. Or something.

Above us, the world we knew had already begun to shift.

Below us, it waited.

And I felt it in my chest—that silent scream beneath the bones of the world.

The myth wasn't history anymore.

It had awakened.

NINETEEN

THE TOMB

"THE HIDDEN WORLD"

The dark was like a never-ending void as the stairs kept going. Allison lit a few torches so we could see. The warm light illuminated the passage, revealing damp, uneven stone walls, some parts covered in moss so thick it looked like velvet. Thin roots dangled from the ceiling, twitching slightly in the warm air like veins seeking a pulse. It was cooler down here than on the surface, but the moisture was dense and clung to our skin. With each breath, it felt like inhaling time itself—ancient, wet, and patient.

In the distance, I began to hear it: the faint trickle of water echoing ahead, like a lullaby from the bones of the earth. Evelyn's hand remained firmly in mine, grounding me. Lucas and my mother walked behind us, quiet, and Allison and her men flanked the rear, their torchlight bobbing like fireflies with bad intentions.

"How much further?" Lucas whispered. His voice was a thread in the dark.

I shrugged. "Could be a few feet. Could be a mile."

Would the passage open into something monumental—or deliver us to oblivion? We had no way to know. Still, we walked forward. The torches burned, the stone sighed, and the old world waited.

Then the passage ended.

We stepped out, and the chamber took our breath away.

It was vast, a subterranean cathedral untouched by time. The domed ceiling arched high above us—at least three stories if not more—its surface intricately inlaid with mosaics of iridescent tile and metallic leaf that caught the torchlight in flashes of violet and gold. Between the mosaic panels, veins of luminous mineral webbed outward like lightning frozen in stone, pulsing gently as if the rock itself breathed.

From four high alcoves carved into the chamber's upper reaches, water poured in graceful arcs. Each stream emerged from the hands of towering stone sentinels—humanoid figures carved with solemn, ageless expressions. Each stood with arms outstretched, palms tilted downward as if blessing the space below. Their armor was stylized and ornate, unlike any culture I could place—half nature, half starfire, etched with flowing runes that shimmered faintly in the torchlight.

The water flowed from their palms in measured streams, striking the stone pool edges with melodic splashes, creating a soundscape that seemed more symphony than noise. The pools encircled the entire room in a continuous ring, their mirrored surfaces reflecting a distorted heaven beneath our feet.

The mist hovered like memory itself, clinging to skin and fabric, glittering with motes of unseen light. The air felt dense with history, fragrant with an earthy perfume of minerals, moss, and something sweeter—almost like citrus and myrrh. It made me dizzy for a moment, not from exhaustion, but awe.

High above, birds darted between the crevices and roosts—living proof that this place had endured in secret for longer than any of us could grasp. They called out occasionally, sharp notes that echoed with eerie clarity through the hollow vastness. Nestled in corners were flowering vines I couldn't name, each bloom glowing faintly with a phosphorescent blush, as if the chamber itself had bled color into their veins.

It didn't just feel ancient. It felt aware. Alive. And it watched us as surely as we watched it.

"It's beautiful," my mother whispered, her gaze climbing the chamber walls like they were holy scripture.

"Not bad," Allison admitted, walking slowly around us, her usual edge softened by awe.

"This puts a new meaning to the word 'tunnels,'" Lucas murmured, his voice reverent.

I nodded. Legends of secret passageways beneath the university had always floated around—smug whispers about secret societies or civil rights history. But this? This was something else entirely.

"Here we thought they were small," I said.

Evelyn and my mother broke away, moving toward the carved stone, running fingers along faded glyphs, deciphering what they could with fevered attention. They looked like children at an open-air bazaar of wonders, overwhelmed and insatiably curious.

Allison observed them too, but with something different in her expression—no smirk, no irony. Just quiet satisfaction, as if even she wasn't immune to the magic here.

Lucas and I moved to the nearest waterfall. The water spilled in crystal sheets, its mist a cool balm on our faces. A shallow pool bordered the chamber's edge, perfectly clear. Silver-scaled fish darted just beneath the surface.

Lucas knelt and dipped his hands in, letting the water wash over the grime of our journey. "Incredible. The water is so pure."

"I guess we found how they got around the water table," I said, scanning the architecture.

The layout wasn't random. This was engineered—meticulously. And impossibly old. Far older than European colonization. Even the Mississippian cultures, powerful and enigmatic as they were, seemed too recent.

"I don't think this was built by any people we've ever documented," I murmured. "This feels... older. Like something we forgot how to remember."

As Lucas and I walked along the edge of the chamber, I noticed faint carvings etched into the walls, half-hidden beneath blankets of moss and trailing vines. They were elaborate, spiraling patterns that hinted at ancient scripts—something neither of us could decipher, but that hummed with the quiet weight of story.

"Can I ask you something?" Lucas said as we wandered.

"What's up?"

"You and Evelyn?"

"Yeah." I smiled, the answer coming easier than I expected. "I think all this time I was so in my head about how it would fall apart… I forgot how it feels to let something hold me together."

"You look happy. I've never seen you this way before," Lucas said, watching me with a soft, knowing smile. "It fits you."

I glanced over, surprised by how deeply he saw me. He always had, I realized. I just hadn't let myself notice.

Even with ancient secrets pressing in around us, even with danger just a corridor away—I felt lighter. Not safe, not free. But grounded. Like I had something to lose. Something worth fighting for.

"Hey, look here," Lucas said, pointing toward a narrow arch partly obscured by overgrown ivy. We brushed it aside and found a small doorway leading into a side room.

Inside, it was dark. The torchlight barely reached past the threshold. I stepped in, squinting—then paused. The center of the room began to glow.

At first, it was subtle—like embers awakening from centuries of sleep. A soft golden shimmer pulsed at the center of the room, then began to spread outward in slow, deliberate waves. The walls, previously shrouded in shadow, bloomed to life. Thousands of tiny lights blinked into existence, swirling upward like a slow exhale of the stars themselves. They hovered in the air, moving in gentle spirals, casting reflections on our faces and across the polished stone floor.

Each point of light shone with its own hue—icy blues, amber golds, silvers like the edges of a dream. The lights didn't flicker randomly; they moved with intelligence, forming patterns that revealed themselves as constellations—familiar and foreign alike.

"Whoa," Lucas breathed, his voice reverent, the awe in his tone mirrored in his wide eyes.

We stood at the heart of a celestial engine. Above, below, and all around us, constellations rotated slowly, impossibly, each suspended in the air like it had always belonged there. Orion stretched overhead, bold and eternal. Cassiopeia curled to our right, her stars like jeweled thorns. Other constellations I couldn't name traced across the far walls, interconnected by threads of starlight too precise to be random.

This wasn't just a map—it was a living archive. The constellations moved as if charting time, the room responding to our presence, as though the act of observing had summoned it to life.

I turned slowly, fully surrounded by the cosmos. "Whoever built this didn't just study the stars," I murmured. "They understood them. Lived with them. This… this is ancient astronomy. It's art, science, and memory woven together."

I turned slowly, the illusion surrounding me completely. "Whoever built this understood the stars better than we do now," I murmured. "This… this is ancient astronomy. Precision we still don't match."

"Who needs an observatory when you can just come to see this?" Lucas said with a grin.

"I wouldn't mind having Astronomy down here. Beats trying to squint through a telescope."

Lucas nodded, and we stood a moment longer, letting the room soak into us. The sky above, and below. Past and present blurred.

Then Evelyn's voice called from the main chamber. We left reluctantly, stepping back through the archway.

My mother and Evelyn stood before another room—this one lit only by torchlight. In its center stood three stone sarcophagi, each massive and carved from a single slab of polished basalt. Their surfaces were etched with symbols and motifs worn by time but still potent with purpose.

Moss veiled parts of their lids. Vines curled along their bases like green ivy tattoos.

"It's just amazing," my mother whispered, stepping forward, her fingers brushing reverently along the edge of one.

"Who knew dead people could be thrilling?" Allison quipped as she passed, but her voice lacked its usual bite.

Evelyn remained close. "Hey, can I ask you something?"

I nodded as we moved a few steps away from the others.

"What are we doing?"

"Still working on it."

"Well, hurry it up," she said, her voice low but sharp.

"Trying," I answered, meaning it more than she knew.

She looked at me softly. Nothing malicious, more of a sense of worry. I could tell by how she was fidgeting; she was on edge, always looking out. Waiting for something to happen. I took her hand and held it, trying to comfort her. It was cold, but she smiled at me.

"It's okay, we will get through this," I said to her.

"Just promise me we make it out," she said, and I nodded in agreement. I did hope we would get out of here. I just knew that if we did, we might be different.

Lucas walked over and noticed us.

"Your mother found something you should see," he said. Evelyn and I looked at each other, wondering probably the same question. As we followed Lucas back to my mother, she was bent over, brushing away dirt from one of the sarcophagi.

"Come look at this," she exclaimed, pointing to the symbols she was able to clear away. They were very worn and hard to see, but I could make out some of them.

"What language is it?" I wondered, hoping my mother would know. From the look on her face, however, it seemed that she had no idea.

"I don't know, but it's a fantastic discovery." My mother was already at work trying to write things down as she looked even more closely at them. Evelyn joined her, each comparing notes. Part of me noticed how much they were the same, in regards to their pursuit of knowledge. However, I was sure Evelyn had other things up her sleeves. Hopefully, something that could help us.

I lingered, stepping forward until I stood directly beside the sarcophagus. The symbols seemed to blur the longer I looked, like ink underwater. I reached out slowly and let my fingers touch the stone. It was smoother than I expected—cool, but not cold. As my palm made contact, a flicker of something stirred in my chest. Not pain, not heat—just... a ripple.

For a heartbeat, the world dimmed. The noise of the chamber receded. I felt—not saw—flashes: a vast tree breaking under fire, three silhouettes kneeling in ash, their hands outstretched toward a silver flame. Then it was gone. The torchlight returned. The sounds of notes and scribbles resumed. But the hum lingered in my bones.

When I looked up, my mother was watching me. Her eyes weren't focused on the sarcophagus anymore—they were on me. Her expression had shifted. Not curiosity. Not confusion. Recognition. Her lips parted like she was about to speak, but then she turned away, almost too quickly, scribbling down another note instead.

I pulled back, unsettled but trying not to show it. Whatever that was, it hadn't felt hostile. Just old. And waiting.

Lucas even looked worried, but we walked out of the main chamber, leaving them to study away.

Allison and her men were setting up something in the center of the large chamber. Lanterns were being assembled, a portable heater unrolled, rations organized with an eerie professionalism. The flicker of firelight played across their features—focused, armed, and alert. This wasn't just camp. This was a war footing masquerading as rest.

"Hey, handsome," Allison called, her voice light and commanding. "Why don't you two give us a hand setting up camp? We're staying here tonight."

I hadn't realized how much time had passed. Even with no signal, my phone's clock still worked. It was late—too late. The weight of the underground pressed heavier now. I nodded slowly. There wasn't much else to do.

As we moved toward the gear, I glanced back one more time at the sarcophagi, half expecting them to shift, to breathe. They remained still. But something inside me knew the night wouldn't end without them finding a way back into my thoughts. Or into my dreams.

The camp was set up in a big circle with a fire in the middle. Allison seemed to have everything planned—down to tents, food, and even medical kits. She knew we would be down here for a long time, and she came prepared. Part of me was glad she did; a little comfort could go a long way. Luckily, there were some old wooden crates or something in one of the rooms near the chamber that we could burn, giving a little warmth to the cool air that lingered down here like breath held too long. Allison was even generous enough to share some sleeping bags she had brought. Like she knew—had known—we were going to need them. I thanked her, even though part of me wanted to push it all back at her. Even if it meant sleeping on the stone floor. But then I thought of my mother and Evelyn. They deserved something soft. Some comfort in this buried world.

A simple meal was made by one of her men—Griffin, I think. It wasn't Lucas-level cuisine, but it wasn't terrible either. Smoky, salty, warm. It grounded us in something real. Afterward, we sat around the fire, the heat flickering against the ancient walls, the glow catching in the sheen of condensation above. Some of her men patrolled the surrounding edges of the chamber. I couldn't tell if they were guarding us or watching us. Probably both.

"So, what lies beyond here?" Allison asked, breaking the long silence. Her voice was even, but something about it was different now. Less venom, more curiosity. The flamelight softened the angles of her face, casting gentle shadows over the edges of her calculating expression.

I hesitated, then answered. We were all in this now.

"There are four trails," I said, staring into the fire. "One of strength, wisdom, will, and truth."

"Sounds... mythic," Lucas murmured. He was trying to make light of it, but the edge in his voice betrayed the nerves underneath.

Confusion flickered across several faces. My mother's expression tightened. She sat straighter. She didn't like where this was going. I couldn't blame her. Neither did I.

"It would make sense—to test worthiness," my mother added, her voice clipped, professional. But there was something else there. A weight she wasn't sharing.

I glanced at her. She looked away too quickly.

"Test worthiness? Like a rite of passage?" Evelyn asked. She was leaning forward now, brow furrowed.

"Maybe," I said. "Or maybe it's a trap."

"Oh good," Griffin muttered from his seat, poking the fire with a stick. "Tests and traps. Classic combo."

"This should be fun," Allison said, stretching her legs out toward the fire. "Seems like we're going to have an eventful day tomorrow."

There was a hint of something else in her tone. Not sarcasm. Not excitement. Almost... weariness.

I looked at her, trying not to let the anger surface. We were only here because of her. If anything happened to Evelyn or my mom or Lucas, it would be on her.

"Only because of you," I said.

Allison looked over at me, then down at the fire. Her smirk faded.

"You can't expect things to be hidden forever, dear," she said, her voice quieter than I expected. Then she stood, dusted off her pants, and walked away toward her sentries. Not triumphant. Just... tired?

I breathed deeply, trying to extinguish the heat rising in my chest.

Evelyn's hand found mine. Her warmth cut through my frustration. My mother caught the moment, her gaze thoughtful. Her shoulders were straighter than before, but her eyes were shadowed. She was proud of what she was discovering, yes—but wary of what it might cost.

"Promise me something," I said. "Promise me we'll all get through this together."

"Of course," Lucas replied instantly. The others nodded.

"Besides, you can get us through this. I know you can."

I hoped he was right. I didn't feel it.

"He's right," Evelyn said. "And I'll be right next to you the entire time."

I turned to my mother. She met my gaze with that familiar softness I'd seen through every stage of my life. The same unwavering belief.

"You must trust yourself, because we all trust you," she said. "You can do this, Phoenix. And we'll be here for you."

Her words settled like warm weight in my chest. Familiar. Reassuring. Terrifying.

"I think we should all get some rest," she said, standing. She gave me a small smile—one I'd seen after scraped knees, nightmares, and graduation speeches—before disappearing into her tent.

Lucas was next, giving a nod before heading to his own space.

Evelyn stayed beside me. She leaned her head on my shoulder. Slowly, I rested mine atop hers, letting the silence carry us. A calm, quiet rhythm. Her breath, my heartbeat.

Eventually she shifted, looked up at me. I leaned forward, kissed her gently. She smiled and nestled into my chest, arms curled around me.

"I believe in you, Phoenix," she said, still watching the flames. "I'm with you till the end."

"I know," I whispered.

We stayed there for another hour before finally heading to the tent. One sleeping bag, big enough for two. I didn't think we'd sleep—but somehow, we did.

That was until the dream began.

TWENTY

NIGHTMARE

"DREAMS TEND TO TELL STORIES"

All that lay in front of me was darkness. Not just a lack of light—but a presence. Heavy, absolute. I couldn't even see my hands or feet as I walked, though I wasn't sure if I was walking at all. It felt more like floating, suspended in ink, every step soundless, weightless. An endless void stretched around me in every direction. Where should I even go? Was there even a destination? The worst part wasn't the emptiness—it was the feeling of being completely alone. Not just solitude, but abandonment. As if the world itself had turned away.

Cold—

Darkness—

Silence—

The words echoed, unbidden. Not spoken aloud, but pulsing through my bones like remembered pain.

I reached out with trembling hands, desperate to anchor myself to something. But there was nothing. Just the vast, indifferent dark pressing in around me. I couldn't even feel the clothes on my body. I sensed I was clothed, but the fabric had no weight, no texture. It was as if I'd been stripped of everything but thought.

A memory flickered—my professor, Dr. Dawson, reaching for me with blood on her hands. Her lips moved in warning, but the words never came. Was this what she saw before the end? Was this what took her?

I remembered falling asleep next to Evelyn—her warmth, her breath against my chest—and now, this. The sudden, cruel cut of absence. How had I gone from that fragile peace to this void?

Then, a thread of hope: light.

Distant and dim, like a candle on the horizon of eternity. I moved toward it, though my steps made no sound. It remained far for what felt like hours, or seconds—time meant nothing here. I just needed to reach it. Needed to know I wasn't trapped forever in this dreamless dark.

Then came the sound—soft, deliberate. The rhythmic drip of water striking stone. The first real thing.

I turned toward it, adjusting my path. My senses sharpened. The sound grew clearer, and finally, I felt it. Cool, clean water traced over my fingers. I dropped to my knees, cupped my hands, and touched the smooth pool that had formed beneath the dripping source.

That meant a ceiling. That meant walls. This place—had form. Had limits.

I rose and kept going, always toward the light. My hands grazed the air until they found something new. Solid. Stone. It was jagged at first, like a natural cave, but the longer I followed it, the more deliberate it became. The stone grew smoother, structured. Square grooves, intentional joins. Block by block, it whispered of human—or inhuman—craft.

I traced its length with my hand, and as I did, I swore I felt something beneath the stone. Not warmth exactly, but... energy. A low thrum. Like the heartbeat of something ancient.

The water had faded behind me, swallowed by the dark. Now I had only the wall and the flicker of growing light ahead.

And something else.

A presence.

Not seen, not heard. But felt. Like breath on the back of my neck.

My pulse quickened. My footsteps faltered. A coldness touched my spine—not the ambient chill of the dark, but a directed cold, like fingers trailing up my back.

This wasn't just a dream. It wasn't memory.

This was a warning.

I pressed on. The light was closer now, gold and flickering like firelight behind a doorway.

But I didn't feel saved.

I felt judged.

The light finally broke the darkness like a whispered promise. As it crept into view, a massive door revealed itself—etched into stone, its face covered with intricate carvings that spiraled outward like veins or roots. The designs felt ancient, older than language, humming with a history I couldn't grasp. There was no paint, no vibrant hue, only the gray of time and erosion. Moisture had carved tiny channels through the surface, giving the impression that the stone itself had wept for centuries.

Beside it stood a single torch in a bronze sconce, its flame swaying gently. I stepped into the light and, for the first time since the dream began, saw my hands. They were mine—scarred, tense, trembling slightly. My clothes were exactly as I remembered them: the same hoodie, the same jeans. Yet they felt like a costume on borrowed skin.

A breeze slipped through the cracks of the stone door, brushing past me like a sigh. It wasn't cold in the normal sense—it felt ancient, like something long buried was breathing just beyond the threshold. I could taste salt and dust on the air, and something else, too. Mourning. The grief was palpable, and not mine alone. The very walls seemed to hum with it.

Driven by a mixture of dread and compulsion, I reached out and lifted the torch. Its warmth didn't comfort me. It only threw longer shadows. Still, I stepped forward, pressing the door open. It gave way without resistance.

The hallway beyond was narrow, its walls smooth and unbroken. The incline began almost immediately—subtle at first, then steeper with each step. The path forced me upward like I was being tested, made to ascend into something I wasn't ready for. Each footfall echoed like it was being judged.

That strange breeze still pressed at my back and pulled at my chest in turn. It felt like lungs exhaling around me, as if the space were alive. My torch cast flickering patterns across the walls, making the stone seem to ripple, like it was watching me.

There were no markings, no guidance. Just stone and slope and silence. But I began to feel a pressure behind my eyes. A hum—not heard, but felt—like memory or a name just out of reach.

I don't know how long I walked. Time unraveled here, coiling into itself. Minutes could have been hours. Hours could have been none at all. The fog wasn't around me—it was inside me, blunting thought, dulling emotion, numbing everything but that rising thrum.

And still I walked.

Silence—

Cold—

Death—

Standing before me was yet another door, this one made of wood. Carved beautifully with etchings of a massive tree in its center. Around it stood so many, but they seemed sad, and I felt the same grief and couldn't understand why. This whole area seemed that way, like a great sadness was here. Why, why did it feel like that? Why was the weight of the air so filled with grief? What was beyond these doors that made it so?

Before I could even think, I pulled at the door, and it opened easily. Taking those effortless steps inside and not looking back. The more I moved, the weight of sadness and grief made it difficult to walk. Like it made the air thick until it was hard to breathe. It was slowly suffocating me until I could no longer hold it in. At the very center, the room was warmly lit by torches. The stone walls were colorless with no decoration. In the center stood four things that made my heart stop.

Four stone rectangles stood evenly spaced in the center of the room. I couldn't mistake them. They were coffins. This was the sadness and grief that I felt. The same that weighted the very air around this place. Now the only question was, who were they? Who lay in this tomb? I crouched down to see if any markers remained that could tell me who were now dead. As I looked, I found nothing, not a single thing that could help me identify them. Who were these people, or was there anything in the coffins at all? There had to be something, so I looked at the room, hoping there was anything that could help me understand.

I used the word "understand" a lot, like trying to make sense. Why was that? Why did I even try to understand sometimes? I should just leave this place and never return. Walk away, because in truth, it probably did not even matter. What could I do to save these people anyway? They were already dead. All I could do was nothing. Nothing could change these people's fate. Yet I still had to know. I needed to see who they were, and for some reason I felt drawn to them. Like I knew them.

I did the one thing every nerve in my body screamed against. My mind howled with protest, but I couldn't stop. I had to know. Who were they? Why did this grief feel so personal? Like a memory I had never lived but couldn't forget. My fingers, trembling with dread, found the edge of the first coffin. I gripped the stone and pushed.

It resisted me—like it knew I shouldn't—but I forced it open. Light crept in slowly, like a whisper of truth. And there, lying still in cold stone, was Lucas. His body limp, a dried wound barely hidden beneath his hand. It looked so peaceful… so final.

My knees buckled. I dropped beside him.

Cold—

Limp—

Silence—

Death—

"No," I whispered. The word fractured in my throat. "No, no, no—"

Grief slammed into me like a wave. I couldn't think. Couldn't breathe. My best friend, gone. No reason. No warning. Just a corpse in stone. My heart clawed in my chest, searching for denial. For anything.

But the silence offered no mercy.

I staggered to the next coffin, mind screaming against every step. I opened it slower this time, already knowing what I'd find.

My mother.

Her face was soft in death, as if she'd merely fallen asleep mid-study. There was no pain on her features, but the ache in my chest turned unbearable. My protector. My guide. Gone. I let out a sound—somewhere between a sob and a scream—as tears streaked my cheeks.

"Why—how—?" I couldn't even finish the questions. I was unraveling. Piece by piece.

The third lid was heavier. Or maybe my strength was failing. But I had to see. I had to know.

When the lid shifted, and the light fell across her face, the last of my restraint shattered.

Evelyn.

She was still, her beauty untouched by death. But the fire that had always danced in her—gone. I reached down and took her hand. Cold. Empty. Nothing. A hollow shell of the woman I'd just held beside me hours—no, moments—ago.

I fell to my knees between the coffins, surrounded by the people I loved most.

"I was supposed to protect you," I choked. "All of you. I was supposed to keep you safe."

Tears blurred everything. I couldn't breathe. Couldn't think. Only the endless drumbeat of loss echoed inside me.

Cold—

Limp—

Silence—

Death—

There was something else, however. One more coffin. It sat at the end like a punctuation mark on pain—silent, patient, inevitable. I pulled myself together, every joint trembling, breath stuttering as I staggered toward it.

Who could be left?

A friend? A forgotten face? My father?

I reached for the lid, and dread pooled in my stomach. The stone resisted, not with weight, but with intent—as if it wanted to stay closed. As if it knew what I was about to see.

But I opened it.

The torchlight spilled in, illuminating the final horror.

Me.

It was me.

I recoiled so violently I nearly dropped the torch. My own lifeless body lay still in the stone, eyes closed, hands crossed, a slight crease in the brow like I had died mid-thought. My skin was pale, waxy. My face emptied of every fire, every flaw. Hollow.

Cold—

Silence—

Death—

A scream built inside me but couldn't escape. My throat locked, my chest seized. I stumbled back, but my eyes couldn't turn away.

I was dead. Gone. Forgotten.

Every fear I carried—the ones I buried in silence—came rushing forward. I had failed. I hadn't saved them. I hadn't saved myself. I hadn't become anything worth remembering.

Tucked in the hands of my corpse was a scrap of parchment. Shaking, I plucked it free, the paper soft as ash.

He died losing the people he loved. They died before him as he was unable to save them. He died a broken and worthless soul.

The words hit harder than any wound. They were truth wearing the face of cruelty.

My knees buckled again. I collapsed fully this time, hitting the floor with a gasp that wasn't pain—it was surrender. My chest heaved, but no air came. My hands clawed at the ground. My vision blurred until even the flicker of the torch was gone.

I broke.

There was no sobbing now. No resistance. Just silence—internal and absolute.

This is how I die.

Not in battle. Not in sacrifice. But alone. Forgotten. Worthless.

My mind spun with memories—my mother's smile, Evelyn's warmth, Lucas's laughter—and one by one, they faded, like firelight smothered by ash. I was the end. I was the ruin.

But even in that void, a thought sparked.

This isn't real.

A fragment of awareness. A thread of defiance.

If I were dead, how could I know it?

Somewhere, buried beneath the despair, that sliver of reason ignited. I wasn't dead. Not yet.

I pushed myself from the floor with trembling arms and stumbled forward blindly. My breath came in gasps. I didn't know where I was going—I just knew I had to move. Had to flee.

I ran.

Down the hall. Through the grief. Screaming until my throat tore raw, until my voice was no longer my own. It wasn't just sound—it was a fracture in reality, like I was tearing myself out of existence.

I ran from the coffins, from the words, from the reflection of my own failure. From their eyes. From my own dead face. My body wasn't just broken—it was undone. A thread yanked from the fabric of everything I believed about myself.

I stumbled, feet catching on stone, hands slapping against the walls, skimming moisture-slick surfaces that felt like skin. The air pulsed with memory and judgment. Every step forward felt like falling backward.

Then the ground vanished beneath me.

I didn't fall. I plunged. Gravity forgotten, breath stolen. A silent scream tore through my head. Light and sound vanished.

There was no air, no direction, no up or down—only crushing pressure and cold, suffocating dark. Like being buried alive in a sky without stars.

And then—

Impact.

Stone and flesh collided. My knees cracked against rough ground. My hands tore open on gravel. My voice had turned to ash. My mind was no longer mine—it was a mirror shattered, each shard cutting deeper than the last.

I looked up—and saw nothing. Not even the flicker of a torch.

Just black. Endless. Complete.

And in that blackness, I knew:

This wasn't fear.

This was truth.

The truth that I was never enough. That I would never save them. That I was only ever pretending. A shadow of a guardian. A ghost of a son. A hollow boy masquerading as a flame.

And then, in the middle of that devastating quiet—

I whispered, barely audible even to myself:

"Please... please, someone..."

But no one came.

My scream had become silence.

And the world vanished.

And all that remained...

Was me.

And then—

Something cracked.

Not the floor. Not the air.

Me.

A seam inside my mind gave way. The despair hadn't passed—it had broken open something deeper. Something buried.

And I saw a flicker.

Not light. Not hope. But fire.

A single thread of gold, curling in the black like a wisp of smoke. It twisted through the dark, danced above the stone like it remembered my name.

And something ancient within me—older than grief, older than language—reached for it.

I didn't speak. I didn't think. I simply moved.

Toward the fire.

Toward the truth that hadn't yet burned me.

As I reached for it, it flared—just once—and struck.

And everything changed.

I awoke gasping, lungs straining like I'd been underwater. My skin was slick with cold sweat, the fabric of the sleeping bag clinging to me like a second skin. Evelyn was there—kneeling beside me, hands on my shoulders, her voice low and urgent.

"Phoenix, hey—hey, look at me. It's just a dream."

Her eyes locked onto mine, wide with concern but steady. She wasn't fading. She wasn't ash. She was real.

I surged upward and pulled her into my arms, clutching her like I might lose her again. She was warm. Solid. Breathing. Her heartbeat thudded against my chest like a drum pulling me back to the world.

"You're safe?" I whispered against her hair.

"Yes," she said, arms wrapping tighter around me. "I got you. Everything's okay. You're here—with me."

Her voice was a balm. Soft, grounding. Every word pulled me back, away from the edges of whatever that place had been. I leaned into her, eyes closed, letting her presence tether me to the now.

We sat there for a long moment, the tent dim and hushed except for the faint trickle of water outside. My breath slowed.

My muscles eased. The dream still clawed at the edges of my mind, but Evelyn was the light that kept it at bay.

"I saw it," I said, voice hoarse. "It was so real, Evelyn. Like I wasn't just dreaming—I was being warned."

She nodded, brushing damp hair from my forehead. "Tell me."

So I did. Every shape, every shadow, every whisper that had burrowed into me. I told her about the stone, the presence, the fire. I didn't leave anything out—not this time. She listened, never once flinching or pulling away. Her silence wasn't absence—it was acceptance. When I was done, she pressed her forehead to mine.

"You're not alone in this. Whatever it is—whatever it means—you're not facing it by yourself."

I let that truth sink in. Let it fill the hollow places the dream had carved out. I'd been broken in that world. But here, in her arms, I could still rebuild.

Eventually, she guided me back down. We lay together again, her hand never leaving mine. Her breath steadied, slow and rhythmic, as sleep took her. I stayed awake a while longer, staring at the tent ceiling as if afraid it would vanish, too.

The night was still. The faint, endless drip of water echoed from somewhere beyond the canvas. I inhaled deeply. Counted the breath. Let the reality of this place wrap around me like a second skin.

And finally, I slept again.

This time, there were no dreams.

TWENTY-ONE

THE ARMORY

"THE PULSE OF MEMORY"

I awoke to the sounds of shuffling feet and the rustle of canvas, punctuated by the low murmur of voices and the occasional metallic clink of crates being shifted. The earthy scent of damp stone mingled with the faint tang of burned coffee and leather, grounding me in the moment. The cold of the stone floor beneath us seeped into my bones, but the warmth of Evelyn beside me offset it. Her breath, slow and even against my collarbone, felt like the last remnant of a dream I didn't want to let go.

Part of me wished I could just stay curled up here, wrapped around her like this was some camping trip, not the lead-up to a life-or-death trial hidden beneath ancient stone. Her head rested against my shoulder, her arm draped over my chest, fingers loosely curled in the fabric of my shirt. For a fleeting second, the illusion of peace felt almost real.

"Good morning," Evelyn murmured, her voice thick with sleep as she stirred. Her eyes, barely open, were glassy with fatigue but softened when they met mine. She shifted, her palm flattening over my heart. We stayed like that for another breath, listening to the subtle rhythms of the camp waking up.

"We should probably get going," I whispered, brushing a stray strand of hair from her face. "Sounds like everyone else is already up."

She groaned in protest and turned away from the light filtering through the flap of the tent. I leaned in, pressing my forehead gently to hers, breathing in the scent of her hair—lavender, faintly mixed with ash and old paper.

"Five more minutes," she mumbled, pulling the blanket up over her shoulder like a defiant child.

"I don't think we have it," I replied as our names echoed faintly through the stone passageways. Evelyn sighed and rolled back toward me. Her hand moved slowly across my chest again, this time not stopping until it settled against my side.

"I demand sleep once all of this is done," she said with a weak smile, her voice somewhere between exhaustion and fond exasperation.

I chuckled softly, nodding. "Deal."

We dressed quickly—layers pulled on with minimal grace. The fabric was scratchy against our skin, and the water we splashed on our faces was frigid, jarring us into wakefulness. The morning pastries were dense and dry, leaving chalky crumbs on our tongues, and the coffee was bitter enough to sting. Still, it felt like a ritual—something familiar in a world unraveling.

Outside, the camp moved like a well-oiled machine. The air buzzed with purpose. One of Allison's men broke down our tent with mechanical precision, the fabric folding like muscle memory. The ground where we'd slept was already fading into the chaos.

My mother stood at the center of the bustle, clipboard in hand, barking orders to a young soldier while Lucas stood a few paces behind her, arms crossed, eyes glazed. The image of the two of them together—her fire, his silence—struck a strange chord in me.

And then there was Allison. Dressed impeccably, already alert, already watching.

"Hope you lovebirds slept well," she called, her voice slick with implication as we approached. "Once camp is cleared, we'll press on."

"She's perky this morning," I muttered under my breath.

Evelyn jabbed me in the ribs with her elbow. "Can we have one morning without conflict?"

I straightened, forcing a smile as Allison's sharp eyes slid over us. The others were preoccupied—checking equipment, eating, muttering over maps—but her gaze lingered.

Lucas stood apart, his fingers twitching against his arms in a nervous rhythm. I recognized the tic—he did it when things were too quiet, too uncertain.

Breakfast was a blur of stale sweetness and bitter sips. The coffee tasted like ash bark and scorched earth. Evelyn and Lucas drank it with the same reverence as they might a sacred elixir. My mother, meanwhile, clutched her tin cup like a relic from Olympus.

Allison snapped her fingers, and the group began to form up. We were moving. The corridor ahead was narrow, the ceiling pressing closer, the air tightening like a fist. I took point, naturally—the sacrificial lamb.

The walls whispered as we walked. Old stone. Older secrets. Every step seemed to awaken echoes—footsteps that weren't ours, breaths that belonged to someone long gone. The scent of the passage shifted from dust to metal to something faintly like cedar.

Then the chamber opened before us like a breath held too long.

The scent hit first—oiled metal, old cedarwood, and something faintly metallic, like blood on steel. Torches lined the walls in perfect symmetry, their flames unnaturally still. The chamber wasn't massive, but it felt vast. Reverent.

Weapons lined the walls in curated silence: blades of every shape and age, spears with etched shafts, rows of arrows fletched with black feathers. Armor sets gleamed beneath the firelight. It was a museum, a sanctum. A war shrine.

The others fell into hushed awe. Even Allison paused.

My mother had her notebook out before I blinked. She moved with purpose, eyes devouring every detail. She reached for a Spartan greave and traced the etchings with reverent fingers.

"Phoenix, come look!" she called, beckoning me with the kind of excitement I hadn't seen in years. She practically bounced on her heels, eyes sparkling with curiosity.

I approached slowly, the sound of my boots muted by the dustless stone floor. A bronze cuirass sat on a pedestal before her, its surface gleaming. Etched into the chest-plate was a design I didn't recognize—something that looked like a flame twisted around a tree, coiling skyward with ancient reverence.

"You're like a kid in a toy store," I said, smiling.

"And you're the only one here who appreciates how incredible this is," she replied, not looking up. Her fingers hovered just above the etching, trembling slightly. "This motif… I've seen versions of it before in the Etruscan collection at the Villa Giulia. But not like this. Not this detailed."

"Do you think it's connected to something older? Maybe... someone like the ancient guardians you used to talk about?" I asked, lowering my voice. The closeness of the chamber made every word feel like a confession.

She finally looked at me, her expression shifting—softening into something more maternal, more curious. "It could be. I don't think this is just about preserving artifacts anymore. This—" she gestured around us slowly "—this is ceremonial. Deliberate. Someone meant for you to see this. To stand here."

We stood in silence for a beat. She stepped toward the pedestal again and ran her fingers along the edge of the armor as if it might whisper a secret. Then, as if remembering herself, she turned back and placed her hand gently on my shoulder.

"Sometimes I worry I've pushed you too far into this world," she said. "I brought you into digs, lectures, debates... But I never imagined it would become real in this way. That the past would reach for you like this."

I reached up and touched her hand briefly. "You didn't push me. You gave me something to believe in. And now I have to see it through."

She nodded, her eyes misting for the briefest second. "Then let's make sure you choose right. Not just with weapons—but with everything. We may not get another chance."

"Do you remember when we visited Karnak?" she said, her voice barely above a whisper. "You couldn't stop asking questions about the carvings on the pillars. You wanted to read every single one."

"You let me trace them with your chalk," I said. "Told me they were 'the world's oldest post-it notes.'"

She laughed, the sound bright and unguarded. It bounced off the stone and lingered in the space between us.

For a heartbeat, I was ten again. Sand in my sneakers. Her hand guiding mine across weathered stone. A sense of belonging I hadn't felt in years.

Evelyn drifted to my side, her eyes wide with wonder. She reached out and brushed her fingers along a hanging helm, then down the flat of a sword's blade. The steel was cool to the touch, but her breath caught like it burned.

Lucas stood quietly nearby, tracing a gauntlet's ridges with one hand. His gaze locked with mine. He didn't smile, didn't speak—but he nodded. That was enough.

I picked up a Xiphos. The moment my fingers closed around the hilt, something surged up my arm—a jolt of recognition, like the blade had been waiting. It wasn't just balanced; it felt intimate. Right. The leather-wrapped grip molded perfectly to my palm, and the weight hummed in my wrist like a tuning fork struck.

The blade wasn't ornate. No flourish. Just a line of steel honed with intent. Not decorative—functional. Efficient. A weapon built not to intimidate but to end things.

I turned it over, ran my thumb along the flat edge, the cold metal sending a tremor into my bones. It wasn't pain—it was memory. Something buried in the marrow. I could almost smell salt air, sweat, and iron. Hear footsteps pounding through sand. My breath caught.

Maybe I'd seen this blade in a book. Maybe in a dream. Or maybe some ancient echo deep inside had chosen it long before I arrived here.

"This place just keeps surprising me," I said, voice low, as my eyes swept the chamber again.

"If only people knew what was really down here," Evelyn replied. Her voice was soft, almost reverent.

We walked between the racks like pilgrims before relics. The torches burned steadily, casting long shadows that reached for the ceiling. The air was thick with silence. Tension. Memory.

Then Allison's boot tapped the floor—sharp, impatient.

"We should get moving," she said, her voice breaking the spell. Her men began to fall into line.

As I moved to follow, Evelyn's fingers found my arm. She gave it a squeeze. Her eyes met mine, and something unspoken passed between us.

I turned back once more. Lucas stood at the threshold, half turned. He parted his lips, but no words came. Just another nod.

Behind us, the flame closest to the entrance flickered. A ripple. As if stirred by breath.

The fire had noticed.

And something inside me had begun to burn.

We didn't walk much further when the corridor constricted again before spilling us into yet another chamber. Evelyn and Lucas flanked me closely, their movements tense and wary. I caught glimpses of them as we walked—Evelyn brushing her fingers against the stone wall, like trying to sense vibrations beneath her skin. Lucas kept adjusting the strap across his chest, his breathing slightly ragged. They were watching me, wondering if I still had a plan, if I'd found some hidden path forward in this madness.

I hadn't.

I wanted to lie. Pretend I knew what came next. But the truth was a hollow thing in my chest. All I could do was move forward and hope the next step wasn't a fall into oblivion.

The ceiling began to arch as the chamber widened. Something about this room felt vast yet compressed—like walking into a pressure chamber. The stone was smoother here, plainer, but unnerving in its simplicity. There were no markings. No glyphs. Just seamless, ageless stone that seemed to swallow sound.

The floor stretched flat and immense, vanishing into blackened chasms at its edges. Torches flickered along the perimeter walls, but their flames danced unnaturally—as if trying to warn us, not light the way. The air was thick with a biting dampness that clung to the throat and lungs. Underneath, a faint copper tang lingered. Blood. Or what remained of it long after the spilling.

Each footstep echoed loud and sharp. I could hear the scratch of boots, the whisper of leather armor shifting, even the shallow clicks of Evelyn's necklace against her collarbone. Everything was too loud. Too clear.

Then Allison's voice cut through the stillness. "Just another empty room?" she said, pushing forward with that same unshakable strut. Her men followed like trained phantoms, eyes scanning, weapons loosely in hand.

I didn't move. I couldn't.

The tension in my gut twisted like a blade. My heart was a steady thrum of warning. Lucas drew in closer to Evelyn. When our eyes met, he gave me the smallest nod, but his fingers danced at his sides—his nervous tell from childhood, still unbroken.

"I don't like this," I said, almost without realizing. My voice cracked dry across the space.

Everyone froze. Finally, they listened.

Their heads turned. My mother's brows knit. Evelyn looked at me like she was about to ask a question but thought better of it. Then her hand slipped into mine, firm and warm and trembling just enough that I noticed.

And then it happened.

A glint. Faint, like moonlight on polished stone. A reflection that shouldn't have been there.

Thwip.

An arrow tore through the air like a whisper of death. One of Allison's men collapsed, a bolt buried deep in his throat. He hit the ground with a wet thud, blood seeping from his lips.

"Down!" someone shouted—too late.

More arrows followed. Swift. Merciless. Piercing armor, flesh, bone. A man screamed until it became a gurgle. Another twitched as he fell, limbs spasming from the shock. They fell like paper targets, their bodies buckling under the weight of unseen wrath.

I grabbed Evelyn and shoved her behind a column. Lucas stumbled but ducked beside us, dragging one of Allison's wounded men out of the open. Screams tore through the air, high and shrill and helpless.

And then—footsteps.

Fast. Coordinated. Loud like thunder and silent like ghosts. From crevices in the walls, from behind broken pillars, from trapdoors we never noticed, they came.

Dozens. No—hundreds.

Cloaked figures cloaked in sand-colored wraps, armor glinting beneath like bones made of bronze. Their faces hidden. Only their eyes showed—cold, precise, inhuman in focus.

They moved as one. Not like men. Like a tide.

Allison's remaining men opened fire. Flashes of muzzle flare ignited the gloom, but it didn't matter. The enemy advanced. Silent. Unstoppable.

One by one, they fell. Cut down with terrifying efficiency. Blood spattered the floor, the walls, the torches. It steamed against the cold stone.

I tried to reach Evelyn again, dragging her deeper behind cover. I couldn't see Lucas anymore. My mother was screaming something—I couldn't hear her. My ears rang from the clash of steel, the crack of rifles, the wet thumps of bodies dropping.

Sand kicked up in the chaos. It coated my tongue, stung my eyes, filled my nose with grit and decay. I tasted blood but didn't know if it was mine.

A moment of near-silence fell—then a spear clattered near me.

A second later, everything stopped.

Stillness collapsed onto the room like a tomb slamming shut. The only sound was the rasp of my breathing and the subtle crunch of movement in the blood-soaked sand.

I forced my eyes open.

They were everywhere—shoulder to shoulder, blades drawn, bows slung over backs. A formation of cloaked warriors that seemed carved from shadow. The air around them buzzed with presence, like they were more than just soldiers.

They were executioners.

I searched frantically, my heartbeat deafening.

Then I saw them.

Evelyn, Lucas, and my mother—on their knees, blades at their throats. Evelyn's lip was split. Lucas had a bruise swelling under one eye. My mother bled from her temple, but her spine was straight.

They weren't just hostages.

They were offerings.

The air around me pulsed with something wild and ancient. My hands were trembling—but not from fear. From fury.

I stepped forward.

One of the cloaked figures moved to meet me. He lowered his hood. His skin was weathered like driftwood, his hair steel-gray. His eyes were ancient and alive.

He lifted his sword.

"Choose your weapon wisely," he said. His voice was calm. Cold. Final.

I stood my ground.

"Let them go."

"Your test of strength must be passed—or you all perish."

My blood ran ice and fire. This was the Trial. And we'd passed the armory like children in a museum.

"Phoenix?" Allison's voice drifted toward me. She sounded… human. Shaken. I turned.

She stood untouched. No dirt. No blood. Just watching.

"This is on you," I said.

She flinched.

"You're not going to help them by coming after me," she hissed.

"No, but I'll sleep better."

I pointed toward her fallen men. "You should be over there."

She said nothing. Just stared. Her shoulders sunk. Her mask was gone.

I turned my back on her.

Back to the armory.

Back to where the real war would begin.

To fight. To endure. To protect them.

Even if I had to become something unrecognizable to do it.

"When the fire awakens, it will not ask for permission.
It will remember what the world tried to forget.
And it will burn until the truth stands alone."
— The Guardians

TWENTY-TWO

THE TRAIL OF STRENGTH

"RESTRAINT IS DEEPEST STRENGTH"

I stepped back into the room that held all the weapons, and the air shifted—no longer quiet with reverence but alive with a charged expectancy. Torchlight pulsed along the stone walls, throwing our shadows across the room like wraiths. The scents were sharper than before: oil thick on the leather grips, the copper tang of old blood baked into the metal, and a new undercurrent of ozone, like the room was electrified. The very air seemed to buzz, as if the chamber itself had been waiting.

My boots scraped softly on the stone, each step echoing like a drumbeat. The weight of what I was about to do pressed down, every breath deeper, slower, heavier. I was no longer just a visitor admiring relics. Now I searched with intention, each artifact a possible lifeline. This wasn't a museum. It was a crucible. A place where destinies were chosen.

"What do you think you're doing?" Allison's voice cracked across the chamber behind me. The disbelief in her tone was unmistakable.

I didn't turn. I ran my hand along the handle of a short axe, then let it fall. "He said to choose a weapon."

My fingers found a piece of armor next—a bronze cuirass shaped to fit the torso, unmistakably Greek, burnished to a soft gleam that caught the firelight like living gold. I knelt and lowered it gently to the floor, the clang of metal on stone ringing out like a bell tolling for the dead. The sound sent a chill through me.

Allison stepped closer, her footsteps faster now, uneven. Her voice was taut. "We need to leave. Now. This is suicide."

I looked over my shoulder at her, my expression flat. "And while we do, they will die. Evelyn. Lucas. My mother. You're asking me to walk away from them. I can't. I won't."

She stared, her brow tight with fury—or fear. I couldn't tell which. Maybe both. Her mouth opened, then closed.

"So, you're just going to storm in? Alone?"

"Yes," I said. "Actually. I am."

"You're going to die, Phoenix. And so will they. If you charge out there swinging like some damn—"

"Then I die!" I snapped, my voice rising like a wave. The firelight trembled. "At least I'll try. I won't let them suffer because I hesitated. I won't be that person. Not again. Not ever."

She flinched like the words struck her. Her hands clenched at her sides.

"You're such a stubborn ass," she muttered. But her voice cracked. There was something behind it. "You do realize your life matters, right? That you're not just some expendable hero?"

I stilled. That was the first time she'd said anything like that. From anyone else, it might've felt like comfort. From her, it landed like a challenge.

I turned back to the armor. "I'm doing this. Either step aside or help."

She didn't move. Just stood there, lips parted slightly, like she wanted to say more. But then, slowly, she stepped back.

I pulled my shirt off, the cold air biting at my skin, and reached for the armor. It was heavier than it looked, its weight anchoring me to the moment. As I slipped it on, the plates scraped across my shoulders with a grating groan. The cold bronze kissed my chest, and for a moment, it felt like it might fuse to my skin.

The straps were stiff, resisting my fingers like they didn't want to be bound again. But I wrestled them into place, the buckles clicking into their ancient grooves. Each one a promise. A pact. A burden.

I moved to the weapons. Each blade called to me, but most felt wrong—too long, too curved, too ceremonial. But then I saw it: that Xiphos, short and deadly, its blade gently curved inward. It didn't gleam like the others. It looked... used. Trusted. My hand closed around the hilt.

A jolt. Like static in my fingertips, racing down to my spine. Not pain. Recognition.

The leather grip was molded as if it had known my hand for years. The weight was flawless. The blade, balanced. It hummed in the air with restrained violence. Not built to be displayed. Built to finish what others couldn't.

I drew a breath, long and deep. The scent of metal and sweat filled my lungs. My pulse slowed. The sword wasn't just right—it was mine.

Behind me, Allison spoke again, quieter this time. "If I didn't know any better, I could mistake you for a Spartan."

I turned, and there she stood—not leaving, not running. In her hands, she held a bow. A quiver of arrows slung over her back. Her posture was ready. Her gaze steady.

"I guess this means you're helping," I said.

She shrugged. "Someone's gotta make sure you don't get yourself killed. Besides... I never liked bullies."

I gave a small, breathless laugh. It didn't last long.

In the polished metal of the Xiphos, I caught my reflection. Bare arms, marred by blood and bruises. The armor clung to my chest like it belonged there. My face was hard, alien in its focus. I didn't look like me. But maybe this was who I had to be now.

I rotated my shoulders, testing the fit, the balance. The weight felt right. Real.

Allison nodded. "Let's go get them back."

I turned toward the doorway. As I crossed the threshold, the flame nearest the entrance flared high, casting light across the walls like a silent salute. A ripple in the air washed over me, warm and strange—like something old had taken notice.

The fire had seen what I had become.

I stepped forward, sword in hand.

And the room let me go, like a forge releasing the blade it had just tempered.

They stood there, still as stone, their faces hidden behind tan cloaks, eyes lost in shadow. The air thickened with the breath of waiting violence. My footsteps echoed like war drums as I crossed the threshold, heart hammering with each step. The torches lining the room burned low, their light flickering against the smooth, ageless walls. Every part of this place felt ancient, ceremonial—haunted. I could feel the weight of memory pressing down from the ceiling, soaked into the stone, waiting for a verdict.

The man in the center stepped forward. Taller than the rest. His presence made the others seem like echoes—lesser impressions of something real. His voice broke the silence with a calm finality.

"Your trial of strength will be measured in a battle to the death."

"So be it," I murmured, though my voice didn't sound like mine.

The odds were absurd—impossible, even. A couple hundred elite soldiers, forged in discipline and purpose, trained beyond anything I had ever encountered, and me—a single man, a former martial arts student, whose only weapon now was desperation honed to a razor's edge. This wasn't just uneven. This was mythic in its cruelty.

I wasn't a warrior raised for this. I wasn't bred in the ways of war. I had no divine armor, no shield blessed by old gods. Just breath, blood, pain—and a sword that felt like it remembered another life.

I looked across the chamber and saw Evelyn and Lucas. Bound and kneeling, heads bowed slightly, but their eyes—when they lifted them—met mine with a ferocity that burned. Not pleading. Not broken. But alive. Lucas's jaw was tight, a vein twitching along his temple. Evelyn's lip bled, a thin line that shimmered in the torchlight, but her spine was unyielding. They were beaten, not bowed. They were daring me to be more than I was.

Behind them stood my mother. Her stance, upright and resolute, made her bruises and split skin almost irrelevant. Her gaze locked with mine, not for comfort but for conviction. The unspoken message in her eyes: Do not falter. Not now.

The chamber around us groaned with silence. Torches hissed and spat as if rebelling against the quiet. My heart thundered like a drum-line inside my chest, each beat screaming that there was no turning back. The Xiphos felt heavier now—alive, almost warm. The hilt had molded to my grip by now, not with comfort but purpose. Like it had been waiting for this.

I closed my eyes.

Not to retreat. Not to shield myself from fear.

But to call forth the fury. To dig down through flesh and memory, into something buried. Something feral. I didn't want peace. I wanted fire. I didn't need calm. I needed the kind of silence that came before an earthquake—the quiet before the scream.

I stood at the edge of a threshold not marked in stone but in blood, in sacrifice, in every choice that brought me here. I had no illusions left. No hope for mercy.

I opened my eyes.

And I ran.

I launched forward, boots hammering against the stone like cannon fire, the Xiphos gripped tight in my fist. Each stride thundered through the air, ricocheting off the ancient walls like a war hymn. The line of cloaked warriors rushed to meet me, their momentum eerily silent. Time fractured.

Every detail sharpened into painful clarity. The flutter of their cloaks seemed impossibly slow—like the breath of death itself unfurling. The curved blades shimmered with reflected firelight, catching sparks that danced like fireflies. I saw eyes beneath those hoods—hollow, determined, timeless.

And then they were upon me.

At the last second, I dropped low, dirt scraping my knees, and surged upward in a violent arc, driving my blade straight into the first enemy's chest. The resistance was nonexistent—just the hiss of air as he evaporated into a bloom of ash. His cloak and armor crumpled, ghostlike, to the floor.

He turned to dust.

No scream. No blood. Just silence wrapped in decay.

The suddenness of it buckled my breath. It wasn't death. It was erasure.

I barely registered the awe before instinct snapped back into place. My hands, burning with borrowed memory, seized the falling shoulder plate and swung it like a shield. A spear clanged off the bronze with a jarring crack that rattled my teeth. I twisted hard—muscles shrieking—and redirected my blade toward the next assailant. It carved a clean line across his ribs.

He vanished too, in a slow spiral of powder and silk. The scent he left behind was like incense and scorched parchment. As if history itself had burned away.

Then the silence shattered.

A roar of motion engulfed the chamber as the others surged forward. The trial had begun.

Then chaos erupted.

Dozens surged forward. I parried a spear with a bone-rattling clang, twisted, and drove the Xiphos upward through a throat. He disintegrated, weightless, ephemeral. Sand flew. Ash spiraled. The scent of iron-less dust and scorched linen filled my lungs. My hands ached, fingers bruised from the hilt's bite. The bronze armor clung to me like a second skin, hot and suffocating. Every dent became a tally of the moments I refused to fall.

I rolled beneath a halberd, the steel screaming inches from my face. I rose with a roar and slashed clean through two more. They folded to dust mid-stride. Ash choked the air like battlefield incense.

Allison's arrows whistled overhead—silent and surgically lethal. She stood behind a half-collapsed pillar, her face set in grim resolve. One by one, her shots found marks—knees, shoulders, necks. The soldiers dropped like marionettes with strings severed. But it wasn't enough.

They circled me.

A wall of faceless death, perfectly spaced, blades raised in eerie synchronization. I spun, ducked, kicked the legs out from one, pivoted into a brutal upward stab. Ash exploded. I screamed from the strain, my muscles crying in protest. The stone floor slick with sweat beneath my boots.

I was a storm. A blade moving through water. My vision tunneled. My mind a molten core of instinct. I could see their movements before they made them—every twitch, every feint, every breath. It was more than skill. It was possession. Something else fighting through me.

As if the sword had unlocked something dormant in my blood—memories I never lived, reflexes not mine alone. Each motion echoed with another's—hands that once trained in the desert wind, feet that moved through war generations before I was born. I wasn't just channeling strength—I was reliving it.

It felt impossible, yet undeniable—like the blade had unlocked muscle memories I never earned. Reflexes and timing that should have taken years of training emerged with brutal precision. I didn't know how I moved the way I did, only that it felt natural, instinctual. As if somewhere deep in me, someone else—many someone elses—had fought before, and their echoes now moved through me.

There was no magic spell, no whispered chant. Just something raw and ancestral, as though the chamber itself had chosen to awaken whatever piece of me could survive this. Maybe it was the weapon, maybe it was the place, or maybe I was always meant to reach this breaking point—to find that, in the absence of all reason, something older would rise to meet the chaos.

Not a warrior by training, but by lineage.

A break.

I leapt, vaulting over two soldiers with a twist midair. Landed hard on one knee. My blade drove through another's back and I twisted into the next. Dust. Screams. My lungs burned. My vision blurred at the edges.

Their eyes haunted me—glimpses of gold, silver, empty black. Were they real? Were they people once? Were they watching me from within those cloaks, or were they echoes of forgotten guardians?

Still they came.

The dead fell behind me in heaps that vanished on impact. The Xiphos was no longer a tool. It was an extension of my will. A sacred line that severed death from life. Each slash came easier. My fear faded, replaced by grim purpose.

What would I do for them?

Everything.

I pressed forward through the storm, each step forging a new path in bloodless sacrifice. My hands were numb, my shoulder bruised, my legs streaked with soot and blood. The blade vibrated with each kill. It remembered them. Each one. Their vanishing weight sang through it.

I spun. Parried. Caught a blade against my vambrace. Kicked a man into a column. His body dispersed into mist before he hit the stone.

Then—clarity.

The dust parted.

The one who had spoken first stood waiting, unmoving. Silver hair framed his weathered face like a crown of ice. His eyes held me in place. Not with fear—but understanding. He stepped forward and drew his sword with ritual grace, the motion smooth, sacred. The others stepped back, forming a wide, respectful circle. They knew this would be different.

We met.

The first clang of our blades cracked the silence like lightning splitting a dead sky. Sparks shot outward in brief constellations, and the sheer force of the blow sent shudders through my arms. We circled, slow at first, feet grinding across the ash-slick stone with calculated friction. Every breath felt like a countdown.

He struck first—an arcing downward cut meant to cleave straight through me. I dodged sideways, just barely, the edge whispering past my jaw like cold breath. My counter came sharp and hard, a diagonal slash intended to drive him back—but he didn't stumble. He absorbed it with a pivot, turned, and re-engaged without pause.

His speed was deceptive. Despite his age, he moved with lethal precision. No wasted movement. No flourish. Just grace honed to a terrifying edge. His blade whirled around mine in tight, surgical arcs. I blocked one, two, three strikes—but the fourth slipped through and slashed my upper arm. Pain sang bright through my nerves.

I grunted, staggered. My footing faltered for a breath. He pressed forward with a series of tight feints that forced me into a defensive spiral. I barely parried a thrust to the chest. My legs burned from the effort. My lungs screamed for breath.

Still, I held.

I changed rhythm. Dropped low, swept at his ankles. He jumped—not high, just enough. But it gave me room. I surged upward, slashing toward his ribs. He blocked, but it cost him. I saw his stance shift, the tiniest overcorrection.

I lunged. Our swords locked at the hilts. We were face to face, breathing hard, forearms trembling with pressure. His eyes—those damn eyes—calm as oceans. My own were fire. And then—he smiled. Just a flicker, a twitch at the corner of his mouth. It wasn't mockery. It wasn't triumph. It was recognition. As if, in that moment, he saw me—not as an opponent, but as the answer to some silent question he'd carried for a lifetime. He knew who I was. What I was becoming. And that was all that mattered.

He twisted suddenly, breaking our lock, and his blade nicked my side. I cried out. Blood warmed my ribs, slick against the armor. My grip slipped. He pivoted, came down again.

I fell back, rolled, came up swinging. Our swords met in a blur of light and screeching metal. He blocked but stumbled this time.

Now it was my turn.

I drove him back with reckless force, fury overtaking form. I shouted with each blow, pain and determination fueling every strike. He defended with elegance, but I was the storm now.

One last lunge. A brutal overhead strike. He met it—but the impact jarred his weapon loose.

His sword clattered across the stone.

He dropped to his knees. Head bowed. Hands empty.

And I stood over him, chest heaving, body screaming. The chamber went silent once more—every eye locked on us.

I raised the Xiphos. The dust around us hung still in the air, suspended like a judgment not yet made. I heard no cries. No shouts. No commands.

Evelyn did not scream.

The world held its breath.

But I didn't swing.

I couldn't.

He looked up at me—calm, almost grateful. There was no fear in him. Just clarity. The kind that comes at the end of a very long road.

I lowered the blade.

"It's done," I said, voice raw and hollow. "I've passed."

He nodded once, his voice little more than breath. "Then let the chains be broken."

A sound like shattered glass echoed behind me.

Evelyn. Lucas. My mother—their bindings fell in pieces at their feet. They staggered, blinking into freedom. Allison emerged from the gloom, lowering her bow. Her eyes locked on mine, unreadable.

I dropped to my knees.

And the room exhaled at last. The flames on the torches flared high, not with heat, but with approval.

And somewhere deep in the stone beneath me, I felt it: the armory had accepted me. Not as a warrior.

As a weapon.

His eyes looked at me as he knelt before me.

"You have passed your trial of strength. May it aid you well," he said before he collapsed into dust. No scream, no fall—just silence, and then nothing. As though he had only ever been smoke wrapped in duty.

I turned around and looked at the carnage that followed me. The bodies that had stood like titans just minutes ago were now crumbling, fading into the sandy floor. One by one, they collapsed, their forms turning to dust in a quiet, collective sigh. Even the ones who had held my friends dissolved, their weapons clinking softly as they disappeared into time.

The silence that followed was not peace—it was shellshock. I could hear nothing but my own breath, jagged and dry, and the slow settling of dust. When I looked at Evelyn, Lucas, and my mother, their faces burned into memory. Surprise. Horror. Reverence. They didn't move.

Lucas's mouth was open, his face pale under the grime and blood. His eyes darted across the chamber, not quite landing on me, as if afraid that eye contact might shatter the fragile calm.

Evelyn moved first. Slow, cautious steps. Not like she was approaching her friend—but a weapon still smoking from the last shot. Her hands trembled at her sides. She didn't stop until she was just in front of me.

Her eyes locked onto mine—searching, questioning, aching. Then her hand came up, brushing dust from my cheek. Her touch was warm, and I realized how cold I'd become. My fingers were stiff, wrapped too tightly around the Xiphos.

The sword dropped with a hollow clatter.

I embraced her. Arms around her shoulders, forehead against hers, I clung to Evelyn like she was the only real thing left in this crumbling myth. Her heartbeat grounded me, her breath softened the violent edge still singing in my blood.

She didn't speak for a long time.

"How?" she finally whispered, her voice hoarse, her face speckled with ash and disbelief. "How did you—"

"I don't know," I said, honestly. My voice cracked. I still held her, needing her presence to tether me. That was when the weight of it hit—the realization of what I'd just done. The violence. The ease of it. The terrifying clarity with which I had ended lives, even if they weren't truly alive.

"What did I just do?"

"What you had to," she said gently. "And you were brilliant."

Lucas let out a long breath. His face was flushed, his mouth trying to form words that wouldn't come.

"Remind me," he said eventually, voice thin with awe, "never to piss you off."

That broke something in me. A laugh, shaky and raw, burst out. It wasn't joy. It was relief. Release. Because for a moment, I'd feared they would look at me and see a monster. I feared I might see one, too.

When I looked toward my mother, her hand was still over her mouth. Her eyes glistened with unshed tears. When we locked eyes, she rushed forward and wrapped me in her arms. Her body shook as she held me, and I buried my face in her shoulder.

"You didn't just watch me fight," I whispered. "You watched me become something else."

"You became yourself," she said in my ear. "And I'm proud of you."

Behind her, Allison stepped into view. Her bow was still in hand, but lowered. She looked at me the way a scientist might observe a volcano mid-eruption.

"Not bad, handsome," she said, voice light but eyes sharp. "Where the hell did you learn to fight like that?"

"I don't know," I said again, quieter this time. It was the truth. I'd never touched a sword in my life. But down there, in that chamber, something had awakened—something old and buried and entirely beyond me. The way I moved, the clarity I felt—it was like my body had remembered a language it was never taught. Each strike had felt both foreign and inevitable, like I was channeling echoes through my muscles. I'd never felt this kind of power—and terror—in the same breath. And the scariest part? It had felt right.

"You're a natural," she said, lips curling into a wary grin. "And a bit scary when you're angry."

She didn't meet my eyes. Not really. And maybe that was enough of a lesson for her.

One trial down.

Three more to go.

I glanced down at my arms—lacerated, blood trailing like vines from open cuts. The pain hadn't registered until now. It throbbed, dull and distant. I would need tending. But in this moment, I didn't care.

We were alive.

We walked together out of the chamber, our steps echoing over the broken silence. None of us looked back. Not yet. Ahead lay the trial of wisdom—its shape unknown, its weight uncertain. But I knew this much:

I would see us through it.

All of us. Alive.

That was my vow.

And nothing would stop me from keeping it.

TWENTY-THREE
THE GROVE

"THIS SHOULDN'T BE REAL"

The more we walked, the more pain I began to feel. At first, it had been a dull echo, almost distant—adrenaline shielding me from the full weight of what had happened. But now, as each breath settled and each heartbeat slowed, the numbness retreated. What was left behind was raw and relentless. Throbbing aches pulsed through my muscles, a burn that ignited behind my ribs and radiated outward. And yet, part of me welcomed it. Feeling something—anything—was better than that void. That cold, terrifying nothingness I knew too well. Pain was a tether. Pain meant I was still here.

Evelyn held my hand, her fingers laced through mine. Her warmth grounded me, delicate yet unyielding. The air grew damp and heavy as we continued. The stone blocks beneath our feet were no longer polished and deliberate, but jagged, their symmetry fraying into rough-hewn edges. It felt like we were descending into the bones of the world itself, each step peeling away the pretense of civilization. Just the five of us now. And silence pressed in like fog.

My thoughts spiraled back to what had happened. What I had done. Evelyn had said it was necessary—but what did the others think? Lucas hadn't said a word. My mother's silence—more than anything—gnawed at me. She always had something to say, a lesson or a warning. But now, her eyes were distant, her thoughts unreadable. I feared what I might see if I asked.

The hallway opened into a massive cavern, so vast the torchlight couldn't find the ceiling. The stone gave way to earth, raw and dark. Our lights danced only a few paces ahead, catching glints of mineral veins and damp walls. It was beautiful in a haunting way—like a cathedral abandoned by time. The air was cooler here, and thick with moisture that clung to my skin and hair.

Then something new emerged from the dark.

Tree trunks. Thick, ancient, rising in symmetrical rows. I blinked, unsure if I was seeing right. A forest, down here? Each tree stood like a sentinel, their canopies lost in the unseen sky. The soil beneath our boots softened, cushioning our steps. The smell changed too—moss, bark, decay, and the faint sweetness of something blooming out of sight. The musty scent of wet roots filled my nose.

I paused, instinct tightening my shoulders. We'd been ambushed before. But there was no movement, no sound but our own breathing. This wasn't a threat. It was something older. Sacred.

We ventured onward, deeper between the trees. Long shadows stretched and recoiled as our flames moved. The stillness became its own kind of pressure. Not silence, but anticipation.

With each step, exhaustion clawed closer. My body begged for rest. My feet throbbed, each muscle knotting tighter. My hands still tingled from gripping the sword so tightly. Every step felt like walking through glue.

"Can we stop soon?" I asked, my voice barely carrying.

"Of course," Allison replied without hesitation. We found a break in the trees, a small hollow where we could see clearly in every direction. I collapsed beside one of the trunks, its bark rough against my shoulder as I leaned back. The armor I still wore pressed into me like a prison. No wonder I felt like I was sinking.

"I'm going to find some wood for a fire," Lucas offered.

"I'll help," my mother said, her voice quiet but steady. They disappeared into the woods, leaving Evelyn, Allison, and me behind.

I let out a slow breath, only then realizing how tightly I'd been holding it. The sword lay beside me, unmoving and spotless. No blood. No stain. Like it hadn't just passed judgment. Like the violence never happened, though my body ached with proof.

Evelyn sat beside me, her movements precise. She opened her bag, retrieving something folded.

"I thought you might want to change," she said, handing me a clean shirt. The gesture undid me a little. Simple. Intimate. Human.

"Thanks. Can you help me with this?" I motioned to the armor.

She smiled gently and helped unfasten the buckles, her fingers brushing against my skin as she lifted the cuirass away. The cold air bit at my wounds. She looked down and winced.

"Let me clean these," she said, reaching into her bag again. Alcohol. Gauze. Bandages. She worked quietly but with care, dabbing each wound, soothing the raw edges.

"Always prepared," I murmured, trying to lighten the mood. The sting of the antiseptic made me hiss through my teeth.

She smiled but didn't respond. Her hands moved gently over my skin, wiping away blood and ash. She was close enough that I could smell her—like books and rain. Her presence was a balm I didn't know I needed.

Across from us, Allison sat with the torch still burning beside her, its flames crackling softly. She hadn't moved since we stopped. Her eyes weren't on us, but distant—drawn inward. There was something fragile about her now. She looked less like a warrior and more like a person lost in her own reckoning.

She held her arms around her knees, chin resting on top. In the flicker of the fire, her face looked younger. Haunted. She blinked slowly, lost in some memory she couldn't speak of.

None of us said it, but the battle had changed things. We'd all seen something in that room. And no one walked away from that unchanged.

The flames popped softly, casting golden light across our tired faces. Evelyn wrapped my wounds in silence, her hands gentle and deliberate. Every now and then, I caught Allison glancing our way, her jaw clenched, her mouth a tight line.

I saw something shift in her expression—regret maybe, or longing. She wasn't watching us with envy, but with a kind of mourning. Like she remembered what it was to sit beside someone and feel safe.

The moment stretched, quiet and sacred.

Then, in a voice barely above a whisper, Allison said, "You shouldn't have survived that."

I turned, caught off guard.

"What?"

She didn't look at me. Just stared into the fire. "The trial. You shouldn't have been able to do what you did. I saw you. That wasn't just courage or anger. That was something else."

Her words weren't accusatory. Just... searching.

I didn't respond. Because I didn't know how.

She finally looked up, and for the first time, I saw something close to fear in her eyes. But it wasn't fear of me. It was fear of what I represented. What I might become.

"There's more going on here than any of us understand," she murmured.

I nodded. Because that, at least, was something I could agree with.

The fire crackled on.

And in the stillness of that ancient, subterranean forest, we rested.

Not in peace. But in fragile truce with whatever came next.

Lucas and my mother returned shortly after with a pile of sticks and wood cradled in their hands. I was surprised they'd found anything in a place like this, but the forest, strange as it was, seemed to yield just enough. Lucas moved stiffly, his gait uneven, and as he bent to place the wood near the fire pit, he winced sharply, one hand instinctively going to his side.

"You alright?" I asked.

"Yeah—just... sore," he muttered through gritted teeth.

Before I could step in, Allison rose from where she sat and crossed the small clearing to his side. She didn't say anything at first—just knelt beside him and gently moved his hand away to see the bruise forming beneath his shirt. He didn't protest. Her movements were uncharacteristically tender as she retrieved a small flask from her belt pouch and dabbed a cloth with some kind of salve. The scent hit me even from where I sat—sharp, herbal, and strangely comforting.

"Hold still," she said, dabbing the bruise. Lucas flinched but didn't pull away.

"Didn't think you cared," he said, half-joking.

She looked at him then—really looked at him. "I care more than you think. Just not in ways that are easy to explain."

There was something in her voice, a heaviness I hadn't heard before. As if her veneer of control had cracked. As she finished and stepped back, Lucas murmured a soft thanks, and Allison just nodded before returning to her place by the torch.

Once the flames caught, we could see better. The warm light illuminated the surrounding trees, creating a haunting image of the narrow yet perfect rows of tall trees, stretching into a void that had no end. Yet there was a silence like I had never heard. Like everything was still, and for me the silence had weight. A weight that was slowly building pressure.

I changed into the thin hoodie that Evelyn had given me, which gave me a little warmth as the air around us was cool. Along with the little warmth from the fire as it danced in front of me. I looked over at my friends and mother, all quiet. They had been like this for the past couple of hours, and frankly, I didn't know what to think. Was it because of me, because of what I did? Was it just them taking all of it in?

I was still trying to push out the pain that gnawed at every inch of me, hoping in vain that it would fade. But it didn't. It dug deeper, rooted itself in my chest, and pressed against my lungs like a weight I couldn't shake. Every glance from the others felt like a judgment, even when their eyes looked away. It was like they were all trying not to look directly at the storm they'd witnessed me become.

I couldn't breathe. I couldn't sit still. My legs twitched with restless energy, my mind a spinning blur of guilt, confusion, and fear. I couldn't help but wonder—what did they really see when they looked at me now? A friend? A weapon? A monster?

My skin crawled with the pressure, and my chest tightened until I thought I might scream. I stood abruptly, nearly knocking over my sword. "I need some air," I said hoarsely. Evelyn looked up, concern flickering in her eyes, but she just nodded and didn't press.

I turned from the fire and walked, my boots crunching softly in the loamy forest floor. The dark welcomed me. It swallowed the flickering firelight and wrapped me in shadow. I hated being alone—usually. But now, I needed the silence. The isolation. A place to fall apart without anyone watching.

I didn't understand myself anymore. I wanted them close. I wanted to push them all away. I wanted to scream. I wanted to sleep. I didn't know what I wanted—only that I couldn't sit there, feeling the weight of their silence crush down on me. The battle hadn't broken me. But this stillness might.

The surrounding trees loomed; their shadows floated across the ground as my phone's light illuminated the path before me. The dark, usually a trigger for anxiety, now soothed me in a strange and quiet way. I welcomed its silence. Each step crunched lightly over the soil and dead leaves, muffled by the weight in my chest. I could still see the carnage I'd caused—played back in endless loop inside my head. It didn't feel like something I did. It felt like something I became. That difference terrified me.

The silence around me was deceptive. I wasn't alone. Not really. Somewhere in the forest behind me, they were still there—Evelyn, Lucas, Allison, my mother. And yet I felt separate, like I had stepped out of their world. The horror of what I had done had driven a wedge, invisible but sharp. I could feel it. I wore it like a second skin.

The weight of the Xiphos still echoed in my muscles. Every swing. Every death. The faces of the dust-born warriors haunted me—not because they lived—but because they didn't. There were no cries. No blood. No mercy. I had unmade them. Erased them. With frightening ease.

Maybe I was a bomb. A fuse that had finally burned down. And no one knew how long before I exploded again.

"Hey." A hand touched my shoulder. I flinched before turning. Lucas stood there, eyes catching the faint glow of my phone. His expression was serious, but underneath it shimmered something softer. Concern. Maybe even affection.

"What are you doing out here?" I asked as he fell into step beside me. It was the first time he'd spoken in hours. For Lucas, that silence had weight.

"Thought you could use the company."

The corners of my mouth lifted. A smile, faint and reluctant. "Most people leave me alone. Let me spiral in peace."

He shrugged. "I'm not most people."

We walked side by side, shoulders brushing. It wasn't accidental. The proximity felt intentional. Like he was making sure I knew I wasn't alone—even if I didn't ask for it. Especially then.

"I hope I didn't scare you off," I said after a while. The words were light, a joke on the surface. Beneath, a real fear.

"Scare me? You'll have to try harder than that," he said, and his laugh carried warmth like a candle in the dark.

"Damn. I'll have to up my game."

We walked in silence again. But this time, it wasn't uncomfortable. It was the kind that comes when words aren't needed. When presence is enough.

"I'm not going to lie," Lucas said eventually. "There for a while, I was scared."

"Scared? Of what?"

"You. I didn't think you were going to make it out of there. And if you didn't—none of us were."

His words hit harder than I expected. I stopped walking, eyes lowered. "I didn't think about what would happen if I failed. I just... couldn't let anything happen to you. To Evelyn. To my mom."

Lucas nodded. "And that's why we were scared. Because we know you'd throw yourself into hell for us. Without blinking. Without thinking."

I didn't respond. I didn't have the words. I didn't even know if I deserved them.

"You're a good person, Phoenix. Even when you don't see it. You always care. Even when it hurts."

He nudged me gently with his shoulder. "Remember when I was sick last year? We barely talked, but you still brought me meds. Checked on me. Took me to urgent care. And your car smelled like cough drops for a month."

"Don't remind me," I muttered. "I thought I was going to catch the plague."

"But you didn't. And you still showed up. That meant something. Still does."

I looked at him sideways. There was something in his eyes—open, raw. If he was hiding feelings, they sat close to the surface. But I didn't know how to name them. I only knew they mattered.

"Okay, so I'm a decent human being. Let's not make a big deal out of it."

"Too late," he grinned.

A flicker of pain crossed his face, and he hissed as he adjusted his stance.

"You alright?"

"Yeah. My side's still bruised from where I hit the wall during the fight. Feels like someone shoved a brick into my ribs."

Before I could offer help, he waved me off and managed a smile. "It's nothing I can't handle. Just annoying."

We kept walking until I paused to fix my shoe, hand resting against the bark of a tree. And then everything changed.

A pulse. Like a heartbeat beneath my fingers. Soft. Alive.

The bark warmed. A soft green glow ignited under my palm, light blooming in thin veins through the tree. The glow spread, slow and steady, illuminating the trunk like veins in stone.

I gasped. Not from fear—but recognition.

It was like the sword had awakened rage, but this—this stirred something else. Connection. Roots and wind and breath. I could feel the forest. Its age. Its sorrow. Its patience. It didn't just respond to me.

It welcomed me.

The glow climbed. Up through branches, into leaves that turned shimmering purple and indigo, glowing like stars stitched into the sky.

Lucas stared, mouth parted. "Phoenix..."

And then the light spread.

Tree after tree flared to life in waves. Glowing in synchronized pulses, like fireflies answering a call. Green, blue, violet, silver. The forest transformed into a cathedral of living light. A secret remembered.

We stood at the center of it.

I withdrew my hand. The glow faded slowly, but not entirely. It remained in the branches. In the leaves. Like the forest was keeping a part of it lit just for us.

"See? You're amazing," Lucas said again, voice reverent. But he wasn't watching the trees.

He was watching me.

I turned off my phone's light. We didn't need it anymore. The glow bathed everything in quiet awe. It wasn't bright. It didn't need to be. It was enough.

As we walked back, surrounded by bioluminescent giants, I realized something had changed.

The rage in the battle had made me a weapon.

But this...

This made me different.

And I wasn't sure which one scared me more.

The scent of the fire was in the air as we got closer. The fresh scent of wood-burning always stirred something deep inside me—memory, maybe even comfort. My parents used to build little fires in our backyard. We'd sit for hours looking up at the stars, my dad pointing out constellations, my mom humming softly beside us. This reminded me of that a bit. But now, instead of stars, we looked up at trees that shimmered like constellations themselves—ethereal and glowing, suspended in a canopy of wonder.

"Who turned on the lights?" Evelyn asked as we approached, awe threading through her voice. They were all standing, their faces tilted upward, expressions caught between disbelief and reverence.

"That would be him," Lucas said, his voice touched with pride, but playful as he pointed at me.

"I swear I just touched a tree. That was it," I said, raising my hands in defense, as if I had set off fireworks in a museum. It wasn't like I tried to light the place up. But the evidence was undeniable—the trees blazed with gentle hues of blue, green, and violet.

They laughed—Allison included. Her laughter, though quieter and more measured, was genuine. A soft exhale of disbelief. Maybe even admiration that she didn't yet know how to show.

"Leave it to you to find a light switch," she said from where she sat, arms loosely around her knees. There was something different in her voice—a gentleness I hadn't heard before.

Evelyn walked over and brushed her hand against mine, grounding me. We gazed up together, shoulders touching. My mother stood to the side, still lost in wonder, her eyes reflecting the shimmering lights like mirrored glass. Occasionally she looked at me with a half-smile, something caught between awe and concern.

We eventually settled, forming a loose ring around the fire. Evelyn lay in my arms, her head resting against my chest as we both looked skyward. The canopy above danced with colors like slow-moving auroras, the bioluminescence casting an otherworldly glow that shimmered off her skin and painted her eyes with stardust.

It reminded me of something I'd always dreamed of doing—lying on my back with someone I cared about and watching fireworks. But this was even better. There was no sound to compete with. No explosions. Just the gentle crackle of fire and the chorus of glowing life above. It was peace—the kind that felt undeserved after what we had just survived.

For a time, no one spoke. The silence was thick, reverent. Then, like a string plucked softly in the dark, a voice began to sing.

It was Lucas. He sat near the fire, knees drawn to his chest, arms draped over them. His head tilted back, and his eyes half-lidded as his voice carried—a soft, resonant tenor that made the night itself seem to hush and listen.

"I lay in a field of white, one that was sowed in hate.
drowning, gasping for air
why can't I breathe, why can't I stand?
why can't I live..."

His voice trembled not with weakness, but with depth, emotion woven into every note. I hadn't known he could sing. But here, in this sacred grove, it felt like the most natural thing.

"Those magnolia blooms, even as blood stains,
those pure petals with judgment and pain,
why can't I breathe, why can't I stand, why can't I live
in this world that they create..."

The firelight seemed to flicker in time with the song. Shadows danced across his face, and for a moment, he looked older. Wiser. Like someone who had carried the weight of something for far too long.

Evelyn shifted against me, and I felt the soft hitch of her breath. She was crying. Quietly. The tears ran down her face not from pain, but resonance.

"People just stare, expecting me to belong,
when I don't, they just wish me away,
why can't I breathe, why can't I stand, why can't I live
in this world that they create
why can't I breathe, why can't I stand, why can't I live
in this world that they create.

Just a stranger, lost finding my way, to a land where I could be free…why can't I breathe, why can't I stand, why can't I live,
why can't I breathe, why can't I stand, why can't I live
in this world that they create."

The last note lingered in the air like a thread of silk, trembling but unbroken. It didn't just fade—it settled. Into the corners of the Grove. Into my chest. Into the spaces between what had been and what was still trying to become.

When silence returned, it wasn't empty. It was thick, charged—like the music had shifted something fundamental in the air around us. Like the song hadn't just echoed; it had rewritten the architecture of the moment. I could still feel the shape of the chords in my bones, the tremble of them in my throat, like I'd sung them myself. The lyrics echoed inside me—raw, vulnerable, unguarded.

Because they weren't just his words. They could've been mine. Every note felt like something I hadn't known how to say until I heard it sung aloud.

Lucas looked up slowly, like surfacing from a dream he hadn't meant to share. His eyes met mine for half a second—then broke away, the weight of it too much. Color rose to his cheeks, a flush blooming along the edges of his ears. He gave a soft, nervous laugh and rubbed the back of his neck, as if trying to brush off the moment, to scatter it like dust.

"I didn't mean for it to get that... intense," he said, voice barely above a whisper.

But we both knew he had. And it had. And nothing would be quite the same after it."That was beautiful," my mother said softly, her voice soaked in sincerity.

"Thanks," he replied, voice low, almost a whisper.

"See, you can be amazing too," I added, nudging him gently. He smirked back, a crooked grin tugging at his lips. But something else lingered there too—something quiet and unreadable. His gaze held on mine for just a moment longer than expected, then flickered away to the flames.

I held his look a breath longer. Felt it settle into me. There were things we didn't say. Things we didn't know how to say. But in that glance, something unspoken passed between us—recognition, maybe. Understanding. A thread tying us closer than before, and I wasn't sure I was ready for what it meant.

The silence returned, not empty but full. Full of healing, and warmth, and ghosts that might not be so scary after all.

TWENTY-FOUR

THE TRAIL OF WISDOM

"WISDOM COMES IN ALL SHAPES"

The lights still dazzled me as I stared up at them—ribbons of blue, green, and violet wove through the canopy like a living tapestry, pulsing gently as though the trees themselves were breathing. Mist clung to the air, catching the glow in soft halos, bending and shimmering with every breath of wind that passed through the ancient branches. The air was cool and damp, a balm on my skin after the chaos of the day. Even the silence felt sacred, like the forest had paused just to witness this moment.

Everyone else was already fast asleep, sprawled beneath the sheltering trees, their breathing deep and steady. But I couldn't bring myself to rest. Something inside me resisted the stillness, a quiet unrest that kept my body rooted to the ground and my eyes fixed skyward. So I just sat there, marveling at what I saw, letting the beauty of the canopy wash over me like rain. Of all the things I had witnessed—disasters, revelations, loss, fleeting joys—this ranked among the most profound. And maybe, just maybe, it had less to do with the trees and more to do with who was beside me.

Evelyn.

She was quiet now, her presence a steady, comforting rhythm at my side. Her warmth radiated through the fabric of our jackets, the light pressure of her head against my shoulder anchoring me in the present. I turned my head slightly to look at her, barely moving so I wouldn't disturb her peace. She looked calm, peaceful, like this wilderness had accepted her somehow. Like she belonged here.

And for the first time in a long while, I felt like maybe I did too.

Maybe I was stronger than I believed. Not the empty shadow I often saw in the mirror. Not the broken boy defined by grief or the quiet shell shaped by guilt. Not the disappointment I feared people saw. Maybe—I was something more. Maybe, in this strange and sacred place, I could believe that I mattered.

But the idea of becoming more—of being seen—terrified me.

Because being seen meant being known. And being known meant being vulnerable. And what if, after all of that, they still saw someone unworthy? What if the truth of me—buried beneath years of silence—wasn't enough?

"Hey," Evelyn whispered, her voice pulling me gently back. Her head still rested against me, but her eyes were open now, blinking sleepily up at mine.

"Hey," I murmured back, offering a small smile.

"You're not sleeping?" she asked, keeping her voice low so we wouldn't wake the others. She sounded half-asleep herself, but still aware enough to care.

I shook my head, glancing back up. "Hard to, with all this beauty overhead."

She followed my gaze briefly, then smiled softly. "You still need rest. Even beautiful places lose their wonder when you're sleep-deprived."

I chuckled quietly. "You always know how to make a point."

"It's a talent," she said, laying her head back down and letting her eyes close again.

I sat there for a few more moments, letting the calm settle deeper into my bones. Eventually, I stretched out beside her, pulling my cloak tighter against the chill. Surprisingly, sleep didn't fight me this time. It crept in slow and quiet, and soon enough, the lights above blurred into dreams.

My mind must have wandered farther than I thought as I began to wake. My body was stiff, aching in every joint, unwilling to cooperate. The weight against my eyelids was almost unbearable, as though gravity had grown heavier in the night. I forced them open, inch by inch, until dim light spilled in. But when the blur cleared, I realized something was wrong.

Everyone was gone.

The camp was silent. No murmurs, no shifting bodies. No Evelyn. No Lucas. Not even the echo of their presence. Just me, sprawled beneath the great glowing canopy of trees, the cold bark of the tree at my back, and an ache blooming in my chest.

I pushed myself upright, limbs stiff, throat dry. The air around me was thick with silence—too still, like the entire forest was holding its breath. I turned in every direction, scanning the grove. The ethereal lights still danced above, casting soft hues of violet and turquoise across the leaves. But the warmth of companionship had vanished.

And then I saw her.

She stood not far ahead, cloaked in an aura of ancient stillness. An older woman, her olive-toned skin catching the light, long black hair streaked with silver that cascaded over her shoulder like a river. Her tunic was simple, primitive, like something pulled from the bones of history itself. Yet her presence was anything but faded. She radiated strength—the quiet kind that doesn't need to announce itself.

I stepped forward cautiously. "Who are you?" I asked, my voice barely louder than the leaves rustling above.

She looked at me with unreadable brown eyes, deep and still like old water. "You have shown your strength. Now let your wisdom guide you."

Her words drifted through the air like a breath of smoke—intangible, but impossible to forget.

"Guide me?" I repeated, heart thudding. "To where?"

"That is your test."

And with that, she turned and began walking into the trees.

I didn't think. I just followed.

I had nothing on me but my sword. No supplies. No map. Evelyn must've kept the rest, wherever she was. But this woman knew something. I could feel it in her gait, the quiet authority in her silence. I wasn't about to let her vanish into the forest without answers.

"You never answered me," I called out, trying not to sound accusatory. "Who are you really?"

She glanced back but kept walking. Her steps were measured, deliberate.

"It does not matter," she said after a long silence.

Frustration sparked in me. Easy for her to say—it wasn't her life on the line. If she was leading me to my death, I'd at least like to know the name of the person doing the killing.

"It does matter," I said, more firmly now. "It matters to me."

That stopped her. She turned to face me fully. Her face, though kind, bore the weight of centuries. I could feel it in the stillness she carried, the way she studied me—like I was a riddle she was still deciding whether or not to solve.

"I am a guardian," she said simply. "I have protected this place for thousands of years."

A pause.

"The man from the trial of strength. Was he one, too?"

She nodded once. "He is."

"So, what do you guard exactly?"

She held my gaze. "Something as old as time itself. And only those of the true bloodline may pass these trials."

The weight of her words dropped into my stomach like stone.

"And if we're not of that bloodline?"

"Then your efforts are noble—but futile. Many begin the path. Few come this far."

A twisted kind of encouragement. Congratulations, Phoenix, here's your existential participation trophy.

We walked in silence, the forest closing in like a soft breath. I followed because there was no one else. Because I needed answers. Because I was terrified of being alone.

"You never told me your name," I tried again, voice softer.

She slowed. Turned.

"My name is not important."

"It is to me."

There was a pause—longer this time. Then, finally:

"Diana."

"I'm Phoenix."

"I know who you are."

I stopped walking. "How?"

Her lips almost curled into a smile. "I would be a terrible guardian if I didn't. But now you must find your way."

She stepped forward, touched my chest. Her hand was cold—not unpleasant, just… distant. Like the sensation of water over stone.

"Let the heart guide you."

Then she vanished.

No sound. No light. Just me, blinking in the quiet.

I stood there for a long moment, stunned.

Let the heart guide me? What heart? Mine? The forest's? Some metaphorical concept I was supposed to unravel like a riddle in a children's book?

So I walked. There was nothing else to do.

Hours passed—or minutes. Time didn't obey rules here. My legs ached, and my thoughts spun. I replayed her words over and over, searching for meaning. The shimmering canopy above lit my path, but gave no direction. No signs. No answers.

Eventually, I collapsed beside a tree, too exhausted to keep searching. I leaned back, let the bark dig into my shoulders, and closed my eyes. The ache in my muscles, the pounding in my skull—none of it mattered. For a moment, I just existed.

Then I heard it.

Soft footsteps—careful, deliberate, pressing against the damp forest floor like whispers on old wood. They weren't rushed, but they carried weight. Purpose. A cadence that didn't match any animal I'd heard in this place.

My body reacted before my thoughts could catch up. My fingers gripped the sword's hilt, the chill of the metal grounding me as I slipped behind the nearest tree. Bark scraped my back as I pressed against it, trying to become invisible. My breath shallowed, each inhale catching in my throat, loud against the unnatural stillness. Every nerve lit up with tension, skin prickling with the eerie sense that something—or someone—was hunting.

The footsteps drew closer. Twigs snapped, a leaf rustled. A shadow moved—slow, approaching from the far side of the clearing. My pulse thudded in my ears like war drums. I tightened my grip, bent my knees, prepared to strike. One breath. Two. Then I lunged, blade flashing through the dark.

"Whoa—whoa! Can we not?" a voice shouted, startled and sharp.

Lucas.

The name hit me like a jolt. I froze, blade hovering just an inch from his throat. The moment cracked—then shattered.

I dropped the sword instantly, staggering back as relief surged through me, raw and immediate. My breath came out in a rush, ragged, like I'd been underwater for too long.

"Sorry," I said. "Didn't know it was you. I'm just—God, I'm glad to see you. Where the hell have you been?"

He gave me a look. "What do you mean, where have I been? You guys left me."

I blinked. "What? I woke up and everyone was gone. I thought I was the one left behind."

We stared at each other, both stunned, both realizing the truth.

This trial? It wasn't just about wisdom.

It was about isolation. About seeing what we'd do when the noise stopped.

"This place is insane," Lucas muttered.

I couldn't have agreed more.

And deep down, I had a feeling—it wasn't done with us yet.

"No one left you. I was the one that was left."

"Wait, what?" Lucas said, frowning. I explained everything—the strange emptiness when I woke, the guardian with the ancient eyes, and the cryptic riddle she'd left me about the heart. Lucas looked even more puzzled than I'd felt. He'd woken alone too. No sign of anyone. No guardian. Nothing but trees and silence.

"Strange," he murmured. We kept walking, the forest thickening around us. Every step forward seemed to drag more questions into the air. Questions that clung like mist: Why had we all been separated? Why had I met a guardian when no one else had? Why did it always feel like this place was watching me, not them? I hated being the center of anything. And yet… here I was, again.

Lucas was uncharacteristically quiet. We moved through the underbrush like shadows, the thrum of fatigue rising with every aching step. My legs pulsed with soreness, my gut twisted with hunger, and the sword strapped to my back now felt like a slab of lead.

Eventually, Lucas broke the silence. "Can we stop? Please."

I nodded, grateful. We found a small clearing framed by gnarled roots and moss. A natural hollow, dimmed by a thicker patch of canopy above. No glowing trees. Just darkness and stillness. We'd take it.

Lucas crouched by a patch of earth and started working on a fire. I searched our pack for food—what little was left. Some dried fruit, a chunk of hardened bread, and a protein bar that had seen better days. Not ideal. Not satisfying. But it would have to do. We didn't plan to be trapped here this long.

It didn't take long to get things ready, though our limbs protested every movement. The fire cracked to life, warming our hands and casting flickering shapes against the trees. I passed

Lucas his share of the meal, and we ate without speaking. The silence wasn't peaceful. It was thick. Stagnant.

Lucas sat hunched, eyes locked on the fire like it had answers he didn't. Was he angry? Was it fear? Shame? Whatever it was, it kept his jaw tight and his words buried. I watched him, heart heavy. He mattered. And right now, something was hurting him.

"What's wrong?" I finally asked, breaking the tension.

"Nothing."

His voice was clipped. Distant. Hollow.

"Then why are you so quiet? You're never quiet."

"I can be quiet."

He didn't meet my eyes. Didn't even flinch. Just stared into the flames, his face caught somewhere between exhaustion and resignation.

"That's hard to believe," I said gently.

He gave me a look—one I'd never seen on him before. A look that said, Don't push me. I don't know what I'll say if you do.

But I had to.

"Whatever it is, you can tell me."

His jaw clenched. He looked at me. Really looked at me. And in that long, heavy silence between us, I saw the quiet unraveling—the way his shoulders stayed tense like he was bracing for impact, the way his mouth opened slightly, only to close again. There was a storm in him. A war, twisting behind his eyes. The fight to keep something buried. The fear of letting it rise. The loneliness of feeling like no one would understand if he did.

"You won't understand," he muttered, his voice low, almost defeated.

I could've backed off. Could've let him tuck it all away and wear that mask a little longer. But I didn't. I couldn't. Not with the firelight painting both our faces in soft gold and shadow, not when I'd seen what he was holding back.

"Try me," I said, my voice steady, but not forceful.

He flinched like it hurt. His fingers dug into his knees. His lips pressed together. The fire crackled again, louder this time, like it, too, was holding its breath.

And then—

"Your life's perfect. You've got a great family. You don't care what people think. You're… fearless."

I almost laughed, but not out of cruelty. More from disbelief.

"My life has never been perfect," I said softly. "You're right about my family—they're amazing. But the rest? No. Not even close."

Lucas looked skeptical. So I opened the door wider.

"I used to live in a fog. Depression. The kind that wraps around your chest and convinces you that sleep is safer than being awake. That silence is better than trying to explain why you're hurting. There were days I couldn't move. Couldn't eat. Couldn't smile. I cared way too much about what people thought, and it nearly destroyed me."

Lucas blinked. Slowly. He swallowed hard.

"I never knew."

"Most people don't."

"Do your parents know?"

I shook my head. "I didn't want to put that pain on them. Didn't want them to look at me differently."

Lucas stared into the fire again. But this time, it wasn't a shield. It was a window. I could see him working through what I'd said. Letting it settle into the parts of himself he usually kept locked away.

"Don't let anyone tell you who you are," I said. "Be yourself. And if they can't accept that? Screw them. They don't deserve your story."

He exhaled. Shaky. And then, in the softest voice I'd ever heard from him:

"We're always supposed to be strong. Unbreakable. Like, if we show emotion, we're weak."

"That's a lie. A cruel one. Pretending not to feel? That's what breaks you."

"We never talk about it. Not really. Not with each other."

"We should."

Lucas let out a breath that sounded too close to a sob. And then I saw it—the first tear, sliding quietly down his cheek. His voice wavered.

"You… you really think I should just… be me?"

"Yes. Because I've met that guy. And he's worth knowing."

He opened his mouth. Closed it. Tried again.

"Phoenix… I'm—I'm—"

His throat closed up. He trembled.

I moved beside him. Didn't speak. Didn't rush. Just waited.

Then, in a voice that cracked with courage:

"I'm gay."

I smiled. Not because it was a big deal. But because it wasn't.

"You know… that explains a lot. But thank you for telling me. I'm honored. And I'm proud of you."

Lucas nodded. His eyes were soaked now. But there was something new in them—relief.

"Thanks," he whispered. "You're the only one I've told. The only one who really sees me."

"Hey, Evelyn does too."

He snorted, wiping his face. "Yeah. You two are a unit."

"We're a trio now. Whether you like it or not."

Lucas laughed again, and it was real this time. Light. Free.

I grinned. "Now it's your turn. Go show the world the real Lucas. Don't apologize for it. Don't shrink yourself to fit someone else's expectations."

He nodded again. This time, like he meant it.

Maybe this was the point of the trial. Not wisdom in riddles or puzzles. But in truth. In connection. In the courage to say, This is me.

For the rest of the night, we sat there and talked, unraveling stories we had never dared to share before. The fire crackled between us, its warm glow dancing across Lucas's face, catching in the creases of his hesitant smile. Shadows shifted around the edges of the clearing, but we didn't notice them much—we were too busy letting go of things we'd held too tightly.

Lucas talked first. Not easily, not smoothly—but with the careful, halting rhythm of someone unspooling a part of themselves for the first time. He told me about the awkward dinners his father arranged, always with girls he had nothing in common with, always with expectations hanging in the air like a noose. He mimicked his dad's booming voice, rolled his eyes, laughed dryly—but I could hear the weariness beneath it all. That quiet desperation of trying to please someone while hiding who you really are.

He looked down a lot, hands clasped together, thumbs twitching. Then he admitted to his first crush—another boy from his school. A simple thing, an innocent thing, but it had terrified him. He whispered about the panic he used to feel, how every day was a game of concealment. How exhausting it was, always watching, always pretending.

"I thought if I just acted right long enough, it'd go away," he said, eyes still fixed on the fire. "But it never did. It just got heavier."

I didn't say anything right away. Just let the silence hold us for a beat too long. Then I nodded, slow and solid, like I was anchoring his words into the dirt.

"I get it," I said finally. "You're not alone in that."

And I meant it. Deep in my chest, in a place I rarely let anyone touch, I meant it.

Something loosened in his shoulders. He exhaled—really exhaled—for what felt like the first time. The tension in his posture eased, like armor beginning to fall away, plate by plate. He wasn't smiling exactly, but there was something softer in his eyes. Something clearer.

"I've never told anyone this much," he said.

I shrugged, but gently. "Maybe you were just waiting for someone who wouldn't run."

We both chuckled at that, and it felt good—normal, even. Like for a second, the weight of where we were didn't matter.

Like we were just two people, sitting by a fire, figuring out how to be real.

Eventually, our words faded. The silence that came next wasn't uncomfortable. It was peaceful. Earned. We moved slowly, gathering up blankets and deciding who would take first watch. I volunteered. He didn't argue.

Lucas curled up near the fire, back turned slightly, but his breathing stayed steady. I watched him for a moment, not out of suspicion—just out of care. He looked... lighter. Not fixed. Not healed. But lighter.

"Good night," I whispered.

"Night," he murmured, half-asleep.

Then it was just me. The fire and the forest and the thousand questions sitting heavy in my chest.

The woods around us breathed in long, slow pulses. Trees swayed in a breeze I couldn't feel, and the blue and green glow above pulsed faintly like stars under water. I sat with my sword at my side, the firelight flickering against the blade's edge, and stared into the dark between the trees.

My mind wouldn't stop. I thought of Evelyn—her smile, her hand in mine. Of my mother, with her unreadable eyes and endless secrets. Even Allison, whose role in all this still churned in the pit of my gut. Were they safe? Were they alone, waking up in a strange place like I had? Would we ever get out of here together?

A branch snapped somewhere off to my left. I tensed, fingers brushing the hilt of my sword, but nothing followed. Just the rustle of leaves. It took a minute or so for my nerves to calm and for my shoulders to relax.

The quiet after that was somehow louder.

I tried to steady my breath. I told myself everything was fine. That we'd made it through worse. There was nothing that could hurt us anymore, everyone would be safe. Yet I was here, with just Lucas and had no idea where the others were. Where my mother was again.

But hope—like everything else in this forest—was a fragile thing.

And I wasn't sure yet if I was strong enough to carry it all the way to the end.

TWENTY-FIVE

THE HEART

"PULSE OF THE SOUL"

Most of my watch was quiet. Just the trees, the slow crackle of the dying fire, and the restless hum of my own thoughts to keep me company. Lucas was fast asleep, occasionally letting out a snore that broke the stillness like a punctuation mark in the long sentence of the night. I didn't mind it. Honestly, I welcomed it. The alternative—absolute silence—was louder in its own way. That kind of silence has teeth. It gnaws on the edges of your memories, pulls apart every thought you've tried to shove down deep. It makes you feel like the only person left in the world.

I leaned back against the trunk of a wide tree, its bark rough and cool against my back, and tilted my head to the canopy above. Like skeletal arms, the branches stretched, etched in sharp silhouette against a star-flecked mist ceiling. The lights that shimmered through the trees weren't just illumination—they were alive, shifting colors like oil on water: green like moss, purple like bruises, blue like deep currents. As if: As if breathing, the entire grove pulsed, its heart beating like a forest's own. It was hypnotic. Beautiful. Haunting.

My thoughts kept circling back to Lucas. To what he had shared. That moment between us was more than just a conversation—it was a fracture in the wall we both pretended wasn't there. He had peeled back a layer of himself I hadn't expected to see, and I didn't take it lightly. The way he had spoken—raw, uncertain, like every word tasted foreign in his mouth—it stayed with me. His silence earlier in the night made more sense now. That wasn't just frustration. That was fear. Years of hiding. Of dodging glances and expectations. Of trying to be what people needed instead of who he was.

There was a quiet bravery in his voice. Not the kind that roars or demands attention, but the kind that survives. The kind that says, "Here I am," even when it's terrified. I respected that more than I could say.

He was my friend. Maybe the only real friend I had left. And he mattered to me.

Same with Evelyn. I thought about her too—her warmth, her steadiness, the way she could see through my bullshit with a glance. I had tried to keep her at arm's length, and she had never pushed past it. She just waited. Quietly. Steadily. And somehow, that had worked better than any force ever could. I had spent so long convinced that isolation made me stronger. But maybe, just maybe, connection didn't weaken you. Maybe it anchored you.

I stood up and started pacing the edge of the clearing, my boots whispering through fallen leaves. Anything to stay awake. The cold crept through the thin fabric of my shirt, but I welcomed it—it kept me grounded. I stretched, shook out my limbs, even resorted to pinching the inside of my forearm a few times when my eyes started to drift closed.

Finally, it was time for Lucas to take over. I walked over and knelt beside him, shaking his shoulder gently.

"Lucas," I whispered. "Your turn."

He didn't move at first.

"Lucas," I said again, firmer this time.

"Five more minutes," he groaned, face still buried in the blanket.

I chuckled. "That's what you said last time. Come on."

There was more grumbling, then a groggy curse or two, but eventually he sat up, rubbing his face like he was trying to erase sleep from his skin. I handed him the blanket and dropped into the warm spot he'd just vacated.

"It's been quiet," I told him. "Let's hope it stays that way."

He nodded, groggily wrapping the blanket tighter around himself as he took his place by the fire.

Sleep hit me harder than expected. Maybe it was the residual warmth of the fire, or the knowledge that someone else had my back. Maybe I was just finally letting myself rest. There were no dreams—just the weightless slide into darkness, like sinking into the deepest part of the ocean.

Until the shaking started.

"Phoenix," Lucas whispered, his voice sharp, urgent.

I blinked, heart already thudding before I opened my eyes. "What—already?"

"Someone's coming."

That woke me up fast. I sat up, fully alert now, hand reaching for my sword on instinct. The cool metal grounded me. The air had shifted. No birdsong. No rustle of leaves. Just stillness. A kind of pause in the world that only meant one thing—something was approaching.

And then I saw it. A pale light flickering through the trees, distant but growing closer with every second. It wove through the darkness like it had a purpose. Not a lantern. Not fire. Something else. Something colder.

Lucas crouched beside me, his hand brushing my arm. We didn't exchange words. We didn't need to. There was a clarity in that moment, the kind that comes when fear sharpens everything.

I stepped forward, barely a pace, placing myself between him and the approaching light. My heart was a drumbeat in my ears, loud and insistent. My fingers tightened around the hilt of my sword. I planted my feet in the dirt and watched as the light moved closer, closer still, until I could almost hear the footsteps beneath it.

I didn't breathe. Didn't blink.

I waited, every nerve stretched tight, every muscle ready to spring. Whatever was coming, I would meet it head-on.

The rustling came first. Quiet. Calculated. A breath of movement against the unnatural stillness of the glowing grove. I stepped in front of Lucas, sword angled low but ready. My pulse thrummed against the hilt, my ears attuned to every snapping twig and shift of brush. The fire behind us crackled, a sharp contrast to the silence pressing in from the trees, and I could feel the heat at my back—a reminder that something warm and safe still existed.

"Who's there?" I called, my voice low but firm, not quite trusting the shadows.

There was a pause—then a voice, light and familiar, laced with that unmissable elegance.

"Phoenix?"

The breath left my lungs in a rush. Relief clashed with disbelief as the light filtered through the branches and caught the silhouette of Evelyn, followed closely by my mother and Allison. My blade dropped. My boots crunched across the forest floor as I closed the distance between us, too quickly to seem composed.

She collided into me, and I pulled her into a tight embrace. Her scent—citrus, lavender, and something uniquely her—hit me like a jolt. My chest ached with everything I hadn't let myself feel until now. She was safe. They all were. Her grip on me was fierce—like she wasn't letting go anytime soon.

"Where in the night have you two been?" my mother demanded, arms folded like she used to when I snuck out as a teenager. Her tone was sharp, but her eyes softened the moment she looked me over, as if confirming I still had all my limbs.

"We might ask the same," I replied, giving her a look. "But… I think we might know why."

We gathered quickly around the rekindled fire, huddled close as if the flames could burn away the lingering tension in the air. Lucas and I exchanged glances before beginning—first him, then me, our words weaving in and out as we tried to make sense of what had happened. We spoke of Diana, the strange moment of waking up alone, the ghostly weight of the dreamlike separation, and the message she'd left behind: let the heart guide you. Each detail stirred more questions than answers.

Lucas's voice wavered once as he spoke, but he caught himself. Then, as the firelight flickered against his face, he took a breath. The kind of breath you take before stepping out into open air with no idea what's below.

"There's something else," he said, glancing at me briefly. I gave the smallest nod—go on.

He turned to the others. "I'm gay."

The words weren't loud. They didn't need to be. They were clear. Solid. Real. The truth spoken aloud, without defense or apology.

There was a beat of silence. Not the awkward kind, but the kind where the world seems to hold its breath to see what comes next.

My mother didn't flinch. She simply nodded once, her lips pressing together in the kind of understanding only years could carve into someone. Evelyn reached out, resting a hand on Lucas's shoulder, her smile gentle and grounding. Allison looked at him, nodded once, and said quietly, "Of course you are."

Lucas exhaled like he'd been holding that breath for a lifetime. The shift in him was immediate, almost startling. His shoulders dropped. His jaw unclenched. He looked lighter. Like a boulder had been rolled off his chest and he could finally breathe in full.

He glanced at me. I met his eyes. No words needed.

He was seen. Fully.

And he wasn't alone.

"Interesting," my mother murmured, watching the firelight dance in her eyes. "This person only appeared to you?"

"Yes," I nodded. "She was… not exactly helpful."

"Do you remember what I always told you when reading something difficult?" she said, eyes narrowing with a hint of mischief behind the motherly sternness. Her voice was calm, but it carried the weight of a lesson she had repeated a thousand times before.

I looked up from the fire, brow furrowed. "Read between the lines," I said softly, half to myself.

Lucas gave an exaggerated groan and flopped back onto his pack like the world had just asked too much of him. "How is that supposed to help? We're not decoding Shakespeare."

My mother raised a brow and glanced at Lucas with a knowing smile. "You'd be surprised how often wisdom hides in plain sight."

She turned her gaze back to me—intense, patient, challenging. "But that's for Phoenix to figure out," she added, her tone threading between affection and expectation.

The others looked at me, as if the next step belonged to me alone. The air around the fire shifted, like the forest itself was holding its breath to see what I'd do next.

And suddenly everyone was staring at me again. Like I held a key I didn't remember picking up. It made my skin itch. I stood, pacing without realizing, chewing the inside of my cheek.

Let the heart guide you.

The words echoed again, loud as a bell in my mind. Let the heart guide you. But what heart? Mine? That felt absurd. I wasn't exactly a poster child for emotional awareness. My choices had rarely come from some deep, inner truth—they were reactions, defenses. Survival instincts, maybe.

Still, something tugged at me.

I turned slowly, eyes drawn to one of the trees that stood slightly apart from the others. It loomed taller, its bark darker, almost reflective under the light. My boots crunched on the mossy floor as I stepped toward it, each movement deliberate, unsure if I was walking into wisdom or something waiting to devour me.

When I reached it, I raised my hand—not in confidence, but curiosity. My fingertips made contact. The bark was cool, unnaturally smooth, as if time hadn't eroded it. Familiar, but not quite. It was like touching the pages of a book you swear you've read before in another life.

Then—it pulsed.

Not wind. Not illusion. A rhythmic thump, soft but undeniable. A heartbeat. Real. Steady. Ancient.

I inhaled sharply. My other hand joined the first, palm pressed flat. I closed my eyes for a moment and let myself feel it, like the tree was breathing with me, or maybe for me. With every beat, something passed between us—a flicker, a thought, a memory not mine. I saw roots deep in the earth and canopies stretching toward the stars. I saw storms endured and centuries passed.

Then the forest responded.

Light spilled from beneath the tree, radiating outward in a vein-like pattern, silver-white and pulsing, snaking across the ground like a living map. The other trees shimmered in response, their leaves rustling in unseen wind.

"What did you do?" Evelyn gasped, standing so fast her cloak rustled behind her, voice caught between awe and fear.

"I don't know," I whispered. My hand stayed against the bark. "There's a heartbeat in the tree. And I think… it's letting me see."

Before they could respond, Diana appeared—suddenly and silently, as if she had always been standing just behind us. Her smile was different this time. Not cryptic. Not distant. Genuine.

"The heart guides you, Phoenix," she said. "The wisdom of the grove sees you—and you have passed."

I looked down at my hand, still resting on the tree.

"That's it? That was the trial?"

She tilted her head. "Wisdom isn't always found in action or intellect. Sometimes it's the willingness to feel, to be present, to listen when all logic says to speak."

Lucas blinked. "That's… incredibly vague."

Diana chuckled. "And yet, here you are. Follow the path. Your next trials will test your soul—and your will."

And just like that, she vanished. No flourish. No grand parting. Just gone, like a whisper swallowed by the woods.

"Was that—" Lucas started.

"Yeah," I nodded. "It was."

We packed up camp quickly. No one spoke much—we were all still reeling from what had just happened. The light continued ahead of us, cutting a winding path through the trees. It pulsed faintly as we walked, like it was breathing. Lucas stayed close beside me, and I could feel Evelyn's presence at my back like a tether.

The forest grew quieter the deeper we went. Even the hum of the bioluminescent canopy began to fade as the trees spaced out and thinned. Shadows stretched between them, tall and sharp, and the path ahead glowed brighter the further we walked. There was no moon here. No stars. Just us, and the soft, silvery breath of the forest's hidden pulse.

I turned to look back one last time.

Behind us, the grove shimmered in eerie, perfect silence—tall trees standing like ancient sentinels, their lights rising into the sky like stars that had fallen to Earth. It was beautiful. It was unknowable. It was alive.

I held the image in my mind, imprinting it like a memory I couldn't afford to lose.

I had passed the Trial of Wisdom.

But it had only left me with more questions.

And somewhere deeper in this place, answers were waiting—or something worse.

WE KNEW WHAT WAS COMING.
HE DIDN'T.
NOT YET.

-DIANA

TWENTY-SIX

THE TRAIL OF WILL

"WHERE THE BODY FALTERS, THE TRUTH BEGINS."

The lights from the trees trailed farther behind us as we walked toward darkness. At first, we followed the soft glow, trusting its quiet presence. It was like walking beneath the breath of stars—each step lit by a thread of magic that whispered you're not alone. But step by step, it faded—first to a flicker, then to a suggestion, until finally, we were swallowed whole by shadow.

"Hold my hand," I said to Evelyn, the moment I realized the light was vanishing for good. She found mine without hesitation, and I clung to her touch like it was the last thing tethering me to this world. Her palm was warm, steady, alive. With each step, I focused on that warmth, anchoring myself to her—to us—as the dark closed in.

Then—nothing.

Her hand was gone.

I froze. My breath hitched in my throat. I reached out into the black with a trembling hand, grasping at the empty air. "Evelyn?" I called. No answer. "Lucas? Allison? Mom?" I shouted louder. Silence answered me. A silence so deep it made my voice feel like a sin—like sound wasn't allowed here. Like hope wasn't welcome.

I turned wildly, trying to find even a sliver of outline—anything. I reached forward, behind, spun in a slow, tightening circle, but there were no shapes, no shadows, no walls. Just void. Endless, eternal. A pitch-black ocean that swallowed all light and gave nothing back.

Panic fluttered in my chest. My breathing quickened. My throat tightened, and each breath felt like drawing air through cloth. All I could do was walk. I had no idea which direction I was headed, only that stopping felt like death. Stillness wasn't peace. It was surrender.

So I walked.

Then I ran.

I sprinted through the nothing, my boots hammering against a surface I couldn't see, my footfalls echoing in a place with no walls. I could've been moving in circles, but I didn't care. I just needed to move, to fight, to refuse the stillness. I screamed their names until my voice cracked, until my throat burned raw. I cursed the gods, the grove, Diana, and this damned trial. My voice was a weapon thrown into a well that never echoed back.

I was unraveling. The darkness wasn't empty—it was aware. It pressed against my skin like a vice, whispering doubt into my bones. My mind twisted under the pressure, thoughts colliding, breaking, reforming. Was this what death felt like? An endless fall into silence where the only voice left was your own?

I kept moving, even when every instinct screamed to give up. I couldn't let this be the end. I wouldn't. Something in me refused to break. I staggered forward, half-blind, half-broken. My lungs clawed for breath. My legs screamed beneath me.

And then—light.

A distant flicker. Dim. Almost imagined. A gasp left my chest. I chased it, stumbling, desperate. My feet tangled in unseen roots. My body threatened to collapse with every step. But I didn't stop. The light swelled as I neared, a small circle of illumination cutting through the dark like a knife.

I stepped into it.

Solace.

It bathed me in a soft, sterile glow. I turned, but the source was invisible—no torch, no sun, no fire. Just this impossible light suspended in the gloom like a forgotten star.

Then a voice, calm but firm, rang out behind me.

"You have shown your strength. You have proven your wisdom. Now you must endure and show your will."

I turned sharply. A woman stood just inside the light, dressed in the same ceremonial garb as Diana—but she was different. Her posture held less mystique and more command. Her eyes, sharp and unwavering, locked onto mine.

"My will... of what?" I asked, breath ragged. "Where are the others?"

"The others are not being tested. Only you."

"Then what do you mean, will? What the hell does that even mean?"

She didn't blink. "I am testing your will to live."

The words struck like thunder. My heart stuttered. Cold slipped down my spine like ice water. She said it like a fact. Not a warning. Not a threat. Just the truth.

"Why?" I asked. It was all I could say. All I could think. "Why this? Why now?"

She stepped closer. "Because I know what you've carried. I know what you've buried. And now, you must face it. Not with strength. Not with wisdom. But with the raw, terrifying choice to stay."

I didn't speak. I couldn't.

This trial wasn't about monsters. Or puzzles. Or ancient truths.

This was about me.

And the darkest part I'd never spoken aloud.

She raised her hand.

"Are you ready?"

I didn't answer right away. I just stood there, breathing—long, slow, and shallow. A thousand moments surged through me. Cold tile. Crimson water. A locked door. A scream I never let out. I remembered everything I had tried so hard to forget.

So, all I did was wait—wait for whatever this could bring. How would they even test it? The silence was almost oppressive. My breath echoed in my ears, shallow and unsure. All around me stretched pure darkness, endless and suffocating, pierced only by the faint, flickering light above. I craned my neck to find its source, but there was nothing. No lantern, no sun, no moon—just the illusion of light, suspended in nothing. It felt unnatural, like something holding its breath.

"What happens if I fail?" I asked, my voice brittle as I turned back to her.

"Then you all will stay trapped here, I'm afraid. We can't afford the luxury of failing," she replied. This time her voice was softer, absent of the sharp authority she'd held earlier. It was almost human. Almost sad. "Are you ready?"

I didn't answer right away. I stood there, heart hammering, feeling the weight of the entire journey pressing down on me like stone. This wasn't just another trial. It was the one thing I'd never let anyone see. The one I didn't even want to see myself. I closed my eyes and took a long breath, deep into my chest. Steady, I told myself. Just steady.

"Yes," I said. And that one word cost me more than I expected.

"Very well. Know that what you hear and what you will see are all things you have already experienced."

I nodded, bracing for whatever darkness lay ahead. Pain I knew well. Pain I never wanted to revisit. And then she opened her mouth.

But it wasn't her voice that emerged.

"Worthless idiot!"

It shot through me like icewater in my veins. I knew that voice—Mr. Farris, fifth-grade science. I could see his face, the hard lines, the sneer barely masked as a joke. Then came the laughter—high-pitched, cruel. My classmates. Children, but with the sharpest daggers.

"You will never succeed in life!" the voice thundered again. I flinched, involuntarily, and shut my eyes. But the darkness offered no protection. The laughter built—layered, echoing, deafening. It wrapped around me like smoke, impossible to escape.

"Look, it's Mr. Pee body!" another voice squealed, and that one was even worse. A name meant to humiliate, born from a single, stupid accident. "Mr. Pee body, rounding the corner to die alone!"

Each word scraped across my skin like broken glass. I was back in that hallway. Back in that fourth-grade body. Small. Alone. Fragile.

"Look, it's the twig! Don't touch him, he might break!"

I tried to push the memories away, but they were stronger. Clearer. Realer. I saw my scrawny arms, my too-large t-shirt hanging off my frame like a flag of failure. The playground spinning around me as I wandered alone, the bark of cruel laughter following like a shadow.

And then the tone shifted.

"Go to hell, wetback," came an adult voice—male, guttural, thick with venom. I froze. That word—it hit different. Not just cruelty, but danger. That time I ran. I didn't understand it at first, not until I asked what it meant. Not until I realized I was the only brown kid on the block.

"Watch out, you don't belong here!"

More voices.

"He's probably a bastard. Damn colored pedigree."

Middle school whispers. Adults who forgot—or didn't care—that I could hear them.

"Look at him, alone."

"Don't be like him."

I remembered that one. A mom pulling her kid away in the grocery store. All she saw was my skin, my name, my silence. Not the kid who just wanted peanut butter.

The weight of those words—decades of them—settled like a vise around my chest. My lungs tightened. My throat burned. I couldn't breathe.

"Stop," I whispered. But it was like shouting into a hurricane.

Worthless child.

Bastard.

Wetback.

Scrawny. Ugly. Big ears.

The labels exploded in my ears like gunshots. My body trembled under the barrage.

"Why is he even alive?"

And that one—

That one broke something.

"STOP!" I roared, my voice cracking like thunder.

But they didn't stop. They multiplied. Surrounding me. Consuming me.

"No one would miss him."

"They wouldn't even know he was gone."

I felt it then. A fracture in the dark. The shift from abstract dread into something painfully specific. The darkness wasn't just pressing in anymore—it was bleeding into shape. Scenes clawed their way out of the void, one by one. I saw the cafeteria, saw myself sitting at the edge of the table with an untouched tray, pretending to read to avoid eye contact. I saw the invitations handed out in class—everyone but me. I remembered the hallway where shoulders bumped me like I wasn't there, where teachers turned away, where I vanished in plain sight.

And then—I saw the bathroom.

The linoleum tiles, cold and glossy. The smell of bleach. The way the light flickered. The way my hands shook. The blood.

So much blood.

The silence that followed, louder than any scream.

That moment—the one I never let myself think about, let alone speak of. The part of my story that lived in the dark, gnawing from the inside. Where I didn't think I'd make it.

Where I didn't want to.

I tried to blink it away, but the tears came anyway—hot, relentless. I didn't stop them. Couldn't. My knees buckled and I crumpled to the floor, hands curled in fists that shook against the ground. This was it. The marrow of my pain. The buried wound. The festering truth I dressed up in jokes, deflection, silence.

"I can't," I whispered, the words barely air. "I can't do this."

And still it came—the memory, sharp and merciless. The red pooling, the cold wrapping around my limbs like chains, the choking sobs I never let out until it was too late.

I wanted to disappear. To vanish so completely that the dark would claim me and never let me back out. I wanted to dissolve into the shadows, to unmake myself so thoroughly that not even memory could cling to my bones. I wanted to stop being—stop existing, stop feeling, stop hurting. I wanted the silence to swallow me whole, to bury me beneath all the noise I'd carried for so long. But instead, I lay there. Shattered. Exposed. The mask I'd worn for years had crumbled, every wall obliterated. I couldn't hide behind jokes. I couldn't hide behind detachment or anger or intellect. There was no performance left, no persona to shield me. Just the raw, naked truth of me. A boy who had once wanted to die. A man still figuring out why he hadn't.

Then I let the scream erupt out of me—not just a sound, but a rupture. A howl born of marrow-deep grief, forged in the fires of years I never admitted burned me. It tore through my throat, raw and animal, vibrating through the void like thunder crashing against the walls of an unseen world. The scream carried every breath I'd ever swallowed instead of exhaled, every word I choked down, every memory I tried to bury but couldn't. It was ugly. Desperate. So loud it made the air itself shudder.

My knees scraped the invisible ground, trembling beneath me. My chest heaved and ribs ached like they were cracked open from the inside. My body seized, shaken by the force of what I had unleashed. I sobbed—wild, brutal sobs that echoed without mercy. The tears came like a flood, not graceful but convulsing. Each one dragged up more pain, more memory, more shame. I wasn't just crying. I was breaking. Splintering.

There was no mask left. No armor. Just me—shattered, bare, screaming into the dark.

And the earth responded. Not with words. But with stillness, like the world itself held its breath. Somewhere in the scream's fading echo, the shadows shifted. I swear I heard the trees groan above me—if there were trees—like ancient things stirred by the weight of my sorrow. As if the land, the myth itself, had paused to witness my breaking.

It wasn't just catharsis. It was reckoning. The kind of scream you only give once. The kind that wakes ghosts and bends fate.

Until, at last, there was nothing left. Just breath. Just the thunder of my own heart. And silence that finally felt earned.

And in that ruin, something stirred. A whisper beneath the chaos. A truth so quiet it trembled:

I chose to live.

But even in the wreckage, I heard something else. A whisper beneath the hate.

I chose to live.

It wasn't loud. It didn't need to be. It was mine.

I chose to stay.

I remembered the blood. The moment I woke. The shame. The regret. The vow I made, alone on that floor.

Never again.

I lifted my head.

The voices kept screaming—but they no longer held me.

"No," I said. Stronger. Clearer.

I rose.

"No. I don't care what you say. I don't care what any of you think."

The air shifted.

"I choose to live. I choose to be. And you—"

I looked at the guardian, her form still surrounded by shadow.

"—don't get to define me."

And then the darkness cracked.

Light.

Real light this time. Not illusion. Not memory. Not the absence of pain, but something beyond it.

Hope.

I pushed myself up, pulled myself together, and faced her, gathering my strength and pushing everything else out. I was going to make my stand here. No one decided who I was other than me. I would show them who I really was. The real me—not the scared one, not the one who had been called hateful things, not the one pushed to the ground and forgotten all those years. I was someone of strength, of knowledge. I was resilient. I was caring. I was loving. And I was going to show the world that person. Whether they liked it or not. Whether they accepted it or not. Whether they even noticed—didn't matter. I had noticed. I had claimed him.

"No," I said again, this time with iron behind the word. "I chose to live."

The screams lowered, retreating like wolves to the edge of the woods, but they still hissed at the edges, still waited to pounce. I took a breath, deep and deliberate, and raised my voice until it thundered across the dark. A sound that didn't echo—it landed, solid, like a weight placed back into the world. I stood tall, facing them—facing every ghost, every voice, every lie that had tried to shape me into something small and silent and disposable.

Somewhere in the void, the ground shifted subtly beneath my feet, as if even the stone listened. The air took on a weight. My skin prickled.

"No, your words don't matter," I yelled. My voice shook with fury and clarity. "I do."

I mattered. My health, my being, my soul—they all mattered. My victories belonged to me. My scars, my growth, my tenderness, my defiance—they were mine. Every breath I had fought to take was mine. No word from a stranger or a bigot or a ghost in the back of my mind would ever own me again. I had lived through the fire. I had stood on the edge of nothingness. And I had walked out of it, still burning. Still choosing.

As I spoke, something stirred in the stillness. The air thickened, humming faintly with energy—like the earth itself was waking. I could feel the heat radiating beneath the surface, ancient and alive. The kind of heat that forges, not just burns.

"You can stop your game," I growled, fire rising in my chest and flickering in my fingertips. "Because I don't care what you or anyone else thinks. I can do whatever I put my mind to. Because

I chose to stay. I chose to lift myself and change. I chose to be myself—and love myself—for whatever flaws I may have."

A pause. A stillness.

The shadows seemed to lean in, curious.

The wind shifted, almost imperceptibly, as though it carried the breath of something older—something that remembered grief and survival and stillness. I thought I saw a faint shimmer of trees, not standing but witnessing, their leaves whispering truths that no voice had dared speak aloud. One branch tilted ever so slightly, as if in solemn agreement. Not a gust, not an accident—an acknowledgment.

A light bloomed from somewhere inside me—not literal, not seen, but felt. A quiet radiance that pressed against the silence.

"I see," she said, her voice gentler now. The voices fell away, vanishing like smoke caught in a wind. Silence blanketed the world again. Her hands folded before her as she looked at me—not as a judge, but with something almost reverent. Something like respect.

"Now get out of my way," I said, quiet but firm. There was no venom in it. Just strength. The kind you earn the hard way, the kind carved by fire and carried by the broken.

"You chose to live," she whispered, like a blessing, like a truth long denied. "And now let it fuel your journey."

Then she was gone—vanished like mist in the morning. Where she once stood, a new light flickered in the distance. Not harsh. Not cold. It pulsed with warmth. With welcome. And it called to me.

I turned to follow it. But I looked back first.

Not because I wanted to stay—but because some part of me knew I was leaving something behind. A version of myself. One built from silence, from shame, from the necessity of survival. A shadow-version that had served its purpose but could no longer come with me. Maybe that part needed a farewell. Maybe I had to mourn it to move forward.

And in that moment, I thought I heard something: a single, resonant note, like wind across old branches or the deep exhale of a mountain. Not a sound, but a memory. As though the forest bore witness—and remembered me.

The warmth ahead was waiting. I squared my shoulders, breathing in the stillness one last time. The silence didn't feel empty anymore.

It felt earned.

I must move forward.

Twenty-Seven

The Trail of Truth

"The Truth Shall Set You Free"

The darkness was fading, and the light became clear—sharper, warmer, more real. I could be okay. I hoped the others made it through. They could be worried sick for all I knew, wondering where on earth I had gone—not realizing I had faced a gauntlet of pain that threatened to consume me whole. Not realizing I had come through fire.

I couldn't even remember the last time I had truly heard all of it, let alone faced the weight of what I had survived so completely. It was like being forced to stare into a mirror long ignored—cracks and all—and not looking away. And yet, I'd made it through.

I knew now that I couldn't look at the trauma as a crutch, something that forever defined me by its sharpest edge. Because, in its own brutal way, it had taught me something. It had carved something true into my core. It had solidified my drive to be better—not perfect, but purposeful. It taught me that I could find light in a world steeped in shadow. It taught me that my will to live wasn't some passive instinct—it was an active choice. A flame I'd kept alive, even in the wind.

As I walked now—step after careful step—I looked back not with regret, but with a strange, fierce clarity. These trials hadn't just tested me. They had revealed me. Each one had pulled something buried from the marrow of who I was. I had found strength—real, terrifying, blinding strength—in protecting those I loved. I had found wisdom not through intellect, but through listening, through surrendering to the deeper current connecting us all. And I had faced the storm of myself—the voices, the wounds, the moment I almost didn't survive—and I chose to live.

Now, the final trial waited. Whatever it held, whatever shadows or truths remained, I would meet it as I was: cracked, mended, scarred, and completely awake.

The light ahead wasn't just brightness anymore. It was warmth. It embraced me. I crossed the threshold and entered a corridor lined with flickering torches, their flames dancing against rough stone. The walls pulsed with age, etched by time and moisture. The scent of moss, damp earth, and minerals filled my lungs. Every footstep echoed faintly, swallowed slowly by the close, winding passage.

The walls felt narrower here, forcing me to walk with purpose, head low, shoulders tense. The corridor curved and twisted like a serpent. Minutes passed. I had no idea how far I'd gone. My own breath was the only sound.

Then, the cave opened.

A new chamber—wider, natural. The rock had softened here, like the bones of the earth had given way. Torches flickered around the perimeter, throwing shadows that danced across uneven walls. But the room was empty.

No one.

I stood still, unsure if this was another illusion, another trick of the Grove.

Was I alone again? Was this part of it?

Then—

"Phoenix, there you are," Evelyn's voice rang out. I turned, heart leaping.

She stepped through the passage, relief written all over her face. "For a moment I thought we lost you. How did you get ahead of us?"

"Wait," I said, confused. "How long was I gone?"

Lucas appeared next, followed by Allison and my mom. He looked me over, eyes narrowing at the sight of my stained clothes, my sweat-dried face.

"Maybe like a minute or so," he said, frowning.

My mother stepped forward, the worry in her eyes immediate. "Are you okay, honey? You look like you've been through hell."

I stared at them, stunned. "Guys... it's been hours since I saw you."

They all exchanged looks. I could feel the tension in the room shift. Evelyn's eyes softened as she reached for my hand, but it was Lucas who spoke next.

"You finished the third trial," he said quietly. The others turned to look at me, concern tightening their features.

I just nodded. What else could I do? They didn't know. They couldn't.

My mother stepped forward again, gently. "What was it?"

I paused, throat tightening. How could I explain it? How do you describe a wound still bleeding?

"A test of will," I said. My voice was calm, but the words cost me. "They threw a bunch of stuff at me, and I had to endure."

There was a pause—just long enough to make me uneasy.

Lucas tilted his head slightly, watching me in a way that stripped past the words. His eyes weren't searching for lies, just truths left unsaid. "Your voice is shaking," he said softly. "You've never sounded like that before."

I tried to laugh it off, but my throat was too dry.

Then my mom stepped closer, gently placing a hand on my shoulder. "Phoenix," she said, her voice the kind she used when I was little and trying to pretend I wasn't hurt. "Whatever you went through... you don't have to talk about it right now. But don't pretend it didn't leave a mark."

Her hand stayed there, warm and grounding.

I blinked—once, then twice—holding everything back with the thinnest thread of composure. The words clung to my throat, too raw to speak.

"I'm okay," I whispered.

No one corrected me. But none of them believed me either.

Allison gave me a sideways look, then smirked. "Well, that leaves one more, handsome. And since the Grove seems to be really into you, I'd guess the finale's your show."

I smiled, weakly, and we turned to move forward.

As we walked, the sound emerged gradually. A deep, rolling thunder. At first faint. Then closer. Louder. Insistent.

The sound of water—rushing, crashing, alive.

The air changed again, thickening with moisture. Every breath pulled in the scent of fresh water—cold, mineral-rich, ancient. The stone beneath our feet grew slick. The walls shimmered with condensation. Droplets clung to our skin like dew, gathering at the tips of our lashes.

We pressed forward. The tunnel narrowed, then widened again. The light of the torches turned golden, diffused by the mist. The roar of the water became deafening.

We turned a corner—and stopped.

What we saw, none of us could've expected.

And it was waiting for us.

Towering waterfalls cascaded from the cavernous ceiling above us, completely covering the walls. The air was cool with a breeze that carried the mist all around us. Even some birds sang; it was only the second time we had seen something living other than a plant. A living, breathing bird flying around in the cave, and it was a sight like no other. It was pure; nothing polluted it, nothing stained its beauty. At the base of the waterfall, a pool with a little island in the center. There on that little piece of land was the last guardian. He stood tall with fair skin as he watched us approach. He did not say anything, just stared—his eyes dark and searching, fixed on me like he was trying to peer through skin and bone to whatever lay buried beneath. His posture was rigid, hands folded in front of him with a stillness that felt deliberate, even ominous. The set of his jaw was tense, and the longer he looked at me, the more the weight of that silence pressed down on my chest like a stone. I felt exposed, as if every scar I'd tried to bury was written across my face and he was reading them one by one.

For a moment I looked towards him and expected him to say something, but he didn't. He had just a look, a studious one. The whispers behind me began to build as they asked questions. I had been the only one to communicate with the guardians, and maybe it would take me to do that here. To reach out and finish this finally. To face what truly needed to be told. I just hoped it wasn't what I feared it was.

"Step forward," the man said firmly. We began to move before we were interrupted.

"Just him," he said, pointing to me. Why me? Why was it always me? Why had all of this been about me? The question clawed at my ribs, gnawing at the raw edges of my thoughts. I remembered the way the guardian in the previous trial had looked at me—not just seen me, but peeled me apart. The screaming. The shadows. The blood I had once tried to leave behind. Was this what all of it had been building toward? Was I some kind of broken compass the grove was trying to recalibrate? My hands clenched at my sides, the skin across my knuckles taut. I hadn't noticed until now, but my shoulders were tight, my posture defensive. Even my breath came shallow, like I was bracing for another blow I couldn't see. Why was it me—why had it always been me who had to endure, who had to bear the weight of the unseen? There had to be a reason. I just didn't know if I wanted to hear it.

I wanted that answer more than anything at this moment. To understand why everything was centered on me this entire time. From being left alone to fight an army. The light turning on with my hand. Reliving the hardships that I had faced, and now it was my truth that needed to be told. This whole time it was me who had been tested. No one else, just me, and I wanted to know why.

I glanced back at the others. Evelyn opened her mouth to protest, but Lucas placed a hand on her shoulder. His eyes were locked on mine. He could see it—see that I wasn't okay. Maybe it was the tremble in my shoulders, or the rawness still clinging to my face. My mother stepped forward slightly, concern etched into her every line, but she didn't speak. None of them did. They just watched.

So, I stepped forward, the water crashing down around me. I began my slow walk into the shallow pool to the island where he stood. Its water was crisp as it embraced my feet, soaking my socks and shoes. The water never rose above my knee, and soon I arrived at the small piece of land at its center. Around the water fell, surrounding this place, and frankly, it was beautiful and powerful as I looked above.

Now that I was closer, the man that stood in front of me was clearer. He studied me as all the others had. Then he looked out to the others as they stood on the shore. I wondered what he thought. I wondered what he had planned. This was the final test, the one that I had feared from the start. The one that could destroy me, destroy everything that I had built.

"You have shown your strength to battle those who wish to hurt you," he began. "You have learned about the wisdom that you possess and have proven your will to live, to prevail against the hardest odds. Now you must tell your truth and prove your worthiness."

Truth. It was a simple thing, yet we all tried to hide it or change it. My truth was what he wanted. I guessed there were millions of ways I could take that. How much truth did a person have? That could be billions, but I knew which one he was talking about. I knew what he wanted me to say. I just couldn't—not that. No one deserved that pain. There had to be another he wanted, some other truth that I had. Before I could even say anything, I looked back and made eye contact with my mother. If I said it, it would hurt her. It would destroy her, and I could not live with that. Knowing that I was the source of the pain.

"What truth?" I asked, hoping he could shed some clarity on how this would work. I'd noticed that nothing was out of their reach. Yet this one seemed so simple.

"The truth you hid from your loved ones."

"Do I just say it and that's it?" I shot back. By the look he gave, he wasn't enthused about that.

"Yes, you say it, here in front of everyone, and I will know if it's true."

I just couldn't say it! How could I? So, I would just start with something simple and hope that worked.

"I love Evelyn," I said in a clear voice, my throat tightening around the words. I didn't look at her at first—I couldn't. My gaze fixed on the ground, and only after the silence stretched too long did I lift my eyes. Her face was still, searching, like she was afraid of what might come next. I shifted my weight, fists curled slightly at my sides, unsure whether the words had landed as a confession or a crack in my armor. My chest rose and fell with shallow breath, the echo of the waterfall behind me suddenly distant. I had said it, but it felt like stepping out onto a cliff's edge—no ground beneath, only faith.

"I always have, I just never could say it; I was scared of that emotion. Now I can't live without it or her." I meant it; he said he would know if it wasn't true. I did say a truth that I hadn't said. I showed a part of me that I hadn't before in front of people. Someone vulnerable, not always calm and controlled. I looked up at him, hoping he would say something and let this be over. I hoped that was it, the thing he wanted. However, I knew what he wanted.

"That is a truth, but not the one you hide. Say your truth," he replied, his voice tightening, sterner now—not with anger, but urgency. His posture straightened further, like the air around him had shifted, electric and expectant. A subtle narrowing of his eyes conveyed something weightier: this moment mattered. The ground between us suddenly felt charged, as if a storm were gathering, not above but within. The others stirred behind me; I could sense their attention sharpening, the hush before a blow.

Behind me, Evelyn's breath caught. Lucas glanced at my mother, who looked pale, bracing herself. There was something unspoken in the air. They could feel it now—the tension, the weight of what was coming. Something deeper than love. A truth sharpened by years of silence.

I had to think of another one as my heart raced a bit. I was going to have to go deeper. Show something more personal. Hoping that something would be good enough before I had to say it.

"I was hated by people," I began, my voice quieter than I expected. I swallowed hard, a lump rising in my throat as I stared at the ground. My hands trembled slightly at my sides, and I clasped them together to steady myself.

"Hated by people just because I was different, hated because my skin was only a little tanner than everyone else." I paused and glanced up, my eyes flicking to my mother's unreadable face before dropping again.

"Hated because of how I looked. Hated because of who I was, even when I didn't know myself." I looked back after, and I could see my mother's face, stone-cold. Frankly, Lucas was the same, and even Allison was showing no emotion. I would have expected that she would find satisfaction in that.

To be honest, that was more than I ever wanted to share. It was revealing and I hated it. It showed a part of me that was insecure, one that was weak. Yet I knew it wasn't good enough. It wasn't what he wanted, and I looked up at him, pleading with my eyes. Hoping that would work, hoping he would accept it and spare me from the pain that I was going to inflict, the pain that almost destroyed me.

"That is a truth, but not the one that you need to say," he said, and I sensed he was getting frustrated. "Perhaps some motivation will help you."

"What?" I replied, scared. That was when I felt the chill in the air as the water froze around me. At first, I didn't understand how that would motivate me. Then I noticed how the ice traveled and where it was heading. Lucas, Evelyn, Mom, and even Allison. "No. Stop."

"Tell your truth or they die!"

"Stop, they don't deserve--" I pleaded with him. Don't make it about them, it is all me. Put the pain on me and no one else. I wanted it all to end.

"Phoenix," Evelyn screamed as the ice came closer. It traveled from the water to the land and began to surround them. I looked over to him, pleading. Not this! Why? Why do this? Why all of this? Why was that damn thing still haunting me? It was past, it was done, and nothing could change that. There had to be something else, but I couldn't think of anything. I could tell him how I sneaked out of the house, or the time I hid a failing grade from my parents. However, I doubted that was what he wanted me to say.

"Just say it, it's not that hard," Lucas said as the ice started to cover his feet. They all tugged at it and tried to free themselves from it.

"Phoenix just say it!" Evelyn said as she struggled.

"I can't, I can't say that," I said, trying to think of a way out. Phoenix, you crazy bastard, you know very well there is not one. Yet I fought with myself. Trying to keep it all away.

"Say your truth!" The guardian spoke again as the ice grew around them. They struggle and it pained me more than the pain that I was feeling inside. There screams echoed as the ice climbed higher, hurting them as it grew. My body ached at the thought. Thinking about it how it had happened. How I had felt that day, how it made me feel every day after. I wanted this to stop, I wanted it all to end. I couldn't take it. I couldn't say it.

I heard their screams; I heard their struggles as my mind slowed. The world didn't seem to exist when I thought about it. Thought about that day. The day my view went black. The day I woke up on the floor with the red pool around me. The pool of my blood pouring from my nose. The bottles littered the ground and counter of the bathroom. I felt the empty feeling that swallowed me. I felt the hopelessness that engulfed me. I could feel every ounce of pain as it flooded back to me.

I remembered pulling myself up off the ground, scared and bursting into tears. Knowing full well what I had done. Regretting what I had tried to do. The screams were getting louder, and I felt the tears fall. My insides burned. It was consuming me, the memories of that day. How I looked, how I felt, how I cleaned myself. Making everything look perfect so no one would know. Scrubbing my blood off the floor. While wrapping my head around it. Telling myself to be better. To never do that again. Swearing not to let anything push me to that point again. Promising never to tell, never to share. A secret to be kept until I died so that no one would feel that pain.

"Phoenix, say it, please," Evelyn yelled. She was scared, and as I looked back, the ice growing over her torso, over all of them.

"Just say it, I promise it will be okay," Lucas said. I couldn't do it; I just closed my eyes, but their struggle and screams were getting worse. I wanted to block it all out. I hate this! I hate all of this! I wanted it to stop. It needed to stop. The ember was lit and there was no stopping it as the wildfire erupted and spread throughout me.

Truth–

Pain–

Silence–

Release–

"I TOOK MY OWN LIFE!" I screamed and collapsed to my knees. The tears flowed from my eyes. My voice was broken. I was broken.

"I just wanted to pain to go away¬. I hated myself as much as everyone else," I cried. I was on my knees, broken, revealing everything. There was nothing else, like I was bare to the world. It was then that I noticed the silence. It was just the water. No one spoke as everything seemed frozen.

"The truth shall set you free," the guardian said as I looked up at him. His face was solemn, yet there was a softness. Empathy.

I just had one last thing to say, to make sure, but I needed to say this for my sake. "I took my life," I said, my voice catching halfway through the sentence. My throat tightened, and I struggled to breathe. The words burned like acid on my tongue. "And I can never forgive myself for it."

I blinked hard, trying to force back the tears, but they came anyway—hot and relentless. My voice dropped to a whisper, brittle and hollow.

"I am not worthy." My shoulders hunched as if the shame alone might crush me. I didn't dare look at anyone, afraid of what I'd see in their eyes—pity, disgust, or worse, understanding.

"You are more worthy that you will ever imagine." He spoke once more, but this time there was a more serious tone. One that I had not heard before. How would he even know? I was the one that had to bear this pain, I was the one who suffered under its weight, and now I pushed that pain to the ones that I loved.

Then I did the challenging thing and looked behind me. There they were, just staring. Evelyn was crying, Lucas stood there, not saying a word. Allison looked away, not even making eye contact with me. My mother just stood there, her hand covering her mouth and tears in her eyes. That was the image that hurt the most. Seeing the pain on her face. Her son just told her the worst possible thing. I could never give her the bliss of not knowing back. The innocence was gone. It was out there, and I couldn't put that back in the bottle.

She began to walk slowly over to me, hesitating for a breath before stepping into the water. Her brows knit together, her lips parted as though she wanted to speak but couldn't find the words. One cautious step after another, the water rippling around her legs, she crossed the distance, her eyes never leaving mine. I just sat there on my knees, trembling, barely able to lift my gaze.

When she reached me, she paused again. Her eyes searched my face—full of grief, confusion, fear—and I saw something shift in her: not just pain, but resolve. She placed a trembling hand on my shoulder, her touch soft but certain. The mist clung to her hair and lashes, giving her an almost ethereal glow, and I could see in her eyes the thousand unspoken questions, the silent scream of a mother wondering what she missed.

I wanted to say something—to tell her she hadn't failed, that it wasn't her fault—but the words stuck in my throat. She pulled me into an embrace, her arms wrapping around me as though trying to hold me together, as if afraid I might fall apart again. I buried my face in her shoulder and let it all out—the sobs, the gasps, the years of silence. I cried into her, and she held me tighter with each breath I lost, as if refusing to let me go ever again.

"I'm sorry. I'm so sorry," I managed to say, but she shook her head gently.

"Don't be," she whispered. "You survived. You found the light. I'm just so happy you're still here. You made your own way—and I'm proud of the man you've become. Be proud too. You didn't just come back. You rebuilt—stronger."

Evelyn knelt beside us, wiping her face with her sleeve. Her eyes met mine, and through the tears, she smiled.

"I love you," she said. "And I'm here. For all of it—the beautiful and the brutal. You're the rock that didn't shatter. You've changed, Phoenix. You grew—not in spite of the pain, but through it." She leaned in, resting her forehead against mine. I never expected this. I expected people to walk away—to turn from the weight I carried. But they'd stayed. They saw me.

Lucas stepped forward next. By then, I had found my feet. He didn't say anything at first—just looked at me, letting silence speak.

Then: "See? Always feels better after," he said with a crooked grin, throwing my old words back at me. "That's why I looked up to you. You didn't need to be perfect. You fell. You bled. But you got up—and kept walking. That's what strength looks like."

My mother stepped in close, her hand brushing away the last of my tears.

"Be the light, Phoenix," she whispered. "Even in the darkest nights. Be the one others look for."

And I understood. That had always been the call. Not perfection—but presence. Resilience. The choice to shine, even in shadow.

I smiled then. Not wide, but honest. It was only then that I realized—I'd passed the trial. The last one. I looked over—and caught the guardian's gaze just as he began to fade into the mist. There was a smile on his face. Approval. Maybe peace.

A low roar began to swell around us.

Allison nodded toward it. "Okay, handsome—hate to break this up, but… look."

We all turned. The waterfall before us was shifting. Its curtain split, revealing a stone opening beyond it—veiled all this time, now glimmering with golden light. The air stirred, thick with moisture and magic.

The way forward had opened.

Not just in the cave.

In me.

TWENTY-EIGHT

THE BLOOD UNVEILED

"TRUTH IS TO BECOME IT."

The water cascaded around us as we walked through the opening. It rushed across the exposed rock face as the mist hung in the air, clinging to our skin like a second breath. Everything shimmered with a quiet kind of reverence. Everything felt different now. I felt different—like a massive, immovable weight had finally rolled off my shoulders and vanished into the past. For once, I could breathe. Truly breathe. And not just with lungs, but with my soul.

What did this all mean? Why were they here? Why had I passed their trials? Why had they tested only me? Why not Lucas or Evelyn or someone more prepared—more worthy? The questions stacked on top of each other like stones, heavy and sharp, rising in urgency, clawing for space in my chest. I needed answers. Real ones. Here. Now. I couldn't walk another step without knowing why I was at the center of all this.

My mother walked beside me, close enough that I could hear the shift of her breath. She glanced over from time to time. I couldn't read her expression—it was carved from something deeper than thought, a blend of pride and sorrow that warred in her eyes. I'd seen it before—when I was younger and she was proud of something I'd done, but it had cost something deeply felt. Something unseen. I only hoped that I wasn't the source of her sorrow this time. I thought about what I'd told her—the worst truth a son could admit. And yet, there might have been pride in that knowing. In the fact that I had survived. That I was still here. Still hers.

Evelyn and Lucas flanked us, silent. Allison eyed the surroundings warily, her posture coiled, alert, ready for anything. Evelyn's hand slipped into mine. Her fingers wrapped around mine with the gentlest pressure—a tether to this moment, this place, this life. Her touch was life. Quiet. Warm. Sure. And I held on like it was the only thing anchoring me.

The corridor widened into a massive hall, an ancient cathedral of stone and memory. Its towering walls were intricately carved with murals that depicted a time of harmony and stillness. Scenes of lush valleys, rivers teeming with fish, skies painted in gold and indigo. Despite their age, the colors in the murals remained almost impossibly sharp—like the memory of that world refused to dull, refused to be forgotten. Pillars lined the path ahead, firelight flickering between them. The torches cast shifting shadows, drawing our eyes toward the chamber's end.

There, framed by a towering waterfall that tumbled from the ceiling like liquid glass, stood a small raised platform. The air around it shimmered, humming with something more than moisture. It pulsed.

We walked slowly, cautiously, the silence stretching tight around us like skin around a bruise. And then I saw them—the guardians. Four of them. They stood like statues at the far end, positioned in front of the platform. Hands clasped, eyes calm, shoulders square. They didn't blink. Didn't breathe. They simply were—fixed points in a story I still didn't fully understand.

Then, one by one, they moved.

"You have shown us your strength and skill in battle," said the first guardian. His voice was steady. Then, without warning, he knelt.

My stomach clenched like a fist.

"You have learned from the world around you and shown us your wisdom and graciousness," Diana said. She too stepped forward and knelt.

"You have proven your will to live, even through the darkest moments of your life. You endured. You rose again," the woman from the Trial of Will said. She bowed low.

"Finally, you have spoken your truth. You are worthy," the final guardian said, his voice rich with something close to reverence.

And then he knelt too.

Goosebumps rose along my skin. My mind reeled.

"Worthy of what?" I asked. My voice barely made it past my lips. "I don't understand."

Diana lifted her head. Her eyes shimmered. "You are the son that was lost. The one that shall awaken. You are—"

My mother took a step back.

Evelyn's hand slipped from mine.

Lucas and Allison stood frozen in place.

Their eyes weren't on the guardians. They were on me.

"What do you mean?" I asked again. My heart hammered in my chest. My thoughts churned like storm water. Behind the guardians, on the platform, a staff stood upright. Simple. Unadorned. Hewn from rough wood—but glowing with something old, something alive. And it resonated. I could feel it like a second pulse, like it was waiting for me.

"You are a descendant of the three shamans. The ones buried in this tomb."

The coffins from the first chamber. It clicked. But the lineage—that didn't.

"That's not possible," I said. "My family... my family came from Europe. My parents—"

I turned to my mother.

"Right, Mom?"

She didn't answer. Didn't blink. Didn't even breathe.

Her silence hollowed something inside me.

The last guardian spoke. "There is one more truth to be told."

But his eyes weren't on me.

They were on my mother.

Time cracked.

"Mom?" I said, and my voice cracked with it. "Tell them. Tell them it's not true. Say I'm your son."

Still nothing.

Then she blinked.

And a tear fell.

"Phoenix," she whispered. Her voice was a ghost. "I need you to understand."

My throat tightened.

The envelope in her office. Veronica's warning. The weight of a silence too heavy to hold.

"That's what the envelope is, isn't it?" I asked.

She nodded. A pause. A breath that ached.

"Yes, dear," she said. "But you are still my son. Always."

My knees wobbled. My chest went cold.

I wasn't a Knight.

I wasn't who I thought I was.

I was a borrowed name. A secret wrapped in love. A lie built into a legacy.

My voice came out small. Hollow.

"Are they... alive?"

"No." It was a quick answer, and part of me was relieved to hear it. Maybe it was the fact that I didn't have anyone out there that I didn't know. That maybe the best thing for me was to be adopted. So that I could at least have a family. One that cared for me, one that loved me.

"They died when you were young. Your mother was my best friend, and so, I took you in and raised you."

"Why didn't you tell me?"

"Because your bloodline is special—descended from a lineage that once held the staff centuries ago, a power bound to myth and feared by those who understand its reach—and people would kill over it. That's why I changed your last name and made it seem like you were mine. Because you are and always will be. I am so proud of you." Her face showed how sincere she was. All I could do was embrace her because I still loved her, and she was my mother. Even if we weren't related by blood, she did raise me, she did care for me, she would still be the person I would always go see on holidays. The person that would support me and care for me. My family.

Her body relaxed now like the weight had been lifted. Knowing that I still cared for her and didn't hate her for it. How could I? She has been nothing but the best, even on the days I was frustrated with her. However, my sights were set on another. Someone who pushed this.

"You knew!" I scowled and faced Allison. She stood there, dignified like she had done nothing wrong. My blood boiled at the thought that she had used me, because of this. The very thing my parents tried to protect me from. She had to pull me out, manipulate me just to get what she wanted.

"Yes, I figured it out," she said, backing up a bit as I began to approach her. Wanting her to suffer. To know the pain that she had just put me through.

"How dare you? How dare you put us through this?"

"You needed the push, Phoenix," she said, but for the first time, there was a waver in her voice—like even she wasn't sure if what she had done was right. Her eyes darted toward the ground for the briefest of seconds before she met my glare again, her jaw tight with conviction fighting guilt. Her voice was louder than it had been before. "You needed to know!"

Oh, how I hated her. She thought herself important. Like she had to right to interfere with my life.

"You killed for this." My voice was rough as my volume rose, feeling the energy build through my bones.

"I didn't kill her, that's not how I work," she replied, and there the calm was in her voice that I hadn't seen before.

"Then who did?"

"I don't know, but you needed to learn this. You needed to be found."

"Why?"

"Because it is all starting. Don't you see? They're coming. My employer plans—"

"Plans to what?" I said. "Use me? Use whatever the hell that is over there? The thing that only I can get." I walked closer to her, making her feel my presence. I wanted her to be scared, I wanted her to know how angry I was.

"Phoenix, calm down." This time it was Evelyn. However, I disregarded it as the heat burned inside me, ready to consume all that was in front of me. The person that caused me and my family harm.

"They want to awaken him!" she yelled back. "I had to do something, you're the only one who can stop it. Phoenix, please take it. You have to trust me, they want you!"

There uneasiness building from behind me as the guardians all shuddered. My mother looked scared, something I had never seen. Even though all this, she had looked confident. Something Allison said scared her, but why?

"Who's coming?" I asked as I was inches away from her. Then I heard it. A loud noise echoed in the chamber. I looked down and saw that blood oozed on Allison's side. She touched it and looked at me. She was frightened, she was scared, and now she was broken.

"I am not who you think I am," she whispered. Who? Who did it?

"Pity," a loud voice rumbled. "Looks like I have to clean up a mess."

Allison collapsed to the floor as my mother and Lucas rushed in, trying to hold her and stop the bleeding. My hands were covered in blood as Allison took my hands, but my attention was fixed to the group of men that now stood towards the back of the hall. One in the center was smirking, and a gun was in his left hand as he just looked over at me.

"I guess you're the one?" he said.

"Who are you?"

"Well, I was her boss. Seems like I need to do some hiring. The name is Kane, and you are going to fetch that for me." His large build was hard to see with his dark skin blending in with the low light. His head was bald, and he wore ugly cargo pants and a bullet-proof vest. The other men were dressed in black, the same as all the other collective members we had dealt with.

"Why in the hell would I do that?" I took a half-step forward, my fists clenched so tight my nails dug crescents into my palms. My voice cracked—not from fear, but from the sheer pressure building in my chest. My eyes locked on Kane's, burning with fury, daring him to push me one step further. I looked down and saw my mother's face. Allison needed a hospital and fast, or she wasn't going to make it. Even as I wanted to let her just lie there bleeding, I couldn't. I couldn't do it.

"Because if not, everyone dies."

Why was that always the motivator? Like, seriously, it was getting annoying. That was all I had heard. His men began to rush forward and surround us. The Guardians retreated towards the staff. Making sure it was protected. I tried to fight them off as they came, but there were too many. They moved in around my mother and Lucas. Evelyn tried to fight some of them off as they moved in around her. Kane came closer as the dust settled. I glanced back at the Guardians, and it was Diana who looked at me. She nodded, and I knew what she meant. Trust, trust that there was always a plan, trust her?

"Okay," I said, and Kane smiled. "I'll get it."

"Good boy," he said. "Now fetch." Oh, how I was going to make him pay for the comment. I was no dog to be ordered around.

I turned and walked towards the platform, not sure what was going to happen. It felt weird walking towards it, and it was only a few seconds before I was at the foot of the stairs. The staff was about two flights up. The others stood just a few steps down from there. Would they even let me cross?

Diana seemed to wink at me, which made it seem like they would. I just hoped they had a better plan. Something up their sleeve that could get us out of here. So, I began to ascend. Up to a staff that, for all I knew, was just a piece of wood. All the fuss for it, all the fuss about me. What made my blood so different? What ancient thread tied me to this moment? I couldn't even say. Maybe it was destiny, or maybe just manipulation wrapped in myth. Either way, I felt both fear and awe pressing in on me—an invisible weight bearing down from centuries of expectation. Did I even want to carry it?

My slow ascent felt like a royal ascending to the throne. Everyone was watching as they held their breaths. Wondering what would happen when I reached the top. As I got closer, my heart pulsed, and I could feel it. Like every move made it beat louder. The emotions in the room flooded around me, and even the air held its breath. Like the world around us was waiting. Anticipating this very move, this very moment. Maybe this was where I was supposed to be.

For years, I ran away from all the pain, from all the suffering. I sealed myself off, not letting anyone in. I hid, covering myself in a facade of calm and collection. When deep down I was an emotional creature. One that wanted to live, to show joy, to cry, to love. I ran away from people who cared about me because I worried that I would hurt them, give them the pain that I held inside.

I made it to where the Guardians stood, and they slowly parted. Even with a simple bow, something I was a little uncomfortable with. As I walked past, Diana whispered.

"Let your emotions flow. You are in control here."

I nodded and sauntered up the final steps. Now I could get a good look at it. It was almost as tall as I was, coming up to my shoulders. Simply made of oak. I stepped close as, for a minute, a pulse of electricity linked to me as the feeling shuddered down my back. Then it was gone, and I stood in the presence of it. I paused, looking back as the men surrounding my family and friends. Allison lay dying, bleeding from a wound.

"Now give it to me," Kane said.

I wasn't going to play this game. I was not going to let it define me, or anyone. We were going to play by my rules. So, I took a breath and circled the staff before standing behind it. Feeling it pulse through me, feeling the connection that spurred from it. I let my emotions flow, let them all out. I placed my hand on it and the rush of energy erupted as it flowed from it. I could feel everything, all of it. From the water, the trees, the air. It was all connected, and I understood now what I could do. Now I was going to show them all of me. The cavern trembled, a low hum pulsing through the stone as if the earth itself recognized the shift. The torches flickered violently, shadows warping against the walls like spirits set loose. My eyes glowed—just faintly at first—then surged with a golden light as the staff in my hand radiated warmth, power, and memory. I felt the wind stir despite the sealed space, rustling the fabric of my shirt like unseen wings brushing past. My breath caught in my chest—not from fear, but from the overwhelming force that was no longer caged inside me. I was the conduit now. I was the storm they tried to contain. I was going to be the light; I was going to let them feel our rage.

For a moment, the world was still—too still. The air hung heavy, as if the entire cavern had paused to draw breath. Then I opened my eyes, and something inside me shattered. A tremble passed through my body, like a lightning strike ripping through bone. My chest heaved, and I gasped, a sharp, raw sound that broke the silence. I felt it all at once—rage, grief, heartbreak, and something deeper, older—like the fury of a thousand storms buried in my blood. It surged through me, uncontrollable, and the fire answered. At first, I couldn't tell what was happening, but I soon realized, seeing the fire erupt around me. It rose to the top of the cavern, lighting everything ablaze.

As it moved, the heat wrapped all around me and its pulse. Like a living, breathing thing that obeyed my every thought—like Prometheus' stolen fire given will, like a god's wrath wrapped in flame and fury. It surged not just with heat but with memory, with legacy. This was no mere blaze—it was inheritance, a lineage of power rising through my veins and roaring back into the world. The flames moved through the columns and surrounded everyone. Like a sea that could not be tamed. The heat caused the water to steam. I felt one with it. Every spark, every movement, every flame and every life.

It was my turn to play; it was my turn to rise, and I wanted them gone. So, the flames spread, swallowing all of them in their path. Everyone who wanted to hurt the ones that I loved. They would burn, burn for all the harm they had caused. There was nothing that could stop it as it flooded past them, taking out every single one of them. Some began to run, but the flames were too fast as they engulfed them, leaving nothing behind.

As the men thinned out, I turned my sights towards the intruder, the one who taunted me, and there was fear on his face. He tried his best to flee, to run back to the hole he came from, but I had other plans. The flood of fire raced towards him, slowly catching up with him, and soon he too would join the others.

The flames surrounded them, and I held them off for a second. Letting them circle him, separating him from the world. Letting the fear set in. I wanted him scared—I needed him to feel every heartbeat of the fear he'd carved into others. But even as I watched the flames dance in his eyes, I felt a flicker of something unexpected: not hesitation, but the hollow echo of how far I'd come. My jaw clenched, my hands trembling at my sides, unsure whether I was reveling in vengeance or mourning the parts of me that had to burn to get here. Still, I held my ground. He would feel this. He would know what it was like to stand at the mercy of something he couldn't control. Satisfied, I let the flames devour him as he screamed. Once the screaming stopped, I let the flames cool after, ordering them to return to me as I let them spiral to the ceiling and released them into the air to wither out. Now all that was left was ash, charred stone, and my family untouched.

Knowing that they were now safe, I loosened my grip on the staff, fingers trembling as I finally released it. A strange weightlessness overtook me, as though the fire that had surged through me had taken part of my soul with it when it faded. My legs buckled slightly, and I stumbled a step forward, catching myself just before I collapsed entirely. My vision blurred at the edges, colors bleeding into one another as a sharp dizziness overtook me. The world tilted on its axis, and I instinctively pressed a hand to my temple, trying to steady myself. Each heartbeat felt like an echo ricocheting through an empty chamber, loud and disorienting. My knees hit the stone floor a moment later, the coolness a stark contrast to the burning heat that had just consumed everything. For a long moment, I stayed there, gasping, every breath like drawing air through smoke. The fire had given everything—and taken almost as much. But they were safe. That was all that mattered.

“Have to say, that was a new one,” Diana grinned, approaching with the others close behind her. The chamber still shimmered with lingering warmth, like the air itself hadn’t yet caught up to what had just happened. Her eyes scanned the scorched stone and the embers floating lazily upward. “I’ve seen a lot in this place—but that? That was something else.”

As she stepped closer, the others followed, and I noticed the subtle reverence in their expressions. Not fear, but awe—like they were witnessing not just a person but the birth of something mythic. The ground still hissed in places where the moisture had boiled away. Small flickers of flame clung to the edges of shattered stone, like stubborn memories refusing to fade.

I glanced toward the now-charred pillars, the still-settling dust. The magnitude of what had just occurred started to root itself in my chest—not just a moment of power, but a statement. An unveiling. I wasn’t sure what it made me, but it had left its mark on the world, and the world would remember.

"You are one of us, and now you must protect it. When that time comes, you will guide him here, and you will guard him and the light until you die," one of the other guardians said. I understood now, more than ever, the magnitude of the power it possessed—the way it wasn’t just fire or force, but history and inheritance made tangible. It was more than heat or light. It was the weight of every soul that had come before, etched into the current that had surged through me. It was not merely something I controlled—it was something I had to live up to. A legacy, raw and relentless, forged in blood and willpower. And in that moment, I knew—this power didn't make me whole, but it mirrored the wholeness I had fought to reclaim. For once, I felt like myself, my actual self, happy and no longer lost.

"I understand," I told them.

"Good," Diana said, she turned back toward me.

"That staff," she continued, her voice lower now, almost reverent. "It was once wielded by the First Flame-bearer, a guardian who tamed the wild fire not just with strength, but with understanding. It was buried here long ago, awaiting the one who could awaken its true nature. Not just anyone could hold it—it would consume most. But you... it chose you. Because the fire recognizes its own."

Another guardian added, "That power in your bloodline—it isn't chance. It's inheritance. This staff, this chamber, even the flame itself—it's all tied to the lineage you've just rediscovered. The world tried to bury that truth, but fire never stays buried."

The air around them shimmered as if reality itself bent to their presence. "You must carry that fire now, not just as a weapon, but as memory. As promise."

Then Diana smiled again, softer this time. "And when you need us again, just call."

With that, they faded into the air. I needed to learn that trick.

"I REMEMBER THE SILENCE MORE THAN THE FLAMES.
NOT THE SOUND OF THEM.
NOT THE HEAT.
JUST THE SILENCE THAT FOLLOWED–
LIKE THE WORLD WAITING
TO SEE WHAT I'D BECOME."

-PHOENIX

TWENTY-NINE

THE ROOT AND FLAME

"BROKEN GROUND BURNS BRIGHTEST."

I looked down and saw everyone staring up at me. I ran down to them, making sure they were safe. Evelyn came up to me and smiled.

"Well, look at you. That was bloody brilliant."

"Um, guys, still have someone dying here," Lucas said as we rushed over to Allison. Evelyn grabbed a few things to help stop the bleeding. We needed to get her out of here.

"I am going to take her; follow me," I said, and I picked her up, trying to keep her stable.

"Look at you, handsome, having the last say," she muttered softly. I ran as fast as I could, not to flee, but to save. Allison's body shifted with every step, her weight growing heavier in my arms as unconsciousness deepened. The roar of the waterfalls followed us, cascading like distant thunder down the cavern walls. The bioluminescent glow of the forest canopy shimmered above us, casting flickering light like starlight on the battlefield sands that now lay still—no longer a place of conflict, but one of strange, uneasy peace.

My breath came ragged, my legs burning with effort, but I didn't stop. Lucas ran ahead, clearing our path as Evelyn stayed close, checking for any sudden signs of distress in Allison. We passed the great armory—silent now, echoes of ancient wars resting behind locked cases—and the grand gallery where once the Order honored the legends of the past. Tonight, I wondered if one day, someone would tell our story here too.

The winding steps to the chamber beneath the Lyceum felt like they stretched on forever. I nearly stumbled twice, the pain in my thighs turning sharp with every lurch upward. Evelyn placed a hand on my back, grounding me. "Just a bit more, Phoenix," she said, voice tight with urgency.

At last, the ceiling widened. A shaft of natural light pierced through the cracks above. I could taste the shift in air—crisper, colder, alive. With one final push, I stepped into the light, lungs gulping in the world above like it was the first breath of my life.

We'd made it. But what waited above would change everything.

On the other side of the bookshelf, I burst through with Allison in my arms, barely able to keep upright. Veronica spun around the moment she saw us, her expression flipping from tension to immediate command.

"We need a med team, now!" she barked, already motioning to two guardians. "Get a stretcher and stabilize her vitals. Go!"

As the others scrambled, I gently knelt and began to lay Allison down, brushing a strand of hair from her face. Her eyes fluttered, then closed again.

"Hold on, Allie," I whispered, my throat dry. "You're not done yet. You're stronger than this."

She stirred slightly at the sound of my voice, and I pressed her hand between both of mine before letting the medics take over.

They carefully hoisted her onto the stretcher, rushing her through the broken doors with a coordinated urgency. Veronica turned to me, eyes darting over my bloodied clothes and ashen face.

I was back—back to the world above. One that felt changed forever. One I knew I'd never see the same again.

"Is everyone okay?"

I just nodded, still exhausted.

"They are behind me; glad you guys got my message," I said with a smile.

"You did good," Veronica said as I sat down on the floor, probably staining it with blood. I needed to rest, but I just sat in relief. It was all over. They looked at me, taking a step back. Now realizing what had happened.

"What am I?"

My only answer was silence. I couldn't really tell what emotion they felt. Veronica looked the same, like she knew. From the others I sensed something else. It was how the chancellor had looked at me. It wasn't fear, but he was cautious.

Then more footsteps echoed from below. My mother, Evelyn, Lucas, and the rest emerged, their faces drawn with exhaustion but lit with something else—recognition. I stood, but I wasn't sure if my legs could hold the weight of what was coming.

The chancellor stepped forward, his tone no longer just measured—it carried reverence, fear, and awe. "He passed all four trials. Not just survived them, but commanded them. The Grove chose him. The flame obeyed him. And the staff... it didn't reject him."

Gasps and murmurs rippled through the chamber, growing louder with each echo. Eyes widened, breaths were held. Then, a single voice—one of the elder faculty, weathered and wise—cut through the noise.

"He is a shaman," she said, voice cracking with emotion. "The last of the line. The seal... it's broken. It's coming."

Stillness fell, heavy and absolute.

Another guardian took a step forward, nodding solemnly. "The signs were all there. We just never thought we'd live to see it."

A third dropped to one knee, unprompted. "He carries the soul of the ancients. He is the bridge."

The chancellor looked to me, his voice barely more than a whisper. "It's true then. The bloodline endures."

A beat passed. Then another.

He slowly dropped to one knee.

And the rest followed.

In a wave of motion, guardians, scholars, and keepers of long-forgotten rites lowered themselves—not in submission, but in reverence. The weight of centuries bowed around me, not because of power, but because of what had returned to the world through me.

It was reverent. Silent. A weight of generations bending, not in submission, but in recognition. In vow.

I stood, still battered and breathless, and watched as the very institution that had doubted, prodded, tested me... now knelt.

I turned to see my mother—still standing. Her face carried that same unreadable strength, that quiet reserve I'd known all my life. But beneath it, her eyes shimmered with something else—truth, memory... and perhaps guilt.

She met my gaze and gave a slow nod. "You always were more than we let you believe," she whispered.

Then, without ceremony, she dropped to one knee.

I stared in disbelief as Veronica—strong, sharp, unmoved even in crisis—followed suit. The two women who had shaped so much of my world now bowed before me. Not out of obligation. Out of recognition.

Because they knew. They had always known.

I shook my head, overwhelmed by the tide of reverence rising before me.

"No—please, don't," I said, my voice cracking like something fragile splitting under pressure. My heart pounded against my ribs, loud and fast, like it was trying to break free. I stumbled back a step, arm outstretched—not just to stop them, but to shield myself from what I couldn't carry.

"I'm still me," I choked, struggling to breathe around the truth. "I didn't ask for this. I don't want worship—I don't even understand what this means."

The weight of their reverence crashed against me like a rising tide. I could feel the stories of generations folding onto my shoulders. They weren't kneeling to me. They were kneeling to the idea of what I represented. And I wasn't ready to be that. I didn't know if I ever would be.

They kept kneeling. One by one, like dominoes falling not to a king, but to an ancient truth.

I looked to my mother, pleading with my eyes. "You don't have to—please, I don't want you to."

She didn't waver. Her gaze was resolute but soft, filled with something that almost resembled mourning. She had known, long before I ever did. And in that moment, her silence said what words never could: it was never a choice. It was a truth too old to deny.

The fire may have gone out, but the echoes of what it had awakened would burn forever. The trials were over.

But the reckoning had only just begun.

And then, from the quiet, a voice broke the spell—Lucas.

"What the hell is going on?" he asked, glancing from one bowed figure to the next. His face was pale, his eyes locked on me like I was a stranger.

Evelyn stood beside him, arms crossed. "They're kneeling to him."

"Why?" Lucas said, his voice climbing. "Phoenix... what did you do?"

I opened my mouth, but nothing came out. The chamber pulsed with silence, thick and swelling like a held breath that wouldn't release. My throat tightened, muscles locked. Every word I tried to summon slipped backward, swallowed by the gravity of the moment. My chest rose once, twice, but no sound followed—only the dull roar of blood in my ears and the subtle creak of ancient stone beneath kneeling bodies. The light felt too bright. My skin too tight. Like the world had turned its gaze inward, and I didn't know how to hold it.

Evelyn took a breath and stepped forward, past the kneeling circle, and came to stand in front of me. Her voice was low. "He passed the trials. All of them. And the staff chose him. He's something older. Something they've waited for."

Lucas blinked, his brow furrowed. "A prophecy?" His voice held a hint of disbelief, but there was a tremor beneath it—something softer, more uncertain. His arms slowly dropped to his sides, and he glanced at Evelyn, then back at the rows of kneeling figures, as if some invisible weight had just settled on his shoulders. The sarcasm he might've once used to deflect moments like this was absent. What replaced it was awe—and fear he couldn't quite name.

"A reckoning," she replied, and her eyes didn't leave mine. "But that doesn't mean he stops being Phoenix."

She reached up and touched my cheek. "You're still you. And we're still with you."

Lucas didn't kneel. But he stepped closer.

"If you're carrying the world now," he continued, his voice faltering slightly as he looked at the others, "then let us help shoulder the weight. You don't have to do this alone—not anymore." he said, voice rough, "we'll carry you."

In that moment, I wasn't just the shaman or the chosen. I was their friend. Their son. Their brother.

And that... that was what kept me standing.

Even the air tasted different. Like iron and fire. Like something old had awakened and wasn't ready to go back to sleep. My vision blurred for a second—not from tears, but from something deeper. A tremor in the threads of who I was. I closed my eyes and tried to breathe. Just breathe.

Gradually, the moment passed. Veronica rose first, followed by the others. My mother approached but said nothing. She didn't need to. Her eyes held something between sorrow and awe.

Later, as the crowd began to disperse and the reverent hush faded into footfalls and low murmurs, Lucas caught up to me near the steps. He didn't say anything at first. Just stood there beside me in the fading glow of the chamber, hands in his pockets, his expression unreadable.

"You okay?" he asked finally, his voice low.

I gave a slight nod, then shook my head. "I don't know."

He laughed quietly, without humor. "Yeah. Me neither."

For a while, we just stood there in the remnants of sacred light. The warmth on my skin had dulled to a low hum, but it was still there—like a mark burned just beneath the surface. Then Lucas added, his voice softer than usual, "You scared me down there. Thought I lost you."

"You didn't. Not yet."

He looked at me, seriously now. "Good. Because I think the world's about to get a lot stranger. And I don't want to face that without you."

I managed a small smile. "Guess we're in it now."

Lucas nodded, then pointed toward a small, carved alcove in the wall I hadn't noticed before. "You see that?"

Something had shifted. A crack in the stone glowed faintly, as if lit from within. The shape was subtle—tree-like, with limbs unfurling in curling arcs. It was alive, somehow. Watching.

I stepped toward it, drawn without knowing why. When my hand hovered near the surface, the glow brightened slightly, pulsing in time with my heartbeat. The stone felt warm beneath my fingertips. Familiar. Like something from a dream I didn't remember having.

Lucas stayed behind me. "That wasn't there before."

"I think... it's always been there," I said. "We just couldn't see it."

Outside, wind stirred the air with a sound like rustling leaves. The scent of moss and distant rainfall crept in through the cracks. Thunder rolled softly across the mountains, long and low, as if the sky itself had begun to stir.

I looked up toward the vaulted ceiling, the ancient arches etched with symbols I hadn't noticed earlier. They glowed faintly now, mirroring the pulse beneath my skin.

The reckoning hadn't passed.

It had just begun.

THIRTY

THE WEIGHT OF BECOMING

"THE BOY THEY KNEW IS GONE"

A wine glass sat untouched in front of me, catching the amber glow of the setting sun like a relic from a calmer world. Merlot, I thought. Not my usual. But tonight, its bitterness grounded me, held the storm inside just long enough to keep my hands from shaking.

The sun had nearly disappeared behind the tree line, casting the room in long, fractured shadows. The kind of light that made everything look older, worn. I wasn't the same person who had entered that chamber weeks ago—hell, maybe not even the same one who woke up this morning. Something fundamental had shifted. I felt carved out and filled with something else—grief, power, maybe even clarity. I was rawer, more exposed, but there was strength in that. I'd faced the dark and didn't break.

I'd learned things—about my fears, my temper, my need to always be in control. I'd seen parts of myself I didn't even know were there. The shadows behind the trauma. The instincts I couldn't always explain. Even the flickers of a deeper force that didn't feel entirely human.

No, I hadn't enjoyed the past few days. They were brutal. But they'd taught me something I seemed to forget too often: I could survive. Maybe even rise. Still, some part of me bristled at the quiet. Like the air was holding its breath, waiting for the other shoe to drop. This wasn't the end.

Not even close.

The floor creaked. Lucas stepped in, dressed down, expression tight. He walked to the bar and poured himself a drink—whiskey. Not his usual. That said more than his words ever could.

He didn't speak right away. Just let the silence wrap around us, thick and humming with everything we weren't saying.

"Any word yet?" I asked, watching him settle across from me.

"Still in surgery," he replied. "How are you?"

"Alive," I said. It was the simplest truth I could offer. But what he really meant wasn't about my body. He meant my mind. My soul. And I didn't have an answer for that. Not one I could say out loud.

The truth was—I didn't know what to feel. I should've hated her. Allison. After everything. The lies, the manipulation, the way she turned every truth into a weapon. She used us. Used me. And yet, when I thought of her lying there—cut open, bleeding, fragile—it twisted something inside me.

Was it pity? Guilt? No. It was more complicated than that. Because once, maybe, there had been something real. Or maybe I'd just wanted to believe there was. Either way, I couldn't bring myself to wish her dead.

My foundations had shifted. I was still counting the cracks. But I wasn't sure if the structure underneath had broken—or just changed shape.

"I'm always here," he offered.

I laughed quietly. "You live here."

He grinned and sipped his drink. He looked different too—less guarded, more himself. It was strange to realize how far we'd come. Once, we were just roommates who tolerated each other. Now? He was my best friend. That snuck up on me.

We stayed like that for a while—talking, half-joking. I even asked if there was anyone in his life. Same answer: no. But he admitted to a past relationship, secret and short-lived. We laughed about it, the way you do when wounds aren't fresh anymore.

It was a little after nine when the front door opened. My mother and Evelyn entered, followed by Veronica. Her presence changed the air—she looked rattled, which was rare. Even for her.

"She's out of surgery," my mother said, wasting no time. "Stable. Expected to make a full recovery."

I exhaled. Even with everything—lies, manipulation, betrayal—I didn't want her to die. That kind of hatred wasn't in me. Not yet.

"Glad to hear it."

Veronica stepped forward, her voice tight but measured. "There's something I'd like to discuss with you, Phoenix. If you're willing."

I nodded, wary. "Sure. As long as it's not more embarrassing childhood stories."

She smiled faintly. "I've spoken with my colleagues—and your professors. They're impressed. Extremely. Your performance during the trials, your conduct under pressure… and your swordwork apparently."

That last bit gave me away. The smirks on Evelyn and my mother's faces said it all. I braced myself.

"I'd like to offer you a seat on the Council," Veronica continued. "Permanent. Like your mother. Like me. And if you'd prefer, Mr. Jones may join in an auxiliary role. He's proven… resourceful."

Her words hit harder than I expected—not because of the title, but because of the weight it carried. A Keeper. A guardian of legacy and truth. It wasn't just a seat at the table. It was a vow to protect what remained. To guard the new world we were being asked to shape.

I glanced from her to my mother, then back again. "So... this provisional Keeper thing—it's not just ceremonial?"

Veronica shook her head. "No. It's real. And it started the moment that staff responded to you."

I felt the echo of that moment—the flame, the kneeling, the unbearable silence that had filled my chest like pressure in a deep-sea dive. It hadn't felt like power. It had felt like being chosen by something ancient and impossible to refuse.

"So what happens now?" I asked quietly.

"Now?" Veronica said. "Now you begin the hard part—learning what it means to carry it. Because that fire doesn't just burn for you, Phoenix. It burns through you."

And just like that, the weight of it settled all over again.

I thought of the trials. Of the staff in my hand, the light that hadn't burned me. Of the kneeling. And how none of it felt like triumph—just a responsibility I hadn't asked for, but couldn't turn away from either.

It took me a second to respond. Not because I doubted the offer—but because of what it meant. Responsibility. Danger. Probably getting the hell beaten out of me again. But also answers. A path toward the truth of who I really was. Of the family I never knew I had.

"Does this mean I get to travel?"

"Only when you're not in class," my mother cut in, deadpan. Of course. God forbid I miss a lecture.

"I guess," I said finally.

"There will be people you will have to prove it to that you deserve this, so don't think it will be easy" Veronica said and I nodded.

Evelyn pulled me into a hug. "Welcome to the club."

My mother and Veronica exchanged a look—smug, amused, conspiratorial. Whatever came next, I wasn't going through it alone. And maybe, just maybe, that was enough.

"So that's what we're calling it now? A club?" I smirked. "Pretty sure secret societies don't come with member perks. Unless near-death counts."

They laughed. But I wasn't entirely joking. The Council wasn't just some hidden order with rituals and relics—it was my new reality. My old life, with its normalcy and simplicity, had ended. Maybe this would help me make sense of the questions still clawing at me. Maybe it would give the chaos a shape.

"I think this calls for a drink," my mother declared, then paused, eyeing the glass already beside me and Lucas. "Well, for the rest of us, since these two got a head start."

"Oh, I'll take wine," Evelyn said, sliding her glass toward me. I poured as my mother and Veronica opted for whiskey, joining Lucas. The bottle wouldn't last the night.

Veronica took a long sip—almost a gulp. She didn't speak immediately, letting the burn settle before lifting her eyes.

"There's one last thing you need to know," she said, voice quieter now. She looked at me, then my mother. "Your brother. He's alive."

Time stopped.

The words didn't hit—they detonated. My body went cold, breath caught somewhere between inhale and exhale. My fingers curled tightly around the stem of my wine glass, but I couldn't lift it.

"I didn't even—" My voice cut off.

My mother's expression mirrored mine. Blank with disbelief. "He survived?" she whispered. "I thought—he died. With her."

"He did," Veronica said. "But he was hidden. And he's remained hidden ever since. Now that you know who you are, Phoenix, it's time you know the rest."

The room fell into a hush. No one moved. The air itself seemed suspended, waiting.

"That would make him… seventeen," my mother said, her voice soft but brittle. A fact and a wound wrapped into one.

Seventeen.

I had a brother.

The words echoed, hollow and distant. A younger brother—lost, hidden, erased. Protected. My stomach turned, thoughts collapsing in on themselves like a house of cards in a storm.

All this time, I'd had someone out there. Blood. Legacy. A shared history sealed away like a secret I wasn't meant to know.

And suddenly, all the threads pulled tight.

The Guardians during the trials—their words: Guard him.

It had never been abstract.

It had always been him.

A brother. By blood. And I was his guardian—though I barely knew what that meant. No training manual, no prophecy cheat sheet. Just instinct and whatever scraps of history they let me uncover.

My legs itched to move, to pace, to run. The quiet in the room pressed into my chest. Lucas looked like he wanted to say something but didn't. Evelyn's eyes flicked toward me with a caution I barely registered.

"One question," I said. My voice was calm, but only because everything else inside me had gone still. "Where?"

Not how. Not why didn't you tell me. Just where.

He was seventeen. A kid. And I was the only family he had left. He deserved to know I existed—even if I didn't know him yet.

"All I can tell you is he's safe," Veronica said. "His location was sealed—even from me. Just as yours was, once. It was your birth mother's decision. For his protection."

Even my mother didn't fully buy it. I could see it in the way she stared into her glass, thinking—calculating. Her fingers tapped the base of the tumbler like they were solving an equation. Like the math didn't add up.

Something in her jaw set. Her eyes glinted—not with shock, but purpose.

This wasn't just a revelation.

It was a spark.

And something had just been lit.

But for now, it would have to do.

I was tired. Too tired to pick at the seams of another half-truth. But I knew this much:

This wasn't the end of anything.

It was just another beginning.

"We'll talk more about it tomorrow," I said, finalizing it with a tone that left no room for argument. "After sleep. Actual sleep."

The room quieted, the business of the Council and bloodlines set aside—at least for the night. What followed was something I hadn't realized how much I needed: simple, human connection.

We laughed. We swapped stories. Lucas—wine-drunk and emboldened—shared about a secret boyfriend from his past, someone he'd dated while living with me. I just stared at him, incredulous.

"You're kidding."

"Nope."

"I lived with you!"

"Exactly."

"I swear, I need to start paying more attention."

"Good luck," he grinned.

Even my mother got in on the humor, recalling half-mortifying childhood stories I had blocked from memory. Veronica joined in too, proving that even high-powered Council leaders weren't immune to a little wine-induced wickedness.

Somewhere around my third—or maybe fourth—glass, I let myself relax. Talked more than I should have. Laughed louder than I normally did. For the first time in days, the shadows in my mind took a step back.

It was close to eleven when Veronica called it a night. One by one, we drifted off toward sleep. All I could think about was how good my bed was going to feel. A real bed. Sheets. A pillow that wasn't a rolled-up hoodie or tree root. You don't realize how luxurious that is until it's gone.

Lucas and I stayed behind to clean up. Wine glasses, scattered napkins, a whiskey bottle almost empty. It was domestic in a weird way—normal, almost.

He glanced over at me as we dried the last few glasses. Smirking.

"What?"

"Oh, nothing."

"That's never true with you."

He paused, still smirking, eyes drifting toward the hallway.

"First night back..." he said, drawing it out. "Sharing a bed?"

I rolled my eyes and threw the dish towel at him. "Shut up."

He laughed. "Hey, just saying. Evelyn's back, you're conveniently out of floor duty, and—"

"Lucas."

"All right, all right." He held up his hands in surrender. "Just marking the occasion."

I shook my head, amused despite myself. The worst part? He wasn't entirely wrong.

But that was a thought for another time.

I lay in bed, already wrapped in the familiar comfort of my own sheets—shorts on, blankets drawn up, the room a cluttered mess I'd ignore for one more night. After everything, I was just grateful for a moment to breathe. Grateful for the stillness. My mind knew I'd get restless eventually—too much time and not enough purpose—but for now, this quiet was sacred.

Evelyn arrived a few minutes later, dressed down and soft with sleep. She didn't knock. She didn't need to. This wasn't awkward anymore. I wasn't staring at the ceiling, overthinking every breath. That fear—that I would hurt her, or let her down—had faded into something deeper, steadier.

Now I was just reading. Casual. Comfortable. Content.

"What are you reading?" she asked, curling up beside me.

"Class stuff," I replied. "Can't exactly flunk out after being offered a Council seat."

She laughed, her smile tugging at the edge of my mouth. She leaned into me, her presence warm, familiar, anchoring.

"Only you would be doing homework after everything that happened today," she said. "That's just one of the reasons I love you."

I looked down at her. "I love you too."

I kissed her. Her lips—soft, unhurried—met mine like a promise.

For a while, we just lay there. I kept reading, and she rested against my shoulder, occasionally peeking at the pages and throwing in commentary that sparked tiny debates. It felt… right. Two history nerds bickering about Latin conjugation while wrapped in a blanket. Honestly, it was perfect. Maybe the best thing that had happened to me in a long, long time.

Eventually, she slid a hand onto my chest and pushed the book gently down.

"Okay," she said, her voice velvet. "I need you to put that down."

"Why? I was really enjoying those translation notes."

"Oh, I'm sure you were," she said, straddling a smirk. "But I think you'll enjoy this more."

She leaned in, lips meeting mine again, this time deeper. Her body moved against mine, soft heat building between us as her hands traced bare skin. We moved closer, instinctively, as if nothing else existed. As if the world—its secrets, its relics, its broken truths—could wait.

"I think you're right," I murmured, setting the book aside and reaching for the lamp.

The light clicked off.

And for the first time in days, maybe weeks, there was no burden. No mission. No war between darkness and light.

Just us.

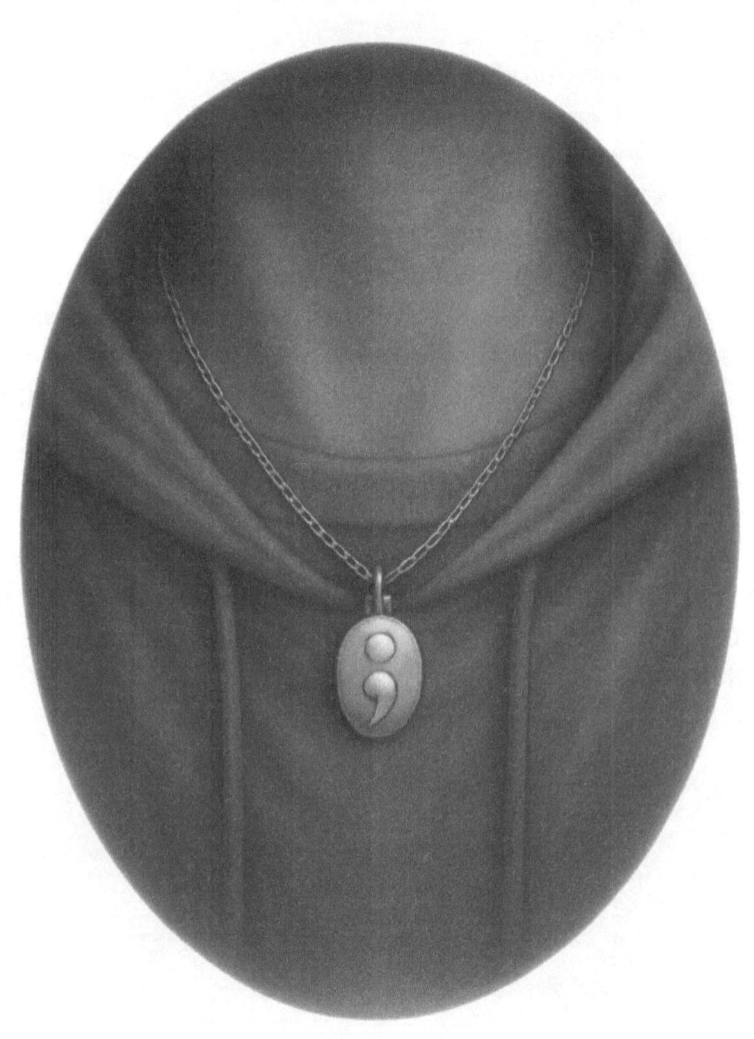

THIRTY-ONE

THE LOST SON

"HE WAS NEVER LOST.
ONLY WAITING TO BE REMEMBERED."

Three days had passed since the tombs. Three days since my world split open and something older, deeper, and terrifyingly real crawled out from beneath everything I thought I understood. Since then, time had unraveled strangely. The hours felt slower, heavier, like each one was filled with new questions and invisible burdens. My mother had returned to Memphis, to my father—who, apparently, had been more anxious than anyone. When he knew we were safe, it was like the tension drained from him all at once, like someone had unplugged the pressure valve on his entire world.

I spent a day with them. Not just existing in the same space, but truly inhabiting the weight of what had passed. We talked—deep, soul-baring conversations that cracked open every carefully constructed silence between us. We faced the raw things: the secrecy they had held out of love and fear, the adoption that had given me a name but not the whole truth, the blood in my veins that carried echoes of something ancient and wild—something that did not belong to them, yet never diminished what we were.

There were tears, pauses where words refused to form, and touches that said more than apologies ever could. But there was no blame. No shame. Only love—love that had bent under pressure but never snapped. It was messy, yes. Human. Full of ache and grace. But it was real. They saw me—fully. The fractured boy who had clawed his way out of shadow and flame. And I saw them—not as gatekeepers of my past, but as the anchors who chose me, raised me, and never once let me go.

I was their son. In every way that mattered. And I always would be.

He found out about Evelyn and me, of course. And—of course—he had something to say about it. Something like, "Could've saved yourself a lot of drama if you'd just figured that out a year ago." Classic Dad. Full of wisdom, low on subtlety. I laughed, rolled my eyes, and didn't argue. Because he was right.

We were happy. That was the strange part. Amid all the fallout and fatigue, I felt lighter around them. No longer walking on the edge of some unspoken cliff. My mom was already talking about remodeling the bathroom—said she was tired of the paint color and tile grout. I think it was her way of reclaiming normalcy. I told her, for the thousandth time, that none of this was her fault. I think this time she finally started to believe me.

Allison, though… she vanished. One day, she was recovering in her hospital bed. The next? Gone. I had come to visit her. Just a gesture. Closure, maybe. But she'd slipped out, leaving behind only the faint scent of antiseptic and a wave of unfinished business.

Some part of me—some stubborn, wounded shard—knew we'd meet again. I just hoped it wouldn't involve another round of chloroform or underground crypts. And I kept thinking about her last words—"they want him awake."

Who? What?

That question circled my mind like a vulture, persistent and foreboding. I wanted to believe the nightmare was over. That the flames had died down. But clouds gathered on the horizon, slow and sure. Something else stirred. Something that had waited a very long time.

The staff—my link to the trials and everything they meant—was no longer in my hands. I left it with those who had guarded it for millennia. If they could hold that line through fire and shadow, they could hold it again. The entrance was disguised now, not with a bookshelf but with a painting of the White Sycamore. A symbol. A warning. The carpet had to be replaced. Blood never did come out.

And the Council? That part came with its own version of reality—a reality filled with red tape, rituals, and eight-hundred pages of procedural doctrine courtesy of Veronica. I made it to page ten before genuinely questioning if power was worth the paperwork. Bureaucracy, I was quickly learning, didn't wield swords or conjure relics—it wielded footnotes. Still, I had my first assignment over winter break. Classified. The word alone gave it gravitas, like something out of a spy novel. Even better—I wouldn't have to do it alone. Lucas and Evelyn were coming with me. Apparently, mythic responsibility was best handled as a group project.

Lucas, of course, suggested matching jackets—black with embroidered flames. I said we'd look like a band, but not the good kind.

Evelyn and I also managed our first real date. No fleeing. No spiraling guilt. No cryptic disappearances. Just two people who had survived the impossible and decided to hold on to something normal. Something tender. We talked about history, debated over wine, and shared silence without needing to fill it. It was real. And, yeah—my dad had been right about acting sooner. But thankfully, he'd never get the satisfaction of hearing me admit it out loud.

Now I sat in the Grove, nestled against the curve of an old tree's root, watching the light bleed across the sky in a slow, cinematic symphony of gold, fire, and amethyst. It was the kind of sunset that didn't blaze—it smoldered. Quietly, reverently. Each color layered over the next like a prayer whispered to the horizon. Leaves blanketed the grass in rust and amber, their curled edges crisp and whispering with each faint breeze. The lingering impressions from last week's tailgate still dented the ground, ghost-like, marking another life that felt impossibly distant.

A whisper of wind coiled through the trees, carrying the scent of firewood smoke, burnt cinnamon, and earth still damp with memory. Somewhere nearby, a distant cheer echoed faintly from the stadium—low and warm, the pulse of a town still alive. Autumn had arrived in full. My favorite season. Not just for the air or the colors, but because it always felt like the world exhaling. Like even time itself paused to inhale the decay and beauty and let it linger just a little longer.

Everything about this moment felt suspended—fragile and whole. Like if I moved too suddenly, it would all collapse back into the noise. So I stayed still, heart quiet, letting the sky burn above me in silence.

"Hey, you," Evelyn said, appearing beside me with a pumpkin spice latte in hand.

"Where did you come from?" I took the cup. Warmth seeped into my palms, grounding me in the moment.

"Can't drop in on my favorite Flame-keeper?"

"Technically provisional."

"You're still mine," she said, and that was that. We sat in silence for a while, the sky turning bruised and brilliant, the light folding in like wings.

"You know Lucas says we're going 'groveing' and that I have to take you to a game," she said.

I groaned. "That's not a word. And he's going to regret introducing you to campus slang."

She grinned. "You'll show me, won't you?"

"Only if I get to laugh when you realize how serious people are about tailgating."

We laughed, and the wind danced through the trees like a hush settling over a long story. It felt like closure—but also like a door opening into something unknown.

"It's been a hell of a semester," I said quietly.

"Yeah," she agreed. "But some of it was good. Really good." She took my hand.

"True."

There was more I could say. About the pain. About the transformation. About the echoes of power that still hummed under my skin like a quiet storm. But for now, this silence was enough.

She pulled something from her pocket—a cloth satchel, smooth and purple.

"A gift," she said.

"Did I forget an anniversary or something?"

"Just open it."

Inside was a silver necklace, simply made but beautiful. The pendant was small. A semicolon.

I stopped breathing.

"Because your story doesn't end here," she said. Her voice was quiet but steady. She believed it. She believed in me.

She helped me put it on. The chain was cold, but it warmed quickly against my skin. I knew then—I'd never take it off.

"Thank you," I whispered. "I love it."

We sat together, watching the sky bloom into stars, each one stitching itself into the indigo fabric of night like an ancient language only the brave could read. The hush between us wasn't just comfort—it was sacred. A silence born not from emptiness, but from a fullness too vast to name.

In that stillness, something in me finally landed. Not peace, exactly. Not in the way most people meant it. But purpose. A new gravity.

I had walked through the fire, let it strip me down to ash, and somehow still rose. Scarred, yes. But alive. Reforged. The kind of rebirth that doesn't come with trumpets—but with tremors.

I had chosen life. Not because it was easy. But because it was mine. And I was done surrendering pieces of it to fear.

I wasn't healed. But I was healing.

I wasn't whole. But I was worthy.

I was the flame that refused to die—

The kind that didn't just burn.

It remembered.

And my story—

Was far from over.
It was just learning how to speak;

Acknowledgments

First and foremost—to you, the reader.

Whether you're discovering Phoenix for the first time or returning after the first edition, thank you. There's no greater gift than someone choosing to spend time in the world I've built, and no deeper joy than hearing that a character I've carried alone is now alive in someone else's mind. That kind of connection? It's everything.

But books don't just come from inspiration—they come from community. And I've had the immense luck of being surrounded by people who helped shape this story into what it is.

To my parents—thank you for always encouraging me to chase what I love, even when it's hard, even when it fails. You've been my biggest supporters, through every phase of this dream. And yes, even my brother helped. (Please don't tell him. His ego does not need the boost.) To my extended family—your perspective, your stories, and your belief in me have been steady anchors.

To my friends, thank you for your patience and your honesty. Noah, for reminding me the world is meant to be seen—not just imagined. Emma and Addison, for letting me shove early drafts at you and still speaking to me afterward. Rebecca, you read the bad stuff—all of it. You stuck around anyway.

To Beth—mentor, teacher, and light in the dark. You heard the heaviness in my early words and told me to keep writing anyway. I still remember that. And I carry it.

To the University of Mississippi—thank you. This story doesn't just take place there. It grew there. The Lyceum may be fictionalized here, but its weight, its roots, its mythic pull—those are real. Ole Miss will always be my writing home. It's where the myth took root, and I'll carry that with me in every story I tell.

To my CREI family—you were the constant during chaos. Dills, Rollins, Maddie, Kierra, Danielle—thank you for grounding me while I tried to rewrite myth. You've shown me what support looks like day in and day out, and I'm lucky to call you part of my circle.

This second edition also wouldn't exist without the remarkable people who gave their talent and time to elevate it further. Thank you to the brilliant team at Miblart, whose original cover brought Phoenix Knight into the world with beauty and strength. And to the designers and creatives at The Scriptorium, who reimagined that vision for this new edition—you've helped bring a myth to life.

To Alexandra and Kim, your editorial insight helped shape the prose, sharpen the pacing, and (most importantly) teach me how to get out of my own way. Your fingerprints are all over this book, and I'm grateful.

And finally—Phoenix.

You stubborn, relentless, frustrating character.

You broke me a dozen times just so I could put us both back together. You've taken me to places I didn't want to go and made me write things I didn't want to admit. And yet—every time—I come out stronger on the other side. You're more than a character. You're a mirror, a spark, and a reminder that some stories demand to be told, no matter the cost.

Even in this second edition—especially in this second edition—you were a pain in my ass. But now, I hope you shine brighter. I hope you finally feel whole.

We've only just begun.

About James Ungurait

James Ungurait is a Mississippi-born author whose work blends literary fiction with mythic resonance and emotional reckoning. His stories often explore identity, silence, inheritance, and the quiet struggle to become who we are beneath who we're told to be.

Phoenix Knight: The Lost Son was James's first published novel, originally released in 2022. This second edition represents a complete reimagining—reshaped in tone, structure, and purpose. What began as a young adult fantasy has grown into something far more personal: a story about truth, power, and the cost of remembering who you are.

James is also the author of I'm the Same, a literary novel praised for its emotional intensity and quiet devastation, exploring themes of grief, survival, and connection in the wake of catastrophe.

He holds a degree in History with a minor in Creative Writing from The University of Mississippi, where much of his early storytelling voice took root. He now lives in Hattiesburg, where he writes, rewrites, and occasionally argues with characters who refuse to stay on script.

Find him online at www.jamesungurait.com or on Instagram @jamesungurait.

About Ungurait House

Books Built to Endure

Ungurait House is an independent publisher dedicated to literary fiction, fantasy, and lasting storytelling. We believe great books don't chase trends—they challenge them. Every title we release is crafted with intention: from the words on the page to the weight in your hands.

We are not a traditional press, and we are not self-published. We're something else entirely—fiercely independent, vertically integrated, and reader-focused.

Our imprints include:

Ungurait House, for fiction that reckons with identity, survival, and the human condition;

and IRONWAKE, for bold, mythic fantasy with a literary edge.

Each book is designed and typeset in-house, printed to last, and available through bookstores and our direct shop.

To explore our catalog or unlock exclusive editions, visit:
unguraithouse.com

Follow along @unguraithouse
For press: media@unguraithouse.com

www.ingramcontent.com/pod-product-compliance
Lightning Source LLC
Chambersburg PA
CBHW020915310726
48980CB00011B/891/J

* 9 7 9 8 9 9 9 3 8 0 9 1 3 *